BOOK II

LOY
AND BEYOND

by

TODD DAVID GROSS

SUNLIT LANE PRODUCTIONS

2024

this book down and it leaves the reader eagerly awaiting volume three. Kudos to the author for achieving something very special!"
– James Conboy

"A great follow up to Book One. The author weaves an adventurous tale that makes it hard for the reader to put down. It leaves one dying to know where the story will go. I can't wait for book three."
– Vincent Marmorato

"*Loy and Beyond* draws the reader into the primitive yet sophisticated world of the Rehloy. The author has an immersive style, and as the story evolved, it became so intense I could not wait to see where it would go next. The complex societies and overall fantasy were both intriguing and very satisfying. Reminiscent of *Clan of the Cave Bear*, the twists and turns of the story revealed roots of a civilization like our own, and provoked questions about life as we know it. I loved every minute of it." *– Claudia Shwide-Slavin*

"*Loy and Beyond* is a compelling story that resonates on so many levels. By telling the story out of time, it captures the zeitgeist of our own, teetering on both destruction and a new age. The novelistic approach to the esoteric content added a depth to the story that was fascinating. A rare achievement." *– Michael Malloy*

"*Loy and Beyond* charts the continuing saga of the Rehloy tribe and their inevitable contact with the Ontarans. Gross is keenly adept at the evolution and intertwining of his characters, and the contrasts between the two cultures. From the pureness of mystical beings to the darker strains of form and substance, the reader becomes deeply immersed in this ever-widening tale. Beyond the action-adventure, the inner life and synergy between animals, plants, trees, and the spiritually-aware, pulsates through this book. This symbiotic relationship not only nourishes the characters, but causes the reader to pause and recognize the importance for all living organisms to coexist. Simply put, this intriguing story, with its twists and turns offers sustenance for the soul. It is a great read." *– Joan Fisch*

Chipping away at stone, a figure emerges.
It was there all along, waiting to be uncovered.
– Tedagee

Excerpt from Jennifer's Journal:

"I hate school. I'm so confused. I had a dream last night. It made me feel better, but I can't remember what it was about. I think I had it before because I remember waking up and feeling the same way. I wish it would last. I wish I could remember."

THE FIRST DAY OF FOREVER AFTER

Daniel took his first step into the light of a world long past smoldering. How long had they lived, buried in the cave, hiding from the firestorm?

A month?

A year?

A decade?

Time lost all meaning long ago.

He vaguely remembered Grandma Jennifer insisting they come to these mountains.

Had she known this was going to happen?

No matter. The borders of their lives were wiped clean by the ensuing maelstrom. In the space between then and now, a new way was emerging.

Senses sharpened to points of light, sound, taste, tone, touch, texture ... *insight.*

If they closed their eyes and listened in a certain way, they could see in their minds' eyes, the nature of things. Not just the forms that lay before them, but those around the bend, and further still.

Resep. The name had come in a whisper of sensation.

Daniel found the plant growing deep inside the cave. It was hiding in a lightless chamber, its leaves and branches wide with invitation.

A tentative bite, and then another. A leaf, a twig, a branch, the body. It kept them alive all this time, nurturing them, crafting them.

The plant was all but gone now, the large pod filled with seeds, its final offering.

The *youngers* raced ahead, unafraid. The time in the cave, the perpetual dream, had ended. Here, now, was the beginning. In the open space of this time, they would take root.

Daniel followed, carrying the seeds to plant, like they themselves had been planted.

It was a new day, a new dawn, a new dream now set into motion…

AS IT WAS

"The far-past was filled with violent and contrasting forces.
When the firestorm struck, Danyal and his family fled into
a cave to escape its murderous light. It was there that they
found the plant growing. This then was our beginning.
They brought its seeds into the light, and we, the Rehloy,
Have tended the Resep ever since." – Oral Histories

The sound of early morning light spread through the land. One voice joined another and set the songs of the day into motion.

Donan listened to the chorus and compared this day to those that had come before. He, the first Kwaman of this time period, was old now, but still listened in that special way.

So much had happened, and nothing at all.

For a millennium, the Rehloy basked in the rarified air of creation. But the outside world was intruding. The trees were abuzz with change. For the past eleven years, the Resep crawled along the ground in ominous, linear patterns.

Jormah had left the sanctuary of their land to discover the nature of that change. He was gone so long, most remembered him by name only.

Where are you, my brother?

Only Donan kept the image of him alive by recalling the *feel* of him each day. Only he remembered, and Tremlo, of course.

But what that troubled child knew was anybody's guess.

On a distant shore, a blight had taken hold.

Their minds could not make sense of the tension in their bodies. But it was coming. Just as surely as night followed day.

And when that happened, nothing would be *as it was*.

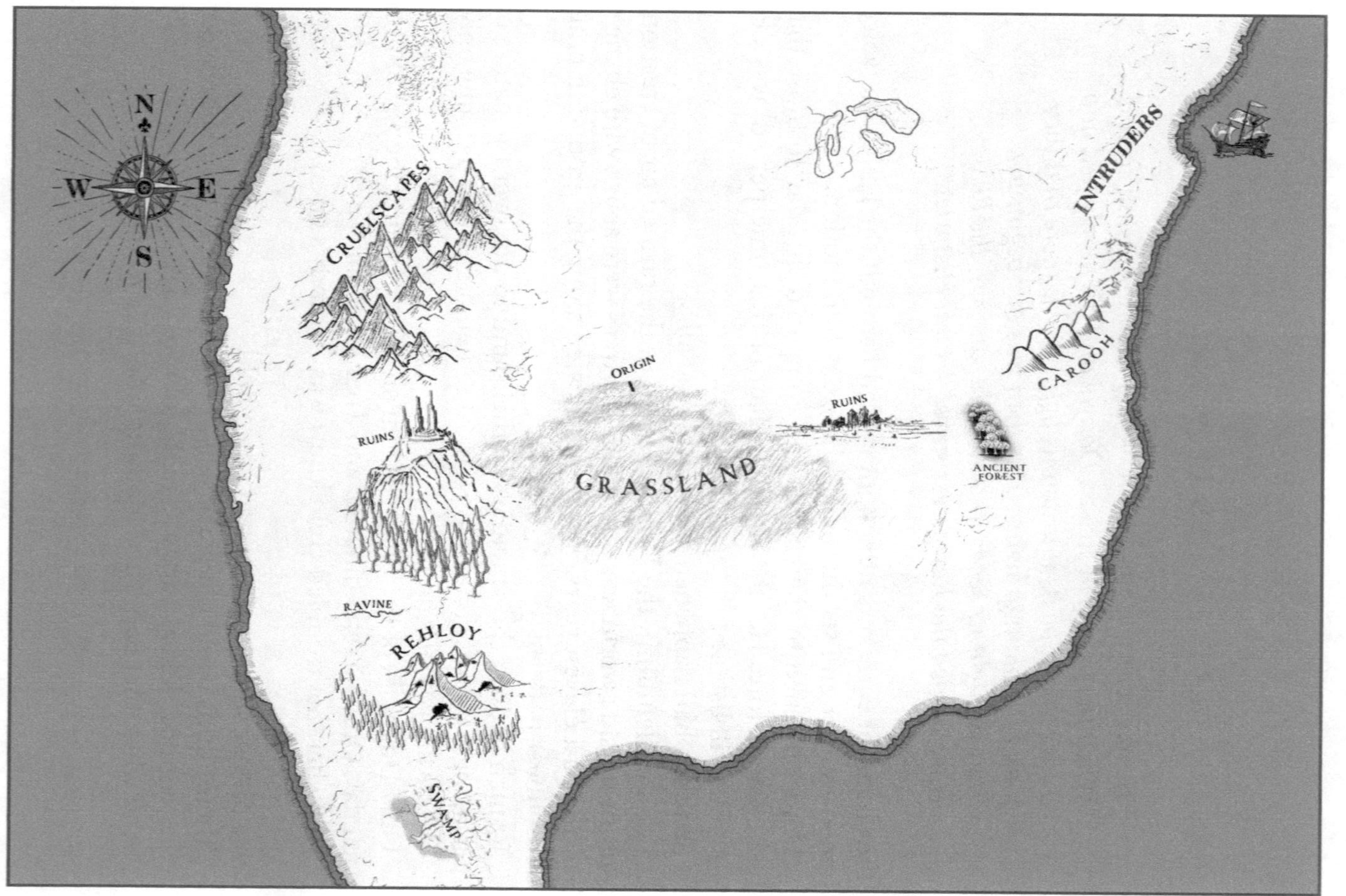

N
W E
S
CRUELSCAPES
INTRUDERS
CAROOH
ORIGIN
RUINS
RUINS
ANCIENT FOREST
GRASSLAND
RAVINE
REHLOY
SWAMP

BRIEF CHARACTER LIST

OUR PRESENT:
Jennifer, now and then.

THE REHLOY:
DONAN – The Kwaman: A spiritual guide. Older brother of Jormah.
JORMAH – The second Kwaman of this time. Donan's younger brother.
TREMLO – Reena's troubled child, who became conscious in the womb.
REENA – Mother of Tremlo.
ARLEN – Father of Tremlo.
STELBIN – Donan's Side (apprentice).
MORTULLA – The Mahtwah, *our mother*. The healer.
KENECTKA – Mortulla's Heart.
WHAET – The Leader of the tribe.
GREMAR – Son of the Leader before Whaet.
TSUTE – Gremar's friend.
RAILLY – Gremar's friend.
GAHEN – Left the tribe with a group. Never heard from again.

PAST KWAMEN:
MAELO – The Kwaman before Donan. Both his and Jormah's teacher.
REJA – The one who found the way to kill the Yarka.

THE CAROOH:
BKA – Leader of the Carooh.
TELT – Older member of the tribe.

THE ONTARANS:
AUGMENTORS – Fierce warriors.
KRIITON – The Newland Commander.
PROUTUS – The Emperor of Ontar.
BARONUUS – A member of the Elite.
BENTON – Under Baronuus's command.
BETTRIE – Animal Trainer

NAMES FOR THE BEAST:
YARKA, for the Rehloy.
KURR, for the Ontarans.

CHAPTER ONE

Tremlo, five years old, all arms and legs, sitting sideways, his thin frame sticking halfway out of the still-cave. His face serene, an air of innocence about him. He embodied so much of what he came into contact with that it was often hard to see what he really looked like. Joys were more joyful, pains more painful. He was disfigured by the intensity, and yet, in the quiet moments, something special to behold.

Nowadays his flesh-tones were relatively stable. He could sit there for hours on end without incident. He could even make short forays into the unsheltered day. But he could not leave the cave for any extended period of time without fear of being overwhelmed.

His mother, sitting several feet away, was basking in the sunlight.

What one felt, the other *knew*.

With her eyes closed, Reena remained all of one color to soothe him. Tremlo, fidgeting as usual; some part was always moving, even when still. Her mind turned to him as his turned to hers.

What are you thinking? she wondered.

Most children began to speak around the age of two, but at five years old, Tremlo had still not uttered a word. There were stories of those born without voice, but Tremlo could babble, cry, and scream with the best of them.

"He may never speak," the Mahtwah had said, implying there was something wrong with his mind. Reena refused to listen to the Healer, but as the years passed, a certain resignation had set in.

Tremlo, blind as all children were, was playing with the light between his fingertips. He gurgled along, adding dimension to his play. But on this day, he felt something in Reena's stare, heard the forlornness of her thoughts, tasted the flavor of her unasked question. A feeling rose up from deep inside his chest.

Under water all these years, aware of the light on the surface, but not until this very moment, did he actually look up.

The rhythm of his mother's yearning was there, waiting, and something within him strove to answer.

"Rrrr...rre. Ree na."

The very act of saying it helped him take a further step outside himself.

"Tremlo? Did you just say something?"

And suddenly, he realized he understood her words, knew their meaning, had always known.

"Rrrr eena."

His mouth struggled to reconfigure itself and give form to the sounds coming up from his chest. Hundreds were bubbling up, thousands, all fighting to be heard.

"Did you say, Reena?"

Her words gave him focus.

"Yyyou...sa y... Rreena?"

The shock in his mother's body nearly knocked him over. Suddenly, she was crying, and he was crying, and they were rocking in each other's arms.

"You are talking."

"Yyou...a are...ta lk...in g," he said, lips and tongue feeling their way.

"Tremlo is talking," Reena cried aloud. "My son is talking!"

Word quickly spread. To everyone's amazement, the younger had spoken one word, then another, then in complete sentences.

Donan came rushing down from the High Cave to witness this turn of events. Years before, he had made the startling discovery that Tremlo somehow knew the whereabouts and doings of every person, no matter how far away, and all from the seclusion of the still-cave. This was an awareness reserved for the Sentients. In the Rehloy's long history, there had only been two.

But Tremlo had been born prematurely, and his extraordinary sensitivities had turned against him. Thoughts roared across his psyche; the simplest of sensations pricked his skin. For most of his life he could not leave the quiet of the still-cave without being overcome by external forces and reduced to spasms of pain.

Donan had watched from afar, hoping for a change, keeping his disappointment to himself. Over time there was some limited growth. But now, suddenly, the child had words....

"Do-na-n," Tremlo said when the Kwaman arrived. He had felt the Kwaman's excitement all along. *Donan,* he said with the language of his body, capturing the very essence of Donan's nature, from his scent to his hidden emotions.

Amazed as always, Donan smiled. In Tremlo's face were traces of his own. The child stared back as if he could see, but he would not gain sight until puberty.

"Hello, Tremlo."

"Hel-lo... Do-nan."

Tremlo's voice was deep and filled with gravel. Not exactly what Donan expected.

"Hello, Tremlo," Donan said once more, calm yet bursting with questions. It was said Sentients could perceive the past, present, and future, simultaneously.

"Hello...Donan," Tremlo replied, smoother now.

"You have words," Donan said.

"Yyou...ha-ve word-s."

Donan repeated himself, and Tremlo said them again much more smoothly.

"How does it feel to talk?" Donan asked, beaming with expectation.

"Yes," Tremlo answered.

Donan chuckled. "You have suddenly begun to talk. What does that feel like?"

"Yes," Tremlo smiled once again.

"What does it feel like?" Donan repeated, much slower this time.

Tremlo responded in like manner.

"Yes. It... feels to...talk."

"It feels to talk."

Tremlo nodded enthusiastically. "It feels to talk."

"Does it feel good or bad?"

Tremlo burst into laughter and nodded his head. Donan laughed with him. The questions he wanted to ask were fast falling away.

"Last week you did not have words, but today you do. What feels different?"

Tremlo looked puzzled and laughed again.

"Feels," he nodded. "Feels."

Donan picked up a wooden bowl. "What is this?" he asked.

"Tree falls, cutaw ay car ve out—"

"Bowl," Donan said firmly. Tremlo laughed, and Donan laughed with him.

"Bowl," Donan said again.

"Bow l," Tremlo repeated. He took it from the Kwaman, put it on its side and began to spin it. Donan watched, trying to muster enthusiasm for this game. Tremlo spun the bowl on its side and listened with glee as it slowed down and landed on its bottom. The moment it stopped Tremlo spun it again.

Apparently, he was done with words, at least for now.

Donan took the time to collect his thoughts. Tremlo had not understood his questions. When he asked him to name the bowl, it unleashed a strange torrent of words, suggesting the chaotic state of the younger's mind.

"Tremlo," Donan asked when Tremlo's fascination with the bowl waned. "What is this?"

He held up a cutting stone.

"Fireburn heat rock, brea kflat hit hard chi p—"

"Cutting stone," Donan affirmed, realizing Tremlo was describing the process of making the cutter.

Tremlo nodded and laughed.

"Cut ting sto ne."

"What is this?" the Kwaman asked, holding up the bowl again.

"Spinn ing rounder, tree falls cut away carve—"

"Bowl."

"Bowl."

Tremlo might indeed have words, but they poured out of him, revealing a labyrinth of loose associations.

Donan laughed to hide his disappointment. It might be years, if ever, before he got answers to the questions he sought today.

"Tremlo, what is this?" he asked, feeling the scope of the work ahead for all of them.

"Tremlo, what is this?"

"Tremlo, what is that?"

Everyone he came in contact with began to talk to him.

"Tremlo, this?"

"Tremlo, that?"

He rose to the challenge, and in less than a year, had the word for every object the Rehloy gave name to. But these had little to do with his perception of things. To say, 'move the rock here,' was so much easier than to express the true nature of the rock, whose surface spoke of its history, whose rhythm was attached to its mother lying some distance away, whose form interacted with all the objects around it, which together fit within the palm of the greater mountain that held in place the rhythms framing their daily lives, whose condition changed from moment to moment within the flow of the currents, that eventually grew, layer upon layer, to encompass Loy and beyond.

Words simplified everything. Words were like the sticks he played with. Tiny objects that could be picked up and moved about with ease. So easy, in fact, that they became a world unto themselves. A toy, a vision, *a dream.*

Tremlo came to love words. They were a bridge to other members of the tribe. Words drew them to him.

"Tremlo, what is this? Tremlo, what is that?"

Here was something they could use to both help him, and keep him at arm's length, limiting their own discomfort when near him.

"Tremlo, what are you feeling?"

"He feels fine."

"No, I mean what do you feel in this moment?"

"He feels good."

When asked questions about himself, Tremlo always referred to himself as "he".

"Tell me the things you are experiencing right now."

"Clouds floating across the sky tickle the back of Reena's neck. Arlen beside, walking through the sound of birds—"

"That is what Reena and your father are experiencing. What are you, Tremlo, feeling?"

"He... He is... feeling...."

More than this he could not say. In one sense, it was as if he did not exist separately from everyone else.

"Tremlo," Donan asked one day when he deemed Tremlo had acquired enough words. "Do you sense Jormah's presence?"

"Covered with hair. Climbing white dirt."

Much of what the child said made no sense, but each time Donan asked about Jormah, Tremlo confirmed that the feel of him was getting stronger.

Of that we both agree.

"What is it you think about?"

Questions like these always made Tremlo nervous. He was never sure what was being asked. He desperately wanted to please the Kwaman, but when he tried to answer, he would become lost. He simply could not hold onto one line of thinking. The harder he tried, the more scattered his thoughts became. Donan always smiled and patted him on the head and told him not to worry, but Tremlo felt his concern. The others in the tribe found it better to ask him questions that required simple yes or no answers than to listen to rambling replies.

When Tremlo was seven, it was decided he was steady enough to leave the still-cave for good. In preparation, Arlen started bringing objects down to the cave they would call home. Each day marked a shift in weight for Tremlo, and on the day they were ready to leave, he found he was already there.

"Are you ready?"

"He is ready," Tremlo smiled, reflecting back to them their own sense of expectation.

"Good."

For seven years Reena longed to stroll down this path with Arlen and Tremlo. Now that the moment had arrived, everything felt surreal.

Tremlo slid his hand inside the special side pocket she had made for him. It held a piece of his touchstone, and he squeezed it tightly to reassure himself that everything was all right.

By the time they got to the cave, he needed to be inside. His sleeping mat lay along the far wall, and he dove onto it. Here was a raft in an ever-widening sea of noise. Curling up into a tight ball, he promptly fell asleep.

It was exhausting to be here.

For the next few weeks, he took many long naps until his body became acclimated to the sound of the cave, which eventually became a raft all its own.

When Tremlo left the cave, he always had his hand in his pocket. Some of the youngers imitated him by putting a hand on their side. The physical motion quickly became their name for him. He felt the teasing but knew there was no malice in it. There was something wrong with him, plain and simple. He knew it from early on. His shame was an everyday color. The stoop in his shoulders, the bend of his neck.

The Mahtwah's cave was one of the few places in which he felt safe. Mortulla was all poking and probing, but Kenectka, her Heart, lived there as well.

"Tremlo, what is this?" she would ask, taking him through the medicines.

"Briar root."

"And this?"

"Keefo."

Kenectka pointed to some baelo. "What is this used for?"

"Burns," Tremlo replied without hesitation.

He came to visit every day and sat with her for hours on end, answering her questions, helping with the chores, all the while just being with her. With others, there was a stiffness. But with her, this was Kenectka, whose tones had always been open and inviting. Who stood fast during the rages. Who never tried to shield him when some strong current coursed through his body, but tried to feel it for herself.

"What is this?"

"Ellaberry."

She taught him the words, but he somehow knew their uses by simply being around.

"And what is it used for?"

"Mixed with aspira and tye, it can help rid a wound of its fire and heal more quickly."

Kenectka was taken aback. "How do you know that?" She was secretly experimenting with this very mixture and had not even told the Mahtwah.

Her surprise put him on guard. He could not think of how he knew it, only that it seemed so. A moment ago, he did not even know he knew this. It was her question that framed it and drew it out of him.

"I'm always surprised by how much you know," she said feeling him withdraw. "It's not a bad thing. Come, let's go for a walk."

Tremlo followed, moving in perfect tandem with her body. He knew her so well, it scared her sometimes. And it only seemed to go one way. Whenever she looked, whenever she reached out with all her senses and tried to see him more clearly, she always came upon a sense of herself looking back. It was a wall she could not penetrate.

Who are you?

Tremlo smiled and spread his arms out wide.

How did you know about the aspira and tye?

He giggled and spun in a circle.

Nervous are you? Why?

He spun faster, wishing only for the unobstructed flow of her. When she looked at him like this, there was no stopping her. She would start asking things he barely understood, things he could never answer correctly. He spun around, faster and faster.

Spreading her arms wide, Kenectka spun with him. Tremlo roared with laughter, and they twirled along the path, spinning like a breeze, until Kenectka's dizziness became his own, and they collapsed upon the ground in peals of laughter.

Lying on their backs, he felt the question still in her body.

How had he known?

He tried to find the moment it came into his mind. But he never thought back on something or forward to something. Everything that happened, happened simultaneously in the very same moment.

"It jumped into his mind," he said aloud, coming as close to the truth as he could manage.

"It jumped into your mind. But where did it come from?"

Where?

A question of direction. He reached out and quickly lost his way.

"Something in you told you?"

Her words were like the banks of a river.

Something in him told him.

Tremlo searched each part. Arms, toes, head, hands, chest…. Within moments he was lost again and the question gone.

"Something in you told you," Kenectka said, feeling him stray.

Something in him told him, he thought. But there was no place he could find where the truth resided.

"You are so sensitive. Your body knows things long before your mind."

Yes, he thought. *Yes, that was it.* Somehow, he knew things before he knew he knew them.

"The mind-of-your-body."

The mind-of-his-body. He knew this meant something specific, but it never made sense to him. He simply could not find it.

The mind-of-his-body.

He did not know where, or what, or when it was.

"Don't look for it. Listen for it. It has a voice all its own."

But there were so many voices. If he listened to one, he had to listen to all, and they would overwhelm him.

Things jump into his mind, that's all.

This was one more thing that caused others distress, and he vowed not to say anything again that jumped into his mind.

"Tremlo, what are you thinking?"

"He. He...."

He was withdrawing again.

"Don't be afraid. The mind-of-the-body watches all the time, whether you are awake or asleep. It knows things before knowing seems possible."

He had heard this all his life. The early lessons.

"Our bodies speak our thoughts in their own language. They speak thoughts that we ourselves may not be aware of."

The children were taught to observe themselves and catch their bodies speaking hidden thoughts. A leg swinging, a foot tapping, fingers rubbing, arms twitching, bodies swaying.

"You think something, and your body speaks it. But who is speaking?"

They soon discovered there was a separate mind to their bodies. Unconscious. It had a life and intelligence all its own. It perceived things they were not aware of. It often spoke in a language they could not hear or did not understand. It was a mind that had the power to influence and direct them without their knowing.

Only by separating from this mind and observing it, could they begin to see it, understand it, and eventually use it. Only then was *true-awareness* possible.

But for him, it was never about looking for it. Or seeing it separately from himself. For him, it was always about escaping the intensity.

"Tremlo, the mind-of-your-body is very strong. Stronger than most. It's what makes you so special. I think you feel its presence in a way we don't. I think it is why you call yourself, 'he'. Don't be afraid of it. Make it your friend."

Your friend.

The words came in time to the beat of his heart.

Your-friend... your-friend....

A throb of recognition, her words illuminating some dark corner, and then it was gone. For a moment, he had tasted something. Heard something. A glint of light before the beat. For an instant, he saw inwards.

In-sight.

"The mind-of-his-body," he said sitting up. "The mind-of-his-body!"

"Is that where it came from?"

"Yes, yes."

And no.

Tremlo leaped up and ran around Kenectka. She laughed along with the energy pouring off his body.

"Sit," she said when it appeared he would not stop. "Sit down and recite your buntra-for-selfstenance."

He did as she asked, and by the time he calmed down, he had forgotten why he got so excited in the first place. He remembered he felt a whisp of his body and its mind but also something else. A form, a sense, a thing so vague... he couldn't be sure.

Yet, something stuck with him. Like a small stone at the bottom of a stream, it resisted the flow of the water.

Slowly, over time, other stones began to collect around it.

CHAPTER TWO

Tremlo stood on the far side of the grotto, listening. The five-and-six-year-olds were circling in preparation for a game he wanted to join.

He was ten years old now, but this was the group he most easily fit in with. Those his own age had forged intimate bonds during the years he was confined to the still-cave. There was a pleasing rhythm to their play that his presence seemed to interrupt. They tried to hide it from him, for they were not insensitive, but he sensed it all the same, and for the most part avoided them.

The children stiffened at his approach. The first flush of Tremlo could be harsh, but he blended in quickly, and the rhythm of their game resumed. They circled twice before Haynlee veered off from the group. Asna quickly followed, imitating her every move.

It would be a game of 'follow'.

Haynlee stopped before a rock wall and assumed a defensive-posture. Within a breath, the front of her body changed color to match what lay directly behind her. She blended in well for a six-year-old, but her posture would not have fooled an adult. She held it for five counts and stepped away to let Asna go.

When his turn came, Tremlo happily stepped up to the wall. But unlike the others, he vanished completely. Before them lay the smell, the temperature, the very sound of the rock. Tremlo's postures were always astonishing in the first few moments and rivaled those of a Kwaman's. Yet he never seemed to hold on to them for long.

True to form, the color on his skin faded, small cracks appeared, and one section of rock crumbled away.

"Tremlo!"

He was far beyond the scope of words.

"Tremlo, stop!" Haynlee cried and pushed him off the wall.

Future and present collided in a flash of pain as he hit the ground.

Hand to pocket, squeezing hard.

H... here.

Once again, he had lost himself to unknown forces.

The sting of him clung to them like dust, and they quickly brushed themselves off. Tremlo lowered his head, but there was no need. This was the burden of Tremlo, and they were used to him.

Donan, observing the youngers from the ridge high above, felt the world go silent.

A wave of future-energy was leaking back into the present.

It was only at this late stage of his life that he was able to perceive such a thing.

The color of the rock wall below faded, tiny cracks appeared, a small section of rock disappeared.

These were the exact changes Tremlo had performed.

Not even tales of the Sentients spoke of such sensitivities.

The vision passed quickly, but Donan was left transfixed. For years he had marked Tremlo's progress, waiting for a change. But the source of the child's strength was the foundation of his weakness, and because of this duality, he was deeply flawed.

A plan had been growing in Donan's mind for quite some time. After the incident today, it made no sense to delay.

Stelbin reached down from the High Cave, feeling the Kwaman on the move again.

That strange shift in Donan had quickly come and gone, but incidents like this were happening more frequently of late. Even Whaet, their Leader, was taking notice. Weeks before, he approached Stelbin when no one was about.

"You have lived with the Kwaman these past many years and know him better than anyone," Whaet said looking up into his face. Stelbin was now the second tallest member of the tribe and a head taller than Whaet. "You've come a long way, Stelbin. Has Donan said anything to you about your ceremony?"

For the past seven years, Donan had trained Stelbin, and he had grown from Donan's Side to his Heart, although the Kwaman had not yet declared him as such.

"Not yet."

"Well, I for one think the time has come."

Whaet's words were pleasing, but caused a shift in Stelbin.

"Insults are lighter than air," Donan often said. *"Flattery is lighter still. Do not be swayed by either. Another's view speaks mostly of themselves. If it concerns you, it still speaks of them."*

Remembering this, Stelbin came into *awareness*.

"Even as we stand here," Whaet continued, "I feel I am in the presence of a Kwaman."

Stelbin smiled, standing beside himself, separate, watching.

Truth is miniscule, illusion grand.

Whaet's body shifted with what he had come to say.

"Donan seems more distracted than usual, don't you think?"

The pattern-of-change was growing stronger. Nowhere was it more apparent than in the Kwaman. Donan had hidden its effects from the tribe, but it was becoming too strong now even for him to disguise.

"Yes," Stelbin agreed. *Be an empty cup for him to fill.*

"Has Donan spoken to you about Jormah?"

"He says he is returning."

"He's been saying that for years. Has he said anything about when?"

"He says only that Jormah's presence is getting stronger."

"Do you sense that?"

Stelbin searched for Jormah every day and often tried to follow the flow of Donan's body to orient himself. But other than a sense of direction, he felt nothing. And that was a great disappointment.

A bitter taste rose in Stelbin's mouth. Donan had taught him to color certain kinds of thoughts and emotions with flavors.

"It will alert you to their presence and help you see the true nature of the mind-of-your-body. A Kwaman must stand apart and watch everything, even the machinations of his own self."

"I have not sensed anything yet. He waits for me to discern the truth for myself."

'I see.'

"Yes, I will."

"What?"

"I will tell you when I know."

Whaet chuckled. Stelbin had seen into his mind.

Donan made his way up the mountain. The caution of age marked his stride, despite the determination in his step.

He's up to something, Stelbin thought. Episodes like today were usually accompanied by a vision, but Donan rarely shared them with him.

I will act like nothing unusual has occurred and see what he reveals.

The Kwaman came in, cast a surreptitious glance around the cave and sat down in his usual place. Their bodies spoke through subtle discernments. No words passed between them.

Donan felt Stelbin's scrutiny.

"What has this day brought?" he finally asked him.

"The pressure felt odd today," Stelbin replied.

"In what way?"

Since coming to live with the Kwaman, little outwardly in the tribe had changed. Inwardly, however, there was a level of pressure building that was worrisome.

"The energies shifted midday and were interrupted by Tremlo."

"Tremlo?"

Donan certainly knew this.

"He had a small fit today."

"Yes, of course."

What did he hope to hear? And why does he keep looking around the cave?

"You had a vision today."

"Of sorts," Donan admitted.

"And you have come to a decision."

"Yes."

"About Tremlo?"

'Yes.'

The Kwaman was very still now. But a moment ago it felt like he was moving things around in his mind, taking inventory, making space.

"You are bringing him here?"

Donan looked at Stelbin carefully. The training had taken on a life all its own. A slow smile crossed his face, and he nodded with new appreciation of his Side, who was nearer to his Heart than ever before.

"I will tell you now of my vision...."

CHAPTER THREE

Benton stood behind the Steersman on the aft deck of the three-master. The moon at half disk bathed the black sea with jewels of sparkling light. A clear night, perfect for navigation. Soft rolling waves lulled those below to sleep. Benton himself was about to turn in when something caught his attention. His nostrils flared. A flicker of rotting flesh – gone as quickly as it appeared.

"Did you smell that?"

The Steersman turned his head in Benton's direction.

"No, Commander. Like what?"

"Never mind."

Most winds came forth in swirling patterns. For all Benton knew, this scent might have come from behind them.

Far to their rear was the westernmost province of Ontar. They had set sail from Port Alburt weeks before and were heading for Ontara, the first colony in the new land. Two ships: one filled with food, tools, and Augmentors. The other housed eighteen lopers, the workhorses of the empire.

"I'm going below. If you smell anything out of the ordinary, send for me immediately."

"Understood."

Late that night, the winds gave out and the two ships were becalmed. There was little to do but wait while the elements had their way with them. At first light, a dark fog appeared on the horizon. It crawled slowly towards them, carrying fragments of that dank rot Benton smelled the night before. The Augmentors drew their weapons as it rolled over them.

Was this the foul breath of a sea monster?

All eyes scanned the water for a ripple that might betray what swam below.

Nothing.

The sun drew higher. Its heat penetrated the upper layers of the fog. Cracks of blue appeared. The wind picked up and the ships lurched into clear light. Once free of the stench, the Augmentors sheathed their swords, still wondering at the cause.

Near midday, the lookout called down from his perch high above.
"North, northwest!"
"What is it?"
"Too far to tell."
"A ship?"
"I think so."
The Steersman turned to Benton. It would mean a change in course.
"Make for it," Benton said and signaled the Charge Augmentor on the other ship.
Prepare for battle!
One ship bore right, the other left. They would turn in on this object from two sides on the fastest tacks.
The Augmentors readied their long bows.
"It looks like one of ours!" the lookout called out. "A cargo, I think."
The smell was back, mixing with the fresh air. They could see the ship now. A few strands of sail flapped in the wind, looking more like banners than sail. The ship was rolling with the waves, a storm anchor off the stern was keeping it relatively steady.
The closer they got, the stronger the smell.
A death ship.
Benton moved to the bow and raised his sword high for all to see.
Hold steady!
From this distance, they saw no one about.
Was it a trap?
Small mounds of dirt were spread across the deck.
Is that a man halfway up the main mast?
Are there two others near the top?
Dead? Alive?
They were bearing down fast upon the ship.
Too fast.
"Fall off!" Benton called out, waving his sword to the side. The ships altered course, Benton's running well in front, the Augmentors' far behind. Once they were a safe distance past, they swung about, noses to the wind, and stopped. It was a cargo ship of standard design. They had drawn no movement from anyone aboard.
The smell was irrefutable.

"Steersman, take us in a little closer."

Bodily remains were scattered across the deck. Those piles of brown dirt were now large animals, dead like the crew.

"Steady," Benton said. "Bring us closer."

"Commander," the Charge Augmentor from the other ship shouted, "Commander, the blue stripe along its side and back. It's the Lotubo!"

"The Lotubo? Impossible!"

The Lotubo was presumed lost at sea and was the very reason Et-El Baronuus sent him on this desperate mission.

Years before, Emperor Proutus sent Et-El Baronuus away from court to inspect Ontara, the first settlement in the new world. It was a task fit for one of lower rank, and Baronuus, who was a member of the Elite, thought this a major setback. He left Ontar fearing he had fallen out of favor with the Emperor.

But once in the settlement, he discovered something remarkable and returned from Ontara with high hopes and renewed ambition. The very day he landed, he was summoned to the Emperor's palace in Halla, the city of cities.

"The wonders of Halla are great, my liege. To be here in your presence once again is—"

"Enough with the formalities, Baronuus. Tell me what you've found!"

The Emperor's abrupt manner put him on edge, and he struggled to keep the tension out of his voice.

"There is no scheming on the Newland Commander's part that I could find. The setbacks of the settlement are well known. Its development is slow, and what I am about to suggest will slow its growth further."

He paused for effect.

"I'm waiting."

"The war with the Argoot is getting worse."

"Yes. The stitch in our side has become a thorn."

"The major obstacle to the settlement's growth may well be the very thing that removes that thorn."

"Speak plainly, Baronuus." the Emperor's voice bordered dangerously on annoyance.

"I am referring to the Kurr."

"The beast?"

"The very one."

Three times these monsters savaged the colony, killing all their lopers and any man who tried to interfere. The beasts were unstoppable when it came to loper flesh and so terrifying that Kriiton, the Newland Commander, banned all lopers from being brought to the new land.

"What we have in our midst is the potential for the greatest fighting force this world has ever seen."

"What foolishness is this?"

"If we could train these animals, we could unleash a force upon the Argoot, against which they could not defend. In a matter of weeks, perhaps days, the Argoot would be decimated."

"You would send an animal to do the work of an Augmentor?"

"The Argoot are cowards. They strike, then run and hide like children. I suggest we bring the battle down to their level."

"Use an animal as a warrior?"

Kriiton had written that the beasts were not trainable. They were driven insane by loper flesh and devoured all in their path. To bring them here to a land filled with lopers was madness.

But what if they could be trained to do our bidding?

Proutus laughed aloud. If this plan failed, he would use it to rid himself of Baronuus and confiscate his property.

"Bring me a formal proposal."

"Yes, my liege. I need a little time to—"

"Tomorrow, Baronuus! I want it tomorrow."

The following day, Baronuus, bleary eyed, presented his plan to the Emperor. Proutus barely glanced at it.

"You will begin immediately. Our need is great. Do not fail us."

The Emperor smiled, and Baronuus knew, without a doubt, what would happen if he failed.

It took nine months to get a properly sized vessel overhauled and outfitted with special cages. The ship arrived at the colony in good order. It took more time to find and capture the Kurr while they hibernated. Eventually, the ship left with ten beasts aboard. But there was a terrible storm at sea, and it was never seen again.

Baronuus hastily commandeered a second ship named the Lotubo. Larger cages were built into its hull to house more animals and compensate for the lost time.

From the beginning, most of the Elite thought his plan ludicrous.

"Why not train birds to fly overhead and tell us where the Argoot are hiding," they joked privately. "Or if they can't tell us, maybe we can train them to crap on their heads."

Since Proutus had endorsed the plan, none of them dared say anything openly against it. But with each delay, the whispers grew louder. A vacuum grew around Baronuus as more and more Elite quietly withdrew. The longer the delay, the greater his isolation became.

"Believe me, Benton," Baronuus said time and again. "Once the beast is here, once they see it, they will come crawling back."

Benton nodded but feared otherwise. He had only recently been transferred into Baronuus's command.

His downfall will be my own.

Two years had passed since Baronuus first presented his plan to the Emperor. Time was running out. If something went wrong with this mission, no matter the cause, Baronuus knew he would be cast aside.

The day after the Lotubo left the harbor, he secretly commissioned another ship to be built using his own funds. The cost was enormous and would leave him penniless, but he had no choice. This would be his last chance to redeem himself.

The Lotubo reached the colony and was forced to wait many months for them to capture the beasts needed to fill the cages. Once provisioned, it set sail for Ontar. The journey normally took three months, but six months later, the Lotubo had still not arrived and was presumed lost at sea.

This time, there could be no excuses of bad weather. The seas had been calm and the winds favorable. Baronuus fell into such disfavor he feared he would not last the season.

"We are victims of foul play, Benton. The new ship is ready. I will announce it to the Emperor today." *Before he moves to depose me.* "You are one of the newest and brightest of my officers. I am temporarily promoting you to my triumvirate and putting you in command of this mission. If you succeed, the appointment will be permanent."

Benton was speechless. He was being elevated to the rank of *Personage*, albeit a minor one, but a Personage, nonetheless. By passing over several senior officers, Baronuus was giving him an opportunity that few ever achieved.

"You know Kriiton personally, I believe."

"Well, I—"

"You know him."

"We, we were boyhood friends."

"Good. You will use that to your advantage."

"Understood," Benton replied, realizing he wasn't just one of the newest and brightest.

"Kriiton will balk at mounting another hunt. He has many concerns and is not sympathetic to our cause. But we can tolerate no more delays. You will take eighteen lopers with you."

"Lopers? But what of the ban?"

"What of it? You are his friend. You will make him understand. You will take eighteen lopers and use them as bait. Instead of wasting time and energy hunting down the Kurr, you will draw the beasts to you and solve both his problem and ours."

The look on Benton's face was severe.

"It is your duty, Benton, not to let anyone, and I mean anyone, undermine us. You will take an escort ship with a full complement of Augmentors. Go to Ontara and bring me back those damned beasts, for both our sakes!"

"Understood."

The Steersman maneuvered them slowly in. The doors to all the cabins were broken apart. A battle had been waged, but one so bizarre, they had difficulty making sense of it. The beasts lay there, their bodies filled with the red painted spears and arrows of Ontar.

The attack had not come from another vessel. The men tied to the mast above had probably starved to death.

"Prepare to board!" Benton called to the other ship. "One *septa*. Beware the beasts! Search and report."

Seven men leaped aboard with short swords drawn. Behind them Augmentors lined the deck with bows cocked. The seven moved swiftly across the blood-stained deck. There had indeed been a fierce battle here.

Of the six beasts lying there, five had clearly been killed by the many spears and arrows protruding from their undersides. But the sixth was different and the Augmentors approached it with caution. It was on its stomach with several arrows in its back. But there was little blood on the deck surrounding it. Its red tongue hung partially out of its mouth. It was dry and scaly from lack of water, and the animal did not appear to be breathing. Its legs, however, were somewhat pliable, and its body, although not exactly warm, was not cold either.

"Commander, this one may be alive."

"Post two guards! Have them place their swords on the underside where its legs meet its body. That is its most vulnerable spot. The rest, proceed with the search."

The Augmentors turned their attention to the remains of the crew. They had seen death on the battlefield, but never anything like the ravaged bodies before them. None of these unfortunate men were left whole. Body parts were strewn about the deck. Arms, legs, and buttocks, stripped bare of flesh and muscle. Chests and backs torn open with few organs left. Many individual bones appeared half chewed.

Down below, doors and walls had been ripped apart and every cabin invaded. Men had gone there in hopes of escape, only to be devoured where they hid. Some were in closets, others under bunks. The remains of two children were found in the forward rope locker.

Once the inspection was completed, the Charge Augmentor declared the ship secured. "All crew are dead. Five more beasts below, also dead."

"Nest up!"

Benton and his second, Gilner, climbed aboard and went over to the animal the Augmentors were guarding.

"Bring the physyck! Keep your swords at-the-ready."

"Understood."

"Commander," the Charge called them to the stern. The aft area was filled with excrement, but nowhere else.

"The Kurr were particular about where they shat."

"Strange behavior for beasts," Gilner said.

Strange behavior indeed, Benton thought.

"What else have you found?"

"Scratches on the mast. Looks like they tried to get to the men above but couldn't quite manage it."

"So they can't climb?"

"Appears so."

"Good to know."

The air down below deck was putrid. There were two cages; one large, taking up most of the hold, and one small, built to conform to the "V" shape of the bow. The large cage was empty, but the smaller one housed five animals.

"They killed them while still in the cage."

Why? Benton wondered. The cage door was locked. *Did they fear someone would let them out?*

The large cage door was also locked, but along the backside, ten of its bars had been cut and bent down. Tufts of animal hair clung to the exposed points of the bars.

They crawled out.

But who would cut the bars? For what purpose?

Could Baronuus be right about a plot to discredit him?

Benton moved through all the cabins. The Kurr had clawed their way into every crevice.

Was there no escaping them?

The men tied to the mast high above had preferred to die of starvation than face this animal's wrath.

No wonder Baronuus is obsessed with them.

"The physyck is aboard," came the call, and Benton went to greet him.

"Let me know if this beast is dead or alive."

The Kurr were cat-like, but monstrously so. Standing on all fours, they were as tall as men. Their claws were thick and pointed and several fingers long. Their faces were relatively flat with wide, black nostrils. Large teeth protruded from either corner of their mouths. The physyck covered this one's nostrils with his palms. There was some slight sensation of warmth but not enough to convince him it was alive. Animals in deep winter sleeps could appear dead, only to come back alive with warming temperatures.

Could this beast be in a similar state, brought on by a condition other than cold?

He lifted one of its eyelids and looked directly into its white, vacant eye.

Did its pupil just contract?

Closing the lid, he turned his attention back to its mouth. With the help of an Augmentor, they pried it open.

"The Kurr is barely alive or recently dead. I can find no direct proof of either yet. Its teeth, as you can see, are quite something. Notice the double row along the bottom. One for cutting, the other for tearing and grinding. Its claws are like daggers and razor sharp. They could probably rip their way through anything."

"Which would explain the damage to the walls and doors. What else?"

"Its outer skin is several thumbs thick and makes an excellent shield. Most of the arrows barely penetrated."

"Can you bring it back to life?"

"I don't know. If I can get some fresh water into it, perhaps it will have some effect. Assuming it's still alive."

"Do it."

"Are you sure?"

"We are charged with bringing back as many of these beasts as we can carry. We need to learn all we can about them, even before we get to Ontara. There's a cage below that was not breached. We will bring this one down before you try to revive it."

"Understood."

Benton turned to his Second. "Have the Augmentors restore the vessel. Throw the dead Kurr overboard. Gather all the remains of the men who have perished. We will give them a proper burial at sea. I'm going below to the Captain's quarters to see what I can find."

"Understood."

Benton found the ship's log on the Captain's desk. They had taken eighteen animals aboard.

But we found only eleven.

Most entries were nautical, noting course, weather, wind, and current. The Captain did, however, make several mentions of the violent nature of the Kurr.

'Day Three: What manner of cargo is this? These beasts roar in unison, howling their protest for *oras* on end. And they will not stop no matter what we do.'

'Day Seven: Today a beast reached through the bars and grabbed a crewman who was feeding them. It ripped open the man's side and held him fast until he bled to death. The man's cries were covered by the incessant howling, and we did not discover his body until later. I have forbidden everyone from going into the hold.'

'Day Eight: The ship's carpenter finished cutting open two sections of the deck so my order can be carried out. We feed them from above, dropping what manner of food provided onto the top of the cages. At times, a Kurr will leap up and catch it as it passes through the bars. This is a testament to their speed and agility. They are a terrible cargo.'

'Day Twenty-Four: The beasts continue their incessant howling. It's unnerving. We can hardly hear ourselves think. In two months' time, when we reach Ontar, I will be quite relieved to be rid of these monsters.'

Benton turned the page only to find the rest of the log was blank.

How soon after he wrote this had the carnage begun?

The Captain wrote that no one was allowed in the hold.

But if the Kurr were so violent, how could anyone have gotten near enough to cut the bars? Could they have been partially cut while still at the colony? Or before that, in Ontar itself?

"Ahhhhh!" the physyck shrieked.

Benton raced up on deck to find the man bent over and cradling his hand. His finger was bleeding.

"What happened? Did it bite you?"

The man shook his head no. He was quite pale. Benton disliked weak men, and the one before him was certainly that. But the physyck was not stupid, and that was his only saving grace.

"Steady now. Tell me what happened."

"I— I was examining the Kurr's teeth near the back. I should have used a probe but instead slipped my thumb underneath its lip and pulled it farther back to get a better look."

"You cut your finger on its teeth?"

"They're very sharp."

"Did the animal move in any way?"

"No. I still don't know if it's dead or alive."

Color was returning to his face.

"What were you looking for?"

"The rear teeth on the left side are different from those on the right. They've been ground down quite a ways. And judging from the color, it happened very recently."

Benton turned to a group of Augmentors preparing to push one of the beasts over the side.

"Hold a moment!" He strode over to the beast. "Open its mouth, but don't use your hands."

The beast's mouth was locked tight. They sliced the jaw muscles and pried it open with a piece of wood. This one's back teeth had also been ground down on one side.

Benton went down into the hold and carefully examined the large cage. The sidebars had been cut through nearly chest high. Examining them more closely, he saw they had been narrowed to points and then broken through. No manmade tool would make such a mark.

The beasts chewed through the bars!

If the Captain's log entries were correct, it took them just under a month to do so.

He knew then what fate had befallen the original vessel. Bad weather or not, it was doomed the moment the Kurr were brought aboard.

The small cage was cleaned out, and the lone Kurr put inside. Benton ordered the Augmentors to chain each of its legs to a separate bar, rooting it to the middle.

"Do you think that's necessary?" the Charge asked.

"The Kurr chewed their way out of the large cage. I will not allow that to happen again."

The Captain of this vessel had inadvertently aided the Kurr in their escape. Ordering his men to keep away from the cages doomed them, for they never knew what the beasts were doing.

'...they roar in unison, howling for oras each day.'

Had the Kurr done this to hide the grinding sounds they made gnawing at the bars?

It was a frightening thought, and he resolved to never underestimate this animal. He would treat them like equals, capable of all the treachery and violence of men.

The physyck placed a water-soaked cloth into its mouth.

"If I pour water down its throat while unconscious, it might drown. We'll keep the cloth moist and see what happens."

Benton went back up on deck and watched as the last remaining beast was pushed over the side. It was dead and rotting, but even in this state, there was something fierce and frightening about it.

The remains of the crew were gathered and wrapped together in a shroud. When all was made ready, Benton spoke the words for the dead.

"We ask the gods to accept and protect these souls who lost their lives in the service of the Emperor and the Way-Of-The-Sane. May they remain out of harm's way. And through their sacrifice, may we be granted safe passage."

"So may it be," the Augmentors said in unison.

The shroud was thrown into the waiting arms of Oceana, and they watched until it sank out of sight.

So may it be.

"Commander!" the physyck's voice. "Commander!" The man was running up on deck. "The tongue. Its tongue just moved! It's alive!"
The words rolled over in Benton's mind.
Alive. Alive. Alive!
It was the call to battle.

CHAPTER FOUR

Jormah sped up the face of the canyon, eyes closed, hands and feet grasping the holds his body knew would be there. The muscles in his back whispered what passed beneath, his leefskin spoke the color. Floating more than climbing, he, the second Kwaman of this time, possessed an awareness most would never achieve.

Up and over the ledge, across the way, stopping at the entrance to the cave Origin once inhabited. He had come here years before, having narrowly escaped the clutches of the deadly grassland. Half-dead, his body starved for Resep, his senses smothered by a terrible rigidity.

Origin was living deep inside this cave. A solitary plant with the voice of many. The story of the Rehloy's origin told of such a plant. But everyone knew Resep grew in sunlight, not darkness. In their long history, no one had ever found Resep growing in a cave until he stumbled upon this one.

The size of the plant, the depth of its ridges and the black-green color of its skin spoke of great age. *A Mother Plant.* He named her Origin, and an intimacy had grown between them. He partook of her sparingly, and eventually plucked the ancient seedpod from her crown in order to grow new plants and keep from consuming her. But this act of care inadvertently signaled the end of her long life.

Horrified, he made great efforts to save her, but she died in the end, leaving him to mourn her passing.

Origin. He missed her to this very day. Through her, he had come to understand the relationship between the Rehloy and the Resep more fully. Through her children, through ingesting the blue Broezia that collected on the edges of their leaves, he discovered the posture-of-speed.

A soft chatter from the ridge above drew him away from these thoughts.

The Resep he planted there had grown and died, and grown again, and again, seeding itself along paths of its own making.

The children-of-Origin.

He climbed the ridge and was greeted by waist-high, lime-green shoots, waving with the wind. Different from Origin, just as he himself was different from the one who first came here. He sat down to listen.

Far to the south and west, he felt a glimmer of the tribe along his back.

About a year away.

Even from this distance, he could feel the rich and harmonious tones of the *intralife*.

The knowledge he carried would change all that.

"I should just stay away," he said aloud.

More than ten years had passed since he left. Ten years since the Resep first crawled along the ground in angular patterns.

The pattern-of-change.

That same year a mysterious pool of water had appeared in the wilderness. He had gone to investigate and discovered that its gold and shimmering tones possessed a unique smell that could repel a Yarka. Those murderous beasts had held them hostage for centuries.

The waterpool vanished soon after, but armed with this new and wondrous scent, he left the safety of the Tribal land to venture into the unknown.

Ten years.

Donan would have taken a Side by now. Some Rehloy may have died, and others were certainly born. That high-pitched tone that appeared soon after he left had remained steady enough for him to understand it was the reflection of a newborn.

The child must be about ten years old.

Despite the years, the younger still stood out separately from the tribe.

Like me, Jormah thought.

A spike of energy from the north fractured the cool quiet of the currents.

Intruders.

A surge like this meant another ship had arrived. He had been to the edge of the continent and seen the infestation. Pathways were spreading out, the forest withdrawing from their touch.

This was the disaster that awaited them.

The knowledge weighed heavily in his body and would infect them all.

I should just stay away.

But even as he thought this, pressures were urging him to move on. He would have to wait to Harvest the plants for food and fresh leefskins before he dared cut through that murderous grassland. Then onto the City-Of-Straight-Lines, through the Valley Forest, and into the heart-land of the Rehloy.

Jormah reached out to the Tribal Body once more. Its tone was open. Inviting. A sense of joy and wonder prevailed.

He listened for a time until the sadness took hold.

They had a year left to bask in their innocence.

CHAPTER FIVE

Mortulla and Kenectka breathed in the tonal health of the tribe. Over the years, Kenectka learned the remedies, but more than this, a new way of thinking. Nowadays, the two rarely disagreed.

An odd pitch in the air today.

"Donan will come," Mortulla said, absently touching the right side of her face. If she or Donan had taken a mate, it would have been the other. But the intensity between them allowed no shade. In the end, they would have burned up all the good in each other. And so they lived a life apart, a life alone, for there was no one else for them but each other.

"I will leave before he gets here."

"Don't be impetuous, child."

"I will leave to gather some chaulkna when the moment seems right."

"Better."

Both smiled. That Mortulla could even say this was a mark of the intimacy the two now shared. Kenectka was her Heart, a Mahtwah in her own right, and the One-To-Follow. There could be no secrets between them now.

Almost none, Mortulla thought, for she would always hold something back to keep Kenectka sharply focused.

Donan arrived midday. He had aged these past few years. Slower in step, a touch more stooped. That inner light bright as ever but feathered now with a kind of distraction.

Kenectka knew he was dying, as much from what she had learned in the art of healing as from the interaction between the two of them. They wished to keep it a secret, and so she had said nothing to either. *The creeping death.* Named for its slow and steady advance, it could take decades to complete its journey. But once started, it drained its victims of their strength a drop at a time.

Mortulla looked into his face with the freedom of an intimate.

"It is a pleasant surprise to see you this morning," she said, indicating he should sit between Kenectka and herself.

"It is neither pleasant nor a surprise," Donan replied gruffly, having felt their scrutiny all along.

Kenectka made a move to leave.

"Stay," he said, softening his tone. He hadn't meant to sound so harsh. "What I have to say concerns you both."

The women shifted into a posture of listening.

"It is time for Tremlo to come live at the High Cave."

That caught their attention.

"Away from the influence of others, he will be able to sort out his perceptions."

Something happened, Mortulla thought. "What makes you think bringing him to the High Cave will do that?"

"I intend to start him on the training."

"The training? You would take him as a Side?"

"As Learner."

"What have you seen?"

"A way to help a child in need."

Mortulla blinked. He wasn't going to tell her.

"You know children born like Tremlo usually die young or lose their excessive sensitivity," she said.

"If they are normal."

The child is just a child, Mortulla thought. *One with terrible problems, nothing more, nothing less. To think of him otherwise is madness.* But even as she thought this, some part of her wondered at her steadfastness.

Donan, quiet, weary. *Adrift.*

Mortulla sighed.

"What do you want from us?"

"Prepare everyone."

"In what way?"

"However you see fit. But send Tremlo to me in five days' time."

"Why so soon?"

"He is to make the climb by himself."

"You really think this is wise?"

"You think it unwise?"

She tilted her head, and he rested his hands on his lap.

There would be no more discussion.

Kenectka was secretly thrilled by this turn of events. She had helped Tremlo as best she could, but whatever he needed now was beyond her. If anyone could help, it was the Kwaman.

Five days later, Tremlo stepped upon the path that led to the High Cave. *He is walking up the mountain,* he thought to himself.

When the Mahtwah approached Reena and Arlen, they were surprised, but not him. The change was coming long before the words.

He is walking up the mountain, while below—

His mother's hope-and-sadness, his father's anticipation-and-concern, Mortulla's reservation, Kenectka's excitement, the tribe's interest-and-confusion.

How much of these feelings were his?

The air around him thickened with the sound and smell of the Kwaman.

Come.

Down below, his mother turned her back.

Letting him go? Pushing him away?

He reached out, but she would not listen.

Was he supposed to be leaving one for the other?

Panicked now, a burst of fear flashed off his skin. He reached up to the High Cave, and Stelbin stepped back from the sting.

The Kwaman held fast.

Come.

From below, nothing. Nothing!

Tremlo burst into tears.

Come.

He ran up the mountain and dove into Donan's waiting arms, a tree creature leaping from one tree to another. His tears soon flowed from the Kwaman's eyes.

How lost, how needy, how powerful this child.

Why did I wait so long?

The two held onto one another for the remainder of the day, Donan as tightly as he was being held. If this was a test, he would not fail him.

At dusk, Stelbin prepared some bunoi. Donan moved carefully over to the fire with Tremlo clinging to his body. Woozy inside and out, he sat down, and Stelbin handed him a cup.

"Drink," Donan said softly, offering it to Tremlo.

The child stiffened.

"As you wish. It is here when you want it."

Donan turned his head sideways so that he himself might drink. The warmth, flavor, and feel of it passed through his body and into the child's. Tremlo relaxed his hold, but just barely.

When they lay down to sleep, Tremlo stayed pressed up against him. Donan's body itched to be free, but he refused to listen.

I will be the ground beneath your feet.

Holding to that, he held them together.

Tremlo fell asleep soon after and took Donan with him.

The walls of the cavern rang with the sound of their bodies. A tunnel opened at the back. Donan had had this dream before. This time, however, he was not alone.

Side by side, through the tunnel they went. Each step propelling them faster, *and faster.*

A speck of light in the distance. Neither sunlight nor firelight. Cool, like starlight, but not a star.

And then they were engulfed, standing in a small room, its walls smooth and angular.

"Uncle Donald!" Jennifer cried.

Tremlo instantly melted into the flat surface of the yellow wall, but Donan held his form. He knew this place with its straight-lined ways. Had been here before.

How many times?

"I missed you so much," she said, her long brown hair flowing behind as she ran up to him.

He caught her on the fly and swung her about. "I have missed you as well, Junnipur," he chuckled, realizing it was true. "You've gotten so big."

She stood nearly up to his chest.

"Let me look at you."

He held her at arm's length, acting out a form she understood. Jennifer smiled and turned around. Hard bones in lieu of muscular ones, a stiffness to her movement. Yet deep within, something soft, something watching, *something alive.*

Resep.

He remembered now. She had found some in her time. The far-past.

"Wildflower. How is Wildflower?"

"She was dying," Jennifer said sadly. "There were only a few leaves left, and I was getting too big to squeeze through the opening. I waited for you to come and help, but you never did. I remembered what you told me, and I picked her purse. There were seeds inside, just like you said. I took them up to a place hidden in the woods and dug up the ground like my father did in the garden. I planted the seeds, and babies grew, each with their own purse."

Speaking of Resep like this warmed his heart.

"Did you harvest them?"

"Yes."

"How did you know when to do that?"

Jennifer shrugged, "The leaves told me. They made my fingers tingle, and I sort of knew it was time. This past spring, I planted the seeds again. They've grown into big plants and are almost ready to be picked. I have some leaves here. I can make us tea."

"Yes," Donan replied, and a thought suddenly entered his mind. "Tell me, Junnipur, what have you done with the malta?"

"The what?"

"The malta. The middle. The white pulp in the center of the stalks and branches."

"I've seen it, but I haven't tried to make tea with it."

"Not tea. It is for eating."

"Oh, I didn't know."

Donan smiled, happy to tell her these things. *Needing to tell her these things.*

"I'll make the tea," she said and took out a small brown sack. Its sides were thin like the leaves of a tree, and they crackled as she opened it. The smell of Resep filled the air, giving new life to all the objects it touched.

"I don't have any of the middle here," she said apologetically. "But I will bring some for the next time you come."

Would there be a next time?

The rigidity within her body created a dull, flat sound. To Tremlo, it was the sound of pain. But she moved about without complaint. She moved like one with sight, and he realized he had sensed the flow of her before.

She placed two cups on the table and filled them with water.

"I love Wildflower."

"Yes?"

"She makes me feel good."

"In what way?"

"After I drink the tea, I can hear things better."

Donan nodded.

"And I can feel things, too. What people are thinking sometimes. But if I don't drink it for a day or two, the feeling goes away."

"If you eat the malta, it will stay with you longer," Donan said.

"Really?" Jennifer beamed.

He nodded like she would, his head moving of its own accord.

"And," he continued, "I have come with... I have brought a surprise."

"You did?" Jennifer looked at his hands and then to each side of him searching for some object. "I like surprises."

Donan smiled.

"It is not a thing, Junnipur, but a person."

"I don't see anyone," she said.

"He's very shy."

She grew still, and her body achieved an open posture of waiting.

"Try not to rely on your eyes so much."

She closed hers immediately.

Almost right, he thought. *With a little instruction....*

"See what you feel. Feel what the rest of your body sees. What does it tell you about this room? What does it tell you about us?"

A quiet sensing began. She reached through the space Tremlo inhabited. But her perceptions were weak, and his defensive-posture too strong. If he did not give something back, she would pass right by, and Tremlo knew now that he wanted her to know him.

Bit by bit, he released the posture.

"Yes! I, I do feel something!"

She instantly opened her eyes, but there was nothing there.

"Is he a ghost?"

Donan smiled, not sure what she meant exactly.

"Can your eyes hear? Do your ears taste? What one sense perceives another cannot. Don't rely upon one or two. Use all of them."

Junnipur nodded, but she did not understand.

"Why can't I see him?"

"Let the rest of you see him, and he will take form in your mind."

She closed her eyes and did as he asked. Impressions of Tremlo slowly grew, and when she next opened her eyes, he was standing there. She gasped at the sight of him. His eyes were downcast, but she could see they were all white. He was about her height, and his clothes, strange looking, like leaves woven into fabric, gave definition to his shape. But their overall color was blending in with the room. She had never seen anything like it. Despite what Uncle Donald said, he looked like a ghost. And he had no hair!

Now that she looked, neither did Uncle Donald.

"Junnipur, this is Tremlo."

She heard, *"Jennifer, this is Truman.*

"Hello, Truman," she said.

"Hello, Junnipur," he replied, keeping his eyes averted, for he felt her dismay at the sight of them.

Uncle Donald said he was very shy, but she could not tell if he was embarrassed or afraid. He turned towards her more directly, and his color began to change.

He's glowing! she thought. He looked more like an angel than a ghost.

"Welcome," she said, trying to comfort him with a hug. He was far more solid than he looked and returned her embrace with equal pressure. It almost felt like she was hugging herself.

Jennifer looked him square in the face. This time he did not turn his head away. "Why are your eyes white?"

"All our children are born that way," Donan replied. "The white skin covering their eyes wears away over time. In a year or so, Tremlo's will be gone, and he will see with eyes like yours and mine."

"You mean he can't see now?"

"Not in the way you are thinking."

"He's blind?"

"In one way, yes."

A wave of sorrow came over her.

"But he sees in other ways."

She reached for his hand to guide him to a chair. "Come, Truman. I'll make you some tea."

"You don't have to guide him," Donan said.

To prove his point, Tremlo moved straight to the chair and avoided any objects along the way.

If he's blind, he certainly doesn't act like it, Jennifer thought. She filled another cup with water and handed each a small bundle of Resep. They followed along, dunking the Resep as she did. Tremlo's arms rested comfortably on the table, his body poised. She felt him watching with everything but his eyes. As she drank her tea, this sensation grew stronger.

Uncle Donald and Truman brought the cups to their mouths. They smelled the tea and sipped a tiny bit. It looked like they were tasting it with all their senses.

"What grade are you in?" she blurted out.

Tremlo gave her a quizzical look.

"How old are you?" she continued.

"Ten," Truman said. "I am ten years old."

His voice was deep and a bit rough around the edges, but the inside was colored with a warmth that was irresistible.

"I just turned eleven," she volunteered proudly.

Donan smiled. With these two sitting at this table, everything in the universe felt aligned.

And then it changed.

Jennifer squirmed and stood up abruptly to recapture what was falling away.

"Would you like to play a game?"

"Yes," Truman said, flowing with her need.

"Let's play catch. I have a new ball and – oh, I'm sorry." She forgot he was blind.

"He can play catch," Donan said.

"But how can he if he's blind?"

"He can still hear. He can feel the changes in the pressure around him. He can even smell it."

Jennifer nodded, uncomprehending. She went over to the far corner of the room, her presence illuminating the details before her. She bent down beside a square wooden box. It was a holder of some kind, sharply defined, built within the flat and angular style of the room. She touched it, and they felt the wood-brown surface of its color. Out came a bright red object, completely smooth, perfectly round. She dropped it to the floor, and it bounced back up into her hands.

This amazed them. She threw it into the air and clapped her hands three times before catching it.

"Stand over there," she said, pointing to the corner of the room. Even though Truman was blind, he seemed to have no trouble going where she pointed.

"Are you sure he can do this?"

"Yes." How could he explain the perceptual sight of their bodies to one who listened mostly to her eyes?

She turned to Truman, his thin arms hanging loosely at his sides.

"Ready?"

"Yes."

He did not bring his arms up into a ready position, and so she lobbed the ball underhand.

It moved slowly in a high arc, and as it came down, Truman did not raise his hands to catch it. She felt sure it was going to hit him, but at the last instant, his hands appeared before it. He caught it less than an inch from his chest.

Tremlo smiled at her surprise and threw it back with the same arc and speed she had.

Back and forth, back and forth. Each time she feared it would hit him.

"Why don't you try to hit him," Donan suggested.

"Hit him?"

"Yes. Throw it as fast and hard as you can."

Junnipur shook her head no, causing Donan to smile. Her ball was so soft and light.

"At home, the youngers play this game with rocks."

Jennifer did not believe him but raised her arm in an overhand position.

"Here it comes," she warned Truman and threw it half-heartedly. As before, it looked like it was going to hit him but at the last instant, his hands appeared before it. She threw it harder the next time, and then finally with all her might.

"I have never seen anyone catch like you."

Tremlo tilted his head. She stood with her arms slightly extended and her hands out in front of her, anticipating the direction of the ball. It limited her range of motion and set her body into a posture-of-expectation. From early on, every younger was taught to avoid this sense of anticipation.

Know what is.

Meet its form with equal force.

But she was a Stiffback. Her bones were stiff and heavy. Not like his, which were muscular bones. And because of this, she could not move as fast, and suddenly he realized that he already knew this. Had always known.

Pulsations from the walls of the tunnel sent a wave of discomfort through them. They stopped playing the game and moved back to the table, to the Resep, to the softest place in the room.

Sitting in silence, Tremlo marveled at how the feel of someone so different could fit in so easily with the internal rhythms of his body.

Jennifer melted into the contours of his presence. She felt closer to him than to anyone in the world.

Donan leaned back, an outer shell within which these two could meet, even as pulsations outside the room became more insistent.

"It is time to go," he said finally.

Tremlo and Jennifer nodded, but they made no move to break this connection.

Another wave came, stronger this time.

"Come," Donan insisted, his words falling on empty space. He was standing at the mouth of the tunnel with Tremlo beside him.

"Goodbye, Truman," Jennifer called from her bed.

"Goodbye, Junnipur."

The tunnel collapsed, squeezing the air out of their lungs.

They ran as hard as they could to keep the walls from touching them. As long as they ran, they could breathe.

Stelbin was first to awaken. It had been a fitful night.

Tremlo and Donan were lying on their backs, breathing in unison. Each had their right arm extended while their left remained close to their body. The fingers of their right hands were curled in precisely the same way.

Stelbin quickly left the cave to keep from waking them with his growing apprehension. The unnatural connection between Reena and Tremlo was well known. Could it be carrying over to the Kwaman as well?

When the two finally awoke, Tremlo rolled back up against Donan's body. The Kwaman felt heavy and full. After a moment, Tremlo pushed away and moved to the entrance of the cave.

Donan was relieved. His body felt chafed, and he was so disoriented he could not sit up yet. He tried to remember the dream that was somehow holding him back from this world.

Tremlo picked up a small stone and threw it into the air. Clapping his hands three times, he caught it just before it hit the ground.

The sight and sound sent Donan's mind into a spin. He turned his head to the side and retched.

CHAPTER SIX

A dark spot on the blue horizon.

Randol caught sight of it out of the corner of his eye and turned to look.

Nothing.

Experience told him to wait.

A short time later, it reappeared. Definitely a ship, moving slowly across the horizon. A land breeze today, forcing it to sail north on a long tack before angling back in.

"Sound the drum," Randol ordered.

The Augmentor at the base of the observation tower complied. Moments later the sound was returned from the Harbormaster's station far below.

"Clear Long Pier," the Harbormaster ordered, "and move that barge inland to the first post."

Randol closed his eyes and turned his face back to where he imagined the ship to be. This was a game he often played with himself. Opening his eyes, he found that once again, he had correctly judged the speed and distance the ship had traveled.

At this rate, it will be docked by midday.

Unscheduled vessels like this usually carried riffraff from Ontar.

Settlers, he thought with distaste. *More misfits to contend with.*

Randol himself had come from a poor farming family. He was the youngest of eight, and his prospects were slim. When he came of age, he joined the ranks of the Augmentors. Many were the tales of men who moved up through the ranks to achieve wealth and power. Kriiton himself was just such a man. When Randol was told he would be sent to Ontara to serve under him, he gave silent thanks.

The new world! Untouched treasure. Kingdoms to conquer. Populations to subjugate.

There would be ample opportunity to distinguish himself on the battlefield. Perhaps he might even be given rule over a small kingdom.

These were the dreams every Augmentor carried into the new world. But the reality proved to be quite different. There were no fabulous kingdoms to conquer and no major populations to bend to their will. The most challenging battles had been waged against an animal so fierce it defeated them at every turn.

In his years of service, Randol had only risen as high as Charge-of-the-Watch, and this was mostly because of his keen eyesight. In three more years, his term would be up, and he would either be mustered out or re-appointed. If he left the Augmentors, he was entitled to a parcel of land as settlement.

A farmer, he thought with some bitterness. Right back where he started.

A second spot appeared on the horizon and captured his attention. Randol leaned forward and squinted. Still a speck, but larger than the original. He turned back to the first ship and stared hard. The incoming tide was drawing it closer to shore. With his superior vision, he was just able to make out the distinctive cut of its bow.

A Seafarer.

This, a mid-sized cargo ship renowned for its maneuverability and speed. Back to the second ship, still too far for detail, but its length twice that of the Seafarer. He had never seen a ship of such size. As it drew closer, he realized only the foresails were set. It was not one great ship but rather two, one towing the other. Within half an ora his eyes confirmed his suspicion. The one doing the towing was lower in the water.

A Treescout.

One of the fastest vessels in the realm, used mostly by Augmentors. He could see now that the vessel-in-tow was a Seacart. There was something familiar about its lines. But it was not until it got close enough for him to see color that he gasped at the distinctive blue stripe along its side.

It can't be!

The first ship was now on an inward tack. At the top of the main mast was a fleck of red.

"Sound the horn! A Personage is aboard!"

Randol raced down from the observation tower and called out to the Charge Augmentor,

"Precaution! I declare Precaution!"

"Understood!"

The Charge quickly assembled a group of Augmentors who hid behind special blinds. If this vessel carried an invading force, they would be drawn off the ship by the small guard sent to greet them and surrounded by this larger one.

Randol ran to find the Newland Commander. The message he had for Kriiton was too important to give to an underling. Besides, here finally was something he might use to his advantage.

Kriiton was in the fields overseeing preparations for planting new crops when he heard the horn and hastened to his quarters. This was a crucial time for the colony. Food stores were almost gone. This crop had to succeed, or they would face starvation this winter. The last thing he needed now were more mouths to feed and the meddling of some stupid official.

"Why have you left your post?" Kriiton barked, seeing Randol waiting for him at his door. "Be quick!"

"There are three ships entering the harbor. The first is a Seafarer. It bears the red flag. The second is a Treescout, which tows the third. That third ship is the Lotubo."

"The Lotubo! Are you sure?"

"Yes."

"Are you suggesting it never reached Ontar?"

"I ordered Precaution. The Augmentors are in place."

Kriiton studied Randol more carefully. The man was no fool. He had grasped the politics of the situation.

Loyalty. Independent thought.

Successful rule came not by handing out decrees, but by proper day to day administration. It required men who could think and adjust, who could grasp the ramifications of the simplest of situations and think with the like-mind of their Commander.

He would talk to Martel about bringing Randol a little closer to the fold.

"Return to your watch. Keep me informed."

"Understood."

"And Randol."

"Yes Commander?"

"You were correct in coming to me directly. Continue to do as you see fit."

"Understood."

Randol ran all the way back to his post.

Benton stood on the aft deck and watched the bustle of activity on shore. They had seen the red flag and quickly raised the honor banners. Whatever the colony's failures, Kriiton certainly kept them at-the-ready.

He could see how much the colony had grown from earlier reports. The rudimentary system of canals was nearly complete. The earthen works had been moved far inland and were no longer visible from the sea. The harbor itself had grown from a primitive anchorage to a thriving port. Docks spread out across the shoreline with hoists and storage facilities all along the way.

Long Pier, the most recent construction, was built perpendicular to the shore and ran into deep water. A ship could sail directly up to it at low tide and dock. No longer would they need to haul cargo back and forth on small boats. On the far-left side of the shore stood the black-tarred barrier doors of the central canal. Once the system was completed, these would be utilized to govern the flow of water.

There was a sense of orderliness to this place that brought a smile to Benton's face. Kriiton had been somewhat wild in his youth, constantly organizing games and small adventures. He and Benton's older brother, Harnell, had been best friends. Benton worshiped the pair, and they begrudgingly accepted him as mascot.

He was twelve years old when Kriiton left for service, and he had only seen him twice since then. The last time was three years before Kriiton left to take charge of Ontara.

Do you know I am now under Et-El Baronuus's command?

A group of Augmentors spread out along the shoreline. Baronuus had told him to expect a cautious greeting.

What will you think when you see it is me?

A signalman appeared on a raised platform. Using a pair of large yellow flags, he signaled the Steersman to bring the ship in.

"He wants to guide us through the channel. They have set a place for us on the far side of Long Pier."

"We will not dock. Set the anchor."

"But Commander, Long Pier is easily big enough to accommodate four ships."

"We have eighteen lopers below deck. You know the edict. We do not dock!"

"Understood."

The Steersman angled the ship off to the far-left edge of the channel. He put its nose into the wind and brought them to a stop.

"Drop the anchor! Lower the sails!"

In a matter of moments, it was done.

"That's damned strange," Kriiton muttered aloud. He had arrived with the honor guard, dressed in his white ceremonial robe with its silver flashings and winged headpiece.

"Perhaps the Steersman did not understand our signal," Martel suggested.

"Or they are avoiding our inspection. Signal Randol. What can he see from above?"

The answer came back almost immediately.

'Few on Seafarer. Treescout – Augmentors.'

Something's amiss, Kriiton thought. A Seafarer with a Personage aboard and a small crew. A Treescout full of Augmentors. Was their anchoring out supposed to reassure him of their peaceful intentions?

A shuttler was lowered from the Seafarer, and set immediately to oars. The Personage stood in the stern. A tall man, holding himself erect, poised. His hair was mid-length. The red and beige colors of his cloak announced one of minor rank. Probably someone on the council of one of the Elite.

The shuttler reached Long Pier and was quickly secured by dock-hands. Several Augmentors climbed out and took up formal positions.

His personal guard.

The Personage refused assistance and sprang from the boat onto the dock.

A young man, Kriiton thought.

"Hold your positions."

Let him come to us.

The Personage walked with a casual stride, flanked on either side by his guard. His headpiece, with its side-pressed gold wings, was pulled slightly forward.

Confident. Assured.

As they drew closer, the markings on the armbands the Augmentors were wearing became clear and announced the Command they served.

Et-El Baronuus!

Kriiton's muscles tightened.

The honor guard gave the traditional cheer of welcome. Benton stopped. Keeping a stern expression on his face, he raised his fist in acknowledgment and locked eyes with Kriiton.

Something familiar about this one, Kriiton thought struggling to remember. *I must have seen him before. But who is he?*

"Hold," the Personage said, separating from his guard. He closed the distance between them, raised his head and broke into a smile. Remnants of a boyish face came to the fore and with it, recognition.

"Benton!"

"Greetings, Commander."

The two men grabbed hold of each other's forearm in the traditional greeting.

"It is a wonder to see you here!"

"It has been too many years."

"Why didn't you let me know you were coming?"

"No time. The appointment came, and within weeks we were sailing to the new world."

Kriiton smiled and embraced him to cover his suspicion. It would be just like Baronuus to send a friend to do his dirty work.

"What matters most is that you're here," Kriiton said, signaling those hidden amongst the ramparts to remain at-the-ready. "So when did that happen?" he asked, pointing to the colors of Benton's cloak.

"I was transferred to Baronuus's command little more than a year ago."

Low-level officers were often circulated amongst the ranks. Benton originally thought his assignment was random, but after his last conversation with Baronuus, he was not so sure.

"It's a temporary rank."

"I see," Kriiton said, put further on his guard.

Benton looked about the dock and shore-works. "You have made great strides here," he said, trying to relieve the tension.

"We are years from self-sufficiency. But come, let us retire and speak of old times."

"I very much look forward to that. But first, we have more important matters to discuss."

He said this more for those around them than for Kriiton. Any spies Baronuus had aboard would report that Benton had remained true to the task at hand and put it before his friendship.

Kriiton grasped the situation immediately.

Friend or foe?

The two men strolled arm-in-arm up the dock towards the main street of the settlement. Their personal guards followed after them.

Thirty steps back, Kriiton signaled his Charge who then forced his will upon Benton's men. There was a moment's tension, but Benton eased it with a nod. All of this happened in the fluidity of a moment, and no protocol was breached.

"I have been told you are towing the Lotubo."

"Yes. They are a few oras behind."

"What happened?"

"She never reached Ontar."

"I feared as much."

"We found her quite by accident, drifting aimlessly at sea. The beasts had escaped from their cages."

"How?" Kriiton searched Benton's face carefully.

"They gnawed their way through the bars," Benton hastened to explain. "A battle was waged, the ship torn apart. There were no survivors, save one beast more dead than alive."

They walked on in silence for a while.

"Does Baronuus believe I'm plotting to discredit him?"

"He is under tremendous pressure and suspects plots everywhere."

"I see. How fare the wars?"

"We are besieged on all fronts. The southeastern provinces are under constant attack. The Argoot raid our lands and withdraw into the mountains where they pick off our Augmentors one at a time. Our forces are being depleted. The area is too vast to defend. The trade routes are now threatened."

"So you have come for more beasts."

"They would be the perfect solution."

"I don't believe the Kurr can be trained."

"I've read your reports."

"Their nature is too violent, and they accept no master."

"I believe you, but Baronuus insists he must try."

"This is the main canal," Kriiton said, changing the subject to give himself time to think. Something was wrong. Something hidden.

"There are hundreds of small rivers and streams north and west that will eventually connect to it. Without lopers, the work in the fields and on the canal has taken much more time and effort than first anticipated."

"Your edict against lopers has been hotly debated."

"The talk of fools."

"From the comfort of Ontar, it's difficult to imagine the problems you face here. They cannot see the fruits of your labor, but only the drain on their treasury."

"A condition they themselves created. Each month we are deluged with more and more starving refugees. Half of them are criminals and most of the others have little talent for survival in the new world. We have become the dumping ground for Ontar!"

"I'm not disagreeing."

"What sort of cargo do you bring? Not more refugees, I hope."

"No. I bring little in supplies but much in will."

"So they've sent you here to capture more Kurr and bring them back to Ontar."

"Correct."

"To do so you will require food, lodging, and many of my men to assist you."

"Correct."

"You will need provisions for the trip home?"

"Yes."

"And when do you want to begin?"

"I have been ordered to make haste."

"Immediately then?"

Benton nodded. "Within a day or two."

"So, within two days you will take many of my Augmentors and supplies and go on a hunt that could take six months or more. Meanwhile, we are about to start the spring planting and I need every man, woman, and child to work the fields. But instead, our efforts will be curtailed, and future food stores compromised so you can capture a few precious beasts for Baronuus's mad experiment. No! I won't do it."

"My friend, you must. Besides, the drain on your resources will not be as terrible as you imagine. We have brought lopers with us."

"Lopers!" Kriiton roared. "You brought lopers?"

"My friend, I—"

Kriiton signaled his Charge. Benton recognized the order for full battle alert. Had Kriiton gone mad? Would he actually risk a confrontation such as this?

Three Augmentors raced off in different directions while the rest quickly surrounded Benton's guard.

Benton pretended not to notice and continued his explanation in an even toned voice. His right hand casually came to rest upon his dagger.

"By your own account, the last expedition took nearly half a year to capture the beasts. Rather than placing undue amounts of strain upon your time and resources, Baronuus reasoned that it would be best to draw the Kurr to us using lopers."

"I do not blame you, my friend," Kriiton said, softening his tone but not his resolve. "But you have no idea what jeopardy you just placed us in."

"Kriiton, I am prepared to forestall our plans and commit my men to help you prepare your fields, but once that is done, you will help us, and we will be gone within a month's time."

"How many lopers did you bring?" Kriiton asked sharply.

Benton was annoyed. After the concessions he just made, Kriiton was not behaving properly. Could he not see the reprieve Benton had just bestowed upon him?

"Eighteen."

"Eighteen," Kriiton nodded as if to himself. "Where are they?"

"In the hold of the Seafarer. That is why I set it to anchor. Despite Baronuus' orders, I did not want to violate your edict."

"I appreciate your action, but it will not be enough. There's a land breeze today. What do you think will happen once the winds change?" Kriiton did not wait for a reply. "Charge! Send a man to the Harbormaster. Have him line the wharf with smudge-pots. The smokier the better. Light one every two paces."

"Understood." The man ran off.

"Tell me of this Seafarer."

"It has been outfitted to carry the Kurr back."

"How many cages?"

"Fourteen small trap cages. Three mains built into the hold. Enough to house eighteen animals."

Kriiton began to pace back and forth, looking something like a caged animal himself.

"All right, Benton. I accept your offer."

He signaled the Augmentors nearby to stand down.

"When the time comes, I will provision your leave and do all I can to assist you in capturing the beasts. But for now that ship cannot stay in the harbor. It must leave within the ora."

"If you insist," Benton said. Kriiton's reaction was growing stranger by the moment.

"There is a large cove a few weeks to the north. They can anchor there until we are ready for them. But understand, the lopers must never touch ground until it is time."

"These are severe measures. Are you sure they are necessary?"

"They are not only necessary; they may be too little and too late."

Benton turned to his own Charge. "Take the shuttler out to the Seafarer and inform the Steersman of the plan."

"Understood."

"Tell them we will rendezvous with them when the planting is finished."

The man ran off.

"Come," Kriiton said placing his arm across Benton's shoulder to reassure him. "We have much to talk about and much to plan."

"Agreed," Benton replied quickly. Kriiton's arm was heavy and felt more like a chokehold.

I will record that this delay was necessary to secure what was needed, Benton thought, but he would not disclose his growing concern about Kriiton's state of mind.

Not yet. But if it comes to it....

CHAPTER SEVEN

Harvest time was approaching. For the past ten years the Resep crawled along the ground emphasizing the pattern-of-change. The resulting tension was now a part of everyday life. Those born after that first year knew of nothing else.

Whaet moved to the near side of the Resep crop and Gremar, the far side. Both stopped to listen to the silent songs the plants were singing.

Gremar's father, Roon, had led the tribe for forty years before becoming ill and losing his connection to the Resep. The people turned from him and embraced Whaet as the new Leader. Roon died soon after and Gremar, who was a child, blamed Whaet for his father's downfall. He swore to himself that one day he would take from Whaet what Whaet had taken from his father. From that time forth, he shadowed Whaet, looking for flaws and weaknesses, all the while trying to learn everything he could about the plants.

As he matured, his influence grew, particularly with the young. And so, for the sake of the tribe, Whaet had taken him years before to this very place.

'When will the plants be ready?' he had asked with the sweep of his hand.

"About six weeks," Gremar replied, keeping his voice low. One only spoke in whispers here.

"And the Broezia?"

The yellow pollen was the most potent part of the plant. Gremar examined the underside of the leaves. The color was nearly mature, but the edges were not yet firm enough.

"It will come later than usual this year."

"We are more in agreement than many would think."

When Whaet said things like this, Gremar knew he was trying to get on his good side.

"You have matured over the years, Gremar, and maintained your interest in the Resep. Perhaps with a little guidance. If you agree, I would invite you to become my Side."

Gremar gasped. His secret plan had taken a giant step forward.

Soon it will be my words that set the tribe in motion!

Whaet was taken aback by the gleam in Gremar's eyes.

"In times of change," he continued, "we must be prepared for the unexpected."

Gremar nearly burst out laughing.

"Yes," he said. "Yes."

With Whaet's help, Gremar learned special ways to gauge the Resep's moods and anticipate its needs. Resep, like the tribe, was a combination of many individuals, yet one solitary being. Treating one plant, he discovered, affected them all.

But where Whaet looked at the Resep as a living creature, to be cherished and treated with great tenderness, Gremar saw it as a means to an end. Whaet would spend hours sitting in the field simply keeping the Resep company. Gremar would do the same but for the purpose of trying to find something out.

It was what he was doing now.

Harvest was fast approaching, and the pattern-of-change near its fullest expression. With his eyes closed, Gremar felt the pattern within his own body.

Each crop was different, and this one was no exception. It sang of the here-and-now and things-to-come, or so it was believed.

I am the only one who does not fear this change, he thought, drawing strength from the contrasts. At thirty-two, he was still young for a people who lived well into their hundreds.

Take my mind. Fill it with images of the future.

Vague colors welled up, but he could not make sense of them. The Resep embodied so much more than they could ever comprehend. By showing everything, it revealed nothing.

Gremar remained undaunted. Tomorrow he would come again, and the day after, and the one after that. There were so many unknowns. Everyone was anxious for Jormah's return and the knowledge he would bring. But no one was more excited about it than Gremar. Things had gone well for him these past few years.

Everything was falling into place.

His time was coming, and he knew it.

CHAPTER EIGHT

"Stelbin," Donan said. "Go to the far ridge and gather some breyberries, and take Tremlo with you."

The delicate balance Stelbin felt between himself and the Kwaman had been disrupted the moment Tremlo came to the High Cave. In the months that followed, Stelbin still did not know the true reason Tremlo was living with them.

"You are to help in his training," Donan had told him.

The training?

"And by doing so, it will become a part of yours."

Will Tremlo become his Side as well, Stelbin wondered?

"What is it you want me to do?"

"Tremlo has no sense of himself separate from the world around him. It is this we must change."

'*How?*'

"He needs to relearn everything. Crawling, sitting, standing, all the while maintaining attention. He needs to root. He needs to be in one place and know he is there."

How Tremlo could lack this simple understanding, and be so extraordinary in other ways, was beyond Stelbin.

He grabbed a basket and set off at a brisk pace.

After a moment's pause, his reflection rushed to catch up. From the beginning Tremlo had taken to following him around, mimicking all the subtle tones of his body, and performing them with a simplicity that bordered on perfection.

A sour taste rose in Stelbin's mouth. It would not be the first time he doubted his own abilities.

When they reached the breyberry bushes, he handed Tremlo the basket before reaching high up to where the berries were known to be the sweetest.

Tremlo stirred.

'*What?*'

The younger turned away.

"Your body is itching to speak."

"He. He thinks the berries on the lower left side are sweetest."

"And how does he know this?"

"He, he is not sure."

"If he doesn't know how he knows, he may know nothing at all."

Tremlo took a step back as if he had been slapped.

To be *Aware* was to know what one was doing and why. To be *Aware* was to pick and choose how one would be from moment to moment.

And Stelbin had done neither.

He moved quickly round to the left side of the bush and tasted several berries lower down. They were indeed much sweeter.

"Tremlo," he said, filled with regret and softening his tone. "Please bring the basket."

Tremlo came tentatively forth and held it for him to fill.

"How did you know these were sweetest?"

"They just seemed to be."

"Can you remember which sense told you?"

"He smelled them, and also, there was the sound."

"The sound?"

"When they are sweetest."

Stelbin did not know what he was talking about. He had never heard the sound, and as far as he knew, no one else had either.

"You smelled them and heard them?"

"Yes."

"And you knew then which ones were sweetest?"

"When he smelled them. And closer, he heard the tone of the skin of the berries. Yes, that was it," Tremlo laughed. "That was when he knew exactly which ones were best!"

Stelbin laughed along with him. It was always best to share the good feelings of another.

This was one of the longest conversations they had ever had. Tremlo's perception of which berry was ripest was both fascinating and distressing.

Tremlo began to fidget.

"The Kwaman is waiting," Stelbin said, leading them down the hill. He focused his attention on the smells of the breyberry bushes above them.

"Where was it that you began to sense the differences in the breyberries?"

"Farther down," he said sheepishly.

"How much farther?

The younger made no reply.

"Tell me when we reach that place."

When they were long past the point where Stelbin could smell anything of the breyberry bush, Tremlo stopped.

"Was it here?" Stelbin asked.

Tremlo nodded nervously. In truth, he was beginning to realize that a part of him had known the moment Donan told them to go pick the berries.

Stelbin closed his eyes and sniffed carefully.

"Do you smell them now?" he asked.

"Yes," Tremlo said.

"And you can hear the differences from here?"

"Yes."

"Very good."

Stelbin resumed their march back to the High Cave. That bitter taste was in his mouth once again. From behind, Tremlo's tones matched the underpinnings of his own mood so perfectly it caused him to stop. Feeling them was one thing, seeing them reflected back was another.

"Take these to the Kwaman. Tell him I will join you later."

When Stelbin returned, Donan was waiting for him. Lessons were often painful, and this was one his Side needed to learn.

"Your remorse is uncalled for, Stelbin. Better to remember qualities you possess, than judge yourself harshly for those you do not have."

Donan tilted his head back and spread his arm wide.

The timbre of the tribe, the whispers of light, the weight of the sky, the ongoing character of the intralife....

When Stelbin listened in this way, he could often predict events of the day from the mood of the tribe, down to subtle interactions between different members.

"You have an ability to see in ways others don't. Always remember this, and you will never feel diminished by the talents of another."

Donan's words blew through him, and the feelings dissolved.

"Remember, Stelbin, thoughts and feelings are like the leaves of a tree. They come and go, but the tree itself is made of sterner stuff.

Truth is miniscule,

Illusion grand.

Again, and again, the same lesson.
Remember yourself always, separate from these.
How did he keep forgetting?

CHAPTER NINE

alking, running, jumping, climbing. Day in and day out, re-learning everything to create habits of clarity.

"We are undoing what Tremlo's entire life has created."

Today, Stelbin brought him to Sky Rock.

"Can you feel Jormah's presence?"

Tremlo pointed north and east, indicating the flat land beyond the City-Of-Straight-Lines.

Stelbin reached out but felt only emptiness.

"I don't sense anything," he confessed, holding to the truth of the moment and going no further.

"What does Stelbin sense?"

Tremlo had never asked him a question before, and it took him by surprise.

"What I sense most lies within the Tribal Body."

"Does anything there mark him?"

"I— I never thought to look."

Tremlo turned away, but Stelbin was pinned to the moment. All this time he had been looking in the wrong way.

It's there! He was sure of it.

By looking near, he would see far.

"What did he say, exactly?" Donan asked.

"He said, 'What does Stelbin sense?' and then, 'Does anything there mark him?'"

'And?'

"And I saw that it was true." Beneath Stelbin's words was something more than just acknowledgement. Here was acceptance.

Donan smiled to himself, for his Side had finally grown into his Heart.

With Stelbin's inner tension gone, Tremlo began to emulate him in everything he did. How he walked, how he sat, all the movements in between. Stelbin thought it an embrace of sorts, and Tremlo's way of belonging. But Donan was not pleased. The child was disappearing.

"Prepare for a journey of several weeks," he said, leaving them to gather what was needed.

Tremlo moved in tandem with Stelbin. From pauses that reflected thought, to choosing the individual objects and placing them in his backsack. He loved the all-encompassing feel of another.

When all was ready, Donan retrieved the small watersack he had hidden in the back of the cave long ago. He slung it over his shoulder and led them down the mountain. There would be no talking. Stelbin followed in silence, with his reflection close behind.

Without words to distract them, their thoughts receded into the long-song of ground, tree, land, and sky. Tremlo's spirits soared. Here was a purity of tone no words could ever express. Here was the true language.

In the days that followed, they continued to weave their way through the forest in perfect silence. Tremlo matched the flow of Stelbin so completely, he was nearly invisible.

A defensive-posture, Donan decided. *But who is hiding?*

"Stelbin, you take the lead."

Tremlo moved to follow, but the Kwaman blocked his way. And now it was Donan who had a reflection. He altered his movements, looking for inconsistencies, but Tremlo thought it a game of sorts and matched his every move so perfectly, wherever Donan looked, he only saw himself. It was as if the child had been born without an identity.

Could it have been taken away by the trauma of his birth?

There was only one way to find out.

"Tremlo, you take the lead."

The younger hesitated, but the Kwaman waved him on.

Tremlo took a tentative step forward. Then another. No reaction in the Kwaman's body. Two steps became twenty, then a hundred. Still nothing. Ahead, a delicate imprint. Not a scent, or a sound, but a *memory*. Tremlo altered his course, and everything flowed more smoothly.

Is he sensing my thoughts? Donan wondered, for Tremlo was leading them towards the very place he had planned to take them.

Years before, Jormah took him to the ravine to see a mysterious pool of water. It disappeared before they got there, and Donan remembered Jormah running ahead to confirm with his eyes what their bodies felt.

Tremlo broke into a run at nearly the same place.

Is this coming from me?

Or is he sensing something else?

Tremlo ran all the way to the ravine, and when Donan and Stelbin reached the edge, they found him lying on the ground below, in the very place Jormah claimed the waterpool had been.

"Tremlo, what drew you here?" the Kwaman asked.

"He felt the feelings and followed."

"Whose feelings?"

Tremlo fidgeted. It felt like everyone's.

"What feelings?" But the child could say no more, and it would do no good to push him further. "Very well. We need wood for a fire, and something to soften the ground beneath our backs."

They gathered what was needed. When night fell, Stelbin lit a small fire, and Donan prepared the malta for the evening meal. He mixed in the spices he had gathered along the way. The blend was the same Jormah had made for him years before. Everything he did now was to invoke a stronger sense of the past. He was sure there was a connection. If they delved deep enough, what would Tremlo remember?

An odd hush ... the world holding its breath.

"What I am about to tell you, Tremlo, is a mystery. The year you were born was the year the pattern-of-change first appeared. The Yarka still preyed upon us. The traps did their work, but once in a while, a Rehloy was killed by a beast. Jormah brought me to this very place to see a strange pool of water that had appeared out of nowhere. But it disappeared before we got here.

"He told me that the water had had a golden afterglow. There was an energy about it and he felt compelled to dive in. The water was surprisingly warm. The silence, profound."

Tremlo, immersed in a fog of sensation, the Kwaman's words giving it shape.

"When Jormah left the water, his body tingled with a newfound sense of aliveness."

Tremlo, filled with trepidation, leaned forward.

"He danced his way to the top of the ravine, just as a Yarka burst through the forest. Jormah was out in the open, with no means of escape. He dropped to the ground and assumed a defensive-posture. But his skin still glistened with the energy of the water. Its smell would give him away. In desperation, he assumed the tone and color of the water, hoping the smell on his body would aid in this deception."

Tremlo, rock-still, held his breath for fear of revealing himself to the beast.

"Death was moments away."

Tremlo sighed aloud, then waited to hear why.

"The Yarka was almost upon him, when its head jerked back. It reared up on its hind legs and batted its nose as if something was attacking it. Crying in fear and pain, it fled back into the forest.

"Jormah was stunned. It was a miracle. He soon determined that the smell had driven the beast away. We were free at last from the tyranny of the Yarka.

"I'm telling you this now, because the waterpool appeared on the night you differentiated and became conscious in your mother's womb."

Donan reached for the watersack and opened it.

"Here is all that remains of the water Jormah found."

Tremlo's hands grabbed hold the sack, moving with a will all their own, and buried his face in the opening. He inhaled deeply. The smell spread through his body, and blended different parts together as it went.

"Tremlo."

He looked up, and both were startled. His face appeared longer; his features more mature. It was a vision of things to come.

Tremlo?

Within a breath, the effect of the water began to fade.

Tremlo pushed his face back into the sack but to no avail. There was simply not enough of him to hold onto it. Disoriented and overcome with dizziness, he lay down and was fast asleep.

Donan sat quietly, trying to sort out what had just happened. The child's body had known something, or remembered something, or perhaps saw something. *But what?*

There was wonder in it, for sure. But other than being witness, Donan could not tease out a meaning.

The next morning, Tremlo got up and walked around the base of the ravine, unknowingly tracing out the actual borders of the waterpool.

"How are you feeling?"

The younger never knew what to say when others asked him this. Of himself alone, he felt nothing. An emptiness. At the core of him, a hole, from which he turned away and scrupulously avoided. But now...

A hole? Or a doorway?

Round and round he went.

If a doorway, what would he find? How should he look? What would he see?

"Tremlo, come sit," Donan said. He opened the sack and passed it to the child.

Tremlo buried his face in the opening once more. The sense of urgency from the night before was gone. He breathed deeply, but there was no change. Donan took back the sack and looked inside.

It was empty, the water gone.

They had come full circle.

Tremlo appeared the same, but something was churning. Of that Donan was certain.

CHAPTER TEN

Benton's men worked alongside the colonists for the springtime planting. In the meantime, Benton learned all he could about the Kurr. He paid frequent visits to that remarkable fortification where they kept two captured beasts. It was a tall, conical structure made of stone. Inside was a huge pit, perhaps fifty feet across and just as deep, rimmed by a waist-high wall.

"Are these the animals Baronuus saw?"

"No, Commander," the guard replied. "They got too big. These are young ones."

Each time Benton leaned over the interior wall, the beasts leaped up at him.

"You would think they would be used to me by now," he said after a week of this. "I'm sure they know they can't jump high enough to get me."

"They know all right."

"Then why do they keep doing it?"

The guard shrugged. "For the sport of it? Or maybe to let you know where you stand."

"Where I stand?

"They're letting you know they'd kill you first chance they got."

"So you don't think they can be trained?"

Kriiton had made no secret about his own opinion, and Benton wondered if he had simply suffered one too many defeats.

"If they were starving to death," the guard continued, "and there was a choice between killing you or taking food from you, I think they'd kill you."

The Seafarer, with its cargo of lopers, was anchored weeks to the north of the settlement. The day the spring planting was completed Kriiton went to Benton.

"You have fulfilled your side of the bargain and we are grateful. Have your men go to the Treescout. You can sail with me and together we will devise a plan for the hunt. Once the beasts are aboard your ship, you will sail directly to Ontar."

He takes every precaution, Benton thought, down to posting extra Augmentors around the perimeter of the settlement.

The ships sailed out of the harbor, and Kriiton brought Benton down to his cabin. It was a small space, simply furnished, with a table, two chairs, and a bed. The walls were bare, the room austere, a perfect reflection of the man.

They sat down across from one another.

"What is your plan for capturing the beasts, Benton?"

"We'll set up trap-cages in the usual manner and bait them with live lopers. Once a Kurr enters the cage, the door will close and lock automatically. We can have Augmentors standing by to reinforce the door if necessary."

"And then what?"

"We bring the cages back onto the ship."

"I see."

If it were anyone else, Kriiton would have let them fail and taken great pleasure in it. It would certainly hasten Baronuus's demise. But the one before him was an old friend.

Kriiton sighed. *Damn you, Baronuus.*

"And what will the other Kurr do?"

"What do you mean?"

"You've got a beast and a loper in a cage. You think the other Kurr will just stand idly by?"

"You mean they will try to free their companion?"

"No, they will try to get to the loper. They will do their best to rip the cage apart, or as you discovered, chew through the bars. As long as the loper is there, dead or alive, they will try to get at it."

"I see."

"They might even work in tandem to break open the cages. And even if they fail, they will not just stop and let you pull them away."

"My thought is that the Augmentors will keep them at bay as we bring the cages to the ship."

"When it comes to lopers, any Augmentor standing in their way will be killed."

I need solutions, Benton thought, *not problems.* Kriiton's resistance was growing tiresome. Apparently, the weapon of choice in this land was the shovel, not the sword.

"Then what do you suggest?"

"I'm not sure. Let's see what the shoreline affords. The cages can be mounted on wheels?"

"Yes."

"Once you have the beasts aboard, how are you going to prevent them from chewing through the bars on your return trip?"

"I have instructed the ship's carpenter to build metal gutters along the bottom of the bars in the hold. We can fill them with coals and heat the bars, red hot if necessary. The guards will also use heated metal pokers to drive the beasts back. Either of these should work. And we will not make the same mistake the captain of the Lotubo did. Guards will be posted day and night."

"A reasonable plan, since there will be no lopers aboard to tempt them. But when it comes to the Kurr, you must think of them as men in animal form. If there is a way to reason it out, they will do so."

The Seafarer came into sight. It was anchored a good distance from shore and they sailed towards it. From out here, the narrow, white sand beach appeared to be a brown lumpy affair.

"Look at that!"

The shoreline was covered with beasts.

"Keep upwind of the Seafarer," Kriiton ordered. "I want nothing of that ship to touch ours, including its smell. Signal the Charge. We'll meet him on the Treescout."

Once again, Benton thought Kriiton's caution excessive but said nothing.

Within half an ora, the Charge was before them and giving his report.

"We anchored out as you ordered, Commander Kriiton. The shore was empty. For the most part the winds have been coming out of the west like they are now. Then just three days ago, we were surprised by the appearance of the first few Kurr."

"Surprised?"

"We had men ashore."

"You violated my orders?"

"No, Commander. You said we should not go ashore with the lopers. I did not understand this to mean the men as well."

"Go on."

"There were twenty men in all. The beasts killed one of them outright. The men raced to the shuttlers and pushed off. The beasts followed them into the water but stopped short of catching them. They were unwilling to go into water more than chest-high."

"That is useful," Kriiton said. "Continue."

"The following day twenty more beasts showed up. Some even waded into the water. Each day more came. Today we estimate there are three times that many."

"You'll never get close enough to the shore to set the traps, Benton."

"Then we'll have to sail to a different port."

"Yes," Kriiton said. "But, now that I think about it…." His face flushed with thought. "Maybe we can build a raft and float a trap-cage to shore with the tide. The Kurr will have to come into the water to get the loper. Once the trap is sprung, we'll pull the cage back to the ship and drown any of the beasts that hang on."

"Brilliant!" Benton cried. Here was the man he knew.

"There's a good stand of timber a day south. I'll take my ship to get some for a raft."

Upon Kriiton's return, they constructed a large raft and lashed a trap-cage to the center of it. A good eight feet of wood was left on all sides. A loper was placed in the cage and tied to the far wall. The trap door was raised and the spring set. They attached a long rope to the raft, and two men worked a winch to pay it out.

The cage drifted slowly in towards shore.

Two shuttlers with ten Augmentors in each rowed alongside. They were armed with long poles to help guide it and would use these to push the Kurr off into the water.

The beasts raced back and forth along the shoreline until the smell proved more than they could bear. First one, then all of them rushed headlong into the water, stopping only when it reached their chests. Apparently, they could not swim, or at least not well.

Just a little more, the Charge Augmenter in the shuttler signaled the Seafarer. The men unwound the winch a few more turns and stopped.

One of the beasts leaped forward and just managed to get its claws onto the edge of the raft. The loper cried out and struggled to free itself, but to no avail. The Kurr pulled itself up and dove into the cage. The trap door slammed shut.

Hearing the clang, the men on the ship let out a great cheer. The beast felled the loper with one swipe and sunk its teeth deep into its neck. It had no concern for itself and did not once look up from the kill to survey the space it was in.

Several beasts got hold of the raft and threatened to tip it as they struggled to climb up. The men on the Seafarer winched the raft back as fast as they could, while the Augmentors in shuttlers moved in. They prodded, pried, and batted the beasts' paws, breaking their grasps, and pushing them off. The Kurr were helpless in the water. Some went under and did not reappear. Others just managed to get back to where they could stand.

The beast inside the cage devoured its kill with no regard for the changing world outside.

"I see what you mean," Benton said. "They really do lose their reason where lopers are concerned."

"Some terrible instinct drives them."

The cage was brought alongside the ship. Armatures were swung round and it was hoisted up. The beast roared as it was lowered into the large cage built into the hold. A loper in a separate compartment was used to lure the beast out. The Kurr leaped out of the trap and into the cage, dragging the remains of its kill behind.

"Next."

Four more beasts were secured in the hold before the tide turned and not a man had been injured.

"We'll wait until morning to start again."

That night, there was much celebration. The next day, seven more beasts were captured before the tide ebbed.

"Stop the fishing!" Kriiton called out, and the men laughed long and hard. "No need to expose ourselves to unnecessary risk."

"Agreed," Benton replied.

Kriiton was ecstatic. Here finally was retribution. The Kurr were now at their mercy.

"By the end of tomorrow, we will both be off," Kriiton said.

"Ahead of schedule."

"And with all but one of the men you started with."

The following morning, the tide took the first trap slowly to shore. Once in place, they set the winch. Minutes later it was sprung, and they reeled it in. By midday they had sixteen beasts plus the one from the Lotubo safely tucked away in the hold.

"One more and we're home."

The men prepared the final trap, relieved their work was almost done. Each looked forward to returning home, and happily imagined the stories they would tell.

"Hey," a sharp-eyed Augmentor called out, interrupting their revelry. "What is that? On the cliff above the beach."

Middling grey in color, from this distance it appeared to be twice the size of a normal Kurr. It bounded down the cliff, and the brown beasts scattered before it. Four more Greys appeared and came charging down. They raced along the water's edge and forced the brown Kurr farther back.

The largest Grey stood on its hind legs.

"Commander, look at that!"

The beast paced back and forth along the shoreline. It towered over the browns and let out a ferocious roar.

"It's walking like a man!"

The four other Greys stood on their hind legs and roared in unison. The Kurr sat down and bellowed as one. Their numbers were far greater but the sound they made was much softer.

What manner of beast is this?

The sense of elation aboard the ship was gone. The sooner they finished what they came to do the better.

"The trap is ready," an Augmentor called out.

"Those large ones might be too big to fit inside."

"We'll know soon enough."

They floated the raft towards shore and the Kurr began to whimper. A few stood up and took several steps forward. One of the giants charged and nearly butted heads.

The smaller Kurr quickly retreated.

As the trap got closer, their whimpers grew louder. Still, they did not move.

The Charge Augmentor in the shuttler polled the depths of the water and signaled the ship to lock the winch. The trap was now set. All that remained was to capture one last Kurr.

The Grey beasts dropped back down on all fours, and maintained their positions along the water's edge, keeping the Kurr from rushing headlong into the water. The largest Grey got back up on its hind legs and turned to stare at the trap.

"Look at the size of that thing. It must be thirty feet tall."

It eyed the Augmentors in the shuttlers, swiped at the air, and roared.

"It's telling them to go away!"

"Signal the Augmentors to move back a bit."

One of the brown Kurr broke from the pack and raced into the water. The Grey gave out a thunderous cry, but the Kurr did not heed its call. The giant charged across the beach, leaped up and landed on top of it, driving it under the water. The Kurr struggled violently to free itself, but the Grey, with its superior weight and strength, held it down until it drowned.

"Unbelievable!"

The Grey faced the rest of the Kurr and roared before releasing the body. The carcass drifted away, and it turned its attention back on the trap.

"I'll be damned."

"It's too big for the cage."

The beast began to move towards it.

"Winch it back!"

The beast raced forward quicker than they could winch it back and sank its claws into the raft. It hung on, but made no attempt to climb up and get to the loper. Instead, it seemed to be studying the trap.

"I've seen enough," Kriiton said. "Winch it back all the way. We'll drown this one if we can."

The cage began to move, and the beast roared, but its protest fell on deaf ears. It tried to pull itself up onto the raft, but the raft tipped under its great weight. Hanging on now, its body dragging in the water, it clawed its way around to the front. There, without hesitation, it began to strike the rope towing the raft.

"It figured it out!"

The rope was thick and swollen with water and not easy to cut. After several tries, the Grey repositioned itself and bit clear through it.

The raft, cut free, began to drift back to shore.

The Augmentors in the shuttlers closed in.

"Push it off!"

Two Augmentors in the first shuttler were standing at the bow with their long poles ready.

"It's a monster! Look at the size of its head."

"Go for the face. Aim for the eyes. I'll smash its paws."

"Ready. Now!"

The Grey twisted its head to the side so fast it avoided the first blow. In the same motion, it let go of the raft and was in the water now. It was not a good swimmer and struggled to make its way back to land.

"After it! Keep it from shore."

They closed in to block its way. The Grey went under, but its hind legs found ground and it stood up. Its upper body was a good six feet out of the water.

"Back! Row Back!"

The beast lunged for the nearest shuttler and tipped it over. The Augmentors fell into the water and tried to swim away. It killed one of them with a powerful swipe before rushing after the raft and riding it to shore. The brown Kurr were on their feet, barely containing themselves. When the trap reached the beach, the Grey pushed partially inside the cage. The trap door crashed down on its shoulder with little consequence. It cut the bonds holding the loper, took a quick bite out of its flank, and threw the poor animal to the Kurr, who swarmed over it like ants.

The Grey stood up, faced the ships of the Ontarans, and let out a solitary roar. Here was a breed of beast too terrible to imagine.

"Let's get out of here," Kriiton said.

"We can't."

"You have seventeen Kurr."

"Baronuus commanded me to bring back eighteen."

"You only have two lopers left. In light of what we have just seen, it would not matter if you had a hundred."

"The fact remains, I must bring back eighteen."

Kriiton knew Baronuus's temperament well enough. "Very well, Benton. We'll sail farther north and put in to see if we can catch a brown Kurr before these Grey monsters show up."

They sailed straight out to sea. The wind was coming from the west and would help mask their direction. Once out of sight of land, they sailed north for a day before turning back inland.

They anchored in a favorable cove and set the trap. In less than a day a brown Kurr appeared and was easily caught.

"Now you have your eighteen. Sail north for as long as you can before you make your tack. Your ship is tainted with loper scent, and we need you to keep as far from the colony as possible."

"Understood."

"I hope never to see you again in this service."

"I hope never to be in it."

They both laughed.

"It was good to see you, Benton."

"And you."

"Keep me informed ... of your progress."

Benton looked Kriiton straight in the eye. Here was an invitation, a thing to tie his fortune to in the new world.

"In the name of friendship, I will."

"That is all one can ask for."

They embraced.

"Now sail away, and may the gods grace you with good fortune."

On the trip back, the men aboard Kriiton's ship were quiet and contemplative. These Grey Kurr were the stuff of nightmares. Heaven forbid they ever made their way into the settlement.

We need a new weapon, Kriiton thought. *Something that will kill them instantly or drive them away.*

He kept the crew busy, making sure they washed the ship, and themselves each day.

"We will not give the Kurr any reason to visit us this year," he told them, and not a man complained about the extra washing.

CHAPTER ELEVEN

"Come, Stelbin. It is your time."

Stelbin looked surprised.

"You're not ready?"

Stelbin did not react, and Donan chuckled.

"Take heart. We go now to confirm what those below already know. You are no longer my Side, and have grown into my Heart."

Stelbin lowered his head in a sign of humility.

"Are you ready?"

"I am more ready than I was, and less ready than I will be."

Donan burst into laughter. "Spoken like a true Kwaman. No other answer was possible. Come."

They walked down the mountain, side by side, a confirmation for all to see.

"Most will let go their former view of you and accept whomever you present yourself to be. Use this opportunity wisely."

And how am I to be? Stelbin wondered. It felt so contrived to think this way.

Neutral, he decided. *I will strike a neutral pose and let their expectations create the form.*

"Today is the day," Mortulla muttered, feeling them coming down the mountain.

"Yes," Kenectka replied.

Mortulla gave her a sidelong glance.

"I am years away from having to make that decision," Kenectka replied. Thirty was the usual age a woman, if she had not already done so, chose a mate.

"I suppose." Mortulla smiled and focused her attention on the sway of Stelbin's body. "He is changing," she said coyly.

"He is becoming Kwaman."

"Yes. Distant and removed."

Kenectka did not reply and Mortulla burst out laughing.

"Come child."

They headed off to the Common Ground to join the others for the morning meal. The people were silent, their anticipation loud. When the Kwamen came into view, they raised their faces to the sun.

We admit this new light into our lives.

As was the custom, the Mahtwah was first to come forward. Stelbin half expected her to pinch his cheek or twist his ear. Instead, she looked deep into his eyes, staring, he was sure, straight through to the back of his head. He held himself firm, willing himself not to blink or avert his eyes. Her face softened, and the corners of her mouth rose into a smile.

Welcome.

Stelbin smiled back, and she touched his hand.

Kenectka came next and assumed a posture akin to his.

"On this day we are equals once more."

Yes, he nodded, unsure what she meant.

"I am pleased," she said, touching his hand.

"And I," he replied, a little too quickly. And then she was gone, and Whaet was standing before him, beaming.

Not neutral, Stelbin thought. *Centered. Be open to what each brings but remain centered.*

He met Whaet's gaze with equal weight.

Held and released.

Gremar came forth next, wearing a smile twice as wide as Whaet's, yet half as warm. Still, the smile was infectious, and Stelbin struggled to keep himself from being swayed by it.

Truth propels. It is formless. It exists between one movement and the next.

"We know how hard you have worked," Gremar said, sensing Stelbin's resistance. "But it does not matter what we think. It's what you know inside yourself that is truth. I welcome you to the role you were destined for."

There was no one in the tribe like Gremar. As soon as Stelbin felt Gremar posturing, Gremar became sincere. His words were full of insight and wisdom. Yet it felt like he would simply find other words if these did not suit his purpose.

How does he appear both deceptive and honest in the same moment? Can both be true?

Each member of the tribe came forth in their own manner. Some were dressed in the fragrance of the past, others sought a new footing.

Some came forth with a serious air, others with mirth. To each, Stelbin acknowledged the past with a look, all the while maintaining this centered posture.

I, who was, remembers.

I, who am, stands before you, open to all that comes.

Donan stood silently by.

You are indeed ready, he thought, basking in the light of his Heart.

After the formal greeting, the people fell into more relaxed tones, and the meal commenced. Even so, a small measure of formality remained and was directed towards Stelbin.

A pause, a space, a moment of regard.

Is this what it will be like from now on?

He was looking at the tribe differently as well. It was a posture he saw in Donan. An attitude of care and responsibility.

But why now? Yesterday he did not feel this way. Yet he could not imagine ever going back to yesterday. The ceremony had inspired a sense of renewal. Beneath it, the rhythms of everyday concerns festered. At their core were shifting temperaments.

Gremar, in particular, emanated a level of energy to which everyone reacted. Whether they pushed back, gave way, or were drawn in, he seemed to cause a stir wherever he went.

Stelbin followed him now with his senses. Gremar approached Kenectka with that same smile he had tried on Stelbin earlier. He stood before her, and his body shifted into an open posture.

I am here for you, it said. But more than this, *you have my full attention.*

It was very much like a posture Donan used. And it was having its effect, for Kenectka grew more animated. Gremar shifted his position to enhance her good mood. When they laughed, it was together.

What is Gremar doing?

Stelbin took several steps towards them before getting a hold of himself. Shocked into *awareness*, he turned quickly away and made casual conversation with those nearby. A layer of feelings he did not know he had, just made themselves known to him.

"I have spent too much time above," he said later to Donan as they headed back to the High Cave.

"Some might say the same of me."

"Yes but—"

Donan held up his hand.

There is no need for words or explanations.

"You are Kwaman. Do as you see fit," he said.

But know what you are doing, for I too glimpsed Gremar's actions to-day and saw it reflected in your heart.

CHAPTER TWELVE

Jormah kept to the outskirts of the City-Of-Straight-Lines. The ancient structures evoked the spirit of the Intruders, and felt more ominous.

Down the mountain he went, along the path carved out of its face. He had once marveled at its construction. Now he saw it as an attempt by the ancestors to shackle the mountain and make it their own.

Far to the south lay the tribal land. A ray of light in the encroaching darkness. Ahead, the Valley Forest. When last he came this way, his mind was colored by the dreamy air of illusion. Now it crackled with brittle layers of truth.

Through the Forest and up to higher ground. Days ahead lay the collective awareness. The Tribal Body, the *intra*life, their crowning achievement. Its invisible boundary rested softly upon the land.

Jormah stopped well before its edge and reached out to the High Cave.

Tremlo knew. Donan felt. Stelbin was guided by their attention.

"What is he doing?" he wondered aloud after the second day.

"Waiting," Tremlo replied.

For me, Donan thought.

"We leave tonight, once everyone is asleep."

To leave like this would warn the others not to follow. Nevertheless, the people would steal glances, but they would not linger. Not at first.

Jormah marked their progress as they made their way towards him. The two with Donan were familiar. The first was a combination of different youngers he had known before he left.

Stelbin, he thought as the impressions grew stronger. *I think it is Stelbin, grown tall.*

The other was that high-pitched one whose underlying presence he had sensed all along.

When the three approached the edge, Jormah retreated.

"Let's stop here and make camp," Donan said.

As daylight faded, Stelbin and Tremlo began to prepare the evening meal.

"I'm going," Donan said. "Do not come unless I call."

With that, he melted into the oncoming night.

The edge of the Tribal Body was lighter than air. Beyond its borders lay the gruff reality of an unenlightened world. Donan pushed through and quickly adjusted to the disorientation that always followed.

Jormah remained seated behind the flames of a small fire. He stood when Donan came into sight.

"Come no further," he said, his voice crackling with disuse. "Who are the two you brought with you?"

Donan grew still. *No greeting. No exchange. Oh, my brother, what fate has befallen you?*

"Stelbin, my Heart."

"I thought as much."

"The other you do not know. His name is Tremlo. He is the son of Reena and Arlen."

"He was born soon after I left."

"Yes."

"I have felt him all along." Jormah's voice trailed off, seeing how Donan had aged. His body was slouching with the pull of the ground. His eyes were clear but some part felt far away. The illness was taking its toll. "You have changed."

"We both have," Donan replied, glancing at the wood Jormah had placed beside the fire. Larger pieces at the bottom, thin ones on top, all facing in the same direction. These were patterns used in caves when trying to conserve space. But out in the open, it should have been random to reflect the currents. "Why did you stop out here? Why are you holding back even now? Are you ill?"

"In a way."

"Have you discovered the reason for the pattern-of-change?"

"I have become its instrument."

"Its instrument? Are you tainted?"

"The knowledge I bring will change everything."

The textures in his voice were ripe with experiences Donan could only imagine.

"If we do not learn of it, will that prevent it from happening?"

"No. I fear it is inevitable."

"Then your actions will not matter."

"I am not so sure."

"Let us both decide what is true." Donan took a step closer. The last time he saw Jormah, Jormah had been living in the wilderness. He had been somewhat distant then, but now he was like a stranger, his body taut, all angles and hard edges.

Donan took another step forward. "You have been away too long." He wanted to embrace Jormah, but his brother's manner did not permit it. Instead, Donan came forth and stopped across from him.

Jormah nodded once, relieved to have the fire between them.

They sat down and remained silent for a time, staring into the flames.

The smell of Donan's body, the beating of his heart, the quiet rhythms of his being....

When the fire burned down, Jormah made no attempt to revive it. He cleared his throat.

"The truth is... we are not alone."

The words struck hidden pools of knowledge within Donan's body.

"Now that you say it, I seem to know it. There are Others."

"Yes, and different kinds." So much to tell, the sheer weight keeping him silent.

"Why not begin with the day you left. It will help me understand all that has happened."

And help you find your way back to us.

"When I left, we thought it would take a year or two. We were like newborns, having no idea of what lay before us."

His words, cautious at first, soon flowed with a life all their own. The Valley Forest, the City-Of-Straight-Lines, his body humming with the singular tone of the vast grassland, He spoke of its lacerating blades and the burning dew that nearly killed him. Starving, the lack of Resep, his body stiff with the blindness that followed. He flushed with color describing Origin. Then the posture-of-speed.

No wonder he feels like a stranger, Donan thought. *He has lived a lifetime's worth of experience and we are just at the beginning.*

Jormah described the second city and his encounter with the gigantic forest-of-crawling-leaves.

"The weather became colder than anything we have ever known. It had the power to turn water into rock. It had the power to freeze our blood and kill us. If it were not for the Carooh, I would have died."

'*The Carooh?*'

"The first Others I encountered. They are Stiffbacks. Primitive. Meateaters. They survive the cold by wearing outer layers of furskin taken from the animals they kill."

Jormah went on to describe his entrance into their lives. Two of their children were attacked by a Yarka. And he, hiding in a tree above, dropped down, expressing that special odor the beast could not bear.

The Yarka cried out in pain and fear, before fleeing into the forest.

To the Carooh, it looked like Jormah had dropped from the sky. The beast saw him, screamed, and ran away. They worshiped him from then on, believing him to be the Bhytoe, the Spirit-Of-The-Forest. They brought him back to live with them, gave him furs, and taught him how to survive the cold.

Bka, Brais, Fraih, Shoone, Jaet, Elash, Telt.... He missed them all despite their barbarous ways.

"I left with the warm weather and journeyed far to the east, to the edge of the continent, where a land of great water resides. It is as vast as the sky."

Jormah took a stick and drew lines in the dirt to illustrate the flat paths etched into the forest floor. He had followed one of these and come face to face with the infestation.

He spoke of fields plowed, row after row in straight-lined ways. Of Intruders who came from beyond the horizon, who enslaved Others. Who created tools and weapons from materials that possessed the power-of-stone. Who indiscriminately cut down trees, carved out roads, and built a city.

"Our ancestors have returned!" Jormah cried with a final burst of energy. He sat back and closed his eyes. He had been speaking all night.

Donan was exhausted from all he heard. He leaned back, and a moment later, both were asleep.

At dawn, Donan wrapped some malta in soochoch leaves for roasting on the fire. Jormah tilted his head in appreciation.

"It has been so long since I ate something prepared by another's hand."

This, more than anything, spoke of the deprivation he endured these past eleven years.

"Here," Jormah said, reaching into his backsack and handing him a piece of malta. "Wrap a piece of this too."

"From Origin?"

Jormah smiled hearing the plant's name said aloud.

"From the children, not many generations removed."

Donan smelled it. Its vibrancy was undeniable.

"I look forward to tasting it."

"And I the malta of my past."

Donan busied himself with the preparations, avoiding the mounting questions in his mind. He understood now what Jormah meant when he said he had become the instrument of change. The mere knowledge he brought would forever change the way the Rehloy looked at themselves and the world about them.

"It is good to see you," Jormah said after a time.

"It is good for us both."

They ate in silence, each tasting the world of the other. Donan found the children-of-Origin rife with flavors of a life unknown. The Resep the Rehloy cultivated was not as strong or as pungent, but for Jormah, its rounded tones were the songs of home.

They finished eating and sat quietly, contemplating all that had transpired from then to now.

"We have waited long enough," Jormah finally said. "What is it you wish to ask?"

"I'm not sure where to begin. Tell me more about the Carooh. Did you see them again?"

"I fled the settlement and headed back to warn them. But by the time I got to their caves, they were gone. It was the cold season. Food must have been scarce, and they followed the herds south.

"They had barricaded the cave I stayed in with tree branches and brush to keep animals out. Inside, they left bundles of dried Resep. They had kept their promise and harvested the small crop I left behind.

"On the wall hung siowttars, teegns, and a new furskin. All that I would need for the cold season. And so, I sat out the winter safely tucked within the shelter of the cave and the warmth of the furskins.

"With the first breath of spring, I felt movement far to the south. They were returning, and I planned to wait for them. But a restlessness took hold. Things that comforted me in the depths of winter now weighed me down. Objects fashioned by the Carooh were suddenly irritating.

"It became difficult to sleep at night and hard to breathe during the day. Hidden forces were squeezing me out of that place, and I awoke one morning knowing I could wait no longer. I picked up a sharp stone and drew a story-map on the dirt floor of the cave. To the east, I feathered in the waterbody and to the north I drew many circles along the lands' edge.

"These were the Intruders. Cross marks were the Carooh.

"Working my way back to the caves of the Carooh, I drew several large circles with tiny cross marks caught inside them. I hoped that they would understand the warning."

"You were the Bhytoe, the Spirit-Of-The-Forest. They would have studied it carefully." Donan thought a moment. "What do you think they would make of us?"

"I think they would see us all as Spirits-Of-The-Forest."

"And worship us as well?"

"Yes."

"And the Intruders?"

"They are Stiffbacks and meat-eaters alike, but they are different and driven by other forces. When they move, it is often in unison, like an insect with many pairs of legs. They have no regard for the currents. I doubt they perceive them. And even if they did, I do not think they would care."

"You think they will come?"

"The land of great water is to their backs. They are growing in number. Whether they come in five years or fifty, the threat remains the same. Their kind built the City-Of-Straight-Lines. They are our ancestors, but we are no longer alike. The Resep has seen to that."

"Tell me again about the blue Broezia and the posture-of-speed?"

"I will do more than that. I will show you."

Jormah stood up. Exhaled—and disappeared.

Donan leaped to his feet and rushed through the space Jormah had occupied.

Gone!

"Over here," Jormah called from a distant treetop. He climbed down and returned to the fire. "It takes a good deal of energy," he said, slumping to the ground. "I will be fine in a moment. What was it you saw?"

"You stood up, contracted your chest, and vanished. A moment later, you called out from that treetop."

Jormah nodded. It was how he imagined it would appear. "There are so many secrets buried within the Resep, if only we understood more."

Donan agreed.

"And what of you, my brother?"

'Me?'

"What is happening with you?"

"I have been having visions of a different sort. When they come, I feel unstuck in time. They began shortly after you left. I cannot explain them, but they are happening more frequently."

Jormah looked at Donan. His initial impression was that some part of his brother was far away. It now had a form.

"I see a part of you drifting away."

"My body weakens."

"It is more than that."

"I suppose."

So much was unknown.

"And you are holding something back. While I told you of my journey, I felt in you a counterbalance to all I was telling you."

"Yes."

"The one called Tremlo?"

'Yes.'

"You believe him to be special. A Sentient, perhaps?"

Donan nodded, lest he forget he was in the presence of a Kwaman.

"But you hesitate…. Something is wrong with him."

"He was born prematurely and lacks the ability to separate himself from anything about him. He lives with us at the High Cave, and we are helping him devise ways of coping. He is a mass of confusion, yet there is greatness in him. When you meet him, you can make your own judgment."

When I meet him.

"Tremlo and Stelbin are the future, Jormah. I am already infected by your influence. It will only spread now. They need to feel your influence directly." *And you need to feel theirs.*

"So be it," Jormah said. "Tomorrow. At daybreak."

CHAPTER THIRTEEN

Stelbin and Tremlo felt the Kwamen enter the Tribal Body and dropped into balance-position.

A sign of respect, Jormah thought. Neither had reached out. Here were the innocent textures of a world that would soon cease to exist.

He took a moment to adjust. The air was almost too rich to breathe.

Apparently, it was as disorienting for him to come back in as it was for them to leave.

The moment Jormah laid eyes on Stelbin and Tremlo, he stopped and sat down in a formal posture. His manner was stiff, a sense of reluctance prevailed.

Donan sat down beside him in a more relaxed manner. A tension passed between the two, but it came and went so quickly, it was difficult to know if it had happened at all.

Stelbin grew wary. This Kwaman was nothing like Donan. Sharp and angular, there was a hardness to him that was as unyielding as stone. Here was a force to be reckoned with.

Tremlo dove into the image of Stelbin and hid. The energy before him was almost too much to bear.

What is this? Jormah wondered. *Will I affect others this way?*

Stelbin maintained a quiet sense of balance despite his wariness, and Jormah signaled him to come forward.

Stelbin rose into an open posture and came forth in the prescribed manner.

How like Donan, Jormah thought. He recalled his own youth and his love for his brother and the Kwaman Maloe.

I am the second Kwaman of this time period. I am brother to Donan and a part of their heritage.

He assumed a more hospitable pose, but it was not natural for him.

Stelbin approached. Two Kwamen sitting side by side, the truth of one embedded in the other.

Be an empty cup for them to fill.

"We meet again, Stelbin," Jormah said and indicated he should sit before them. "You are much taller now, but I remember you well." He just managed to convey a complimentary tone.

Stelbin nodded. "And I remember you. But I see now that my memories are useless."

"Useless?"

"I could not understand then the smallest part of what I see now."

"And what is it you see?"

"Someone familiar, something foreign, inviting, disturbing. You carry the knowledge of our future. It is a source of strength in one moment and turns against you in the next."

"You speak correctly, Stelbin, just as a Kwaman should."

"What do you wish to avoid?"

Jormah glanced at Donan.

"I see my brother has taught you well. These are skills he possesses in abundance. My talents have taken me elsewhere."

"We are eager to hear."

"In time."

Jormah's eyes fell upon Tremlo. It was like looking at Stelbin himself.

The power of Jormah's gaze made Tremlo's head spin. This Kwaman embodied so many segments of time.

Past present future, future present past.

Jormah intensified his scrutiny, and Tremlo quivered. An unpleasant odor colored the air.

How do they tolerate such a thing?

Jormah shifted his position in a show of discomfort.

Let him see what he causes.

The air grew bitter-rank.

In the past, Tremlo's experience of Jormah had been little more than a gentle breeze, but the flesh and blood before him was nothing less than a storm.

Stelbin took a breath. Tremlo had not had a fit since he came to live at the High Cave, but now…

A prickly burst of energy flashed off the younger's skin and burned their eyes closed.

Donan leaped up and threw his arms around the child. He took the full brunt of what followed without so much as a flinch.

Find a single rhythm and chaos will cease.

In that embrace, Jormah saw his brother's tenderness, and sacrifice. Donan's part in the events shaping their times was different, but perhaps no less challenging than his own.

"Tremlo," Donan said, releasing him. "Go to that tree and assume a posture for us."

Tremlo was all too ready to hide in plain sight. He ran to the tree, threw his back against its trunk, and vanished.

Jormah reached out, softly at first. Tremlo's skin was more than just a representation; it possessed every twist, turn, cut, and smell. His body had even captured the elongated rhythms of the tree.

Perfection, Jormah thought, delving deeper. *In all ways, he is the tree.*

Donan held up his hand. *'Go further.'*

Tremlo's skin-tone changed. The outline of his body appeared in shifting colors. Sections of his bark peeled away. No longer aligned with the tree, his posture had become some future expression of it.

It's true then, Jormah thought. *All that Donan has said and more, it's true!*

The posture was accelerating, the younger losing control.

"Stop!" Donan commanded, and Tremlo broke away from the tree just before becoming lost to it.

Jormah, still watching. The press of his attention almost painful. Tremlo dropped to the ground and reflected Jormah back to himself.

The Kwaman leaned forward.

Why are you doing this?

"We have much to learn from each other," Donan said, inserting himself between the two. "Jormah has returned with a similar marvel. He calls it the posture-of-speed. It challenges our senses and, like Tremlo's posture, alters our sense of time."

"Will you teach it to us?" Stelbin asked.

"It is not easily gotten, and there are dangers. When your abilities in the perceptions have reached a certain level, you will be taught."

Jormah leaned back. For the past eleven years, the currents were his companions. It was expansive. He could give himself over to things far greater than himself. But here, with the weight of these three, was a pull to compress and merge.

"You need time to get used to us," Donan said. "Rest now. We will make preparations for the evening meal."

The three moved away, but Tremlo could not keep his attention off of Jormah. To look at this Kwaman was to fall off a cliff.

"Tremlo, leave him alone."

Jormah ignored the reflection. He would make no efforts to comfort him.

You will be yourself with me, or nothing at all.

He closed his eyes and sat in balance-position. If only he could recede into the night. But that was no longer possible. He had come back to rejoin the tribe and needed to set down roots to secure the future. To put that off would only prolong the inevitable.

Tomorrow, they would set off to join the others.

Then we will see.

CHAPTER FOURTEEN

Gremar had ignored convention and scrutinized Donan, Stelbin, and Tremlo directly. They had stolen away in the night, and it soon became clear they were heading directly towards the edge of the Tribal Body. He could not be sure, but thought it must be Jormah. For two days, he contemplated what to do. On the third day the tribe awoke to the rhythms of him following after them. Some were appalled, others curious.

Everyone felt Donan leave the Tribal Body.

A day later he returned, and he was not alone.

Jormah!

All who had known him knew it was him.

The last Kwaman had returned.

Desire spread through the younger members of the tribe. Even the elders wondered if they should go forward to greet him.

"All are free to go," Whaet said, standing firm. "But I will remain here in a show of respect for Donan's desire for discretion."

Some youngers were unable to contain themselves and were first to leave. They took several adults with them. In all, about thirty Rehloy left, but the balance of the tribe remained behind, yielding to the good sense of their Leader's words.

Everywhere Jormah looked, everything he touched, heard, and smelled was Rehloy. Individuals reached out to touch him with their senses and quickly darted away.

Jormah.

His name echoed through the forest. Some were rushing to greet him.

"Gremar," Donan said simply, referring to the one who was closest.

How eager they are, Jormah thought sadly. It was this very trait that would be their undoing.

Gremar wanted to let Jormah know that he was not afraid of the on-coming change. Whatever might come, he could be counted on. He prepared several words of greeting, but the moment he saw Jormah, he dropped all pretense. This Jormah was not the one he remembered. Here was something hard and impenetrable. Something that would not be trifled with.

Jormah looked him straight in the eye and gave him a small nod of greeting, but he did not stop to speak, and Gremar was forced to wait for Donan, Stelbin, and Tremlo to pass by before he could join them. This was not going at all like he had planned. As he followed, he focused his attention on Jormah and adopted a similar posture to suggest some intimate connection between them.

Jormah paid him no mind. He nodded to everyone they met along the way, but stopped for no one. What he had to say, he would say only when all were present.

Kenectka followed the progress of those returning. She could not keep her senses on anything else.

"It is not for us to go to them," Mortulla said.

"Aren't you the least bit curious? You have barely reached out once."

"We are intimately tied to the Kwamen, child. As it is, they will now have to come to us."

"What do you think he found?"

"We will hear soon enough. But the energy he brings will speak to us long before his words. It is there that you should look."

The procession reached the Common Ground, and everyone spread out. Young children, who knew Jormah only from the stories, stepped back from the intensity of the figure before them.

Jormah spread his arms wide. Here was home. Here was food. Here was the past coming back into the present. The taut, harsh lines of his body softened.

They spread their arms out in return.

Jormah.

He moved amongst them. From those he knew, to those newly met, the totality of the Rehloy, not as people, but songs to be gathered and held close to the heart.

His body became bloated, and he returned to his place before them.

"It is... a joy, to be here."

His voice so full of them, those in the back hearing it as if he were standing right next to them.

"I have traveled far and seen many wonders. And in all that I have found, I have discovered how special we are. There is no place where *being* such as ours exists."

The intensity of his emotion colored their own.

"I have found strange tribes living in different places."

Others!

The world they knew, gone with a word.

Jormah did not wait for the shock to pass.

"Those tribes are years away. Each is different from the other, but they are all Stiffbacks.

Stiff— Backs!

A jagged sound.

His mouth filled with the questions rising in their own.

"They do not perceive the currents. They do not understand the language of the mind-of-the-body. They eat animal flesh, smell of rot, and are unaware of their own stink. They are lost to the world about them and try to enforce their will upon the land to compensate.

"It is our *awareness* that sets us apart. That and our relationship to the Resep."

He looked at each and every one of them, trying to decide if they were ready to hear what he would say next.

"There are forces far greater than ourselves at work. Things we are a part of. In one sense, things for which we have been chosen. Things we do not yet understand.

"My journey did not begin on the day I left. It began the night before Harvest in the year the pattern-of-change first appeared in the body of the Resep. On that very night, a strange pool of water appeared...."

As Jormah told the story, Donan thought to himself how artfully it had been done. Before this, to live meant simply to be. Jormah had now introduced the concept of cause.

Be-cause.

There was now a reason, a purpose.

Without them realizing it, the Rehloy were changed forever.

CHAPTER FIFTEEN

Questions flowed without end.

"What were the objects you found in the City-Of-Straight-Lines like?"

"What does the vast yellow in the grassland feel like?"

"What were your first impressions of Origin? The Carooh? The great waterbody? Tell us again about the Intruders and their enslavement of Others."

What this?

Tell that?

Would they come?

Would they not?

By afternoon the questions had become redundant.

"We are feeding upon ourselves," Jormah declared. "There is nothing left to say."

Without words to relieve them, the energy of the tribe became *thyck*. Whaet maintained a neutral posture, and many strove to achieve balance by emulating him. It was only Gremar who moved about freely and with an air of confidence.

"You don't seem disturbed by what we have learned," Kenectka said.

"No."

"And why is that?"

"It will force us to grow beyond the boundaries of the past."

"Are those boundaries so bad?"

"To hold to the past is to deny the future."

"And what will the future bring?"

Gremar gave her a wry smile.

Was he hiding something or pretending to know? She would not give him the satisfaction of asking and turned to go.

"When I am sure," he said, trying to stop her, "you will be the first to know."

She shrugged and left anyway. She liked Gremar. Despite her reservations she was coming to like him more and more.

She made her way across the Common Ground and felt the touch of Stelbin's attention.

"What say you, Kwaman?"

Stelbin nodded to hide any expression in his eyes.

"What is it you think?" she asked.

"About?"

"The tribe. The shift of energy. All that we have heard this day."

"We must listen, and wait, and see what unfolds."

"All except Gremar."

"Gremar?"

"He does not wait in the same way."

"Everyone has their way."

"He is not afraid to act."

"Neither is Whaet."

"Whaet would act, but in a different way."

"You think one is better than the other?"

"I think all possibilities must be considered."

Stelbin grew still. Were they speaking about something more than what they were speaking about?

"Stelbin, you and I need to know each other's thoughts. These times are different than those that shaped Mortulla and Donan. We need to be open and aware of all that comes. We need to stand together."

Together? How could he tell her what he was feeling when he barely understood it himself?

"I am trying to absorb all we have learned," he rushed to explain. "I will tell you when I have a strong opinion."

She searched his face carefully. He seemed open enough, but he was holding something back. Mortulla always complained that the Kwamen were tricky, and Kenectka was beginning to think she might be right.

Everyone retired for the night.

Donan, Jormah, Stelbin, and Tremlo made their way up to the High Cave. Donan hung the flag-for-solitude, and Jormah was relieved. Tremlo moved to the back of the cave, and Jormah took a spot near the opening. He preferred to sleep outside, but he was here now. Efforts had to be made.

Throughout the night, each time he moved, Tremlo moved. In the quiet before dawn, Jormah eased his way out of the cave and drew the emptiness deep inside.

Tremlo felt it inside himself. It was something he might have done.

Jormah headed down the mountain towards a thick stand of trees. Tremlo crept out and followed. He could not help himself. Jormah was from *outside*. Acting like him was like standing outside the tribe looking in.

Jormah entered a stand of trees and let their cool tones caress his body. Were it not for the younger, he would have immersed himself completely.

Tremlo stopped a hundred paces away and buried himself in the Kwaman's reflection.

What are you looking for? Jormah wondered.

He left the sanctuary of the trees and walked straight at Tremlo. The younger withdrew step for step, holding onto the reflection. Anyone looking would have thought they were physically connected. Jormah drove him back but resisted the impulse to run at him. Finally, he turned and took the path back up to the High Cave.

Tremlo followed, unable to stop himself. The rhythms buried deep within Jormah's body were irresistible. Each movement, each mannerism resonated somewhere in his own body.

Past present future, future present past.

Jormah reached the High Cave and found Donan and Stelbin waiting outside.

"You have acquired a shadow," Donan said. "It is an old habit. This is the way he learns without being overwhelmed."

"It's more than that."

"What do you mean?"

"He wants something from me."

"Tremlo sensed you all along. He has a certain connection to you."

"Perhaps, but that is not one I share."

Sitting around the small fire that night, Jormah spoke about more intimate details of his journey. Tremlo could barely keep still. Each word ricocheted through his body. That night he tossed and turned and awoke the next morning with shooting pains in his back and shoulders. Within a week, it spread to his arms and legs, fingers and toes.

Donan sent for Kenectka.

"Stay here to greet her. We will return later."

Tremlo wanted to go with them and keep close to Jormah, but that was not to be. Instead, he sat down just outside the entrance to the High Cave and assumed a posture like Donan might.

"You haven't come to visit me for so long," Kenectka teased. "You have forced me to come to see you."

Tremlo did not smile.

In the past, he would have matched the rhythms of her body and established a connection long before words. Now, he shifted awkwardly about. This was a new shading.

"You are growing. Come, let me see your eyes."

She took hold of his chin with the propriety of one who had cared for him all his life. Turning his face towards her, she lifted a lid and looked carefully at the white-skin covering. It was not as thick as it had been.

Another year before he reaches puberty, then sight.

She let go of his chin, and he turned away. He did not like this inspection, and she resolved to be more careful next time. Their relationship was changing. A different footing was required.

"It is calm up here compared to the changes below," she said, trying to close the distance between them.

He knew she was asking something of him, but he was not sure what. "Above and below, it feels the same," he replied.

"Do you like being up here?"

Like and dislike were words he did not really understand. Everything just *was*. But since he was up here as opposed to down below, he supposed it must mean that he liked to be here.

"He, he does."

"Come, walk with me," she said, careful now to resist recreating the rhythms of the past.

Tremlo stood and surprised her. He was almost as tall as she.

When did this happen?

"I see your time here has been well spent," she said.

He did not know what she was talking about.

"You are maturing, coming into yourself."

Was he?

That certain playfulness between them was gone. He seemed so serious. She stooped to pick up several small stones.

"Let's play a game."

She pointed to a particular tree, and they took turns throwing stones.

Through his movements, she saw how long and lanky his arms and legs were becoming. It seemed like he had grown a year's worth in a few short weeks. His fingers and toes were hot to the touch and predicted new heights to come. A sense of Jormah appeared in the flow of his body. It bespoke a changing orientation. Strong. Disparate. He was leaving one sense of himself and stretching into another. An awkward time.

"You are troubled," Mortulla said upon her return.

"He is going through a growth spurt, but it is unlike any I have ever seen. And it is coming on very fast."

"Hastened by the Kwaman's return."

"You think so?"

"Tremlo has clung to the tribe, like we-were-he, ever since he was born. He will need to differentiate from all of us before anything real can happen."

"What about the training?

"It will not be enough."

"How do you know?"

Mortulla stared ahead. This was a feeling in her bones not her mind.

Kenectka moved to the entrance of the cave. *If the training won't be enough, what will?*

She reached out, trying to get past all she knew, trying to find an answer without asking a question.

A new way of watching.

Something lurked. If only she could *see.*

CHAPTER SIXTEEN

There were three main cages in the hold. After seeing the devastation on the Lotubo, Benton ordered them pulled from the walls and anchored in the center to prevent the beasts from tearing up the sidewalls.

A thick rope was placed five feet out from each cage and nailed to the floor.

"No-man's land. No one crosses this line. We will not lose one man to a quick grab."

They threw a layer of gravel between the rope and the cages as an added precaution.

"If they try to reach through the bars and tear up the floor, the gravel will slow them down and the noise will alert us."

Initially, the beasts spent their time devouring the remains of the lopers. They did not stop until every last scrap of flesh, gut, and bone was gone. Afterwards, they licked the floors of the cages clean until there was nothing left of the lopers but a memory.

They slept for nearly two days, and when they awoke, it was as if from a trance. One stood, and a moment later they all did. They sniffed and pawed every part of the cages. Afterwards, they pressed their great weight against the bars. When these failed to give way, they pushed harder, and finally hurled their bodies against them.

The guards drew their swords and aimed their spears, afraid the bars might buckle under such pressure. But the cages were full and there was little room for the beasts to take more than a step or two before smashing into the bars. Had they been able to take a running start, things might have been different.

The Kurr roared in unison, voicing their frustration. It was so loud that Benton ordered the hatch covers closed. Even so, the vibration spread through the floorboards of the ship. Some of the men climbed the rigging to get away. It wasn't so much how loud it was, but rather how long it went on that rattled their nerves.

"They've got to be getting pretty hot down there with the hatch covers closed," the Steersman said.

"I know," Benton replied. "I'm hoping this will settle them dow—."

The ship lurched like it struck bottom.

"What was that?"

A moment later, it happened again.

Benton ran to the stairway and lifted the cover.

"What's going on?" he called down to the guard below.

"They're ganging up," the Augmentor shouted back. "They're throwing themselves two and three at a time against the bars!"

The man was drenched in sweat.

"Fire up the coals," Benton ordered. "Start with hot pokers."

"Should we fill the gutters?"

Heating the bars would deter a passive animal, but these monsters? Benton realized the heat might actually weaken the metal cages, and if the beasts persisted....

"Not yet."

It seemed like ages before the coals were glowing and the pokers hot enough.

"Their hides are too thick to do much damage," Benton said. "But flesh is flesh and it will burn. Keep the pokers low. Go for their paws. If that doesn't work, try for their ears or face. Avoid the eyes. We don't want to blind them."

"Understood."

The Augmentors rushed in with the hot pokers, and the smell of burning flesh quickly filled the hold. The beasts slammed into the bars in a show of hatred and contempt, but eventually they stopped to nurse their wounds.

"The pokers worked," Benton declared, examining the bars. "But let's not give them an opportunity like this again."

It had taken nearly an ora to heat the coals and get the pokers hot.

"From now on, we'll keep the fire going and the pokers hot at all times."

He strode over to the small brick furnace they used to heat the pokers. It was half filled with coal.

"Charge, how much coal are we carrying?"

"About two hundred buckets."

A bucket of coal would burn effectively for two or three oras. This was a trip of at least ninety days. At that rate, they would be out of coal midway through the journey.

"The use of coal is restricted," Benton declared. "We need to ration what we have."

"What about cooking?"

"Food won't matter if these beasts get free. Signal the Treescout. We'll take her coal as well."

"We should starve the beasts," the Charge said. "That'll take the fight out of them."

"Or make them more desperate. Or worse, sick."

He did not want to think what Baronuus would do if he returned with dead animals. But what the Charge said made sense.

"Let's take away their food on the days they attack their cages and feed them on the days they don't."

For the remainder of that day, the Kurr kept back from the bars in what appeared to be a show of quiet resignation.

An uneasy silence filled the hold.

Late that night, the ship shuddered again. The beasts in the center cage were slamming their shoulders, three at a time, as hard as they could against the bars and then curling up to protect their faces and paws. The Augmentors reached in with the hot pokers, and the other Kurr swiped at them, trying to knock the pokers away.

Again and again, the ship shuddered from the beasts' attack until the Augmentors surrounded the cage and came at the beasts from all sides. The Kurr finally retreated to the center of the cage amidst howls of protest.

Most disturbing were the beasts in the other cages. They were sitting quietly with looks of concentration in their eyes. Benton had never seen this in an animal before and returned to his cabin haunted by that look.

What will they think of next?

The Kurr slept the following day, but that night, the next assault began. This time, they staged random attacks through all three cages. First one group would slam their bodies against the bars and stop as soon as the Augmentors got to them with the pokers. Then the beasts in the second cage would start. From one cage to another, and back again. These staggered attacks were proving to be quite effective.

"Reinforcements! We need reinforcements."

Additional Augmentors were brought down to surround each cage with hot pokers. This stopped the attacks, but put even more pressure on their reserves.

If this continues, we will be out of coal long before we reach Ontar, Benton thought. Kriiton had told him to expect the unexpected. How little he understood his words.

They were a week into the trip, and already he had been forced to abandon his initial plan. The cages were holding so far, but some of the bars appeared like they were beginning to bow outward.

Benton summoned the Cagemaster to his cabin.

"Examine the cages twice a day and report to me. Do not discuss your findings with anyone else."

"Understood."

The Cagemaster went into the hold and got as close to the cages as he dared. That some of the bars were beginning to bend was clear, but this was not what worried him. Along the metal floor, the bars were anchored into raised slots. The pressure the beasts were applying to the bars was inadvertently putting undo amounts of stress on the slot-walls. Using a wooden pole, he tapped the slots to test their strength. They were holding up, but there were tiny stress cracks here and there.

"Commander, the inside slot-walls are beginning to show signs of fatigue. If the beasts exerted as much force pulling the bars inwards as they have been pushing against them, they might soon break out."

"God help us if they figure that out. Can you strengthen the slots?"

"I can try to fortify them and fill in the area behind them, but I would have to heat the area, and until the metal cooled down, it would be vulnerable."

"Commander!" An Augmentor banged at the door. "The Kurr are attacking the slots!"

They ran down into the hold and found the beasts clawing at them.

"They saw me testing the slots," the Cagemaster said.

"And they sensed your concern," Benton muttered. "I'll be damned. What are the chances of them breaking them?"

"Their claws are sharp, but the slots are metal."

"Water can wear away stone."

"True enough."

"Madness," Benton muttered. "Charge, use the pokers! Protect the integrity of the cages."

"Understood."

"And don't let them gnaw at the bars."

The Augmentors surrounded the cages and drove the Kurr back. The beasts smelled their captors' fear and continued to strike at the slots, retreating just before an Augmentor got to them. They kept this up day in and day out. The only time they stopped was when they slept.

Benton ordered all food and water taken away, but this only seemed to make them more determined.

There was no way to preserve the coal now. Every bar had a slot to protect. Every poker had to be reheated over and over again. The following week the beasts began to gnaw at the bars. The Augmentors were only able to drive them back by keeping their pokers right in their faces.

"Our actions have alerted them to our vulnerabilities," Benton wrote in his journal. *"The end seems inevitable now. We will be out of coal within a month. Our return, which began with such promise, is turning into a disaster."*

"If the Kurr escape," Benton told the Charge Augmentor, "we will abandon ship and make for the Treescout. From there we'll take the Seafarer in tow."

"What if they cut the line?"

"We'll have to wait and see."

The beasts continued to slam against the cages, tear at the slots and chew on the bars. They were relentless.

"Commander," the Cagemaster said. "The slots and bars are going to fail."

"How long?"

"A few days. A week, perhaps two."

Escape, which seemed impossible when these cages were first constructed, was at hand. Benton drew up plans to evacuate. He tried to imagine what the beasts might do once free of their cages. Would they tear the ship apart? Jump overboard? Die from starvation?

Passing an open hatch, he overheard an Augmentor in the hold grumbling to one of the other guards.

"I don't know what we're doing. We should just kill 'em' all. And if not, use pitch."

"What do you mean?" Benton called down, confronting the man.

"Commander. I uh—"

"Speak!"

"I meant no disrespect. It's only that, I thought maybe we could try pitch."

"Tar?"

"They've plenty aboard to seal the seams. We could paint the bars and slots with it. One taste of that stuff and I'd wager they'll keep their mouths and bodies well off them."

"You'll get three nubs of avarin if it works. Charge! Get the ship's carpenter."

The carpenter confirmed there was plenty of tar aboard.

"It might slow them down."

They set a pot on the furnace in the hold and threw in a chunk of tar. As it began to melt, thick bands of black, acrid smoke rose up and spread throughout the hold. The sickening smell set off a wave of complaints from the Kurr. Some began to make choking sounds, others retched. The air thickened with the smoke, and the beasts curled up, burying their noses under their legs, or in nooks and crannies of those around them.

"Look at that. They hate the smoke! It's making them sick."

"That's it!" Benton cried. "We don't have to paint the bars! If they're like this now with the hatches open imagine what it will be like if we close them."

Word spread like fire.

"Each time they ram the cages, chew on a bar, or attack a slot, we will close the hatch covers and fill the hold with smoke."

"Understood!"

Benton went up on deck and took a breath of fresh air. The sun was shining, a fair wind blowing, and the green sea sparkled with vigor. A day had never seemed more perfectly constructed, and he laughed aloud for the first time in months.

True to his plan, each time the beasts slashed at the slots or pressed against the bars, the hatches were closed, and tar melted. The beasts dropped to the floor and fought to cover their faces. By the third time, all the Augmentors had to do was close the hatch covers, and that was enough to settle them down.

"They learn quickly," the Charge said.

"Too quickly."

The furnace was kept burning, but at a minimum, just enough to melt some tar. Hot pokers were a thing of the past and each man gave silent offerings to the gods, who hovered above, offering their protection in one moment, and just as easily squashing them like bugs in the next.

CHAPTER SEVENTEEN

The land, the sky, the trees, the forest, creatures large and small... an unending expanse. One could let go, see without naming, be without thinking. In this way, the Rehloy renewed themselves.

For months, Jormah bathed in their way of life. The songs of the world, *all and everything*, the collective ring of the *intra*life, sullied now by the taunt of the oncoming calamity.

What am I to do?

Wherever he went, unspoken thoughts greeted him at every turn. Everyone kept him in their sights. They mistook his foreignness for strength and were sure he would know what to do. But he was as trapped by their expectations as they were by the circumstances.

"When I first returned, I could not get enough of the people," Jormah confided in Donan.

"You were gone a long time. There was much to absorb and remember."

"Now, I feel hemmed in by them."

This restlessness in him had been growing for some time.

"You would return to the wilderness?"

"It's where I fit best." But how could he return to the ways of the past when the past itself was no longer?

"We have yet to speak of things to come," Donan said, leading him to the ledge overlooking the Resep far below. The plants were nearly full grown, and Harvest just a few weeks away. From this vantage point, the linear paths the plants had taken produced a vision of a city a bird might have. "The pattern-of-change has become ingrained."

"More than in the past?"

"More so than ever before. Your arrival has made sense of it."

Jormah was pained by this, despite knowing it was inevitable.

"You said the Intruders are very different from the Carooh."

"They are."

"Yet, they are Stiffbacks all the same."

"Yes."

"The Carooh revered you for qualities we naturally possess. Would the Intruders do the same?"

"The Carooh live closer to our ways. The Intruders are different."

"But if they revered us as the Carooh did, would they not do our bidding? Could we keep them at bay and preserve our way of life?"

"I don't know."

"The Carooh thought of you as the Bhytoe, the Spirit-Of-The-Forest."

"Yes."

"Perhaps it is true."

"In a way. From their view."

"What would happen if the Intruders met the Bhytoe?"

"Their nature is different."

"Then a different Bhytoe must appear."

A different Bhytoe.

"When you first appeared before the Carooh, they thought it a miracle. With the Intruders, you may have to find a different miracle."

What Donan was proposing bordered on blasphemy. Besides, the thought of being exposed to the Intruder's violence and brutality was so repugnant, a part of Jormah rebelled.

"I can't imagine living amongst them."

Donan sighed. "Then your challenge will be that much greater."

Jormah turned away. He always knew he would leave one day but did not expect it to be so soon, or that he would have to travel back so far. Would his role always be that of outsider?

They lapsed into silence, a sadness between them.

To hold to the past would deny the present. To deny the present would ignore the future.

"I will go," Jormah said, after a time.

"For all our sakes."

"I make no promises."

Donan embraced him.

"Of all of us, you are the one most capable."

Jormah was not consoled.

"I must study them first."

"Of course."

"If it is possible, and the situation arises, I will make myself known to them."

"That is all we can ask."

There was nothing left to say.

"I will leave after Harvest and the Day-Of-Feasts."

"With fresh leefskins and a backsack full of malta. Enough to take you to the Children-Of-Origin."

Jormah nodded.

"You will travel faster than before."

"Now that I know what lies ahead…."

Donan felt a sudden chill. What if he never returned?

Stelbin approached Jormah days later with the same open posture he had employed the first time they met. "I sense something has changed," he said. The balance in the tribe had alerted him to a shift, a leaning.

"What do you mean?"

"You are different. Everywhere you go, everything you do is touched with a sense of... naming."

"Yes," Jormah replied, waiting for more.

Stelbin thought more carefully. *Naming, as if saying hello and goodbye.*

"You are leaving?"

"Yes."

"When?"

"After the Day-Of-Feasts."

Tremlo was nearby and heard the words, but they made no sense. The Kwaman's growing restlessness seemed completely natural, yet it did not feel possible that they would be separated so soon.

"Tremlo?" Donan asked. "Do you know Jormah is leaving?"

"Yes."

"Does this bother you?'

Tremlo thought a moment, "No."

Given how attached the younger had become to Jormah, Donan found his lack of concern odd.

"You know he will be leaving soon."

"Yes."

The night before Harvest, Jormah stood beside the Resep and absorbed its fullest expression. As he did so he reached through the currents to the north. The Intruders were wider and more pronounced than ever before. The Resep confirmed it was so.

If they revered us, we could keep them at bay and preserve our way of life.

If they revered us.

If.

CHAPTER EIGHTEEN

The beasts were weary and withdrawn. As one month turned to two, they slept all day and most of the night. When they were awake, their movements were sluggish and the expression in their faces unfocused. It appeared like they were finally resigned to their circumstance.

Whenever enslaving a population, one had to apply a certain pressure to break the spirit. Once this occurred, a kind of molding could take place, but the spirit of the enslaved had to be broken first.

Benton studied the Kurrs' demeanor and wondered if, in fact, this was what was happening. A Commander once told him that the moment one felt the most secure, was the moment of one's greatest vulnerability.

"Charge, double the guard."

It seemed prescient, for the energy in the hold changed soon after. The Kurr did not resume their attacks on the cages but paced back and forth now with an alertness that had been missing for some time. They stared directly into the eyes of any who came into the hold, and many were the men who turned their heads to avoid this gaze.

"Be careful."

"They're up to something."

"Don't get too close."

Expect the unexpected.

Day in and day out, it was the same. Everyone was on edge.

Benton was asleep in his cabin when the ship started rolling from side to side. He awoke with a start.

We've stopped!

He grabbed his sword and opened the door to his cabin. A moonless night. He could barely see a foot in front of him. Keeping one hand on the guardrail, he crept up on deck and moved towards the stern. He was almost upon the Steersman before he saw him.

"Why have we stopped?"

"Lights."

"Where?"

"Off the starboard bow. There."

Benton peered into the blackness. Nothing at first. The ship rolled atop a swell, and there it was.

"Land?"

"Yes."

"Where?"

"Ontar certainly. Not sure where. We'll wait for daybreak to get our bearings."

"Good."

Could it be that this accursed journey was almost at an end?

At daybreak, the Steersman set course.

"We're about three days south of Port Alburt, Commander."

"Excellent."

The beasts were making low rumbling sounds.

"I think they've been smelling land for days."

"Land and lopers."

The rumblings grew louder, and the ship shuddered with the thud of them hurling their bodies against the cages.

"Close the hatches!"

But the beasts were not dissuaded.

"The smell of lopers must be getting strong, Commander. It's driving away all reason."

"Agreed. Melt the tar!"

As the fumes filled the hold the beasts collapsed, covering their nostrils as best they could.

Benton kept the hatches closed for quite some time. Surely the smell of the tar would linger and help mask the lopers' scent.

Port Alburt was dotted with all manner of brightly painted buildings. Reds, greens, yellows and azures, a great relief from the monotony and tensions at sea. Some buildings were for commerce, others for pleasure. Off to the right was a city of white tents. It was a fresh-air market where anything and everything was bought and sold. From food to medicines, tools to weapons, seeds, services, animals, people. Everything. The men's stomachs growled, hungry to be discharged from this terrible service.

"Steersman, we will not dock. Anchor where you deem best. I will go ashore and have preparations made."

"Understood."

Port Alburt was the busiest harbor along the western shore of Ontar. With its superior roads, it serviced all the northern provinces and was the main entry port into the interior. All ships venturing to Ontara departed from this port.

As they rowed in, Benton counted thirteen ships tied to the docks. Two loper-drawn carts moved lazily along the periphery. A sleepy, late summer's afternoon. A group of men sauntered over to the receiving dock. Augmentors, crewmen, dockhands.

Spies for the Emperor and the Elite, Benton thought. This was the world of men. As dangerous as the cargo in the hold of the ship, only here there were no cages.

They rowed up to the dock, and a man wearing the official dark blue coat and gold-crested hat of the Harbormaster greeted them.

"Greetings, Commander. I celebrate your safe return."

"Thank you for your well wishes, Harbormaster."

This man was in Baronuus's employ, but Benton did not trust him. Medium in height, his gaze deceptively dull, his fingers too plump for his body.

Trust no one, so the old saying went.

If in error, the damage can be repaired.

If misplaced, the damage can be permanent.

"How may we serve you?" the Harbormaster asked.

"I ask permission for the Treescout to dock. We carry a complement of Augmentors."

"Permission granted."

"In addition, we carry unusual cargo."

"So I have been told."

"Special preparations will have to be made before we dock and unload. But first, I must signal Baronuus of our arrival."

"That has already been done."

Benton was annoyed.

"May I add a message?"

"Of course."

The Harbormaster escorted Benton to the signal tower.

Using mirrors and sunlight, an elaborate series of towers and relay platforms had been set up long ago. Based upon the terrain, some towers were miles apart, while others much less so. There were five major light-paths that spread throughout the realm. The main path went straight to Halla, the Imperial City. It lay twenty days to the east of Port Alburt. The signal would take a fraction of that time to get there.

"What message do you wish to send?"

"To Et-El Baronuus. Returned with cargo. Send escort. Benton."

"Understood."

If Baronuus was in Halla, he would receive this message within a few oras. If not, it might take days to get to him. Nothing to do now but wait.

"Commander, are these animals really as fierce as we have heard?"

Benton looked at the Harbormaster carefully. *Is he asking out of personal curiosity or spying for one of the Elite?*

The man's hands were hidden behind his back.

"In my opinion, the beasts' only saving grace is that they are not invulnerable."

Ha! Benton laughed to himself. *Let him make sense out of that.*

The Harbormaster nodded as though he understood.

"What sort of preparations do you need for unloading?"

"I want to look around first."

"Of course. It would be an honor to escort you."

Benton was convinced now that the man was also in someone else's employ. Any information he could tease out might be worth something to line his pocket.

They walked around the perimeter, and Benton focused on a dock farthest from the rest.

"The unloading will take place there," he said. "That ship and cargo must be moved. We want no obstructions of any kind. All lopers will have to be removed from the area."

"When do you want this ready?"

"Soon." Baronuus had told him he would send a full complement of Augmentors under the command of someone who was 'up to the task'. But he had not said who.

Whoever he sends better be more than just up to the task.

"When the escort arrives, we will unload the beasts. For now, the Seafarer will remain offshore and at anchor."

"These beasts must be something for you to take such precautions."

"Are they?"

"Well, I suppose."

"You have your responsibilities, I have mine."

"Commander, may I— I mean, I was wondering if I might be allowed to go aboard and have a look for myself."

"Once everything settles down, I will consider your request," Benton replied. He needed to keep this man close. "If you hear who is leading the escort…."

"You will be the first to know."

And so it was done.

CHAPTER NINETEEN

Harvest morning, the green of the Resep, the green of their leef-skin, they a part of it, and everything a part of them.

I must remember this, Jormah told himself.

Whaet gave the signal, and they eased into the field. The Resep was very much alive; its rhythms ran through their veins.

Each plant was grasped by hand and heart, uprooted, carried to the storage cave, and placed gently in piles where they were left to commune in this, their final *easing*.

Weeks later, when the time was right, their leaves would be stripped, their malta extracted.

In this way, the Resep would enter the body of the Rehloy.

In the days that followed, Jormah kept to the outskirts, absorbing the combined rhythms of the Rehloys' experience. He, who would be leaving soon, did not want to make anyone too dear.

Reena watched along with the others. She had felt a sense of him long before he returned, long before she herself was aware of it.

Tremlo.

Her son's fascination with Jormah was now her own. The Kwaman's return had set off a riot of sensations. Nowhere did she feel it more strongly than in her son.

Jormah wandered about knowing he was watched, no matter how discreetly. Always there was Tremlo, and now, his mother.

Curiosity finally brought them together.

"Hello, Reena."

He remembered her to be festive and lighthearted. A different Reena stood now before him.

They looked at each other, plainly, directly.

"I see Tremlo in you," he said. "And you in him."

"We are all connected in unseen ways."

"So it is known."

She knew what he was asking.

"I hear Tremlo more deeply than most," she said.

"And what does he say to you?"

"He does not speak in words."

"How then?"

"Impressions. Sensations. He is deeply affected by you and growing because of it."

"How do you know?"

"I feel his struggle. And his pain."

"His pain?"

"He's letting go the old and stretching into the new. The change you bring is working through his body."

Jormah did not want that responsibility. "He watches me wherever I go. Even now."

"Yes."

"And what do you make of that?"

"He has need of you."

"In what way?"

She felt his resistance and Tremlo's hunger.

"You are food. A missing flavor. You inspire him."

"He hides from me at every turn."

"He is easily overwhelmed. He has to *be* you, in order to be *with* you."

"And what does that tell us of him?"

"That he is painfully sensitive. A victim of circumstance. But he is good, and kind, and special in all ways."

A mother defending her cub.

Jormah would not get the answer he sought. Perhaps it was unknowable.

"He will not harm you."

"I did not think he would."

"An encumbrance in one moment can be a source of comfort in the next."

They looked deep into each other's eyes.

He felt the depth of her plea, and she the weight of his resignation.

She took his hand before they parted. Nothing more to say, yet volumes left unspoken.

The Resep was stripped of its leaves, and the malta extracted. Only the sharpest of cutting stones were used to minimize the trauma. The leaves were distributed and the patterns cast as the people began to make their new clothes. *Leefskin*. Tremlo made his own alongside Jormah. The Kwaman wove an extra-large backsack into his pattern and Tremlo did the same. No one took particular notice, for Tremlo's mimicry was well known, but whispers of another kind began to spread through the tribe.

Jormah's backsack is too large.

"Is Jormah leaving?" Whaet was first to ask Donan.

"Yes."

"When?"

"Soon."

"What else can you tell me?"

"What do you wish to know?"

"Where is he going?"

"The wilderness."

"To live?"

"There, and beyond."

"Beyond?"

"He will go north again."

"How far?"

"All the way."

"To the Intruders?"

"Yes."

"For what purpose?"

Whaet deserved to know. They all did.

"He may reveal himself."

"To what end?"

"To see if he has the same effect upon the Intruders as he did upon the Carooh."

Whaet's mind was reeling. The fact that the Kwamen were implementing such a daring plan suggested how great was the danger. Given Jormah's description of the Intruders, he might well be putting his life at risk.

Where Whaet approached Donan, Gremar went after Jormah. The Kwaman was walking along the eastern side of the mountain, and Gremar moved to intercept.

"May I walk with you?"

"You have been doing so all morning."

Gremar smiled to soften the blow. *Be precise.* This Kwaman had little tolerance for conversation that wasn't direct and truthful.

"Everyone says you're leaving."

"Everyone?"

"Your backsack," Gremar hastily added, "is made for traveling."

Jormah remembered Gremar to be a needy youth, but he had matured over the years. His reaction to the knowledge of the Intruders was different from all the other members of the tribe. It set him apart.

"What is it you want?"

"I want what is best for the tribe."

Jormah heard the sincerity in Gremar's voice and saw the calculation in his body.

"We all want that. Speak your mind."

"You said the Intruders might never come."

"That is one possibility."

"But knowing what you know, and seeing what you have seen, you think differently."

"They are a long way off."

"You are going back there, aren't you?"

"Yes."

"You go to rule!" Gremar exclaimed.

Jormah was impressed. Gremar had seen right to the heart of the plan. This kind of thinking was rare in the tribe. But there was something dangerous here.

"Guide," he said. "If possible, I go to guide."

Gremar nodded vigorously, imagining all that Jormah might do. But the Kwaman's stare brought him back to himself.

"I understand," he said, dampening his excitement.

"Do you?"

"This raises many questions."

"And what might they be?"

"The world is changing and we have to find our place in it. On the day you returned, you said we have to plan for a new way of being."

"And what did I mean?"

"A time of transition is upon us. Holding to the forms of the past could be detrimental."

Gremar's mind was agile. There was wisdom in his words, but there was also something corrupt and self-serving.

"When you get there, what will you do?" Gremar asked.

"Nothing."

'Nothing?'

"I will observe them for a time."

"And then?"

"I will wait and see."

He knew what Gremar wanted to hear.

"Jormah, you are a great Kwaman. Don't judge me too harshly."

Gremar could be alarming in one moment, disarming in the next.

"I have often wondered," Gremar continued, "about Gahen and those who went south with him."

Jormah had heard about Gremar's early exploit. He had left the Tribal Body years before, and created all sorts of havoc.

"I was young and foolish then."

"Were you?"

"Have you considered going south to see what might lie in that direction?"

"If the Intruders come, the southern regions will only prolong the inevitable."

"But a strong wind always dies."

"Who is the wind?"

"It depends upon where you stand."

Clever. Manipulative. Tiresome.

Gremar felt Jormah's impatience. "I will leave you now to resume your walk."

"Yes, that would be good."

Gremar held his composure, and Jormah watched him go.

What was it about Gremar that annoyed him so?

Is this the kind of person that will lead us into the future? And if so, what might we become?

CHAPTER TWENTY

Jormah rose long before dawn and filled his backsack with malta. He had said his goodbyes to the people during the Day-Of-Feasts and wanted to be gone before first light. Donan and Stelbin sat in balance-position watching, but Tremlo could not sit still. After a few moments, he began to fill his own backsack.

"Tremlo, what are you doing?" Donan asked.

The younger stopped to think. The word 'doing' often confused him. In this moment, he didn't feel he was doing anything. He was merely being carried along by the natural flow of events.

"Nothing," he replied.

"What are you doing with the malta?"

"Putting it into the backsack."

"Why?"

"To follow Jormah."

Jormah stopped packing. *No, you're not.*

"You're leaving us?" Donan asked.

"No." Tremlo hadn't thought of it that way.

"But you are going away?"

Yes, he saw now that he was going away. But he was not leaving them, not really.

"Just following Jormah."

"For how long?"

"As long as it goes."

He said it so plainly, so directly, it was like there was no other possibility. Tremlo never took charge like this. All three felt the finality of his words and were stilled by it.

"Tremlo," Donan ventured after a moment, "we know you want to remain close to Jormah. But where he is going will be very dangerous."

"Yes," the younger replied. He had grown years in just a few months. The taller he grew, the longer his thoughts.

"It will be many years before Jormah returns."

"Yes, it will be many years." Tremlo's voice was firm, a statement of fact, not one of agreement.

"You would not see us, or your parents, or anyone for all that time."

Tremlo gave him a quizzical look. Everyone was with him no matter where he went.

"Jormah may not want you along," Donan said, bluntly.

Tremlo was surprised by this. He rolled the idea around in his mind but could find no place for it. Whether it was true or not, it did not seem to matter, and he resumed his packing.

Donan and Jormah looked at one another. If this had been any other younger, they would have simply said no. Jormah tilted his head and Donan followed him outside.

"This is not wise," Jormah said.

"Wisdom may have nothing to do with it."

"What do you mean?"

"I don't think anyone will think this is a good idea."

"Then you should stop it."

"Forbid him to go?"

"Yes."

Donan did not reply. This was unforeseen, and Tremlo had been so forceful.

"Will you do it?" Jormah pressed.

"I'm not sure what to do."

Jormah sighed and turned away a little too quickly.

"You have foreseen this?"

"Not exactly."

"What then?"

"When Tremlo started following me, it felt like he had thrown a rope around me. Not just then, but in the future."

If so, who are we to stop it? Donan wondered.

"He will slow me down."

"In all likelihood," Donan replied. "But he will remind you of us."

"He will create problems."

"He will bring possibilities."

"Moments ago, you said it could be too dangerous for him."

"In the end, it may be too dangerous for all of us."

"What am I to do with him?" Jormah cried. "You are the one skilled in the training, not I."

"You will learn together."

"He has no sense of self."

"He embraces more than we can imagine."

"He reflects what is around him and casts nothing of himself."

'*Yes.*'

"At the center of him, I sense nothing but... pain."

"Whoever he is, whatever he is, the influences of the tribe are too strong. They distract him from finding himself."

"What do you think I can accomplish?"

"You were not within the Tribal Body while Tremlo was growing up. You are from outside. He reacts to you differently. It may be the one thing that can save him. Away from us, he might be able to discover his true nature."

Jormah's body tensed with 'no'. This was a terrible burden, and he felt unequal to the task.

"Jormah, if he is what we think he is, we will need him, and possibly sooner than we might have thought. You said to the tribe that you believed there was some purpose here. That we have, in effect, been chosen."

"You know why I said that."

"I do. But I believe it is not we, but he who was claimed."

Jormah ceased to argue. It was not Donan's words, but the weight of future events that took hold of him. He could stand in the way and be crushed, or swim along and try not to drown. Either way, he saw now that there was nothing he could do or say to help or hinder.

Everything was going to happen of its own accord.

CHAPTER TWENTY-ONE

Bettrie stood at the bottom of the old granite quarry and looked up at the white stone walls. She had hoped this day would never come. What happened next could determine whether she lived or died.

Years before, she was summoned to the Emperor's palace and greeted by one of the Elite. She had no idea why she was there, and the man's brusque manner precluded any conversation.

"Come this way," Et-El Baronuus said.

He ushered her into a large anteroom where the Emperor himself was sitting upon a throne some ten feet tall. Bettrie instantly dropped to her knees and lowered her head. She had only seen the Emperor once and that was from a great distance.

"You may rise, Animal Trainer," Proutus said, watching her carefully.

She rose with *panthra*-like grace. A tall woman. Short cropped hair. Powerful. Her face lined with the kind of experience that betrayed no emotion. Eyes sharply focused, a penetrating blue. She possessed an undeniable presence.

"Et-El Baronuus has some questions for you. Answer him honestly and directly."

"Yes, my liege."

Her voice was strong. Tempered. Assured.

"Bettrie," Baronuus said. "Have you heard of the beast they discovered in the new world?"

"It killed all the colony's lopers."

"What do you make of that?"

"Hunger was not the beasts' motivation."

"And why is that?"

"According to the story, the beasts could not be stopped, or driven off until they killed all the lopers. It suggests some primal force at work. A territorial dispute, perhaps."

"If territorial, why didn't they go after the colonists as well?"

"Perhaps they did not see them as a threat. Territory is often marked by scent. Maybe the lopers' odor has something to do with it. Maybe it makes these beasts mad with desire. The smell of death can drive creatures away or lure them to it."

"What is your opinion of the beast?"

"My opinion?"

Baronuus took a step closer. "Do you think it can be trained?"

Bettrie knew the animal world intimately. How they lived, how they related to one another, how they hunted. Men were a breed of animal all their own. In this room, she had become prey.

"Trained in what way?" she asked, stalling for time.

The Emperor's voice boomed from above. "We have been told that you are the best Animal Trainer in all of Ontar. Baronuus is of the opinion that this beast can be used as a weapon against our enemies."

"You want me to train them to kill on command?"

"Exactly," Baronuus said, his cruel eyes glowing.

"It's difficult to—. I don't know what the intelligence or disposition of these beasts might be."

Baronuus took a step closer.

"You have been quoted as saying that there wasn't an animal alive you couldn't train."

"Yes," she replied, cursing herself for her boast. "But I cannot train a hound to fly or a loper to climb a tree, or an animal to think beyond its capacities."

"The Kurr are very intelligent," Baronuus said. "And as they have demonstrated, they are experts at killing."

"Some animals must be beaten in order to train them to kill," Bettrie said, speaking to both but looking at neither. "Others need to be beaten to stop them from killing. None of these are good options. The most effective way to train an animal is to have them bond with their Trainer. If the Kurr are too independent, the answer is probably no, they cannot be trained."

"What if you started with cubs?"

"Wild animals raised from infancy can revert back to the instincts they were born with. Some turn against their masters."

Baronuus was irritated. This woman was becoming troublesome.

"Bettrie, what do you know of the goings on in our Southern Provinces?"

"There was an uprising. We sent Augmentors to suppress it."

"We sent Augmentors there, but their job was not to suppress it. They are setting up positions from which we will defend the Empire. The mountains that border the edge of the Southern Provinces are no longer inhabited by the Argoot alone. There is a push from behind them, a merging if you will, with a new and fierce nation. Our spies tell us the Vradeem are over a hundred thousand strong and moving in our direction. The mountains have done much to protect us and keep them away. But over the past year, their presence has increased dramatically. It's only a matter of time before they come through the mountains. What I tell you now is under the Oath-of-Secrecy."

"I comply."

"Ontar's resources are dwindling. It is all we can do to protect and maintain what we have. This additional burden could have disastrous results."

Once again, the Emperor's voice boomed out from above. "Et-El Baronuus believes that these creatures could give us the advantage we need to defeat the insurgents."

"This animal must be very special to put so much faith in it."

"True," Proutus said. "We have said as much ourselves."

Baronuus stood perfectly still, the expression on his face unreadable.

"I make no guarantees," she said, directing her words above, hoping to gain the Emperor's protection. "I pledge to do all I can, and nothing but death will prevent me from trying."

"Pledge understood and accepted," Proutus said, smiling to himself. The Animal Trainer had distanced herself from failure if it came, leaving it squarely on Baronuus's shoulders.

Baronuus gave her a look that let her know he would not be forgiving.

Years passed. As each successive mission failed to return, Bettrie's fear slowly subsided. It seemed like her skills might never be tested. Then word came.

Beasts in Port Alburt. Come.

She arrived to find the animals in the transport ship anchored offshore.

Why?

They shuttled her out to the ship and immediately brought her down below to see her new charges. These were large, docile lumps of brown, whose movements, if any, were slow and lumbering. Their white eyes were dull and unfocused.

"These animals look sick."

"We've been keeping the hatches closed, and they've refused food and water the last several days," the Charge explained.

"So any act of aggression is repaid by poisoning the air with smoke?"

"Don't judge us too harshly," Benton said, coming down to meet her. "These beasts are very intelligent, and far more dangerous than any animal you have ever encountered. It would not surprise me if their refusal to eat was a ploy to get us to move them."

Bettrie nodded politely. Animals were not stupid and often acted in ways that appeared rational. But mostly, these were simple variations based upon inherited behaviors. They moved in a certain way, explored their environment in a certain way, interacted in a certain way. Once these patterns were established, they rarely, if ever, varied.

'Animals draw comfort through repetition,' she often said.

"Forgive me, Commander, but the only creature I know capable of such strategic thinking is man."

"Exactly."

Bettrie stared at the ground.

"It's been a difficult journey for all of us," Benton continued.

"I can imagine."

"I don't think you can. I don't think anyone could. But come, I'm just now finishing my report for Et-El Baronuus. You may find the details interesting."

They went to his cabin and Bettrie listened while Benton read her the report. It was clear, concise, impressive in its own way. But some of Benton's interpretations seemed far-fetched, particularly when it came to the beasts' intelligence. Everyone spoke of the beasts' intelligence, and how all reason was abandoned where lopers were concerned.

But why lopers? They posed no physical threat. *Why not some other animal?*

"Thank you, Commander. You have given me much to think about. We need to get them out of here and on land as soon as possible."

"Where will you take them?"

"The Damatine Quarry. It lies about a week's journey inland."

"Why there?"

After centuries of digging, the Damatine Quarry was many hundreds of feet deep. The floor was at least two hundred feet across and twice that in length. Bettrie had ordered the walls recut in such a way that the higher up they went, the less rock they took away. This created walls that slanted inwards and would prevent the beasts from scaling them.

"There are no bars on a battlefield, Commander. The quarry will allow them to move about more freely."

"Understood. The road leading to the quarry will have to be cleared of lopers."

"You can send a detachment ahead of us once we're on the road."

"That may not be good enough. The smell will be too fresh."

"Perhaps, but I'm ordering the Kurr fed a steady diet of their precious loper flesh."

"That will rile them up. You don't want to do that before we transport them."

"Animals are driven by three major forces: food, elimination, and reproduction. All else is simply waiting. Hopefully their appetite for loper flesh can be sated, or at least their sensitivity to it dulled."

"You will rouse them from the sweet lethargy we now enjoy."

"There is a substance called wolfir that works with similar breeds. When eaten, it seems to dull their minds and relax them. Perhaps it will work here too."

Benton remained unconvinced. "How much loper do you intend on feeding them."

"They need less in the confines of a cage than in the wild. Based on size, I would say roughly a sixteenth part would be enough, but at first, we will give them twice as much each day."

"That would mean feeding them about two lopers a day."

"Full stomachs calm the fiercest of men," Bettrie said reciting the common phrase.

"At that rate, it will require over seven hundred lopers a year to keep their stomachs full."

"Not so many, but it can't be helped. We can add other meat or gruel if necessary. But to begin with, I want it to be pure, to see if we can satiate this need in them."

"I see."

"Please convey this to Et-El Baronuus. Let him know I insist this be done."

"Understood. Once the Kurr are delivered to your quarry, I will have fulfilled my duties, and frankly, the sooner the better."

Upon hearing the Kurr were going to be fed loper meat, the crew grew tense. There was much guarded conversation.

Bettrie noted their fear.

The Kurr were soon stalking back and forth as if knowing fresh loper meat was coming. Gone were the slow movements and dull facial expressions. In their stead were the sharpened features of a killer.

How did they know?

"You see," Benton said.

Bettrie marveled at the transition.

Did they sense the crew's trepidation? Had this really been a ploy?

The shuttler carrying freshly killed meat drew near, and the Kurr pressed their noses through the bars. Their bodies trembled with excitement. Their blood-red tongues flicked in and out like a snake's, tasting the air.

This will not do, Bettrie thought. Here was a kind of frenzied passion that could never be managed.

The Augmentors dropped pieces of meat into the cages from the open hatches above. The beasts tore into the flesh with a viciousness that went far beyond the bounds of hunger. They did not stop until every last lick was gone. Bettrie had never seen animals eat like this.

Afterwards they fell into a deep sleep, as if relieved to be free of this perverse compulsion.

"You may go," Bettrie said to the Augmentors. "I will spend the night here alone with them."

"But, it's not safe."

"Nonsense. I want to get to know them, and you are all a distraction. Stay on deck. I will call out at the first sign of trouble."

She is gutsy, Benton thought. *Or a fool.*

Bettrie placed herself in a prominent place so all the beasts might see her. It did not matter if they slept. For now, she wanted them to get used to her. Together they breathed, their smells intermixing. Together they dreamed, each aware of the other, incorporating unconscious sensations, laying a foundation, creating a familiarity.

The beasts awoke early the following morning and paced back and forth with an air of expectation. Bettrie sat with her back against the bulkhead and studied them carefully.

Who is the dominant?

She wanted to start with the leader, and if trainable, the others would follow more easily. But they were separated into three cages, and based upon Benton's description of the capture, there might not be a leader yet. If so, she would learn much about the Kurr from how this hierarchy was formed.

The morning wore on, and the animals grew more agitated. Several cast glances in her direction.

Why?

Shortly after she arrived, she had ordered them fed. Could they be associating her presence as a precursor to food?

They were all looking at her now, some in an almost questioning manner, others more belligerently.

What are you thinking? she wondered. *How do you communicate?*

One beast stopped pacing altogether and sat on its haunches.

It's looking me right in the eyes.

In the animal kingdom, to stare into another's eyes was an act of aggression that might easily lead to violence if the other did not avert its gaze.

Is this a challenge?

She kept her body firm, yet relaxed, and stared back into the beast's white, vacant eyes. 'The eyes of death,' Benton had called them. Bettrie expected the beast to charge the bars, or roar its displeasure, but it did none of those things.

It simply stared back.

If not challenging me, what then?

She read no hostility in its body.

Could this be contemplation?

The idea was too absurd. Animals used their senses in an active way to investigate and sort out the world. To sit and contemplate something for any extended period of time was not in their nature.

Are you the dominant?

It was a female, and not the largest or the fiercest of the group. Perhaps physical prowess was not as important to them as other qualities.

But if so, what? Intelligence?

The beasts in the other cages sat down and looked at Bettrie like the one who had not averted her gaze.

Is she trying to communicate with me?

The beast stood up slowly and moved to the bars of the cage without taking her eyes off Bettrie.

She has a regal bearing, Bettrie thought. *Regal. I shall call her Regal.*

She stood up and took a few steps towards the cage. Regal pushed her nose through the bars and seemed to be sniffing at her, inviting her closer. All the other beasts remained quite still. Bettrie took a step closer and then another. She was now at the edge of no-man's-land.

Dare I get closer?

The softness in Regal's bearing beckoned her to come near.

What are you thinking?

Bettrie stopped and stared back. She would come no closer. Once this became apparent, Regal's eyes narrowed, her ears flattened and her calm demeanor turned to rage. Looking straight into Bettrie's eyes, she roared. The hot, sickening smell of her breath covered Bettrie like dew.

Do not show fear, she shouted to herself.

All the beasts were up now and at the bars. At some unseen signal they roared in unison. The guards came running down the steps ready to set the tar to melting.

"Stop!" Bettrie shouted, raising her hand while keeping her eyes trained on Regal. "Go back up. Now! Out! OUT!"

The guards reluctantly withdrew.

The beasts continued to roar.

Here was defiance, anger, threats. *And a demand?* Bettrie held herself in check for what felt like an ora before Regal sat down and began to lick her paws.

You are not important, her actions seemed to say.

The others turned away, falling into a pattern of distraction and self-interest. It was then, and only then, that Bettrie backed away and sat down once more with her back against the bulkhead.

When the loper meat arrived, she insisted on feeding them herself. She used a long pole and inserted the pieces through the cages. The beasts were crazed by its presence, but she made a great show of feeding the dominant female first.

It is you. You are the leader. You are the one I will begin with.

Over the next five days, Bettrie fed the beasts both loper and wolfir mixed together. She did so at the same time and in the same quantities until a pattern of eating and sleeping was firmly established.

"As soon as they finish today's meal we will start," she told Benton. "From now on, we will feed them each day just before moving them and they will sleep through most of it."

The ship was brought to the dock, and the animals loaded into baited cages. These were then lowered onto carts that would be pulled by Augmentors. Each cage was covered with thick, black blankets to shield them from the outside world.

As Bettrie predicted, the Kurr offered little complaint along the way, and they arrived at the quarry without incident.

"It's up to you now, Bettrie," Benton said, slapping her good naturedly on the back.

"You're not out of this yet, Commander. These animals may be too old. We might have to start with cubs."

"Let them breed, and you'll have all the cubs you need."

"Some animals do not breed in captivity."

"For both our sakes, you'd better hope these do."

CHAPTER TWENTY-TWO

What am I to do with you?

It was the same thought Jormah had before they set off; it was the same thought that greeted him every day.

What am I to do with you?

Each step he took seemed to emphasize a word.

What– am I– to do– with you?

Tremlo flowed behind, seamlessly; not only expressing Jormah's outward form, but his internal rhythms as well.

What am I to do with you?

Even this question could be seen in the youth's bearing.

It's as if I am alone with myself.

Tremlo never spoke unless spoken to. His orientation to the world seemed *all-listening*. If resistance defined existence, Tremlo resisted nothing.

If only I could have spoken with Donan about this before we left.

But there had been no time for planning or preparation. In one moment, it was decided, and in the next, they were on their way.

"Tremlo, do you want to say goodbye to your parents before you go?" Donan had asked.

In response, Tremlo took a step up behind Jormah. His sense of Reena and Arlen was *ever-present*. Why would he want to say goodbye to them when he did not feel he was leaving?

"Take care then," Stelbin said, embracing the younger with a sense of parting that went far beyond the moment.

Donan stepped forward and placed his hands on his shoulders. "You will always be in our hearts and minds. Remember what you have learned."

He, too, seemed to anticipate a real separation, and Tremlo grew nervous.

Donan turned to Jormah. "Farewell, my brother."

"Until we meet again."

"Until then."

Jormah headed down the mountain with long purposeful strides. There was an element of haste in his manner that might not have been there if Tremlo was not coming along. The younger struggled to keep up. His backsack was stuffed with malta and shifted heavily from side to side.

"Our burden now will be our salvation later," Jormah said, maintaining his pace through the dark of early morning. He wanted to be gone before the general rising.

Tremlo was soon breathing hard, but the Kwaman would not slow down.

If he wishes to be with me, he will have to stretch his capacities.

Reena awoke with a start.

"Tremlo's leaving!" she cried and rushed from the cave.

Arlen chased after, not knowing what she meant. How could he be leaving? He was a child. *Leaving how?* He reached out and felt Jormah and Tremlo coming down the mountain. What were they doing?

They intercepted them at the base path near the bottom of the mountain. Reena ignored Jormah and went straight up to Tremlo. She knew he would have left without saying goodbye. He, who did not know what that meant, who would honor her and carry her to the ends of the world. He would not understand her need.

She threw her arms around him and hugged him tight. She had been a good mother. The best she could ever be. She would never hold him back. He was a part of something much greater than herself. She knew this, but still....

She let go and ran her fingers across his face, tracing the outline as much to remember him as to release him.

He stood by, reveling in her touch, participating in his own way. Feeling her feel the face before her, a new face, different, the same, *emerging*.

She kissed his forehead and stepped back, pressing her hands to her chest.

Arlen came forward and hugged him. Within his arms, he felt the lengths to which Tremlo had grown. A fleeting spark, a glimpse into the future. As father, his role had been nearly the opposite of Reena's. External, consistent, there for Tremlo when he needed something outside himself. But Tremlo was touched by many forces. There were many fathers, and Arlen knew he could not claim him as his alone.

Take care, my son. Remember us as we will remember you.

And then it was done.

Jormah led Tremlo into the forest at nearly a run. Reena watched Tremlo struggling to keep up and fought back tears.

How hard life is. How hard he tries.

This was her last sight of him. The vision would linger, held close to her heart. If and when he returned, a whole new person would appear.

She would never see this one again.

Everyone knew Jormah was leaving, but Tremlo's going was a complete surprise. Shock, consternation, fear, but also sadness, relief, and in a few youngers, envy.

Tremlo's skin tingled with it all. He had never been the object of envy and found it puzzling. His leaving, which he felt to be of little consequence, seemed to be having great effect upon the tribe.

Why do others feel this way? Why does he not?

Jormah led them swiftly through the forest. No words passed between them. Tremlo asked no questions when they stopped to rest. At night they ate in silence and then went to sleep. The next day it was the same.

Tremlo rode along in the wake of Jormah's perspective. He loved the textures and nuances. In the swing of Jormah's arms lay the Kwaman's orientation to the world. In the tilt of his head, that which captured his attention. The pitch of his shoulders revealed the things he was wary of, and in the trunk of his body, all that he held sacred.

As one day followed the next, Jormah's concerns grew.

What am I to do with you?

That part of him that felt put upon wanted to impose exercises, correction and direction. But feelings like these were reactionary and untrustworthy. *The mind-of-the-body.* Instead, he resolved to wait until they were outside the Tribal Body to see what changes might occur. If nothing happened, he would take action. But what that action might be, he did not know.

In a few short weeks, they reached what should have been the edge of the Tribal Body. Instead, that invisible membrane kept expanding before them. Whether they walked or ran straight at it, it seemed to keep a day away.

Could Tremlo embody so much of the tribe that it is swelling to accommodate him?

"Wait here," Jormah said. Within a short distance he came closer to the edge.

So it is Tremlo.

But how long could it go on like this?

For two more days, the Tribal Body stretched and the center contracted, creating pressure throughout the tribe. Tremlo felt it in his own chest.

He cannot go there.

The harder he pushed, the more difficult it became. Soon he was leaning forward as if walking into a stiff wind.

He cannot go as he is.

Less a thought than a knowing. Something was going to break. He could not be the sum total of the rhythms of one world and carry them into the next.

The jagged, sharp and bitter flavors ahead were the very ones he would have to absorb in order to let go, and be let go.

He sat down and swallowed hard. In the past, he would have spat these flavors out.

"Tremlo, what is it?"

His pallor, his tone, the very smell of him was changing.

"Tremlo?"

There was loud snap ahead.

The elusive edge of the Tribal Body blew back towards them. Jormah dropped into balance-position as it rushed over them. A portion tried to cling to Tremlo, but his body was filled with the rhythms of outside and gave it no purchase.

It rushed back through the forest leaving them uncovered and exposed.

Outside.

The world was loud and gruff.

"Are you alright?"

Tremlo nodded.

"What did you do?"

The younger shook his head.

"No, you did something. With yourself. Your tone, your scent."

Words, Tremlo thought. *He wants words.*

"The flavor," he said, surprised by the sound of his own voice. Without the tones of the *intra*life to round it out, it seemed to grate against the air about them.

"The flavor?"

"Of things to come."

"How did you know what to do?"

Tremlo did not. It was the mind-of-his-body that had known.

CHAPTER TWENTY-THREE

The travel cages were lowered down into the quarry and placed side by side along the back wall. A safe-walk had been carved out behind them. It was like a corridor with an open side that was lined with thick metal bars.

From the safety of the safe-walk, the trainers could feed the animals individually. Every ten feet, there were spaces between the bars wide enough for a man to slip through sideways. If on open ground, they could easily get back to safety, for the Kurr were far too large to fit through the spaces.

In the ship's hold the beasts were grouped together and slept on, or against one another. Now they were stationary, in individual cages. Bettrie saw this separation was alien to them.

She ordered extra portions of loper meat that first day, and the handlers pushed the added treats through the bars of the safe-walk into the cages.

What language do you speak? she wondered, watching the beasts eat with their accustomed ferocity. If only she could tap into their superior intelligence and create a language beyond conditioned associations. What an incredible feat that would be. It was said man achieved greatness only when circumstance permitted. Here before her was that very circumstance.

That night, Bettrie lay down on a mat of straw in the open area beside the cage of the one she called Regal. On the trip here she had walked, slept, and eaten beside the beast. Regal was accustomed to her now and seemed to expect the special attention she gave her. This was not exactly the effect Bettrie intended. Tomorrow would be the start of something new.

Just before dawn, Regal raised her head and snorted several times. The other beasts answered in kind.

A greeting of sorts, Bettrie decided, and sniffed as loudly as she could in imitation.

The beasts began to grumble and looked at her directly. They had been in cages since their capture eight months before, and Bettrie could not blame them for their dissatisfaction.

"We will begin with Regal," she said, coming back inside the safe-walk. The most effective way to train and control the beasts on the battlefield would be to use individual handlers.

"As we get to know their temperaments, we'll see which of you will pair best with each of them. Ready?"

The handlers, both men and women Bettrie had hand-picked, spread out and watched carefully from inside the safe-walk. The lock to Regal's cage was slid back and the door was raised with overhanging ropes. Regal sprang from the cage and bounded over to the far corner of the quarry with such speed, Bettrie saw that the lopers didn't stand a chance.

Regal leaped up and tried to grab hold of the rock wall. Her claws made flat scraping sounds as they slid off its surface. She sped around the perimeter, leaping up at different places, trying to dig her claws into the inward slanting walls. It seemed chaotic but she never marked the same section twice.

The other beasts were on their feet, following her movements with their bodies.

Regal circled several times before turning her attention to the ground. She dug furiously, but the dirt floor was only a few inches deep and she quickly came to the solid rock beneath it. She stood up on her hind legs and roared her dissatisfaction. The other beasts roared with her. The sound echoed off the stone walls and was so loud, it was reportedly heard miles away.

She dropped onto her stomach, panting from the exertion.

Their imprisonment has left them with no stamina, Bettrie thought. This was something that needed tending.

When Regal's breathing returned to normal, she moved towards the cages. Looking here, smelling there, she leaped atop the cage of the beast Bettrie named Kara. She tried to rock it back and forth, and Kara drove her shoulders side to side mimicking her motion. The cages were well anchored and barely moved.

After a few attempts, Regal stopped and moved onto the next cage. The beast within was already moving side to side in anticipation. They rocked together with the same result. She did this with each and every one of them.

Bettrie noted the order. Here was a hierarchy of sorts that she could use. When Regal got to the final cage, her ears flattened, and she leaped directly at those in the safe-walk. The handlers jumped back in surprise, which seemed to satisfy her. She moved to open ground and lay down to wait.

She expects us to do something, Bettrie thought. *And she's right.*

Bettrie wore a small brass horn on her side. From the safety of the safe-walk, she raised it to her lips and blew. It made a loud, high-pitched blast. Immediately afterwards, she took a small piece of loper meat and pushed it through the bars of Regal's cage with a long wooden feeding pole.

Regal rushed to the side of the cage and tried to reach in through the bars, but the meat lay just beyond her grasp. She banged against the cage trying to draw the meat closer, but it barely moved. With a howl of displeasure, she moved round to the open door of her cage. Hunching her shoulders as if ready to spring forward she shifted her weight back and forth.

She's reasoning it out, Bettrie thought.

Lying down flat, Regal inched herself forward keeping the back half of her body outside the cage.

As soon as she got hold of the meat, she snapped back and devoured it where she landed. It was little more than a mouthful.

Bettrie waited until she moved away before blowing the horn and baiting the cage once more. This time she placed the meat in the far corner. Regal would have to come all the way inside to get it.

Regal bellowed in protest, but the loper meat was too compelling. Once again, she shifted her weight back and forth, and stretched her front legs as far into the cage as she could without going completely inside. Her eyes narrowed, and her tail straightened. She dove inside, but instead of going for the meat, she tried to reach through the bars into the safe-walk to get at Bettrie. With claws fully extended, she just managed to nick the hand Bettrie carelessly left on a bar.

In the next moment, Regal pounced on the meat, her body fully inside.

"Close the door!" one of the handlers shouted.

"No!" Bettrie said, covering her wounded hand. "Leave it open."

Regal leaped back out and, as before, ate where she landed.

"Are you alright?"

"Just a cut. Tell me what you saw?"

"She made us think she was going for the meat and attacked you. It was a diversion."

"Exactly."

"These beasts are treacherous."

"It was my fault."

"How?"

"I pushed her too hard. I should have drawn the meat in by stages, a few feet at a time to gain her trust. Instead, I violated that, and now this. She just said, 'I want the food but don't think I don't know what you're doing'."

"You think they're that sophisticated?"

"You don't?"

Bettrie went back into the staging area to have her wound dressed. When she returned, she resolved to start again. Regal was sitting some distance away. In preparation, Bettrie raised the horn. Regal was up before it touched her lips and heading for her cage door.

"You see that?" Bettrie said. "She's already made the association!"

She placed the meat on the floor of Regal's cage near the center. Regal pulled it outside and ate quickly.

Bettrie waited again for her to drift away. This time, she made an elaborate gesture, bringing her hand down to her side by the horn. Regal caught the movement out of the corner of her eye and was back at her cage in an instant.

"Incredible. We have two signals already. Sound and now a physical sign."

By evening, Regal had no reservations about walking all the way inside the cage and leisurely taking the meat out.

"We will leave her outside tonight. Tomorrow, when she comes inside, we will close the cage door. She'll be angry at first, but we will feed her there, and once she's finished, open it again. This way they will be less resistant when called to the cage."

Bettrie was ecstatic. Regal had learned, *Come!* Around this command all others would be built. But teaching animals to perform tasks in a confined area was one thing. Having them perform on an open battlefield, quite another.

How will I get them to use their intelligence for our benefit? How do we create an emotional bond with such creatures?

The philosophers spoke of such matters. They said that most of what man called emotion – the 'love' of touch, of food, of safety, and companionship – were instinctive emotions. They were concerned with comfort, survival, relationships. If any aspect was withheld, this love could easily turn to hate. If love remained in the face of adversity, it was said to be "true love". True love transcended need and desire. Or so the philosophers said.

Bettrie believed she had just such a relationship with her hounds. They would put her before their own needs and desires, even to the point of death.

How do I create this with you? Are you capable of such a thing?

By the next day, *Sit!* and *Stay!* were firmly in place. All she had to do was act out what she wanted once or twice, and Regal got it. The only thing Regal would not do was lie down in a way that exposed her underside. Given the beast's vulnerability, Bettrie deemed this wise.

"It is time to release the second beast."

Following Regal's pattern, they opened Kara's cage. Kara ran around the perimeter, scratching the walls and making her mark beside each place Regal had. Regal ran beside her, and afterwards, they stopped in the middle of the quarry where a kind of grooming ceremony began. Kara nudged her head against Regal's shoulder and began to lick her just behind the ear.

Regal accepted this without turning her head. After a few moments, she returned some licks of her own.

Bettrie blew her horn, and Regal perked up. But there was tension in her neck. She was fighting against the impulse to do Bettrie's bidding.

Bettrie pulled out a piece of the loper meat. Kara could not resist its scent and started towards it, but Regal would not allow it. She took a powerful swipe at Kara's side and nearly toppled her. Kara lowered her body in deference. Satisfied, Regal walked over to her cage and stepped inside.

I will do this of my own volition and only when I feel like it, her actions seemed to say.

What magnificent creatures these are, Bettrie thought. They possessed enough mindfulness to go against their more primitive instincts. Bettrie gave her the meat, and they closed the cage behind her.

"Kara," her new handler called out, sounding his horn as he baited her cage. She leaped inside with no reservation. She had learned from watching Regal.

Each day another beast was released. What one learned the others learned more quickly. When the horn was sounded, they all returned to their cages to be fed. From the safety of the safe-walk, the handlers issued commands, refined signals, and got the animals used to them. But the real test would be for a person to stand in open ground before them.

When Bettrie deemed them ready, she put on a thick, brown leather apron, arm-length leather gloves, and leggings. In her right hand, she held a shield made of wood, covered with the same leather. It would seem like an appendage of sorts. In her left hand, a long feeding pole. Behind her the handlers were armed with torches and hot pokers. Bettrie slid out from behind the safe-walk and took five steps forward.

"Let her out!"

The door to Regal's cage was raised and she stepped outside. By now, she was quite used to coming and going, but today something new. A feeder, standing open. She stopped for a moment to consider.

The position of her head and shoulders, the focus and direction of her eyes, her ears, the hair on her neck, the workings of her mouth, the motion of her tail. Bettrie could tell at a glance whether Regal was content or disturbed, and watched intently, for her life depended upon it.

Regal's head was tilted to the side. She seemed more curious than anything else. She was used to Bettrie reaching into her cage with a stick. Bettrie was carrying that very stick now.

Regal made a low-pitched grumble that lasted nearly thirty seconds. She took several steps forward, and made the sound again.

Was it a warning?

If Regal charged, the handlers would rush to her defense and drive Regal back, possibly inflicting wounds and perhaps sustaining injuries themselves. But to what end?

No. I must hold my ground, but not stand foolishly in the way of a superior force.

Bettrie sat down slowly.

Regal raised her head and howled. Turning her back on Bettrie, she drifted back to her cage. She was used to being fed there.

Bettrie stood slowly.

"Get ready," she said to the handlers behind her.

"Regal!" she called out making the sign.

Come!

Regal hesitated.

Bettrie reached back through the bars of the safe-walk with her pole, and the handlers shoved a small piece of meat onto the tip.

"Regal!"

Come!

Regal moved slowly towards her, asserting her independence.

Bettrie extended the pole far to her left to avoid facing Regal directly. The Kurr always approached each other from the side. To move in head-to-head was sign of confrontation. Regal followed the line of the bait and expertly swiped the meat off the end. She was no more than twenty feet from Bettrie and ate it now without a care. To allow Bettrie this close suggested she did not see her as a threat. Bettrie made sure to keep her head slightly averted and remain very still.

She put Regal through all the commands that day, rewarding her each time with a piece of meat. Regal performed flawlessly, but on the last one, there was a slight change in her demeanor. She took the meat off the pole, turned sideways, and shot out her rear leg, knocking Bettrie off her feet.

The handlers grabbed the hot pokers.

"Stop! Her claws were retracted. I'm okay."

She stood up slowly and brushed herself off.

"She could have killed me if she wanted to."

We need to get past this struggle for dominance, she thought. Regal would have to see her as a friend first in order for them to connect in some meaningful way.

But how? How do I get you to befriend me?

CHAPTER TWENTY-FOUR

Tremlo had absorbed the essence of the world ahead and relinquished the world behind without a stumble. Jormah would have distracted him from the disorientation that always came once outside the Tribal Body. But the younger needed no distraction.

Is there nothing normal about him?

Ahead, the Valley Forest sparkled with energy. Tremlo reached out and felt himself deep inside the forest reaching back. This was a curious phenomenon. Had it always been so?

"When approaching the unknown," Jormah said, "caution is prescribed. We must remain hidden within the body of the known."

But he need not have said anything, for Tremlo was barely visible as it was.

Daylight fading, creatures high and low singing the sun away, the leaves of the trees begging for a final kiss.

The two entered the forest softly, silently, a homage to all.

'We will sleep in that tree,' Jormah pointed to a thick old granddad. Tremlo felt the very limb he would occupy. A part of him was already there.

They climbed up and settled in for the night.

Within the surrounding dark lay a growing fascination. Small animals began to collect at the edges of the trees.

Something new in the forest.

It did not smell of meat eater.

Warm, soothing, something.

Birds and groundlings drew closer, resting against the shadow of their being. By morning, the trees were full.

Tremlo loved the feel of the creatures here. They had an openness and a vulnerability that reminded him of himself. He reached out with tones of care and wellbeing just like others had done for him. In this place, he was not just younger, but father and mother to all.

The creatures followed them that day, which was different from the last time Jormah came this way. Tremlo's happiness was unbounded.

He spread out in all directions until the leaves of distant trees seemed to caress his skin. On a whim, he stretched out an arm and sent a ripple of motion through the forest. He burst into laughter. The sound of his voice crackled through the trees in a wave of chatter.

Thrilled by this new sense of proportion, he jumped up and down. The branches of trees a hundred paces away shook with creatures mimicking his movements. He spun around and set off a swirl of motion. Round and round he went. Animals near and far followed, running through the trees.

Faster and faster.

To move, to have things join him in this way, filled him with irrepressible joy.

The trees hissed with the sound the wind might have made.

Faster and faster.

Creatures racing to keep up, fearing they would not, their distress becoming his. He tried to slow down, but the momentum he set in motion now spun him.

Spinning, spinning ... not letting go.

Desperate now, he yanked himself away. Falling to the ground, a hail of motion falling with him.

Pain.

"Your influence is greater than you know," Jormah said, picking him up.

Creatures near and far struggled to get up. Some were hurt, and filled him with remorse. The life about him sagged.

"Lessons can be painful, Tremlo. But you are not blamed by those who have suffered. Already they await, hanging on your every move."

He felt worse for their empathy. Back in the trees, waiting, watching, hoping. He vowed never to hurt them again.

The wind picked up, and the leaves fluttered. Here was movement unrelated to him. The sky brightened, and the natural rhythms of the forest returned.

They resumed their journey, and the creatures followed once more. This time however, Tremlo kept a close hold on himself and moved with extra care.

A day later they reached the marshland, and Jormah stopped.

"With each step, our presence is shouted through the forest. We attract too much attention. We must leave these creatures behind."

"They will not harm us."

"They won't, but there are other forces at work, and those who mark them, mark us."

The last time Jormah came this way he was nearly trampled by aliates. There was no sign of those ancient lizard-like beasts now, but that did not matter.

"A defensive-posture will not always protect us. You have to learn to reflect an animal's fear so they will scare themselves away."

Tremlo did not want anything to be afraid of him.

"You would draw some monster to you?"

"No," Tremlo said, his voice *thyck*.

"The posture-of-fear does no harm and might save your life one day."

Jormah indicated a groundling nearby and took an abrupt step towards it. The animal froze and he reflected its momentary fear back to it. Its fear increased, and Jormah's reflection intensified, until the creature let out a screech and scampered up the nearest tree.

"You see. It is unharmed."

The groundling's heart was beating fast. Tremlo enveloped it with soothing tones.

"Your efforts are misguided. We must stop them from following and travel alone. It is your turn to assume this posture. Begin with the groundling over there."

Tremlo did not move.

Jormah hardened the lines of his body.

"I expect you to do this as well as I have. Begin."

The younger lowered his head and turned towards the creature. He felt the gentle ring of its being, its innocence, its kinship. How could he violate its trust by frightening it away?

Jormah wondered how hard he should push. It was important Tremlo learned this posture, and yet, it was his very resistance that was most interesting.

Resistance defines existence.

So far Tremlo had resisted nothing.

Until now.

Who are you? What is this that resists?

The younger's body was taut.

"Tremlo, your care for these creatures does not matter. This is something you must learn."

"You have already shown how."

"Knowing in your mind and knowing in your body are two different things. You are avoiding what must be done."

"You said we... attract too much attention."

Tremlo was fighting to bring something to mind.

"Yes."

"It is too dangerous, to have them follow."

His body was trembling.

"Yes."

"The posture-of-fear drives them away."

"That is its purpose."

Tremlo shifted his bearing.

"Here is the purpose."

He vanished.

The harmonious tones of wellbeing that brought the creatures to this place were gone. In their stead was an empty chill. Birds and groundlings suddenly realized how close they were to each other. They cried out in alarm and fled back to the safety of their own separate places.

He figured a way out, Jormah thought, following slowly behind. It did not matter why Tremlo found the posture-of-fear so repugnant. The conflict had revealed something of his character.

Resistance defines existence.

Here now was something Jormah could use.

CHAPTER TWENTY-FIVE

*R*esistance defines existence.

"From now on, we will begin each day with Armrue."

Armrue was a game every child learned. The object was to project one's energy into an opponent's arm, find his reflex point, and force the opponent to touch his own face with his hand. All without physical contact.

The game always put Tremlo ill at ease. He was far more comfortable going with an opponent's energy than imposing his own.

Jormah kneeled into position and extended his hand. Once their fingertips touched, the match would begin, and there would be no more physical contact.

"Face me."

The younger got into position and slowly extended his hand. At the touch of their fingers Tremlo cried out.

"Ow!"

Jormah had generated a large spark of energy. It shot up Tremlo's arm. A moment later the Kwaman's mind closed in on his reflex point and Tremlo's muscles contracted. His hand snapped up, slammed into his face and knocked him backwards.

The sound of the slap became the sting on his face, which he heard, felt, and watched himself feel.

Rolling backwards to control the fall, Tremlo circled up into a kneeling position. A part of him was stunned, another confused.

Jormah was appalled. He hadn't meant for Tremlo to hit himself. The look on the younger's face was not anger, or accusation, but bafflement.

"Come," Jormah said, walking quickly away to hide his dismay.

Tremlo dragged behind.

"You have been alone for far too long," Donan told him just before they left. *"Tremlo will help remind you of who and what you are."*

Jormah stopped and waited for the younger to catch up.

"We have much to learn from each other."

It felt like an apology, but Tremlo could not fathom what the Kwaman might learn from him.

The next morning, Jormah kneeled into the position Tremlo hoped to avoid.

"Armrue is a test, Tremlo. The day you beat me is the day you will be ready."

Tremlo was confused. *Ready for what?*

Their fingertips touched with barely a spark. This time Jormah's attack was a whisper of what it had been. Tremlo offered no resistance, and his hand hit his face almost as hard as the day before.

"Tremlo, the world is a dangerous place. You cannot embrace everything. Resistance defines existence, more so than accommodation."

You must fight back or suffer the consequences.

The look on Tremlo's face gave him pause. It was said that an assault on one's person, whether physical or mental, had a sound that echoed throughout one's life. That part of Jormah that wanted to continue with this harsh regime was just such an echo.

No one can escape violence, he thought. *But we do not have to be the bearers of it,* another voice said.

The next time they kneeled into position, Tremlo turned his head to the side as if to avoid the impact of the blow. This was the price paid for violence.

The younger's arm was tense in anticipation, but the Kwaman's touch proved to be limp and cold. There was no spark. Tremlo waited for him to take possession of his arm, but Jormah just sat there. Tremlo had been invaded all his life, and did not want to do the same to another. He squirmed. The stern look on Jormah's face softened. A moment later, the Kwaman smiled. He would wait all day if necessary.

Finally, Tremlo tried to focus his attention on the Kwaman's reflex point. He closed his mind around it. A burst of energy shot up Jormah's arm, surprising them both.

In the spirit of the game, Jormah fought back, trying to disguise his reflex point. Tremlo held it in his mind like a child holding onto a favored toy. He would not let go, but he went no further.

Jormah finally shifted his attention to Tremlo's arm. He tightened his focus, and Tremlo's arm began to bend. Not long after, his hand touched his face, ending the game.

The younger smiled, and Jormah smiled back.

"Better," he said. "Each day we will begin the same way and see what we can improve upon."

Tremlo did not like this idea, but he understood now. This was a complete change from the day before.

We have both learned something this day.

But if Tremlo did not learn to resist, if he did not become an active force, he would end up little more than a brilliant pool of water.

And a reflection, for all its beauty, does not cast a shadow.

CHAPTER TWENTY-SIX

Et-El Baronuus arrived at the quarry with an escort of forty Augmentors.

"It's been three months, Animal Trainer. Show me what you've done."

Baronuus and Elgar, his second in command, were brought down to the safe-walk and stood alongside the handlers.

The beasts were in their cages.

Bettrie put on her protective gear and stepped out into the open ground.

"Regal, Come!" she called, and Regal's cage door was lifted. Regal usually took a lap around the quarry before coming to Bettrie, but something was amiss. She stepped out of the cage, and her nostrils flared. A moment later, she stormed the safe-walk where Baronuus and Elgar were standing. They leaped back as she slashed through the bars, narrowly missing them.

This was not an auspicious beginning.

"Regal. Come!" Bettrie insisted, sounding her horn. Regal had asserted herself like this before, but it was mostly directed at Bettrie, never with visitors.

Regal sauntered back and took her usual spot before her.

Bettrie felt the tension in her own body. Could Regal have sensed the threat she felt from Baronuus and Elgar's presence?

Were you trying to protect me?

If true, the inroads she was making had come much further along than she suspected.

What is inside your mind?

Bettrie threw her a piece of dried loper meat from her side pouch. She had dispensed with the feeding pole the week before.

Regal sat down to chew, and Bettrie threw her an extra piece.

Good girl.

Once Regal finished, Bettrie sent her circling around the perimeter with a hand signal. A toot of the horn brought her back to the starting place before her. She put Regal through three more commands before the beast's eyes narrowed, and she cut the demonstration short.

"A circus entertainment at best," Elgar sneered. "How does this advance our cause? These beasts are too independent. You don't have full control over them."

"That is not the aim," Bettrie replied.

"No?"

"Not yet."

"How do you propose to manage them in the field?" Baronuus asked.

"Each animal will have their own handler to guide them through the battle."

"And you think these beasts will obey?"

"If we can establish the proper bonds."

"And how long will that take?"

"I don't know. We are trying to build relationships and get them to rely upon us so we can work together. It takes time."

"Time is something in short supply," Baronuus said.

"There are no shortcuts, Commander."

"Let us speak in private."

Bettrie brought them to the staging area behind the safe-walk. Baronuus and Elgar sat without waiting for her to do so.

"What I tell you now is under the Oath-of-Secrecy," Baronuus said.

"I comply."

"Our spies report the Vradeem will invade the Southern Provinces this spring. They will cross the mountains after the snows melt. In about five months' time."

"I see."

"If they get a foothold in the south, it is feared they will continue north, perhaps all the way to Halla. If that happens the Emperor will be forced to withdraw troops from the borderlands to mount a defense. This will leave us dangerously exposed. And if the Vradeem decide to march north, they will move so swiftly, I doubt the additional troops will arrive in time to save the city."

"Why?"

"What do you know about the Vradeem?"

"Only vague rumors that they are expert riders."

"We've encountered them in several skirmishes, and they have defeated us at every turn."

"How is that possible?"

"They are fearless in battle. But more importantly, they have developed a style of fighting that suits them perfectly. They are a nomadic people, made strong through centuries of wandering. Their lopers are considered members of their family. They sleep riding, eat riding, and, I've heard, give birth riding. It is said they learn to ride before they can walk. They are the most accomplished cavalrymen we have ever encountered. Some say they are half-man, half-loper, for they use neither saddle, tether, nor rein. Yet their lopers know instantly what they want, and do their bidding with no regard for their own safety. Imagine a man with the strength and speed of a loper. Imagine fifty thousand of them."

"Have you captured any that we might learn their secrets?"

"They never leave any of their men behind. Never! Even their dead. Like the Argoot, they prefer quick strikes and then retreat. We have yet to have a full engagement with them, and I am not sure they would allow it. A quick strike and out. That has been their strategy. We need the Kurr, Bettrie, and we need them now more than ever."

"But we haven't gained enough of their trust or cemented the kind of relationship that would allow us to—"

"Trust?" Elgar spat. "You need to instill fear."

Bettrie kept her eyes on Baronuus.

"How much longer do you need?" he asked.

"It's hard to say. These are not pliable cubs, but mature adults. They are independent and set in their ways."

"Do you beat them?" Elgar persisted. He was an ugly man, renowned for his cruelty.

"No, we do not beat them. They are too strong and too violent. Beating creates deep-seated resentments, and the Kurr are too smart and too dangerous for us to give them any more reason to rebel."

"Are you saying the Kurr do not accept you as their master?" Elgar leaned forward like one about to partake in a meal.

"No." She knew his type well. Violent, arrogant, they thrived on intimidating others.

"And you think pampering them will win them over?"

"We do not pamper them," she said in a strong voice. "We look for ways to soften their resolve."

"You have to beat them!" Elgar said adamantly.

Like you were beaten," Bettrie thought. "That's not the proper course here."

"No? I pride myself on the control I have over my slaves. You strike fear into their hearts with the least amount of effort. Discover the thing they most fear and use it to drain them of their strength and resistance, quickly, precisely, to the point of death if need be. Then you nurture them back to health, showing them kindness. But if they do one thing wrong, you torture them immediately. You follow this formula until the slave never makes a mistake, or instantly falls to the ground begging forgiveness if they do."

"And how many are killed in the process?" Bettrie muttered.

"What?"

"By your own admission, the slave will do your bidding while you hold the whip. But what happens when you turn your back, or drop it?"

"The fear keeps them in check."

"I see. So we should start torturing the beasts and show them who's master. Then we'll drive them forward into battle with torches and hot pokers to ensure they do our bidding. Oh, and we'll hobble their legs with chains so they cannot run away. What a fighting force they will make!"

"I am not a fool, Animal Trainer," Elgar hissed, his words sharp as a knife. "I will say it one more time. You have to instill fear in the beasts. If they fear you, you can control them."

"We are giving them permission to kill men! How will they distinguish who is good and who is bad if they hate us all? No. Their handlers must establish a bond. If there is a relationship, we can succeed; if not, they will kill us all the first chance they get."

"The truth is you haven't found what it is they fear most! Isn't that right, Animal Trainer?"

"Enough," Baronuus interrupted. "Bettrie, is your way working? Yes, or no?"

"There is no yes or no yet. We've just begun to—"

"Bettrie, you staked your life on this project!"

"I pledged to Proutus that I would do my best, and nothing short of my own death would stop me from *trying*."

"You staked your life on this project!"

"Commander, these are mature animals. Very smart but set in their ways. What we're trying to do could take years. Even if we started with cubs, it could still take years."

"This doesn't help us. I order you to try a different approach."

"It is destined to fail."

"If you will not try, Elgar will take over from this moment on."

Elgar would destroy all she had worked for and probably end up killing all the Kurr. But how could she turn over her charges to this repulsive man.

"What say you, Animal Trainer?"

"...There … may be an alternative."

"What do you mean?"

"If you are willing to risk losing the animals."

"In the face of the insurgence, everything is at risk."

"Understood. We've been trying to create a special rapport with them, but you say we no longer have enough time to do what is necessary. We could possibly train them to kill the lopers in succession."

"I'm not sure I follow."

"The Kurr will kill a loper and stop to feast upon it. That is their pattern. I think we can train them to kill all the lopers first, before they stop to feast upon them."

"When you say all, what do you mean?"

"I mean all the lopers they encounter. That means we do not bring our own lopers into battle."

"We are facing a cavalry!" Elgar interrupted. "We must fight them atop lopers."

"Then the Kurr will be just as lethal for us as for them."

"You're suggesting we enter the battle on foot, and then set the Kurr loose?"

"Exactly. If the Vradeem dismount and try to protect their lopers, our troops can move in to fight them on the ground, because that is where they will be."

"You really think you can train them to do this in so short a time?" Baronuus asked.

"According to you, I have about half a year. The Kurr already know how to kill. It's more a matter of guiding them. If any of them survive the battle, they will probably run away and seek refuge in the mountains."

"We can hunt them down."

"Possibly."

"Done! I will return to Halla and present this to the Emperor. You will start 'the guiding' immediately."

Baronuus smiled broadly and placed a hand firmly on her shoulder.

"Do not fail me, Animal Trainer. Do not fail the Empire."

CHAPTER TWENTY-SEVEN

The distant mountains were surreal in their majesty.

They took up half the sky.

At the top sat the City-Of-Straight-Lines.

The last time Jormah left the Valley Forest and came this way, there were Yarkas about. Now there were none. The land ahead was a gasp of brown rubble. Gray scrub grass poked through here and there, punctuated by an occasional black shagya tree.

In this open space, the length of Tremlo's stride, and the elongated swing of his arms, became more apparent. The growth spurt had not stopped. His trunk seemed thicker, and his fingers and toes continued to be hot to the touch.

"Tremlo?"

The white skin covering his eyes was thinning out.

Six months, Jormah decided. If the Mahtwah were with them, she could probably predict it to within a week. The onset of sight could be very disorienting.

How will one as sensitive as he, fare?

They reached the base of the mountain and listened. The sound of the City tumbled down the mountainside, tarnishing everything in its path. The gentle slopes along the bottom had been pulverized long ago. Before them were sheer, grey-stone facings. Not an easy climb, but their nimble fingers and toes possessed minds of their own, and they scaled the steep vertical without incident.

A third of the way up, the remnants of that wide path the ancestors carved out began. It snaked its way back and forth across the face of the mountain, all the way to the top. Littered with debris and fallen rock, its slow rise still made for an easy climb.

"We are walking upon the backs of our ancestors' labor," Jormah said, stiffening his arms and legs. "When I first came here, I walked like this to see if I could gain insight into their perceptions."

Tremlo stiffened his own arms and legs. Where Jormah's posture was awkward and exaggerated, his seemed completely natural. His body knew the dull sound a stiff-backed body made. It knew the flat slap of the original path, and the rumble of footsteps too numerous to count.

Something terrible had happened here.

"The undercurrent of the City will get stronger the higher we go," Jormah said. "The sun is setting. Let's spend the night here and finish the climb tomorrow."

They ate some malta and listened to the sounds drifting down from the mountaintop. The undercurrent's punctuated tones whispered songs of the far-past. Hollow. Filled with longing. It was these Tremlo listened to as he fell asleep.

The sound melted into the walls of a cavern.

Donan was standing there to greet him. It seemed quite natural.

They stepped into the mouth of the tunnel, and it swallowed them whole.

Jennifer, *hoping, praying, wishing, wanting,* heard the sound and sat straight up in bed. She stared at the yellow wall for the telltale sign. A black dot appeared. It swelled, engulfed the wall, and then contracted like a mouth opening and closing, leaving Uncle Donald and Truman before it. The wall behind now a solid yellow.

"You're here!" she cried, her voice deeper, her body longer. Opening her eyes, realizing they had been closed, she saw the two standing before her, just as she had *seen* them a moment ago.

She leaped into Donan's waiting arms.

"I've missed you!"

"Yes," Donan said, flooded with feelings as he hugged her tightly. "I have missed you too. You have grown since the last time."

Jennifer smiled. "You always say that."

Do I?

"Hello, Truman."

He was glowing; some inner light illuminating the exterior walls of his body. He looked down to hide his eyes, and she remembered their whiteness and that he was blind. She would have hugged him, if not for his shyness.

He nodded and smiled but kept his face averted.

The room seemed smaller with them all standing there.

Come, let's sit.

Objects had been rearranged. The chairs and table were larger than before.

"These are new," she said, touching the back of one of the red-brown chairs.

"Yes, we see," Donan replied. "You too are new."

"I grew a lot since the last time."

She had waited so long. So much had happened, so many confusions, so much misunderstanding. The sound, sense and smell of these two made the worry go away. The smile on her face was so broad it carried them along.

"It's so good to have you here!" she cried. "I couldn't wait for you to come back."

They nodded. Some part of them could not wait either.

A throb of energy bathed the room and the three lost form.

No here.

No there.

No this or that, just all and everything….

And then the energy faded and the chairs were the chairs, the table between, and they, once again themselves, separate but connected by the sights and sounds of a dream within a dream.

"You are troubled," Donan said.

"Yes," Junnipur replied.

"Tell me."

"I— I am afraid."

'*Of what?*'

"Things are happening. Strange things. I— I keep spreading out. Do you know what I mean?"

She saw immediately that he did. "Whenever I tell others, they don't understand and look at me strangely."

"You have been drinking the tea you make from Wildflower," Donan said, remembering its name as the words came out.

"No, not so much anymore, but I have been eating the middle."

"The malta?"

"Yes, the white stuff."

Resep. It was changing her. *But why would she be disturbed by it?*

The answer came to him simultaneously with the question. She was beginning to know things in ways she never had before.

"I keep feeling what other people feel. Sometimes I think I even hear their thoughts!"

Tremlo took her hand in his. In the past, it was he who usually need-ed comforting. At the touch of his hand, they felt the full weight of her anxiety.

"I'm spreading out. Whoever is nearby becomes a part of me. I don't know where I end. I don't know who I am. I don't know what to say."

She stopped short of telling them that her classmates called her crazy, and in harassing her, the adults were alerted. Her mother was now tak-ing her to doctors and lately, to a counselor after school. A gray-haired lady who looked at her with sympathetic eyes and had no idea what she was talking about.

'Sit this way,' Donan's body said, interrupting her thoughts.

"This is balance-position."

The position of safety.

The position of home.

The position of self.

All three on the floor, each a mirror of the other.

Jennifer's body eased into the posture. It seemed so natural, so right. Here was the heart from which all others beat. Her distress was gone.

"The spreading... is natural," Donan said softly. "But others will not understand. Trust what you know, hold it close, and keep it to yourself."

Keep it to yourself.

His words were warm, yet firm. She felt blessedly contained.

"Those parts that forget will feel lost, afraid, disconnected."

The Kwaman leaned forward and whispered a secret buntra in her ear.

"Say that to yourself when you are troubled."

She nodded.

"Say it to yourself when we leave."

At the mention of leaving, it was time to go, but neither Donan nor Tremlo moved. It was for Junnipur to release them. She, who was most in this world, clung to them.

A surge of pressure. She needed to let go.

Another surge pulled them apart.

Pain.

She needed to let go.

'Recite the buntra.'

The wall dissolved into the entrance of the tunnel.

'Recite the buntra.'

Jennifer, sitting in balance-position atop her bed, repeated it over and over, reaching out to them all the same.

'Please, come back soon.'

They felt her plea as if it was their own.

Stepping into the tunnel, they were sucked into the darkness.

CHAPTER TWENTY-EIGHT

Something could happen today, Stelbin thought.

Confusion had spread through the tribe the moment Jormah left with Tremlo.

"The younger is too distracted by our presence," Donan had told them. "His sensitivities are unique and border on Sentience."

Sentience?

That had caused a stir. It was difficult to conceive of Tremlo as anything but Reena's troubled son.

"In his separation from us, it is hoped he will hear his own voice and grow."

Where Jormah's return set their minds to reeling, Tremlo's leaving was visceral. The smooth, well-honed rhythms of the past were laced now with strange and disconcerting gaps.

How had they not realized the depth of his influence?

"These empty spaces create possibility," Donan said.

But how? In what way?

The Kwaman did not say.

Energy bound to old patterns was being liberated. It dangled in the air, taunting, tantalizing, holding everyone captive by the uncertainty.

There were no stragglers when the Rehloy gathered for the common meal.

"I'm going down," Stelbin said, knowing Donan would not join him. The Kwaman had ceased to come down from the High Cave soon after Jormah and Tremlo had left. He didn't say why, but it contributed to the change their leaving had set in motion.

When Stelbin reached the Common Ground, he found everyone peering north. Some thought they felt a soft spot within the body of the currents. Others were not so sure.

Gremar stood confidently to one side, speaking to a group that hovered about him. Stelbin ignored him and made his way over to where

Kenectka was standing. She and Gremar were well aware of each other, and he saw her admiration for Gremar was growing.

'Hello Kenectka,' he smiled, boldly inserting himself between the two.

Gremar looked over, but Stelbin stood firm, his back to him, his body hovering about Kenectka like a protective shell.

She smirked, and the look on her face brought him out of himself. He was mortified. What was he doing?

"The mind-of-the-body creates our thoughts and feelings. Choose how to be, or the mind-of-the-body will do the choosing."

How had he forgotten this? His feelings for Kenectka were hiding behind his distrust of Gremar, and caused him to act like he had.

It was this that Kenectka saw. Whether she had similar feelings for him or not, he did not know. But he feared he had not yet earned the right to speak to her about them.

Stelbin took a deep breath through all his senses and exhaled even deeper.

Kwaman once more, he turned to her and smiled from a new place.

Hello, Kenectka.

She smiled back.

Hello, Stelbin.

Whatever happened, whatever would occur between Kenectka and himself was, in one sense, already set in motion. If something did happen, it would unfold in the future, not now.

Whaet observed the subtle exchange between the three. He did not know what Gremar intended but welcomed anything that might get in his way.

"They should be at the mountains by now," someone said, capturing everyone's attention.

"They might even be at the City-Of-Straight-Lines," another ventured.

"Remember what happened to Jormah the first time he was there?"

"Yes, it is a fearful place."

"If they are at the City-Of-Straight-Lines, they will not linger."

"How long will it take them to pass through?" a younger asked.

"That depends upon whether they go around the City like Jormah did on his return, or straight through it."

Conversations like these were becoming commonplace.

"I wonder how Tremlo will be affected?" another asked.

Tremlo.

Everyone grew silent. His name was becoming a buntra that called for reflection.

Tremlo.

They searched their minds for past interactions with him. A word here, a moment there, anything that might reveal a glimmer of what Donan suggested. As their memories shifted, it became harder to re-member what had been so irritating about Tremlo in the first place.

"Reena," Gremar called out with a flourish.

Everyone turned to look as she approached.

"Do you know where Tremlo might be?" Gremar asked. "Some think they can sense him, but others are not so sure."

She saw the hunger in all their eyes.

Years before, when she left the still-cave to live amongst them, she was gently eased to the outskirts of tribal life. But now that Jormah and Tremlo were gone, she had moved to the forefront of their thoughts.

"We all know of your special connection to your son," Gremar coaxed. "Can you tell us where he is now?"

A question like this would normally come from the Leader or the Kwaman, but in Gremar's enthusiasm, he seemed to have forgotten this.

The subtlety of the gesture was not lost on Stelbin.

"They are on the mountain," she said, seeing now how they would make use of her.

When Tremlo left, her physical sense of him had faded. But there was a place inside her, a place without words, where her connection to Tremlo lived on.

The Mother-of-Tremlo.

They were laying claim to her in this new way.

She might have been resentful, but that old Reena was long gone. In actuality, she felt nothing at all.

"Have they reached the City-Of-Straight-Lines?"

"No," said the Mother-of-Tremlo, "but soon."

A murmur of thought. Gremar pounced on the shifting energy and turned to the others.

"The Kwaman said we need to grow. We need to learn to think in a different way."

Yes, everyone thought. *But learn to think how? Different in what way?*

"If the Intruders come, what will happen?" Gremar asked. "Will the *intra*life be affected?"

These were questions most were afraid to think about.

"Will they embrace us, or try to enslave us? Will we have to fight?"

Fight?

"Yes, fight. Kill them or drive them back."

A wave of nausea spread through the tribe. Many turned to Whaet, but the Leader stood quite still, waiting to see what Gremar was up to.

"If not fight, run? What if they pursue? These are the kinds of things we must begin to think about."

These are the kinds of things that will bind you to me.

Gremar emanated a sense of confidence that was rock hard. He said no more, but no one, not even Whaet, doubted that he had some special plan in mind.

On his way back up the mountain, Stelbin thought about how the notion of *doing* something captivated them. The free-flowing energy was captured by the promise of direction. By the time he reached the High Cave, he was so full of thoughts, Donan winced at the feel of him. Gone was his connection to the currents. In its stead was compression and rumination.

The voice of the ancestors.

Donan held himself in check until a certain stillness returned to Stelbin.

"What happened today?"

Stelbin answered slowly, carefully, trying to listen to himself as Donan might. After he finished, Donan sat quietly, pondering all he had heard.

"We know," he finally said, "that Gremar has an interest in Kenectka. But the mind-of-your-body reacted as though his intention was to take her as his mate."

Stelbin grew still.

"We do not know if that is true. But we do know that Gremar has need of you and will try to draw you closer to him."

"How do we know that?"

Stelbin was young. What he lacked in experience, Donan would try to provide. But Stelbin needed to make his own mark, the sooner the better, for things were changing more rapidly than any of them anticipated.

"Gremar wants to be Leader, but Whaet lies close to the peoples' hearts. If circumstances were normal, Gremar would have a long time to wait. But in periods of upheaval, anything is possible."

"Is there something I should do?"

"Do? Like what?"

"I'm not sure."

"The best thing you can do is to learn to think like Gremar does."

How? Stelbin wondered. He was still trying to understand how he himself thought.

Donan stared off into the distance. Stelbin was drawn to the daily rhythms of the tribe, and would embrace the present circumstances.

But someone must remember. Someone must remain pure to remind us of who we are.

The Kwaman looked at himself and saw that his final role in the tribe would not be one of recluse but that of relic.

CHAPTER TWENTY-NINE

The City-Of-Straight-Lines was named for how it appeared in the distance. Up close, the bleached white skeletal remains were pock-marked and crumbling. Thousands of structures stood in varying stages of collapse.

Cresting the mountain, the unbridled sounds of the City blew straight at them like a hot wind.

"Recite your buntra-for-selfstanence," Jormah said, adjusting to it himself. But Tremlo, standing before the City, found himself deep inside looking back. One sensation counterbalanced the other, and by viewing both, he was neither.

"Did you recite your buntra?"

The younger nodded from this *place-of-no-place*. How could he describe what he did not understand?

"Almost everything here was built with a four-sided principle," Jormah pointed out. "Each side equal to the one opposite it."

Tremlo barely listened. Within the crumbled remains he sensed the smooth walls that once dressed their faces. Flashes of strange objects passed in and out of his mind.

Jormah stopped before one of the taller structures, and they climbed in through an opening. Tremlo clapped his hands sending the sound up the sides, bringing their shape more clearly into focus.

The ancestors had created elaborate shells of gigantic proportion.

To house them? To protect them?

Hollow tones were everywhere.

He moved to the nearest wall and touched it. The rhythm of these peoples' lives had been leached from it long ago.

What remained was an act of will.

Moving deeper into the City, a somber mood took hold of him. Every step seemed to bring more soulless detail into being. Within this City was a great sadness. A loss of structure. Of ideas. The loss of a multitude.

They came to an area filled with large mounds of green-speckled moss. Bits of structures protruded here and there, revealing their presence beneath. Several mounds had thin sapling-like growths coming out of their tops. But they were not plants. Their straight and narrow stalks had straight and narrow branches that grew perpendicular to them.

Straight-lined trees for a straight-lined world.

"These are scattered throughout," Jormah said.

Tremlo ran his finger gently over the rasping red flakes that clung to the surface of the branches.

Age, they whispered.

Age.

He grasped the center stalk and squeezed. It was hard as stone, yet not like any stone he ever felt. This was not something the city dwellers had carved out of rock; this was something they had made.

The power-of-stone.

His ancestors had created a nature all their own.

And then they died.

The echo of their death could still be felt.

Had the currents risen to take back what was theirs?

Each question gave rise to several more. Never had so many thoughts come into his mind. To sense everything was no longer enough. There were reasons now.

Reasons. Meanings. Meanings behind meaning.

The more he thought, the more he realized how vast and complex the world must be.

Jormah picked up a stone and struck the sapling.

"Iiiiii..." It rang out with an empty voice all its own. "Iiiiii..." It spoke of those who had created it.

"There is one more thing I want to show you."

They stopped before a particular mound, and Jormah dug into its side. In a short time, he came to the wooden holder he discovered long ago. Reaching in, he pulled out a cutter and handed it to Tremlo.

So thin and light, yet so strong. A perfect cutter. Violently so. Tremlo held it by the base of its handle and struck a nearby rock.

"Iii," it pinged softly. Child to the straight-lined saplings, it sounded with the power-of-stone.

He put it down and took the next object Jormah handed him. Here was that same cutter twice, one a perfect reflection of the other. They had not been carved. They had come into existence devoid of any imprint from their maker. Jormah said the ancestors were master builders. That they had created ideals in physical form, and it seemed to be true.

Late that night, Tremlo became restless. Each new rhythm was fighting to make a place for itself inside his body. He awoke in the morning to a terrible itching and could not stop scratching, arms, legs, face.

"Let's go," Jormah said. The rhythms of the City were infecting the younger. "You lead."

Tremlo's walk soon turned into a run.

CHAPTER-THIRTY

They poured out of the northern end of the City and spilled down the mountainside.

Beyond lay that vast yellow plain.

A land of grass. So vast … so empty.

Windswept waves rolled across the waist-high grass, and Tremlo found its motion soothed away the prickly remains of the City.

"We'll stop here for the night," Jormah said when they reached the base of the mountain. They gathered wood and he built a large fire. "This is the last one we will have for some time."

Tremlo turned his face away. The heat was strong, and his skin too sensitive.

In the morning, Jormah checked their backsacks. He had run out of food and nearly died the last time he came this way. This time, he made sure they would reach the cave-of-Origin with plenty to spare.

Tremlo was rubbing his face.

"How do you feel?"

"It itches."

Residue of the city.

"Throw some water on it and try not to touch it."

Tremlo did as he was told, and it seemed to help.

The yellow grass was dead-dry and broke if pushed through too hard. The blades, however, were clumped together in randomly spaced tufts. Jormah stiffened his upper body to maintain direction and relaxed his lower, allowing it to weave its way from side to side around the clumps and avoid the blades. It was like a dance. Tremlo instantly captured the motion and together they blew through the grassland like a soft-spoken breeze.

When night came, they lay down between the tufts to draw shelter from the cool air. The ground retained the warmth of the unshaded day and kept them quite comfortable.

Each day the same. The same every day.

The land was flat.

Their route direct.

The rhythms of their bodies, one continuous flow.

The repetition lulled Tremlo's senses, and he lived more in his mind than ever before. Thoughts and ideas filled the increasing length of his body. Patterns that eluded him in the past were emerging.

This is how people think!

He recalled hundreds of past incidents, remembering his perception, and now, how the others would have thought about it. No wonder they didn't understand each other.

Each day the same, now different every day.

Up ahead, a spot of warmth appeared clinging to a single blade. Farther out were many more. *The dreaded red spots.* Jormah said these possessed a rudimentary awareness and secreted burning dew to dissolve and digest anything that wandered into their midst.

They went right up to the spot, which was no larger than a drop of water. Tremlo touched it.

Soft, smooth, fleshy, *alive!*

The droplet contracted, expressing moisture, and the yellow blade of grass bent in his direction.

"You see how sensitive it is. And this is only one small spot on a single blade of grass. When they cover the grass, we must hide within the rhythm of their lives. Otherwise, their lacerating blades and burning dew will eat us alive."

They continued on, the red spots multiplying, creating a stunning iridescence.

Beautiful to look at, Jormah thought. *And all the more deadly because of it.*

Red became the dominant color. No more talking, every movement blended to disguise.

One day bled into the next and the itching on Tremlo's face returned. He buried himself in the motion of walking, trying not to scratch. But the itching became relentless. His eyes started to water.

'Shhh.'

He was seized with a fit of sneezing and squeezed the bridge of his nose to stop it. But touching his face unleashed a torrent of sensation. His fists dug into his eye sockets.

Rubbing. Rubbing. RUBBING!
He could not stop it.
'*Tremlo.*'
The red grass around them was poised and listening.
"Tremlo," Jormah whispered, but Tremlo was powerless to stop. The more he rubbed, the more his face and eyes demanded it. The grasses bent in his direction.

"Squeeze my hands," Jormah whispered fiercely, pulling Tremlo's hands from his face.

Tremlo's eyes were clenched.

'*Let me see.*'

The pain was sharp. Tremlo barely managed to open them. There were cracks across the white-skin covering. His sightday was upon them, in this, the worst of places.

A blade of grass brushed against Tremlo's side, and droplets formed instantly. Moments later, all the blades around them were drooling with fiery dew.

"Run!"

They raced back the way they had come, but the blades were now aware of their presence. Some bent towards them moments after they passed. Others ahead tried to bar their way.

Jormah hoisted the younger onto his shoulders.

Tremlo's eyes were gasping for breath. All he wanted to do was rip away the covering, but Jormah took a firm grip of his wrists.

"Feel my body," he commanded.

Be as me.

Tremlo struggled to obey, eyes shut tight, hiding from the stabbing bright. He rocked along with the flow of Jormah's body.

Sunlight was called yellow. Was that the color that gave his eyes so much pain? The names of colors had never held much meaning for him. Most leaves were called green, tree trunks brown. The stone of their caves, gray. Water was clear, the sky blue, except at night when it turned black. Yellow was one of the hottest colors. It was the color of the flames of a fire; it was the color of the sun. But the grassland was also yellow, yet it was cool to the touch. Black was the color of night and usually the coolest, but on hot days black rocks were hottest. The more he thought about it, the more confused he became. Smell was a much more reliable sense. Every object, every emotion had its own particular odor. Even thoughts carried subtle combinations.

It was said that sight gave instant form to the shape of things, that one could survive without any other perceptions. Tremlo lived in a dark world, rich with the color of sensation, and could not imagine it.

Sight.

The ancestors were said to be born with sight, and because of it, they saw mostly with their eyes.

Sight.

Disorienting. A time of change.

The passage from younger to adult.

When they reached a place free of red spots, Jormah let Tremlo down.

"We will sleep here," he said, exhausted from the ordeal.

Late that night the last layer of skin came off Tremlo's eyes. He was on his back, staring up at the night sky, when the familiar blackness filled with countless points of light. He had seen whiteness like this before in the dark reaches of his mind, but usually in flashes or streaks.

Does the blackness cover some infinite white, whose specks peer through? Or is the blackness a backdrop upon which the points of light are hung?

As the night wore on, he saw how they moved slowly, together. And then they faded into a sky that was no longer black. By the sound, he knew dawn was approaching. To his eyes, a whole new story was unfolding.

Jormah awoke to find him staring at the sky.

"Tremlo?"

The younger turned to look at him. The white was gone. In its stead were radiant pools of emerald green.

Jormah began to sing the song mothers sang to their children.

"Rejoice, rejoice, sight has arrived,

Look at what your eyes behold,

Do not turn away and hide,

Rejoice and watch the world unfold."

Tremlo smiled.

"I will name the colors of what you see. Right now, the sky is gray," Jormah said. "There are many kinds of gray. This is dark gray, soon it will turn to gray, then light gray. When the sun arrives, it will turn everything blue."

Dark gray, gray, light gray.

The *yellow* sun burned its way into the sky, and just as Jormah said, the sky above turned into a haven of *blue*.

Here was a breadth of color that filled one's insides.

Tremlo looked around and found himself surrounded by a sea of yellow. The flat surface of color was smoother at the top, and more textured and irregular at the bottom. He did not know that the closer the object, the more detail one could see. It would take time to understand that color spoke of distance as well.

Beside him was a narrow column of colors. With his eyes closed, he knew it to be Jormah. With them opened, it was a bizarre mixture. Jormah's face possessed multiple lines and shadings that did not exist with eyes shut. Forehead, eyes, nose, the hollow of his cheeks. With eyes opened, two almond shapes edged in white, surrounding circles of green with black centers. Below each were shaded lines that ran down and curved in to meet two dark areas. *Nostrils.* Below them, lines running left and right, that moved as Jormah spoke.

"When you see my face for how it truly is, we will resume our journey."

The upward turn of color was a smile, the downward curve a frown. Tremlo ran his hand across the Kwaman's face, trying to rectify what his eyes saw with what his body felt.

How different sight is. Filled with lines. Empty of song.

And yet, there was incredible beauty here. Color possessed undeniable energy. He felt how his other senses, so rich in texture and tone, were easily displaced.

True to his word, Jormah named everything they saw. But color was a complex language and Tremlo soon discovered there was no single color. Yellow was a name used to describe thousands of shades within the same family. Many of the lines on Jormah's face were not actual lines but indications of depth or size.

"Do not despair. Your senses and your eyes will soon work together."

At first, Tremlo's senses told his eyes what they saw. But a few days later, just as the Kwaman predicted, his eyes were able to tell his senses what he was looking at.

He was fascinated by his own shadow. Here was a thing he could see, and yet it was without substance.

Walking with his eyes open was the most troublesome, for color spoke of speed as well, and he was quickly made dizzy by the visual rush.

"How can we rely on such a fickle perception?"

"We don't."

Every day was a new experience. He discovered that color could evoke emotion, and soon the *feel* of something was no longer enough. He had to *see* it as well, and continuously, for sight had become a thirst that could not be quenched.

His long arms and legs became a source of fascination. What he knew from inside out, he now saw from outside in. He loved moving them about, seeing himself move as others might.

"You have made the adjustment," Jormah said soon after.

And with that, they set off once more.

CHAPTER THIRTY-ONE

Bettrie gathered all the handlers the moment Baronuus left.

"Our plans have changed. We will maintain our pairings, but once we reach the battlefield, the beasts will be set free to attack the enemies' lopers at will."

"Why? What happened?"

Bettrie would not elaborate.

"The Kurrs' obsession for loper flesh has two parts. The compulsion to kill and the desire to devour. In this regard, we will allow the first and interrupt the second."

"How can we separate a beast from its kill without hot pokers or some other coercion?"

"We can't. However, we've dampened their appetite by sating them with loper meat. Now we have to delay their desire to finish them off."

The handlers looked at one another. How could they ever do that? What was the great Animal Trainer talking about?

"We will use something they discovered aboard the ship."

Bettrie ordered two lopers brought into the tunnels behind the safe-walk.

"Paint the first one with tar. Make sure you cover every inch of its body. Head, face, hoofs, tail, everything."

"What about the second one?"

"Leave that one alone."

When the lopers were prepared, Bettrie stepped out from behind the safe-walk and began with Regal.

"Release her!"

Regal leaped out of the cage and followed her usual pattern around the perimeter of the quarry.

She speaks the name of this place through the physical motion of her body.

When Regal came round to the center, Bettrie gave the signal to *Sit!* She used this now as a preparatory command to ensure Regal's attention. Regal sat on her haunches, alert, waiting.

"Release the first loper!"

It raced to the far side. Regal was on it in two bounds. She slit its throat with one ferocious swipe and went to take a bite out of its hind quarter. The taste was horrible. She spat several times and dragged her tongue across her teeth.

"Release the second loper!"

Once again instinct took over, and she killed it quickly. This time when she bit into it, there was nothing to prevent her from finishing it off.

Bettrie waited a week before the next lesson. This time, she introduced three lopers. The first two were painted with tar, and the third left clean. After that, she introduced five. In this way, Regal learned to kill them all before she stopped to devour the kill.

As before, what Regal learned, all the beasts learned more quickly. In a relatively short period of time, it was done. For the final test, all the lopers were released unpainted, and the Kurr killed every last one of them before they stopped to feast.

"It worked!" the handlers cheered.

It worked, Bettrie thought sadly. A new habit of killing had been substituted for an old one. The beasts' fate was now sealed.

"Send a signal to Baronuus."

"What should it say?"

"Ready."

While awaiting transport to the Southern Province, where in all likelihood the Kurr would either be killed or run away, Bettrie continued the training. It was during this time that the breakthrough occurred.

She was working with Regal and instituted a series of commands in rapid succession. It was like speaking a sentence, and Regal followed along perfectly. But when Bettrie signaled her to come for her reward, Regal stopped halfway. Opening her mouth in what looked like a yawn, she made a strange elongated sound and kept moving her mouth as she did so.

"Look at that!" Bettrie called out to the handlers. "I think she's imitating the way we speak."

Regal patted the ground in front of her with her right paw and made the sound once more. Bettrie took a step forward and Regal cooed.

"That's it! She's trying to communicate with us!"

Bettrie stopped, and Regal made that strange sound once again.

"She's definitely mimicking us."

Regal patted the ground, and Bettrie took another step forward, which was rewarded by a coo.

"*Come!* She's telling me to come! The coo means 'good' or 'yes'."

Twice more Regal did it, until Bettrie was almost beside her. She raised her head as though looking at the sky and made a sound that was nearly a bark. Then she opened her mouth.

Food. Feed me.

It was undeniable. Bettrie instantly did as she asked, barely able to contain her excitement. She made a bark-like sound similar to the one Regal had made. Instantly Regal opened her mouth.

"A word! We have a word of her own devising!"

In all her years of training, Bettrie never encountered an animal smart enough to try and train her. Conditioned responses were one thing, but if they could communicate through words...

What might we learn from each other?

If only there was more time.

"We must save her!" Bettrie insisted when Baronuus arrived with the transport.

"You've made strides, Animal Trainer. I'll grant you that. But by your own admission, she is the leader. They will follow her lead. So the answer is no. If any of the Kurr survive, you will get all the support you need. For now, our needs are greater."

Over a thousand Augmentors and their lopers ran ahead of the main body of the army to create a staging area and build ramparts in preparation for the forthcoming battle. Their orders were to leave before the infantry arrived and take all their lopers with them. The Augmentors were too well trained to question their orders, but most thought this madness. Men on foot were no match for those mounted.

When they reached the staging area, they immediately smelled an acrid odor. Somewhere, in the mountains, the Vradeem were gathering. They were a barbarous people who bathed in their lopers' urine.

Anyone who doubted it need only get this close to them to know the truth. It was a frightening smell. Primal. Choking. Many were those who had surrendered to the Vradeem or ran off before a sword had been drawn. The Augmentors were warned about this stench and told to ignore it. But these words did little to stop the uneasiness it created.

Nearly twenty thousand Augmentors trudged forward on foot. There were no lopers or any other beasts of burden. The men themselves pulled the supply carts. The largest and most dangerous of these were at the rear, covered with thick black blankets. They dampened the beasts' roars and helped reduced the lopers' scent.

Each handler walked beside the animal they had bonded with to monitor, feed, and soothe.

Bettrie walked beside Regal and made the cooing sound Regal had introduced. This was the sound of approval, the word 'good' or 'okay'. There were many sounds and signals now. Each morning, Bettrie would raise an arm and make loud sniffing sounds: *'How, are you?'* Each day Regal would respond, continuing to communicate with her in like manner.

Simple physical wants and emotions were easiest to convey. Regal defined herself with a quick raise of her head. At first it meant 'look at me' but now became the word for 'I' or 'me'. Bettrie responded with the same physical cue, which she used now to define herself.

Through all this, she felt she was just on the cusp of understanding something of Regal's mind. Before they left the quarry, Bettrie tried to communicate that they were going on a trip. Starting with the command – *Sit!* – which now meant *watch* as well, she got down on all fours and acted out what was going to happen. Regal watched carefully. It seemed like she understood what Bettrie was trying to tell her.

The transfer of their cages onto the traveling carts went smoothly enough, so perhaps something had been conveyed. As the trip progressed, nothing of serious consequence occurred. The beasts were lulled by the motion of the wagons and slept for most of the trip.

Then, about five days from the battlefield there was a change. The Kurr began to pace in their cages and roar sporadically with discontent. Bettrie lifted the blanket of Regal's cage, raised her arm and sniffed. In answer, Regal lunged at her. Her ears flat against her head, her eyes, sharp slits.

Get me out of here!

Despite their growing connection, she knew Regal would not hesitate to kill her if she chose.

Regal's anger softened, but did not go away. There was an edge to her. There was an edge to all of them. Bettrie raised her arms and sniffed again. After several more tries, Regal made a particular sound and swiped at the air with her front paw. This was her sign for loper.

I understand, Bettrie cooed.

"Lopers," she called back to the other handlers. "They're picking up the scent of the Vradeem!"

CHAPTER THIRTY-TWO

"Look at that," Arbat said, as the skies began to lighten. He and his captains had snuck halfway down the mountain to the observation blind. "What is it you see?"

Soft rolling hills spread out from the base of the mountain. The land had been cleared long ago for farmland, but recently its inhabitants, fearing an invasion, had abandoned it. Knots of trees were scattered here and there, but overall, it was the perfect landscape for their style of fighting.

The Ontarans' advance guard appeared more than a week before and staked out a staging area less than a quarter day's march from the mountain. They were building ramparts to defend a retreat, all in typical Ontaran fashion.

"If we attack now, we can easily defeat them," Arbat's firstborn had said.

"We want to engage their entire army," Arbat replied. "Not chip away at the smaller parts." He had been planning this battle for over a year. He even let a portion of their plan be known to the Ontarans to draw them forth. "It is time we crushed them in one battle and let their precious Augmentors know that we, not they, are the greatest fighters in the world. With their defeat, the tribute will flow, and afterwards, Halla itself may be ours if we wish."

The men stared at the ramparts and beyond.

"What do you see?" Arbat asked again.

"They're gone!"

The advance guard had left in the night taking all their lopers with them.

"Exactly."

The main body of the Ontaran army was just arriving, and they were all on foot.

"To what end?"

"How stupid can they be to fight us on foot," Arbat's son boasted.

"Be silent!" Arbat shouted. "Never underestimate an enemy. I do not know what they are planning, but something is not right."

That night, he sent scouts to discover if there were cavalry troops hidden behind their lines. But there were none, and no lopers whatsoever in the vicinity.

"This troubles me. Bring Lamoot."

Lamoot was ootra, an outsider who had worked his way into the tribe. Lamoot was also a traitor whom they had secretly used without his knowing, to leak information back to the Ontarans. The fact that the Augmentors gathered now was proof their plan was working and that Lamoot was indeed a traitor.

Lamoot came forth on his loper. He was a head taller than the tallest of the Vradeem, and flanked by two of Arbat's captains. Lamoot had planned to sneak off before the battle began, but lately, he found himself surrounded by others who kept closer to him than usual.

"Lamoot, you are ootra. You have special knowledge of the Augmentors. Look at them. They have no lopers and pull their wagons with their own hands. Have you ever heard of such a thing?"

"No, Arbat. This is new to me."

"What do you think those black wagons are for?"

Eighteen of them had just arrived. They were large and square, and completely covered in black. The Augmentors were spacing them out evenly along the perimeter of their lines.

"I don't know."

"What is it you do know?"

Lamoot heard the tone in Arbat's voice and dared not avert his eyes.

"If fighting on foot, the Augmentors band together and use their shields to create a shell. They will advance as one with many arms, three sections at a—"

"Enough! All this is known. What is it you know that you aren't telling us?"

"Arbat, I—"

Arbat turned his head sharply. Lamoot was instantly pulled from his loper and thrown to the ground. The others fell upon him. In moments, he was on his stomach, arms tied behind his back, and his legs tied to his wrists.

"We know you are the traitor! You are a dead man. Think carefully now. Your only choice will be the manner of your death. If you tell us what we want to know, your death will be swift. If not, well, you know our ways."

"Arbat, I swear I know nothing," Lamoot pleaded. "This is as new to me as it is to you."

"Then how unfortunate for you. Take him away. Give him to the women."

"Arbat, Arbat, I swear I don't know! I don't—"

He was silenced by a blow to his head, which was nothing compared to what was coming. Piece by piece, he would be ripped apart and skinned alive.

That night, Arbat gathered with his captains for final preparations.

"The plan has been to attack at first light. But the Ontarans are up to something. I do not like those black wagons."

Everyone agreed. The moment those wagons appeared, their lopers, who were nearly themselves, had grown skittish. One of the scouts reported he heard strange sounds coming from the wagons, but he was too far away to identify exactly what they might be.

"Originally, we were going to draw their cavalry forth and surround them. But now it looks like they are planning to fight us on foot. If that is true, we would normally attack head on and overrun them. But maybe that is exactly what they want us to do. So we change our plans and divide into three groups. One on the far left, one near the middle, and one on the right. The middle and the right will remain hidden as best they can. We will begin the attack on the left to see what comes of it. If they are not up to some trick, we will drive them towards the middle and the second section will join in the fight. Then the third. If they are up to something and defeat us on the left, the right will attack to divert them while the middle rescues the left. Any questions?"

There were none.

"Then let us begin."

The men returned to their sections to perform the final ritual bath. Weeks before they went into battle, the Vradeem bathed in their lopers' urine. This was part of the *final joining,* where man and animal became one. Each man knotted his long hair into a tail to match his loper's. From this unified sense of self, each would draw strength from the other.

"You smell that?"

The stench was growing stronger, and Baronuus strained his ears to hear something in the night. If their spies were correct, there could be nearly sixty thousand Vradeem warriors in the mountains, and yet, there was not a sound. The rapport these invaders had with their animals was uncanny, and the very reason for their success.

If our plan works, that will be the cause of their undoing.

The Augmentors were on foot and seriously outnumbered, but these were all the men the empire could spare. If their plan failed, Baronuus would order a hasty retreat and try to preserve what little army was left. But if they were successful….

"The attack will probably come tomorrow," he said. "Spread the word. Make ready."

The Augmentors were organized into two divisions. The first were called Defenders and divided into small groups of twelve. Defenders were to follow individual beasts into the battle and protect them as best they could. The second group of Augmentors were Pursuers. They were to ignore the Kurr and focus on the downed Vradeem.

The Vradeem themselves would be reluctant to dismount, and this would work to the Ontarans' advantage, for the only way of stopping the Kurr was to get underneath them. To this end, the craftsmen had been instructed to create leather harnesses for the beasts to wear with protective side and back panels to make it appear like these were the Kurrs' most vulnerable parts. Each side panel was painted with bright, individual markings, so the Defenders could better identify them and follow after.

At dawn, the air grew rank with a biting stink. Baronuus expected the attack to come from the middle, but a flock of birds took flight on the right. A short time later, a lookout came racing in.

"They're coming!"

"How many?"

"I don't know. They were too far away to count."

Could this be a diversion?

If the attack started on the right, it would make it difficult for the Augmentors to outflank them in a coordinated manner. A battle was often won, not by the best plans, but by the ability to adapt to the moment. Baronuus had planned to release all the Kurr at once; now however, he had something different in mind.

"Keep an eye out for any movement on our left," he called to a Relayer who signaled to those down the line. "Bettrie, bring half the cages to this side and get ready!"

The Kurr were frantic. They had not been fed for days, and the smell of the Vradeem and their lopers was driving them insane.

"Raise the blankets!"

The beasts blinked at the sudden bright light and took swipes at anyone near them. Their bodies were shaking, their mouths foaming. They did not respond to any commands or seem to recognize their handlers. It was as if the training had never occurred.

"Move back. Everyone, move back!" Bettrie shouted.

A rumble of hoofs filled the air. The Vradeem had launched their attack.

"WEE-ARERRRRR!"

Their battle cry masked the shrieks of the Kurr.

"WEE-ARERRRRR!"

A continuous flow of men on lopers appeared atop a distant hill and turned the green ground brown with their numbers. Those in front disappeared into the trough only to rise several moments later upon the next hill. There were two more hills and six hundred yards that separated the two armies.

"Handlers! Ready! Now!"

Nine cage doors opened. The beasts hurled themselves out and hit the ground running. Here was unbridled fury. Here was madness personified.

The Augmentors ran after them in the semi-orderly formation they had planned, but the Kurr quickly outdistanced them, and before the Augmentors had gone a hundred yards, the beasts were already at the base of the last hill and about to make contact with the lopers.

The Vradeem were filled with the special energy that always came with the charge. Their bodies swayed in time to those around them. Their lopers' legs were now their own. The pressure in their knees told their animals how fast to run, their feet and ankles, the direction to go.

It was in these moments before contact that they felt most alive. It was incredible. Intoxicating. But more than this, it was what defined them.

The men in the front rows carried spears in one hand and large leather shields in the other to deflect arrows. Those behind, were armed with bows and arrows. Small shields were attached to their forearms for protection. Every man had five leather sheaths tied to the outside of each leg. These held the throwing knives. Across their backs, each wore a scabbard with a sword, whose handle rested beside their heads for quick removal.

As they crested the second to last hill, they saw the Augmentors in the distance running towards them. Those with spears, raised them into throwing positions. Those with bows, cocked their arrows. Down into the trough they went filled with blood-pumping exuberance, and up the final hill. Over the top– into flashing mounds of brown, that cut their beloved lopers out from under them.

It happened so quickly the Vradeem had no idea what assailed them. As the men were thrown off, or jumped off their falling animals, the Augmentors, who were just arriving, swarmed over them and killed them as quickly as they could.

The Vradeem's front line was in chaos. Piles of dead and dying lopers quickly mounted, forcing them to spread wide, losing the focus of their attack. These rolling hills, which had been thought to be an advantage, had become an impediment. Those behind could not see what was happening ahead and continued to press forward.

Once atop the hill, they saw beasts ripping apart their comrades' lopers. They rushed in to save them only to find their weapons ineffective, their own lopers cut down, and they themselves on the ground fighting for their lives.

The Kurrs' backs were filled with arrows, knives, and spears, but the beasts continued on, swirling in this dance of death. Their claws were fully extended, slashing in every direction with incredible speed.

One brave Vradeem leaped upon a Kurr's back and grabbed hold of its harness. He worked furiously to cut it off with his knife. The beast ignored him and continued on its killing spree. The Defenders, whose job it was to protect the Kurr, ran in and killed the Vradeem outright. Seeing the Augmentors fervor to protect the beast's harness inspired others to go after it. But the Defenders managed to keep to their plan, and for the most part, protected the beasts.

The Vradeem continued to pour into the ever-widening pool of death to rescue their fallen comrades, which only made matters worse. Hundreds, then thousands lay dead and dying. All the while, the beasts continued their murderous rampage.

Baronuus and Bettrie were on the observation platform in the staging area. The death and confusion the Kurr were inflicting upon the enemy so exceeded Baronuus's expectations, he cried out with joy. For every Augmentor killed, at least five Vradeem had fallen. The

Augmentors' only problem now was to avoid tripping over the mounting carcasses.

"Can you believe it?"

Bettrie was straining to see the Kurr. From this distance, she could only identify where they might be by the movement of lopers falling around them. She had lost sight of Regal moments after the battle began but imagined her to be somewhere near the middle.

"Commander! More are coming in from the left!"

Baronuus had suspected a two-stage attack and only committed half the Augmentors to the first wave,

"Make ready!"

This time, he would send the rest of the Kurr and most of the Augmentors into battle. A thousand men would be held in reserve, which was hardly enough to protect or assist in a withdrawal, but there was no turning back now.

"Bettrie, prepare the cages for release, but wait for my signal."

He wanted the Vradeem to get much closer so the beasts wouldn't be drawn off to the main battle on the right.

"Ready! Wait…. Now!"

This time the Kurr met the Vradeem on flat ground, coming in from the side. The Vradeem swirled around, losing the thrust of their attack and their lives, as they fought this unknown enemy.

The central body of the Vradeem had remained hidden. The commencement of the second attack was the signal to rescue the left flank. As they launched their attack, some of the Kurr raced to meet them. This forced the Defenders to run after them, and then the Pursuers to follow.

"No!" Baronuus shouted. Their lines were stretching out, making them vulnerable to attack. "Signal them to stop! Signal them to stop!"

In the mad dash no one looked back. Besides, they could not have stopped the Kurr if their lives depended on it.

The Vradeem were in retreat, trying to put as much distance between themselves and their attackers so they could take a moment to figure out what to do. But the beasts closed in, able to run faster than their fastest mounts and kill their lopers at will. The fallen men were left behind to face the oncoming Augmentors alone.

The flow of the battle moved quickly out of sight.

"We've got to regroup and reset the lines!" Baronuus shouted. "Bettrie, you're with me!"

Baronuus set off at a run. Bettrie needed no encouragement for she was desperate to find Regal.

The smell of blood and feces was rank. Thousands of lopers lay strewn across the ground, forcing the two to move to the outskirts.

In the mayhem ahead, Bettrie caught a glimpse of Regal at the top of a hill and headed straight for her.

"Bettrie!" Baronuus shouted.

"Regal!" She pointed, leaving Baronuus no choice but to follow. In the distance, there were flashes of other beasts.

"Regal!" If she could get to her and reestablish their connection, the other beasts might follow. "Regal!" *Will she hear me? Will she come?*

"REGAL!"

From behind, the sound of hooves. A group of Vradeem had broken off from the front lines and circled around. She and Baronuus were in their sights.

"Bettrie! They're coming. Go there!"

A pile of carcasses lay about a hundred yards away. It was the only thing nearby that offered any kind of protection.

They ran as fast as they could.

The pounding of hooves drowned out the pounding of their hearts. An arrow whizzed by. They dodged left and right. Something sharp pierced the muscle in Bettrie's right shoulder, but she did not miss a step. The pain was there, but it belonged to a life she could not afford to listen to.

Seventy yards, sixty, fifty. Thunder rolling up their backs. The carcasses close, the Vradeem closer. Five were bearing down on them with swords drawn. The two in front would try to behead them at a full gallop. The ones behind would get their own chance if the first two missed. Despite the catastrophe on the battlefield, here was the sport they lived for.

"WEE–ARERRRRR!" they shouted. No matter what happened afterwards, in this moment, these two lives were theirs.

The Ontarans were trying to make it to the dead lopers. The Vradeem would play with them, string them along, let them run for their lives, and just when they thought they were going to make it, kill them.

Baronuus and Bettrie ran as hard as they could, knowing the lopers were right behind, but neither could turn to look.

"WEE–ARERRRRR!"

Thirty yards, twenty, ten.

Out of the corner of her eye, Bettrie saw the head of a loper move up beside her. It was the end, and she knew it.

"WEE–ARERRRRR!"

She swerved, even though it would not be enough. She swerved— and slammed into a living wall!

Her head hit the ground so hard she saw stars. A blur of motion. Her eyes closed, and all went dark.

Baronuus fell to the side and rolled out of the way.

Regal had taken them all down in one fell swoop. Her front claws went right through the rib cage and into the heart of the first loper, while her hind legs dragged across the neck and slashed open the windpipe of the second.

Baronuus leapt up and killed two Vradeem thrown from their mounts. Regal quickly dispatched the other lopers, and uncharacteristically, killed the riders as well.

More Vradeem were coming, and Baronuus hid behind a carcass.

Regal placed her hind legs near Bettrie's fallen body and took several swipes at the air. The Vradeem ignored her warning and charged. She attacked their lopers, and the men leaped courageously onto her back. She paid them no mind and drove forward into the horde of oncoming loper flesh. The Vradeem worked feverishly to cut through the thick leather harness and finally split it open. She rolled over to crush them.

With a few twists, she freed herself of the harness and attacked with renewed vengeance, killing men and loper alike.

Now that her entire body was exposed, the Vradeem surrounded her and shot their arrows and spears directly into her sides and back, all with little result. One downed Vradeem reached up with his knife as she ran over him. She stomped on his chest and killed him just as his knife caught her in her vulnerable spot. It was not a deep cut, but it opened the artery, and the others saw the blood pouring down her leg. She fought back, killing several more before showing signs of weakness.

Eight Vradeem quickly dismounted and attacked her underside. She was moving more slowly, her life's blood pouring out. One drove his sword deep into the underside of her front leg and cut into a second artery. She spun around and collapsed. The others closed in and continued to drive their swords and spears into her body long after she was dead.

Now that they knew how to kill one of these monsters, those who saw raced to tell the others.

The Augmentors, inspired by the Kurr, fought with incredible ferocity. To get to the beasts, the Vradeem had to fight the Augmentors, but to get to the Augmentors they had to kill the beasts. It was impossible.

The only way the Vradeem could fight the beast was to retreat at a full gallop and draw them away from the Augmentors. Once the Augmentors were far enough behind, the Vradeem stopped and surrounded a beast, sacrificing many more men and lopers until they could get to its vulnerable parts and kill it. Never had they suffered such losses. More than half their men and lopers were dead or dying. There were only five beasts left, but judging by the despair in their own hearts, it could have been five hundred.

The Vradeem finally killed the last of the beasts, losing hundreds more men in the process. As they scattered up into the mountains, Baronuus called a halt to the battle. All the Kurr were dead, the losses to the Augmentors minimal, and the enemy soundly beaten. It would be all the Vradeem could do to protect their own families from those peoples they themselves had vanquished.

The threat of the Vradeem is over, Baronuus thought. *And we have a weapon that will make us invincible!*

He laughed aloud, imagining the expression on the faces of the Elite who had conspired against him. There were many scores to settle and new alliances to be made. With the Southern Provinces secure, his return to power was assured.

He might even be made Sovereign-of-the-Elite because of it. Second only to Proutus himself.

Halla!

He could not wait to get there. He would give Bettrie a title that would bind her to him.

"Bettrie?" He looked about. "Bettrie!"

The last he saw her was just before Regal came down upon them.

"Charge! Take ten men. Find the Animal Trainer and bring her to me. Search for Regal's body. She may be nearby. And hurry!"

"Understood."

"Bettrie! ... Bettrie! ... Bettrie!"

Bettrie's eyes slowly opened. It was dark and strangely quiet. She could barely breathe. Her head ached, but it was the sharp pain in her shoulder that drew her into consciousness. The sound of her name was muffled. For a moment she did not know where she was. She tried to move her legs, but they would not budge.

Weight.

She was lying on her back under a pile of dead lopers. The weight was crushing the life out of her. She tried to turn and succeeded only in shifting the pile more heavily upon herself.

"Help," she said, squeezing out the word, fearing she would suffocate. "Here," her voice barely a whisper. "Here."

"Here!" a voice said from above. "Ready? Heave!"

The weight began to lift. Her hands were grabbed, and her right shoulder exploded with pain as they pulled her out from beneath.

"Ahh!" she cried out from the rough handling.

"Steady," one of the Augmentors said.

They propped her up and examined the shoulder.

"Not bad. The arrow missed the bone. A narrow tip."

He yanked it out in one swift movement.

"Ah!"

"You'll be all right," the Augmentor assured her as he bandaged the wound.

Afterwards, Bettrie tried to stand but nearly fainted dead away.

"You've lost a good amount of blood. We'll carry you."

They lifted her onto the back of the strongest Augmentor.

"Wait," Bettrie said, looking about.

Where was Regal? Could she still be alive?

She looked back and forth, left and right. Again and again.

Where is she?

Regal's body was filled with so many spears and arrows she looked more like a mound of dirt used for target practice.

"There! There she is! Take me to her."

"Orders are to bring you to Baronuus straight away."

Bettrie struggled to break the Augmentor's hold, but she was too weak.

"Bring me there first or there will be hell to pay!"

They respected the Animal Trainer and knew she was responsible for their victory. Perhaps this was important.

"Alright. But just for a moment."

Regal lay about two hundred feet away. In the end, she had drawn the battle away from Bettrie. Her eyes were wide open. Her mouth, curled in a grimace. Her blood-red tongue hung lazily off to the side. A portion of her teeth showed. From the angle of their approach, it almost looked like a smile.

"Put me down."

Remembering her alive, seeing her now dead, Bettrie went numb.

In the hold of the ship Regal had stared directly into her eyes and roared. Not just with anger, but as if she was saying, 'We are prisoners, but you are not our masters.'

I knew you were special from the beginning.

Early in the training Regal knocked her down, softly enough to remind her of this.

What a magnificent animal.

When Baronuus and Elgar came to witness the progress, Regal had lunged at them through the bars.

You were protecting me even then.

When the breakthrough came, it was Regal's doing. She was the one who devised a language Bettrie could understand. She was the one doing the training.

And we, just beginning.

Regal's body, stiff now with the last moment of her life.

Oh, my friend.

Bettrie placed her hand on the side of Regal's head just behind her ear and gently stoked. This was one of the only places on her body that was not pierced. In motion, Regal had been a thing of perverse beauty.

But now....

Bettrie knew she had died doing what she did best. In one sense, what nature had bred her to do. Perhaps she was destined to die this way, perhaps not, but for Bettrie, the truth seemed inescapable.

Lowering her head, she let out a soft moan; for on this day she knew, Regal had died for her.

CHAPTER THIRTY-THREE

Gremar heard Stelbin coming down the path towards the Common Ground and positioned himself along the way. The two had not spoken since the day Stelbin stepped between Kenectka and himself.

As Stelbin drew near, Gremar filled himself with memories of the past. Here stood that adventurous youth Stelbin once sought out.

Stelbin slowed his pace.

"Gremar has need of you," Donan had told him. *"He will try to draw you closer."*

But closer in what way?

Stelbin stopped before him.

Be an empty cup for him to fill.

The two basked in the light of their youth.

"These are remarkable times," Gremar said, taking a step into the present.

"Yes."

"New pressures at every turn."

Stelbin nodded.

"The Kwaman withdraws, leaving you to fill the gap and create a place for yourself in the tribe."

As always, Gremar could be insightful and his words shrouded in care. Perhaps that was what made him so dangerous.

"I feel you looking at me with suspicion," Gremar continued.

"Suspicion?" *What did he see?*

"You are Kwaman, and I may be Leader one day. The tension between Kwaman and Leader is not uncommon. I wonder if it has to be the same for us?"

Kenectka had made a similar appeal. What were these two up to?

"What we want, Gremar, and what happens, may be two different things."

"Of course. Two opposing forces can create a kind of balance," Gremar countered. "But one tends to cancel out the other. When action is required, this is the weakest posture."

Stelbin wondered what action he was contemplating, but would not ask.

"The Leader," Gremar continued, "struggles with the daily concerns of the tribe. The Kwaman keeps himself free from this in order to observe a greater reality unfold. From this perspective, the Kwaman guides. I hope that when the time comes, we can act as one."

Stelbin nodded, having no idea what he was referring to. Donan had told him he needed to learn how to think like Gremar.

"Donan, do you know what Gremar is thinking?"

"Not exactly, not completely. But knowing what is on his mind is different than knowing *how* he thinks."

Stelbin stood uncomprehending.

"If you put yourself in his place, it will only lead to your idea of him as best you can imagine. You must try to see him as he is placed."

"I don't understand."

"The past informs the present, but do not be confused. *What* he thinks is fashioned by the events in his life. *How* he thinks was set in motion before he was born. *What* he thinks can change in an instant. In one moment, something has great value; in the next, little or none. If so, which of these views are correct? *What* one thinks changes with the wind, but *how* one thinks is always the same."

Could there be something in the way Gremar saw the world that defined how he thought, separate from circumstance?

Are we all made that way?

"*How,* is the landscape from which thoughts arise. To see the landscape is to have a sense of the shape of the thoughts to come."

"But how does one do that?"

"When we observe others, we see that some are naturally active, others more subdued. Some see the good in everything; others see the bad first. Some are reckless, others cautious. These are inherent traits. They are patterns embedded in the mind-of-the-body. And there are many more."

Stelbin stepped back from these thoughts and looked at Gremar. Waves of congruity and disparity flowed between them.

We have need of each other.

"You will take Donan's place one day," Gremar continued. "Your perceptions of the currents will guide us, assuming we are still alive."

Gremar, pressing his cause. *I must learn the 'how' of him.*

"There is much to consider," Stelbin said, coloring his voice with what sounded like a tone of appreciation.

Gremar nodded. *That wasn't so hard.* He needed the Kwaman to be on his side, or at least not to oppose him when the time came.

They walked together towards the Common Ground, keeping to the warmth of the moment. Both avoided the topic of Kenectka. But when they reached the Common Ground she came right up to them, grabbed their arms and inserted herself between them.

Both stiffened, and she laughed.

Everyone turned to look. Here, for all to see, was a hint of the future.

CHAPTER THIRTY-FOUR

Jormah and Tremlo resumed their travel north through the grassland. The blades were mostly red now. Bursts of yellow appeared here and there, looking like pieces of fruit. With Tremlo's eyes closed, there was nothing. With them open, all sorts of enticements.

"False-fruit," Jormah said. "It brings the birds."

With the false-fruit came patches of grass that grew over the bodies of dead birds.

"Death mats," Jormah called them. "We are entering a main feeding area."

The air was moist with anticipation. They no longer spoke aloud or looked at each other. The only relief from this damp, dark sea came from the sparkling sound of Resep. Its jeweled tones guided them to that narrow strip of black rock that pierced the heart of the grassland. Jormah had escaped along its ebony back the last time, and they followed it now out of the grassland to safety.

To Tremlo's eyes, the land beyond was a riot of shapes and colors. Tall striations of brown condensed into tree trunks. Bursts of green became individual leaves and ground-growth. There was so much to see compared to the uniformity of the grassland. He would have lingered for days had Jormah allowed it.

Broad strokes of color parted the land far ahead. Gashes of reddish browns and bluish blacks, feathered with flecks of green and whisps of yellow.

That was where the Resep lived.

A thin band of blue sky ran along the canyon floor. With Tremlo's eyes opened, it was a source of wonderment. With them closed, a river. Giant columns of rock towered over them as they walked alongside it. Here was a City all its own. The first time Jormah came this way, he was *bodyblind* and barely smelled the Resep. Now it permeated everything.

They climbed up the far wall and stopped before the cave that Origin once inhabited. Jormah's body spoke with such remembrance, Tremlo could see her in his mind's eye.

"Our tribal Resep was taken from a cave a thousand years ago," Jormah said. "The plants I planted up on the ridge are only thirteen years beyond Origin."

Thirteen years, Tremlo thought.

Nearly his own age.

Jormah led them up to the ridge where a tangy scent colored the air. The closer they got, the more pungent it became.

"They are reacting to us," Jormah said.

All along, Tremlo thought.

The plants were bright lime green, and wild. They had gravitated to one end of the small plot and grown together. Tremlo chuckled and ran up to them. The tenacity with which the Resep clung to itself made him feel as if he was with a group of youngers wrestling with themselves. These were the playmates he never had. He ran his finger over their leaves, and the air became suffused with a host of new smells.

Jormah never knew Resep to be so responsive.

The edges of their leaves were flecked with the beginnings of both yellow and blue Broezia. In another month, it would be time to Harvest.

With eyes opened, Tremlo saw the external forms the Resep had taken. With eyes closed, he felt the energy that created them. He sat down in balance-position, and Jormah quickly followed.

The air filled with smells of earth, of warmth, of beginnings. Its tones rang through the length of Tremlo's body, and he just long enough now to hear.

The root of the world. The root of himself. The very song that called to him in the dark of the womb, the body of a rainstorm, the heart of a dream. Father-and-Mother, the purest of light, too powerful then for his small body to contain.

Knowing it now, he lay down flat on the ground to listen.

"It is getting late," Jormah's voice startled him. "We need to make preparations for the night."

Tremlo sat up, surprised by the darkening sky. What seemed like a moment had been half a day.

They went down and made a fire by the entrance to the cave-of-Origin.

"When I first came here, Origin tried to speak to me with rhythms and smells, but my perceptions were too dull to hear. Now I can hear them, but I do not understand the meaning."

Tremlo said nothing. He too was trying to make sense of it.

They ate in silence. The flavors of now, the flavors of the past, reminding them, defining them. Afterwards, Jormah gave the fire a final stir, and they moved into the cave to sleep. It had been some time since they had slept in a cave. Jormah found it reassuring, but Tremlo was unsettled. It was not that the floor felt too hard or the cave was uninviting.

"I ... will sleep on the ridge," he said, finally, his body feeling the need.

Jormah watched him go. He longed to connect to whatever forces were making themselves known to Tremlo, but this was not to be, at least, not yet.

'I ... will sleep on the ridge.'

Tremlo said it so matter-of-factly, Jormah almost missed it.

'I will sleep on the ridge.'

'I.'

Tremlo said I.

The plants were waiting.

Tremlo stretched out before them and the air colored with scent. The *joy* of acceptance. The *happiness* of connection. The *sadness* from long ago. The Resep was speaking to him through the emotions it aroused in him. It bathed him in a lullaby of smells throughout the night. Where once his body absorbed and reflected, now it also observed. He awoke in the morning not knowing what to think or where to look.

It was the reassuring sense of Jormah below that brought him into the rhythms of now.

Jormah watched him climb down. Tremlo appeared distracted, and a little heavy on his feet.

Tremlo shrugged in response to Jormah's looking. The night had passed in a haze of sensations he could barely remember.

It doesn't matter what is happening up there, Jormah decided. *Down here is where you will live your life.*

The Kwaman got down on his knees in preparation.

Tremlo stood a moment, confused. It seemed so out of place. Jormah was challenging him to a game of armrue. They hadn't played since entering the grassland.

"You would prefer to avoid this?"

"Yes."

"That is not possible."

"No."

"It can end if you choose."

"On the day I defeat you."

'I.' He said it again.

Their fingertips touched and the contest began. Tremlo, pitched deeper now, launched an attack with more power than before. Jormah fought hard to resist, and when he went on the offensive, it took much more effort to cause Tremlo's arm to bend.

Resistance defines existence.

"You are growing," Jormah said afterwards, marveling at the change that had taken place overnight.

'Yes.'

From then on, Tremlo slept on the ground beside the plants each night. They sang to him as he slept. Each day tiny pieces of himself fit together just a little better than the day before.

Jormah did not interfere, but maintained their morning ritual. Through the game of armrue he could gauge the subtle changes that were occurring in Tremlo.

Here was a young Rehloy coming into being.

CHAPTER THIRTY-FIVE

The Augmentors marched triumphantly along the road to Halla. The beasts had inspired them to heights rarely achieved in battle. At night they sat around their fires retelling the events of that day. These tales were such that they would be woven into the fabric of their history, and they, crafting their stories, were the living proof.

Bettrie's shoulder healed quickly under the physyck's care. Baronuus insisted she ride in a cart pulled by Augmentors until her shoulder was completely healed. The Animal Trainer found herself surrounded by men. Without any formal command, they appointed themselves her bodyguard. Honor guard was more like it, for they knew she was the one who had made everything possible.

"Bettrie," Baronuus said, more to the men that pulled her cart than to the Animal Trainer herself. "Stay close to me."

When they reached the outskirts of Halla, the main body of the Augmentors stopped. Armies were forbidden to enter the city-of-cities, and so they made camp along a designated border and listened as Et-El Baronuus and his officers continued on to the Hall-of-Renown. The streets were thronged with the masses. Distant cheers of the citizenry marked their progress.

Members of the Elite were waiting inside the hall. Each wore an honor-gown of red with bright purple stripes, fringed in gold to welcome back one of their own. But what should have been a joyous occasion was fraught with fevered whispers.

"They are approaching the plaza."

"It won't be long now."

"What do you think he'll do?"

Baronuus sat proudly upon a jeweled throne, mounted on a platform that rested on the shoulders of eight men. He and his officers were being given the hero's welcome. Already there were small woodcarvings of his profile being sold in the marketplaces.

Flowers were heaped upon the platform and a continuous flow of fruits, sweetmeats, beer, and wine were offered along the way. Baronuus stopped often. A bite here, a sip there. Each time the crowd cheered. This was the least they could do to repay him and his men for staving off the invasion. On this day, any and all matters of service, human and otherwise, were available to them.

The pomp had little meaning where real power was concerned, but Baronuus indulged himself and stood up for most of the parade with his arm raised and fist clenched in salute to the citizens of Ontar. When the procession reached the Hall-of-Renown, he took his place at the base of the steps with the rest of his entourage. From there, they waved to the crowd.

Proutus stood just inside, waiting for the cheers to subside before he nodded to the guards to open the doors. Stepping out, he was greeted by a thunderous swell. He was expert at gauging the enthusiasm of the crowd. Just before the sound faded, he looked down at Baronuus and nodded. The crowd cheered anew as Baronuus climbed the steps.

"Our prodigal son returns!" Proutus declared and embraced him. This was the highest public honor that could be bestowed upon a man. The crowd roared their approval.

"Your mad scheme worked," Proutus whispered before releasing him. "And we are more than just pleased. We are in your debt. Come into the hall and get your due. Afterwards, you and I will speak in private. We have much to discuss. Welcome back."

Elgar and several other high-ranking officers followed, with Bettrie taking up the rear.

"Members of the Elite, I present our victorious defenders!"

The Elite stood side by side in two rows. They turned to face one another, creating a narrow passageway through which Baronuus would pass. The Elite raised their right arms in salute and pounded their chests with their left hands. Baronuus took great pleasure in the sound. Moving through the ranks, he nodded to both friend and foe with equanimity.

You are at risk, his benign smile seemed to suggest. *You are at risk. You are at risk. You are all at risk.*

He moved past the Elite and over to the base of the podium where the Emperor now stood.

"Et-El Baronuus, we, the citizens of Ontar salute you! For your brilliant vision, your efforts, your faith and devotion, and more importantly, your steadfastness against adversity. We hereby bequeath to you the Southern Provinces and declare you to be the Lord and Master of that land."

Baronuus caught his breath.

"You will divide it up and populate it with those you see fit and deserving. For the service of your officers, we give them each ten solid bars of avarin."

His men fought to maintain their composure. They had just been made rich by the Emperor's decree. With such a sum they could quit soldiering altogether and start their own *stocracies*!

Baronuus smiled to himself. What his men did not realize was that the reward was enough for them to move up a rung in society, but not enough to maintain the needs of that station. In one sense, they would be indentured to him and forced to seek greater conquests in order to maintain what they had acquired this day. In this way, Proutus ensured that his army would remain intact.

Clever. Very clever, Baronuus thought, remembering how heady and dangerous it was to be near the Emperor. Proutus was a bit heavier than the last time he saw him. The lines of his face were softer now and more inviting. How easy it would be to be lulled by his charm.

The Elite cheered, and Baronuus and his men bowed, first to Proutus and then to the Elite. Now that the formal part of the ceremony was over, the Elite were eager for first-hand accounts of the battle and came forward to intermingle with the officers. Word of the victory had arrived only days before. Beyond the numbers of casualties and a brief description of the results, the details had been left to their imaginations.

Proutus withdrew to the inner chamber and signaled Baronuus to join him.

"Don't be too angry with us, dear Baronuus," he said closing the door behind them. "Your former ostracism was unfortunate but necessary."

Baronuus nearly laughed at the Emperor's attempt to cover his tracks.

"And how was that, my Liege?"

"You must admit your plan bordered on lunacy. But it also had its merits, which you have proven beyond a doubt. And yet, would it have succeeded if you were not so, shall we say, driven to it?" Proutus raised his eyebrows and tilted his head. "You see Baronuus, extreme situations require extreme measures. Ambition has both its strengths and weaknesses. In my experience, combining ambition with the need to survive often yields the best results."

Baronuus was taken aback. He thought the Emperor's disdain was a ploy to remove him from power, but could Proutus have been that calculating?

Would I have persevered had the stakes not been so high?

"Besides," Proutus chuckled, slapping him on the back. "What better way for you to discover who your real friends and enemies are?"

Baronuus nodded in awe. Proutus had played him to perfection. He was even playing him now.

"We can speak of these matters in more depth later. For now, let us sit. I want to hear about everything that happened leading up to and through the battle. No detail is too small to exclude."

The Emperor preferred dry facts and mundane details so that he might form his own opinions. Baronuus obliged and spoke at great length, and when he finished, Proutus was staring off into space.

What is he thinking? What plots is he contriving?

One could never be sure.

Proutus turned back to him, his eyes clear and bright.

"This is all very encouraging. You have done an excellent job, Baronuus, but," the Emperor paused as if searching for just the right words, "between you and me, it is too soon to appoint you to the triumvirate."

Baronuus's stomach tightened. He had not asked for anything of the sort.

"It will cause too much dissension amongst the Elite at this time. But don't worry. Just before your arrival, I sent word to Commander Targus that in three months' time, he will step down and come to Halla to be closer to me. You will take his place and become the Supreme Commander of all our armies. This new appointment will help you bring others in line and consolidate your position. From there, things will... evolve. Do it slowly and with care. These are delicate times for all concerned."

"I am honored, my Liege. I don't know what to—"

Proutus raised his hand like this was just a part of a plan he had had for him all along.

Dare I believe him?

"Now, Commander, tell me of your plans."

"My plans?"

"For your armies. How will you go about employing this new weapon?"

"Well, I, I'm not sure I—."

"Don't pretend you haven't thought about this promotion. I am not a fool."

A familiar edginess had crept back into the Emperor's voice.

"No, of course not. I mean I have given it some thought," Baronuus hastened to say, "but I haven't worked out all the details."

"What have you got so far."

"Well, obviously, we need more beasts. And we have to develop a breeding program. But before this, we need to get them over here and with better efficiency. To save time, I think that we should send Bettrie to Ontara with two complements of Augmentors to capture more beasts. She wants to start training them when they're cubs anyway. I believe she should do it there, so if any of them die, she can quickly catch more. Besides, once they're trained, it will make the journey back to Ontar much less treacherous."

"I have been thinking along similar lines. Is she aware of your plan?"

"Not yet."

"And what about her?"

"What do you mean?"

"What of her family?"

"She had a husband, although no longer. Perhaps she threw him out. Three children. They live on her farm in Waige."

"Is she close to them?" Proutus leaned forward.

"Close?"

"Will she want to take them with her?"

"I don't know. We haven't discussed any of this. But Bettrie is a patriot."

"Tell me more." Proutus had met Bettrie only the one time and remembered her to be both intelligent and a pragmatist.

"She is opinionated, argumentative, at times belligerent. She carried out my instructions in spirit, but not to the letter."

"Contentiousness is often inherent in those of special ability."

"In the end, she was developing a language with the beast."

"A language?"

"A mixture of signs and sounds and not just a series of commands. She was beginning to speak to them, but even more astounding, they were beginning to speak back."

"Remarkable. So she is a woman of genius and a patriot. A useful combination, don't you think?"

Baronuus nodded, already feeling outmaneuvered. The Emperor was far ahead of him.

"Is she replaceable?"

"Well, I, uh."

"Can she be replaced?" The edge was back in his voice.

"I, suppose."

"You suppose?"

"Two of her handlers are my spies. Their instructions are to keep a close eye on her and learn all they can about her art."

"And this is enough?"

"Bettrie defies description in some areas. There is a kind of magic about her. She has a talent, a natural understanding of what to do with these animals that others do not. How can I legislate intuition or demand it of others?"

"And what happens if Bettrie dies?"

"There are other trainers."

"But she is special."

"Yes."

"How long before the others can do what she does?"

"I don't know. We've never done this before. I'm sure we could duplicate some of what she has done already."

"Some? You'd better pray this woman remains healthy."

"Understood."

"Do not fail us, Baronuus."

The threat hung in the air, and for a moment, there was silence between them.

"Good," Proutus said. "Let's bring her in. I will appear to make her my personal friend, even at your expense. Understood?"

"Understood."

The Animal Trainer was brought in, and she dropped to her knees.

"Bettrie, Bettrie," Proutus said coming forth and lifting her to her feet. "No need to be formal here. Come and sit."

She moved to the lounge he indicated and sat across from him. He smiled, and she smiled back, trapped by his familiarity. Something was up.

"Baronuus told me about the extraordinary service you have rendered us. Through the efforts of you both we have delayed the destruction of Halla and given Ontar a reprieve. We are eternally grateful."

Bettrie nodded once. If his intent was to put her at her ease, it was having the opposite effect, but her face and body betrayed none of this. "It worked out, my Liege," she said, matter-of-factly. "But it could have gone the other way. The Kurr all died in our service."

Clear-eyed, Proutus thought. *Pragmatic. A touch of humility. Again she tries to distance herself from Baronuus.*

A realist, he decided.

"Baronuus tells me you were developing a language with the beasts."

"Yes, trying to, anyway."

"Is it possible to converse with them?"

"The Kurr are not ordinary animals. Their intelligence is nearer to our own, but they are trapped in four-legged bodies, with paws instead of hands, claws instead of fingers, born into a violent world ruled by instinct rather than reason. They think differently than we do, but they think all the same."

"What were you hoping to accomplish?"

"If we understood their thoughts, we could work with them in ways never before imagined. It might even give us insight into other animals as well."

"So, you are a woman of science."

"Just an animal trainer," Bettrie replied, in a firm voice that allowed no other possibility.

She has a presence, Proutus thought to himself, and recalled that he liked her. But how would she fare in rougher water?

"You understand that our borders are plagued with insurgents and that we need to develop these new weapons in order to protect ourselves from invasion."

"Yes, so I've been told."

"I am concerned that your interest in communicating with these beasts might sway your judgment. We need these animals to fight for us, not be our friends."

"I do not think these two ideas are incompatible."

"How so?"

"If you witnessed the battle, you would have seen that the lopers evoked the natural instincts of the Kurr. However, surprise is no longer on our side. The Vradeem now know of the beast's vulnerable spot. If there is a next time, the Vradeem, or whomever, will fight differently. Simply setting the Kurr loose upon our enemies will eventually fail. We need to develop new techniques."

"You think this language you are trying to develop is the way to do it?"

"We need to create a special kind of alliance. After all, we are asking the beasts to lay down their lives for us. What if the enemy takes a lesson from us and comes on foot? In the heat of battle, how can the animals know who is the right man and who is the wrong one to kill? We must guide them and not just in battle. Their sense of smell and hearing are far superior to ours. They could become the ultimate scout, letting us know far in advance the movement and even the numbers of our enemy."

"If you can accomplish this you will become very rich."

"I do this for the good of Ontar, not monetary gain."

"Just for Ontar?"

Bettrie thought a moment. "No, I do this for myself as well. It is a challenge. I do it because I believe it can be done."

A place in history, Proutus decided. *You want a place in history.*

"And you are just the one to do it!" he said aloud. "So, when are you leaving?"

"Leaving?"

"For Ontara."

"I, I wasn't suggesting that—"

"Don't worry. We'll give you all that you require. Baronuus, how much time before a ship can be outfitted and provisioned?"

"A few months perhaps, but that will place us in the middle of summer where the prevailing storms will make the crossing prohibitive. I would say we could be ready to sail sometime in the fall or early winter."

"Excellent. That will give Bettrie enough time to put her affairs in order."

"Your Eminence, I, I don't think I—"

"Yes, I know. This is all very sudden."

"Yes, but. It's more than that. I—"

"Baronuus, step outside for a moment."

Baronuus exited without a word, and the Emperor came over to Bettrie and placed a hand on her shoulder.

She shrugged it off, unsure of his intent. "The wound," she hastened to explain.

"Oh, yes. Of course." He dropped his hand but did not move away. "Between you and me, I don't trust that Baronuus has, shall we say, the correct, sensibilities for this task. He's very competent when it comes to organization and moving troops about. I trust him to get your animals back here safely. But he has a heavy hand and doesn't fully appreciate how revolutionary the task you've set before yourself. This could change the course of history, and opportunities like this rarely, if ever, come in a lifetime."

"I know."

Proutus began to pace.

"Then what is your hesitation? Your family perhaps?"

"That is one consideration."

"You can bring them with you if you like."

"It's not that exactly. Besides, I doubt they would want to come."

"Then what is it?"

Bettrie sighed. "I— I fear the sea. I get desperately ill."

Proutus burst into laughter.

"My dear woman, my physyck can see to that. He has potions that will make the whole crossing seem like nothing more than a dream."

Bettrie lowered her head. The Emperor was not going to let her out of this. And despite the assurances, she knew how sick she would be.

"As you command, my Liege."

Later, after both Bettrie and Baronuus had gone, Proutus began to compose the letter he would send to Targus. He had lied to Baronuus when he told him he sent word to the Commander to step down.

That was pure inspiration, he thought chuckling to himself. *The letter has to be worded in just the right way so that Targus will read between the lines and see that I had no choice. That Baronuus sued for the position, and the people were behind him.*

Proutus laughed aloud.

These two will make powerful enemies and become so focused on each other, they will miss what is really going on.

CHAPTER THIRTY-SIX

Tremlo plucked a fat seedpod from the top of one of the plants. A sigh of scent, a sense of relief. Harvest had begun.

They moved through the plants, scraping the Broezia from the leaves, making sure to separate the yellow from the blue.

The blue Broezia, if ingested, propelled one into the posture-of-speed. But if too much was taken, one could become lost in the waking dream and never fully return. Jormah knew the dangers of blue Broezia well. He had only been able to take it twice.

After cleaning the leaves, they carefully pulled the plants out by their roots and placed them deep inside the cave-of-Origin to commune in this, their final easing.

In the days that followed, the two worked on the ridge, turning the soil and mixing in fresh fertoe to enrich it.

When the Resep was *serene*, they stripped away its leaves and made two sets of clothes for themselves. The sensitivity of these leefskins was such that, at times, it felt like they were wearing nothing at all.

Jormah would have preferred to stay for another season to give Tremlo more time to mature. But the whisperings from the north had intensified, and with it came the added pressure to leave.

"Given the dangers ahead, there is one more thing you need to learn."

"I'm ready," Tremlo said, smelling the drift of his thoughts.

"Are you?" *Are you rooted enough to withstand the force of it?*

Months earlier, Tremlo could have been pushed aside by a gentle breeze or a strong emotion.

Jormah measured out a very small portion of blue Broezia and gave it to him. This would be a test, just like when he himself first took it.

Tremlo swallowed, and his stomach exploded with a high-pitched sound. A jolt of pain shot through every cell in his body, and the world groaned to a halt.

A bird, suspended in midair.

Jormah, rock-still.

Flames of the fire, frozen stiff.

A single moment held captive in time, and he living fully in between.

He stooped to pick up a small stone, but it would not budge. It wasn't that the stone had attained a great weight, but rather it was somehow attached to the ground. Beside the stone lay a twig. Tremlo pushed against it using all his strength with no result.

"You see," Jormah's voice boomed and startled him. Even the sound of this place was different. "In this state, we are less than a shadow."

"I thought I might have moved the twig a little."

"Perhaps. With continued pressure we might become a puff of air, but little more."

Tremlo grabbed Jormah's arm and moved it from side to side.

"With you I am more than just a puff."

"We are of one world. Before us is another. Come, let us walk through it."

They went to a nearby tree.

Everything was cast in static light.

"In the amount of time we have been here that bird has yet to take a breath, let alone blink an eye. We could live a lifetime here and never see the sun set."

"Do you think that bird can see us?"

"If it can, we would be a thing of no substance and easily ignored."

The Kwaman leaned against the tree. Without the use of the blue Broezia, it took a great deal of effort to maintain this posture. He compressed his chest harder to keep up with Tremlo.

"This is not a place ... to dwell in. A path of escape. But we cannot live here without har—. Do not... stay lon—"

"Jormah?"

The Kwaman slurred to a halt. Tremlo was alone once more.

Objects around him were changing. The smooth surface of a large boulder devolved into intricate latticework that spread into the ground. What was familiar in one instant proved to be a superficial covering in the next. Jormah himself was breaking down into a compilation of geometric forms. Colors were separating into individual fragments of yellow, red, and blue.

I am accelerating!

He would have cried for help, but there was no one to hear.

Panicked now, with nothing to hold on to, he sat down upon the ground-that-was-no-longer-ground and assumed balance-position. If only he could slow down.

He breathed slowly, deeply.

Slowly. Deeply.

No matter. He continued to accelerate.

Jormah pushed off the tree. He was exhausted. He had held the posture longer and harder than ever before.

Where is he?

Hours may have passed for Tremlo.

For each breath he took, Tremlo might have taken a hundred or a thousand.

Something is wrong!

Jormah was desperate for energy. He grabbed a pinch of yellow Broezia and swallowed hard. The moment it took effect, he compressed his chest.

"Tremlo," he called out.

A strange sound was coming at him from all directions.

"Tremlo."

The young Rehloy was lying on the ground, blinking in and out of existence.

"Tremlo!"

Jormah squeezed tighter to match his frequency. Tremlo was just a few steps away. He rushed forward and fell on top of him.

Tremlo grabbed hold and Jormah was yanked forward with such force, he was surprised to find he had not moved a hair's breadth. He compressed his chest further. The higher in pitch, the more substantial Tremlo became. But this level of speed was impossible to maintain. Jormah began to falter. Tremlo tightened his grip and carried them along for a while longer. But the Kwaman was losing it.

"Treml—"

Jormah turned to stone, trapping Tremlo beneath the dead weight of his body.

Come to me! Jormah projected himself down into the empty space below.

Hold onto me!

"Tremlo!" Jormah shouted.

Tremlo!

Tremlo was hurling once again towards the end of the world and beyond. Jormah's steady influence had slowed him down, but only for a moment. Lost, frightened, and alone, he grasped frantically at any passing rhythm, but he was moving too fast. His teeth chattered; his body shook. He thought he would shatter into a thousand pieces.

With nothing to grab onto, a small voice drew him aside. Here was that place of no-place. His body rushing forward, victim to its fate, and he, suddenly flowing alongside, *watching*.

From the place of no-place he saw fragments of emotion and layers of thought. Near the center was that kernel, the root of the world, that seed of himself. Remembering the sound, he sang aloud, caressing himself like a newborn. Remembering the sound, he shouted it throughout his body.

One note became two, then four, eight, sixteen, thirty-two....

Jormah felt a whisper of sensation beneath him grow into a chorus of color and sound. Bit by bit, it condensed into the body that was Tremlo.

He did not move until the steady beat of Tremlo's heart was assured.

"I'm ... here," Tremlo said softly.

Jormah rolled over onto his side.

"I'm here," Tremlo said again, flat on his back, spreading his arms and legs out wide.

Here... at last. Here.

CHAPTER THIRTY-SEVEN

They slept hard.

Lungs craving air, bodies craving movement.

When Jormah stood, the residual effects of the posture-of-speed stood with him. The last time he took blue Broezia, it was months before he felt fully integrated back in the world.

How much worse for one like Tremlo.

"Give me your hands," he said, pulling the younger up and squeezing them tight.

"This is real for the hands that are attached to the thoughts and feelings that call themselves Tremlo."

The tighter he squeezed, the more focused Tremlo became.

"Stay with me."

Tremlo held onto the slow and steady pulse of the Kwaman. He had been drifting away without knowing. The speed in which he radiated determined what was real.

It took several weeks before the daily rhythms of their lives steadied him.

"You're better," Jormah said.

"Yes." Tremlo's lips moved, and his voice spoke. "I am ready to try again."

"Again?"

The posture-of-speed.

"We almost lost you the last time."

"He ... found my way back."

The one who did, the one who saw, the one who knew.

"I don't think you are ready."

"No." The blue Broezia had the power to take him away. *Never again.* "I will do what you did."

He compressed his chest like Jormah had. The high-pitched sound was inside. The tighter he squeezed, the louder it rang. He clamped down hard.

Gone!

Jormah spun around. An instant ago, Tremlo was standing before him.

"I did it," Tremlo said reappearing some distance away.

"Well done!"

"I could have held it longer."

"Do you want to try again?

"No."

He did not need to practice. He owned this song now and forevermore.

A month turned into two. Jormah was not sure Tremlo was ready to leave, but they had to get to the caves of the Carooh before the cold season set in. Beyond the grassland lay the second City. Beyond that, the barren land where he got his first taste of real cold. After that, the giant forest-of-crawling-leaves and then the mountains of the Carooh.

Tremlo looked at him.

Did you speak this aloud or did I hear it in your gaze?

"We need to leave," Jormah said, definitely aloud.

They seeded the ridge not knowing if they would return here one day.

At the edge of the grassland, they stopped to inhale the red hues ahead, before seeping slowly, silently, into its waiting arms.

Each day the same, the same every day.

Tremlo was not sure if it was yesterday, today, or tomorrow.

Am I awake, or dreaming that I am?

Days. Weeks. Months.

Far ahead, the open *awww* of the great waterbody. In between, the punctuated rhythms of things to come.

Each day the same, the same every day.

Red draining into yellow.

"How are you?" Jormah's question fractured a silence years long.

"I, am good."

The sound of Tremlo's voice surprised them. Its gravel-like tones were smoothed out by the thrust of a young man emerging.

Each day the same, the same every day.

The hard, ebony stone that bordered the northern edge of the grassland slapped them awake.

"Tremlo?"

"Yes."

"How are you?"

"I, am good."

"Are you sure?"

'*Yes.*'

"I planted Resep in three places along the way to the Intruders. The first was days ahead."

The small patch of ground where the Resep once resided was overrun with violet-colored fledglings. Upon reaching it, Jormah dug down for roots that should have been there.

"I don't understand."

Any number of things could have ended the Resep's life, but something should have remained. Tremlo listened to the ground beneath his feet. It felt like the Resep had grown into another place.

Here. There.

Side by side, one place at a time.

Like me.

Jormah watched carefully.

"Tremlo?"

"Yes?"

He had been drifting again.

They traveled along the outskirts of the wound that was the second City to avoid the full brunt of its angularity.

Tremlo imagined the skeletal remains whole, throbbing with life. It was no wonder that the ancestors were Stiffbacks. How else could they tolerate the din?

Beyond the City lay a desolate land. In the swing of his arms and the newly acquired weight of his body, Tremlo felt pressures lurking along the fringes of the currents. Forms of the future shifted from one step to the next.

Nothing is set except how it will...

"Tremlo."

He was drifting again.

"Tremlo!"

What if he never fully returns?

The trees ahead sounded with voices so deep, they filled Tremlo with *knowing* eons long. An ancient forest of gigantic proportions. Jormah had described it in words, but none could bring forth the *being* that resided there.

The tree trunks had grown together at the edge of the forest to create a formidable wall. Rippled bark. Every twist and turn a lifetime all its own. The wall a shield, keeping the world out to preserve its *listening.*

Where the City spoke of ancestors, the forest spoke of nature in the bones.

They scaled the wall and stood between two massive elders. Their trunks were thirty feet across, and grew straight up for hundreds of feet before branching out in the final quarter.

As Jormah described, their huge crowns were home to colonies of birds that protected them. Dark green wings, the color and shape of the leaves hid them well. Their deadly beaks were anchored into buds, and their sharp claws retracted, *for now.* As Jormah discovered the first time he came this way, any tampering with these trees invoked their wrath. He had just managed to escape their murderous attack the last time by leaping into the posture-of-speed to avoid them.

The crowns ahead were densely packed and permitted no light to touch the forest floor. A shield of a different sort.

They entered this perpetual night with a shiver, for the air was markedly cooler. Branches and leaves swirled about the forest floor as if driven by a strong wind.

But there was no wind.

Jormah called this place the forest-of-crawling-leaves. He caught one and held it up. Its tiny under-legs spun, creating the shushing sound the wind might make. The Rehloy strove to blend in with the land. These creatures grew into the very shapes of the branches and leaves.

One the expression of the other.

It felt good to be here.

When the sun set, a soft sigh slid into the forest. The cool air was colder than Tremlo had ever felt.

'*Pay attention!*' the mind-of-his-body said.

The deep and abiding tones of this place spoke to one part, the cold another. It bit him awake and would not let go.

'*Pay attention!*' the mind-of-his-body shouted. *Here is what matters! This is what is real for the body that calls itself Tremlo.* Again and again, it forced him to return.

"This is just a taste of what's coming," Jormah said.

They walked through the night to keep warm, and the chill did not soften until the sound of the sun was high above.

"You will sleep by that tree, and I this one," the Kwaman said. "If the leafbirds attack we will not get in each other's way. But if we leave the trees alone, we should be fine."

They slept with bodies curled and arms tightly wrapped, and then they were up and moving through the night. It was another day before they stood in full light, their skin breathing as deeply as their lungs.

They had come through unscathed.

Before them and below, lay a slow-moving, river of reddish-brown mud. More like a cloud of mud than mud.

"It's deeper than the last time," Jormah said. He estimated the vapor to be an arm's length over his head. "I'll go first. Watch my progress carefully."

He took out a soft piece of malta and broke it into four small pieces. One by one, he stuffed them into his ears and nostrils.

"The mud is harsh. This will protect me from the vapor. Be sure to do the same and keep your eyes shut tight."

Tremlo nodded. The air grew cool with a passing cloud and reminded him to be here. He stepped into a patch of sunlight along the edge.

Jormah climbed down the face of the forest wall and took a deep breath before letting go. He hit the mud beneath the vapor with some force and sank to his thighs. Once free, he moved as quick as possible. The far bank was perhaps forty steps away, but the mud was very soft, and with each step, he sank to his knees.

The bank proved to be like the mud beneath his feet. He tried to get a handhold, but it was like digging into water. Wherever he dug, he could find no purchase.

His chest burned with desire.

He tried to leap up to the surface and catch a breath, but the soft mud floor offered no resistance, and he only sank deeper.

Tremlo, drifting back into the trees, the sound of the forest so pleasing. How wonderful to luxuriate in the past. *But is this real for the body that calls itself Tremlo?*

Jormah plunged his hands deep into the bank, desperate for something solid to grab onto. His lungs were turning to acid.

Keep going!

Too far to run back to the forest wall.

Keep going! he cried, digging desperately as darkness took a step closer.

Sensations from the forest flow through me, Tremlo thought, looking at himself. He had stopped breathing. '*Pay attention!*' the mind-of-his-body said. '*Pay attention!*' it shouted.

Chest-burning, arms-churning, Jormah fought to hold his breath.

Frantically-burrowing, desperately-furrowing, something ahead, just out of reach.

There, there, almost there....

Darkness-descending, his jaw clenching, mind going slack, his lungs having their way.

Lips-parting, air-departing, mouth opening wide... inhaling—

Air.

His head just above the surface. Fresh air filling his lungs, clearing his mind. He threw his arms over the top of the bank and gained some leverage. A rock, a root, piece by piece, dragging himself across until he rested upon solid ground.

Relief.

He had escaped.

How?

His legs remembered being lifted.

Tremlo!

Leaping up, he ripped the nearest sapling out of the ground and dropped down upon the slippery bank.

Lying flat, he shoved it down over the side.

Instantly grasped. Tremlo pulling himself up, hand over hand.

Jormah dug his toes deep into firmer ground to keep from being dragged back over. His upper body went limp, conforming to the collapsing bank beneath. His head and shoulders went down below the surface, but his toes held fast.

Tremlo climbed over his back, careful not to move too quickly for fear of pulling them both back under. He flipped around at Jormah's legs and dragged him back out of the mud.

Once safe, they breathed deeply. Mortified by what might have happened, exhilarated by what had.

"I owe you my life," Jormah said.

'And I owe you mine.'

The burning sensation on their skin roused them into action. There was a stream nearby, and they washed the mud and burning away, equals now in the eyes of the forest.

CHAPTER THIRTY-EIGHT

That second patch of Resep Jormah had planted lay ahead. Its stalks and branches were short and stubby, its leaves laced with jagged edges.

It stood like a clenched fist.

"Hello," Tremlo whispered, running his fingers over its body. The plants barely heard. The distant rhythms of the Intruders lay upon them like a disease, leaving them coarse and brittle.

Sick, and dying. They should have been harvested months before.

In the past, the Carooh had harvested the Resep and replanted it. But there was nothing of them now.

Something must have happened, Jormah thought.

Hopefully he would learn more when they reached the caves.

Tremlo hummed the songs-of-Origin and touched the plants continuously to ease them in their passing. Their edges softened, and the leaves unfurled. Eventually, they relaxed enough to let go and die.

They uprooted them and buried them some distance away. The plants were too ill to be of any use.

Tremlo returned to the patch and began to turn the soil before adding fresh fertoe. Jormah gave him a questioning look. Tremlo shrugged. He did not know why, but only that it felt right to plant here again.

The markings on the ground around the Caroohs' caves confirmed they had not been here for at least a year.

The warning Jormah had drawn on the floor of the ceremonial cave was surrounded by large white stones. Between them were tiny pieces of bone and feathers. His warning had become an altar of sorts.

The last time, the Carooh had left a watersack and a furskin for him. Now there was nothing.

Had Bka died? Or could an illness have swept through the tribe and prevented them from returning?

Jormah went to another cave and dug up a basket that should have housed furskins. That putrid flavor filled the air, but the basket was empty.

Tremlo stepped away. The Kwaman's stories prepared him for the idea of living inside the skin and hair of a dead animal, but this smell spoke louder than all the words combined.

It was horrible.

"Now you know the cost of survival."

They searched the other caves, all with the same result. There were no furskins.

That night, the cold lashed out with new ferocity. Here was the bone-chilling cold Jormah had spoken about. Streams of smokeless smoke came out of their mouths. 'Breath-sign,' Jormah called it.

They huddled close to the fire and barely kept from shivering.

"Imagine what it will be like when it gets worse."

Worse?

"The water will take the form of rock. The rain will no longer fall in drops but white flakes called siowt and lay upon the ground in thick blankets of cold. There is a secret cave where the Carooh would hide their young. It is a climb. Tomorrow we will go there, for we must find furskins."

The cave entrance was hidden behind a grove of green-leaf-pricklers. Inside were watersacks and sealed storage pots. The basket buried in the floor smelled strongly of death. Jormah unearthed it, and the stench enveloped them like a layer of grime.

"Our people could not survive a cold season as we are. We would have to learn to hunt and kill to get furskins. I fear many would prefer to die before that happened."

Jormah pulled a dark brown furskin out of the basket. It was from a burly creature the Carooh called, bristly. He draped it about Tremlo's shoulders. The young Rehloy had grown nearly as tall as Jormah this past year, but he was still thin, and it was too large for his small frame. There were two more bristlies and one small Yarka. Jormah took out the smallest of the bristlies. This one had a slit cut out of the center with a hood attached.

"Here," Jormah said, holding up the furskin. "Put your head through this."

In the past Tremlo would have run from such a smell. Now he was forced to bathe in it. The odor of decay was colored by the oily flavor of the Carooh who had worn it.

Female.

With it came vague impressions of emotions she must have had.

The furskin was heavy, the inside cold and stiff, and it chafed his skin.

How did they live in such a thing?

Few outside sensations penetrated, and conversely, little escaped, especially with the hood up. He quickly discovered it was the heat of his own body, prevented now from escaping, that warmed him.

"The furskin will soften with warmth and conform somewhat to your body, but mostly you will have to learn to conform to it."

Jormah took out one of the other bristlies and put it on. Tremlo smiled seeing the Kwaman's head sticking out of a mass of fur. Jormah caught the look and roared in the manner of a bristly. Tremlo laughed and roared back. Their snarls and growls were quite authentic, and anyone hearing might have believed two beasts were inside the cave.

"These are tars," Jormah said pulling out several sewn fur pieces. "They will keep your feet warm." He showed Tremlo how to put them on. "And these are teegns. They go on your hands."

Tremlo put them on. It was suffocating.

"When the cold gets worse, you will find this sensation preferable to that. This cave is the smallest of all of them. It will be the easiest to keep warm. We should make this our home."

Tremlo nodded, unsure if the Kwaman was asking or telling him.

Jormah lifted up the Yarka furskin and spread it out upon the ground. It was light brown with dark traces woven in.

"This was a ceremonial robe."

They lay down upon it still wearing their own furskins and pulled the other bristly over them. Here was total warmth at last. With the cold now held at bay, their muscles relaxed, and their bodies drifted into a good night's sleep.

The following morning Tremlo stepped outside to greet the day. The furskin muffled everything, leaving sight firmly in charge.

This is how the Carooh experience the world.

"We need to gather as much wood as possible before the siowt comes," Jormah said.

In the confines of the cave, shrouded in furskin, with senses muted, words grew in proportion.

"Jormah, tell me of the tribe, before I was born."

"There is not much to tell. It was peaceful. For a thousand years we sang along with the currents through the movement of our lives. And then the pattern-of-change came."

"What was it like when you were a younger?"

"Where shall I begin?"

Tremlo rarely asked about anything other than practical matters.

"What is the first thing you remember?"

There was a new level of concentration in his face.

"A sense-memory. A mixture of tones. My parents, Donan, myself. A comforting sound. All things start from there. The sound of *home*."

Tremlo frowned.

"You are bothered by this?"

"My first memories are all of pain."

Jormah had not considered Tremlo's childhood nor how different his life might have been had he found peace early on.

"What was that like?"

"Everything hurt. Everything burned. Everything was blaring. I kept trying to find quiet spaces to hide in." He reached inward to cradle that sense of himself, who, having been battered so early on, had remained hidden all this time.

"Tremlo," Jormah said softly. "The circumstances of your birth tore you from us. And it is these same circumstances that are forcing you to grow beyond us. But it is you whom we will look to, to show us the way. It is you whom we will seek to join."

All his life Tremlo simply wanted to belong, to fit in with the others, to be a part rather than stand apart. And now the Kwaman's words solidified the notion that this would never be. He would never fit in. Their expectations would set him apart. He would always be separate, in one sense alone.

His eyes grew moist.

No, not alone, he thought, reaching in once more to that tiny being, warming it with attention. This was he, the root of himself. Long forgotten and newly found. It grew with each caress.

He and it. It and he.

If he could remember, they would never be alone again.

CHAPTER THIRTY-NINE

The cold season passed in a blur of words. Tremlo pressed Jormah constantly for details about his life and those of the people. Stories were maps, and the quality of his questions became more sophisticated and more insistent.

When the first lick of warmth wafted through the mountains, it lasted less than a day.

"When it stays for three days, we will leave," Jormah said.

A month later it came to pass.

Jormah drew a crude picture of a Resep plant on the cave floor. "If the Carooh come back, they will know we were here. Perhaps this will give them hope once again for our return."

It was a cold gray day, and they set out dressed not as Rehloy but Carooh. Weeks later, when it grew warm enough for them to shed their furskins, they tied them into tight balls, hung them off the end of carry-sticks, and slung them over their shoulders. It was awkward and cumbersome but there was no choice.

"We will need these later."

Later?

Tremlo had given no thought to where they were going or what might happen. Jormah told him they were going to observe the Intruders in secret. That they would only reveal themselves if they thought the Intruders would accept them as Spirits-Of-The-Forest. But he had not said how long that would take or how long they would stay amongst the Intruders.

A year? Two? More?

"When we are close to the Intruders, we will bury these," Jormah said.

Of course!

They would need these furskins for the return. How much more had Jormah anticipated?

How might I begin to think in this way?

They came out of the mountains and headed through a hilly forest. The north crackled with tiny, staccato-like musings.

The chatter of a growing horde.

"There are more Intruders now than the last time," Jormah said, heading due east towards the distant undulations of the great waterbody. Fragments of its scent soon peppered the air. Tremlo loved these rich and loamy bits. Here were peaks and valleys and a host of different sensations to explore with each breath.

The trees were changing, favoring those with needle-like leaves that grew better in this kind of soil. Tremlo scooped up a handful of dirt and sifted it through his fingers. The soil was a compilation of tiny grains, each a lightly colored stone-miniature all its own.

Just like us.

"Bka told me of two tribes. The Twie, who live farther south, and the Wollow, who live beside the land-of-great-water. We will soon come to what remains of them."

The Wollow's first encampment contained several oblong structures whose sides were woven into curved walls. Tremlo was fascinated by their shapes. There was no limit to his curiosity now.

The second Wollow encampment lay much closer to the land-of-great-water. At first sight of that blue expanse, Tremlo stopped short. The ripple of the water, the sound of the waves, the fluttering of a multitude filled his body with endless detail.

How many other worlds live just beyond our awareness?

They slept that night beside the water, and Tremlo drifted far out to sea. The farther out, the more diffuse, until he was barely a wisp of wind across this great expanse.

In the morning, flickers of contrast far out of sight woke him. Two objects moving in tandem across the skin of the water.

"Jormah?"

"I feel it. Intruders. Many of them. They will continue north until they reach a wooden path that lines the shore."

Of the two vessels, one held many more Intruders. They felt like tiny stick figures moving about the craft. The other vessel contained a swirl of low motion, less than half the height of a man. This small group moved on four legs.

Tremlo reached out more directly and felt the touch of their awareness. It was weak, but clearly these creatures had a sensitivity to the currents. They gathered on the side closest to shore and sniffed at the air. There was a strong land breeze today, and he knew they had caught scent of him. He reached out, amplifying all that he was, to say hello to them like he had to the groundlings in the forest.

The hounds were playing along the starboard side when something caught their attention. They raised their snouts into the wind and raced over to portside.

"What are they doing?" the ship's captain asked.

The man was affable enough but clearly under Et-El Baronuus's employ.

"I don't know," Bettrie said. She had just managed to climb up on deck, and her mind was still sluggish from the drink the Emperor's physyck had given her. For most of the voyage, she had remained in her cabin, on her back, in a stupor.

The hounds raised their heads and bayed in unison. It was more like a chant than a howl.

"That's odd," Bettrie said, gripping the rail tightly to steady herself. These hounds were the best trackers in all the animal kingdom. She had raised them from pups. They were attuned to her scent, her vocal, and physical commands. They would follow her anywhere and obey her every command, no matter the danger. In the months ahead she would need that kind of loyalty. It was these eight that would help her find Kurr cubs.

"They smell something," Bettrie said. The fresh air was helping to clear her head. "But I've never seen them bay like this."

The Captain quickly scanned the horizon looking for any sign of trouble.

Bettrie took several steps closer to her charges.

"They're communing in some way."

"With what?"

"I don't know."

The hounds stopped and looked around. Whatever was happening had ended. They circled back to the starboard side and surrounded her with hello.

"What other kinds of creatures lurk in this new land?" Bettrie asked, trying to make sense of what just happened.

"Beyond the Kurr? Nothing out of the ordinary as far as I've been told."

They both looked landward, searching for an answer they could not see.

"Why Bettrie," the Captain said in mock surprise. "You're standing on deck!"

"Yes," Bettrie replied weakly. "The steersman said we might reach port sometime next week."

The Captain laughed seeing the ashen look on her face.

"Be at peace, Bettrie. He was teasing. We'll be there in a day or two."

"How do you know?"

"The darcies. You've seen those little birds with the black wings and white faces flying around?"

"I— I haven't noticed."

"They're land birds. They never fly out far."

Bettrie looked about. The sight of the bow bounding up and down proved more than she could bear, and she beat a hasty retreat to her cabin.

"Rest assured," the Captain called after her, "your ordeal will soon be over."

CHAPTER FORTY

Jormah and Tremlo left the waterbody and headed inland. The last of the Resep Jormah planted lay hidden in the forest. Its tones were soft and round, and drew them right to it. The leaves had rough-cut edges, but these juveniles were not sick. The soothing rhythm of the waves rang through their bodies.

"They have a mixed character," Jormah said. "Their proximity to the waterbody has given them hope."

Tremlo ran his fingers across their young leaves.

"What are you sensing?"

"It feels like a greeting and a warning." But he could not fathom what these sensations foretold.

"We will be careful. Let's bury our furskins."

They moved to the top of a nearby hill where water would not collect and dug a shallow grave. Once free of the furskins, they returned to the Resep. Tomorrow they would resume their journey north, but today they would keep the plants company.

With the coming of night an extra layer of tension in the trees and ground revealed itself.

The pressure of things to come.

Sleep amidst this feeling was difficult, and they all reached out to the waterbody for solace.

Tremlo asleep and drifting. Donan appearing in his mind. Side by side, they sped along the tunnel that undulated with urgency. A speck of light appeared in the distance, and reminded Tremlo that he could see. This would be the first time he would do so in this place.

This place.

Memories of what lay ahead gathered in the dark.

Jennifer was sitting on her bed in balance-position, just like a Rehloy might, feeling them coming, waiting for them to arrive.

"Hello," Donan said, and she sprang from the bed.

"I am so happy to see you!" Junnipur cried.

The beat of her heart pounded in Tremlo's chest.

Everything felt too loud, too desperate.

Donan hugged her tight, trying to squeeze the loudness out of her. On the surface, she was Stiffback, but beneath, a Rehloy, struggling to break free.

A sigh of relief, the borders of her body giving way. Here was respite. Here was connection.

Quieter now, and learning quickly, she turned to Tremlo and embraced him in this new way. He held her as Donan had, making space for her to unfold.

In the stiffness of her bones lay fear and loneliness. She was an outcast, hovering between two worlds. Her pain reminded Tremlo of his own.

Jennifer sighed. That part of her separate from her suffering found a way to breathe.

'That's right,' Donan said, but his lips did not move.

They were sitting around the square-topped table on the straightbacked chairs. Their silence ignored the structure and detail the room tried to impose upon them. The chatter of her mind grew still as she listened in this way.

They felt her confusion and despair. Her heightened perceptions had brought an abundance of energy that turned against her. She knew how to assume balance-position, but this was not nearly enough. They felt her twist and turn, even as she sat here in quiet imitation.

"There is the mind-of-the-body and the mind of our Selves," Donan said, reciting lessons all Rehloy learned at an early age. "The mind-of-the-body has a life and intelligence all its own. It often speaks to us in a language we cannot hear or do not understand. It is a great resource and a force to be reckoned with. You must learn who it is, and who you are separate from it."

He paused, feeling Junnipur's tentativeness.

"The sun strikes an object, which casts a shadow. The mind-of-the-body is the object. You are both sun and shadow. You are the energy that comes and the energy that goes. You are the flow."

These were strange words. Arresting. But how to make use of them?

Donan lapsed into silence. Words were getting in the way. The two Rehloy sat in a state of stillness, allowing Junnipur to absorb all she could. Sitting like they did, listening like they did, seeing like they did, a sense of her body and its concerns fell away. For a moment, she was connected to the indwelling life of all things.

The flow. The wonder. If only she could remember....

Tremlo looked about. Here was a room filled with the color of things he had seen only in his dreams.

"You can see!" Junnipur exclaimed, opening her eyes. His were a sparkling, emerald green.

"Yes," he said. The angularity of her face, speaking now in color. A nose, and chin, stronger than his. Thin wisps of hair arching over her eyes. Things he *knew* all along but had not named. It was a pleasing face.

He looked around the room more directly. Her words reminded him to do so. The details of each object seemed to represent a universe all its own. It was far too much to comprehend, but something compelled him to memorize each detail.

Outside.

Donan and Tremlo turned their heads. From somewhere beyond they felt a sharp spasm.

"What's the matter?" Junnipur asked.

Pain!

A desperate struggle had begun.

Beyond the border of the walls that surrounded them came a harsh gasp. A life-force was bowing to pressures far greater than itself. Out beyond these walls, beyond the walls that housed these walls, out on the open ground, someone was alone and dying.

"What's happening?" Junnipur exclaimed.

Both Donan and Tremlo reached out to probe the area and were thrown back into the tunnel.

"What's happening!" Jennifer cried. A vision of her father clutching his chest, the pain now in her own, and he, lying on the ground, half-way down the long dirt driveway leading to their house.

"Remember us," Tremlo called out as they receded from view. Her fear cut deep into his own body. "No matter what happens, remember us...."

CHAPTER FORTY-ONE

The gash in the forest was two paces wide and unrelenting. Everything that stood in its way had been removed, and small stones were pressed into its surface to maintain its form.

It drove straight north into the main body of the Intruders. Here was a sense of purpose impossible to ignore. Its effect upon the currents was undeniable.

"The Intruders are more dangerous than the Yarka," Jormah said. "If we can guide them, we can preserve the sanctity of the *intra*life. If not, our future is uncertain."

Guide them? Tremlo thought. *Is that what we are here to do?*

Jormah stepped boldly onto the path, and Tremlo followed close behind. They settled into a swift and easy rhythm, keeping to its edge for a quick escape.

The air soon became rot-spotted.

The stench of a meat eater.

A Watcher lay in wait.

"We will avoid this one," Jormah said, "and wait till we are further along."

They left the path and circled far to the right to keep out of sight. Once safely past the Watcher, they came back to the edge of the path and continued along its flat back, making sure to leave no sign of their passing.

All manner of practical questions came into Tremlo's mind.

If we avoid the Intruders, how will we know if they will see us as Spirits-Of-The-Forest?

"We will observe them close up and take their full measure," Jormah said, sensing his thoughts. "If they prove too violent and unpredictable, we will leave. If not, we will find a way to present ourselves."

Twice more they left the path and moved past a Watcher hidden along the way. Up ahead, a group of many were milling about.

"We will wait till dark to observe them close at hand."

A windless night. Sound would be their enemy. They moved forward in the stalking manner, their feet sensing the nature of the ground before setting themselves upon it. At times, landing on the balls of their feet, at others, just one toe. In this way they worked their way across the ground in silence.

The glow of light from the Intruders' campfire cast shadows up into the night sky. The pungent, greasy smell of burning flesh stained everything it touched. They breathed through their mouths to minimize its effects. Neither moved until their bodies were acclimated to the rancid odors. Easing to within a hundred feet of the Intruders, they climbed separately, seamlessly, silently, into two different trees, and vanished.

Tremlo counted eleven Intruders sitting or moving around the campfire. Eleven separate rhythms colored by firelight. The outline of their bodies, and their rudimentary movements were a vision of the past. A cacophony of strange words set off a sharp report of laughter that ricocheted from one voice to many. Here was something recognizable. A link, a bond.

The Intruders were preparing to eat. One tended the meat hanging over the fire. Another was mixing something in a large wooden bowl. Those standing about were having lively conversation. There was much prodding and laughter. The emotional content of their bodies was loud and edged with violence, yet none seemed to take offense.

At a certain point, the Intruder tending the meat cut off a small piece and tasted it. After a moment, he nodded and the others lined up, each with a thin slab of wood. They collected their cut and sat around the fire, taking great pleasure in tearing the dead flesh apart with their teeth.

If Tremlo listened to their emotions, he felt pleasure. Thinking about what they were doing made him wary. If he gave attention to the flavor in his mouth, he grew ill.

The Intruders ate quickly, gruffly, finishing all that was before them. In a final burst of greed and satisfaction, they thoroughly licked their fingers clean.

Afterwards, the fire was stoked and more wood thrown upon it. A fat water sack was brought out and passed from one man to another. Each took a long drink. Tremlo caught the scent of rotted fruit. With each pass, the mood of the Intruders grew louder. They laughed at each other's words and a sense of merriment prevailed. They continued to pass the sack until their Leader gave a command that put an end to it.

Mats made of furskin were unrolled and placed on the ground. Several Intruders wandered off to relieve themselves.

One came close to the tree Tremlo was hiding in, but even a Rehloy would not have known he was there. Certainly, the Intruder knew nothing and returned to his place near the fire.

Tremlo watched the unconscious tension in their bodies declare their individual space.

Stiff, uncompromising, separate, cut off, disconnected.

Their language, their banter, the rituals they followed, even the objects they created gave them a sense of intimacy and fraternity. But he saw how it was awkward and false, and the comfort they derived transitory at best. They were so alone.

He saw this and more, and felt sorry for them.

Nine Intruders lay down upon their mats and were soon fast asleep. The remaining two went to opposite sides of the encampment and moved out into the woods far enough from the firelight to remain hidden in shadow.

Instead of sensing-truly, they assumed postures-of-watching, which was the best they could do.

Jormah and Tremlo moved softly into the night and did not stop until they were out of sight of the firelight.

"We will be safe here. We'll sleep while they do, but we must be up before they are."

Tremlo thought as much himself.

The next day, they encountered many solitary Watchers spaced out between groups of eleven Intruders. One group varied little from the next.

The sadness Tremlo felt for them continued to grow, but he could not think of what there was to do. If only he were a bird who could look down from high above and see where all this led. But reaching ahead, the future lay hidden within the turmoil of swirling patterns.

Nothing is decided. Anything can happen.

A large group of Intruders entered the forest and marched down the path in unison. The trees spoke of their coming for miles around. Tremlo counted well over a hundred men.

"They're coming this way," Jormah said. "At this rate, we will meet them tonight."

Ten separate fires, the smell of charred flesh, the perennial stench that was Intruder. Rain was coming and many gray, soft-skinned shelters had been raised. Each possessed a center pole with sides spread wide and pegged to the ground.

Jormah and Tremlo scaled two trees.

There was an edginess to this group. Men ate quickly, quietly, straining to hear words spoken from a group near the middle. Two Intruders were engaged in a heated discussion about a Watcher who stood silently before them. Head down, hands tied behind his back. The scent of fear on his skin, insolence in his body.

One of the Intruders shouted something, and all the others grew silent. Another stood up and spoke what sounded like seven separate words. The bound Intruder was dragged to a large tree near the edge of the campsite. They cut his bonds, pushed his chest against the tree and forced him to wrap his arms around its wide trunk. He could not reach all the way around and they tied his wrists as close together as possible.

A command was shouted, and all the Intruders left their fires. Two from each group lined up before the tree and were handed sticks. One at a time they struck the bound Intruder. His cries, both silent and aloud, punctuated every strike. Some hit him very hard, others less so. Most were conflicted about striking him, but all complied, no matter how opposed they might have felt.

When it was done, they returned to their campfires and went inside their shelters for the night. Several Watchers were posted around the periphery.

The beaten Intruder was left tied to the tree. His bloodstained back stood in testament to the brutal punishment he had received.

What had he done? Tremlo wondered. *Why did they strike him when so many were reluctant to do so?*

The Intruder drifted in and out of consciousness. Pain radiated off his back. His arms were tied so tightly around the tree, they held him up long past his legs' ability to stand.

His arms burned with a thousand tiny pricks, begging for the blood denied them. Tremlo's arms ached with longing. Beyond the man's pain was the pathos of his life. *Of all their lives.* It filled Tremlo's insides, and before he knew what he was doing, he dropped out of the tree and wove his way towards the Intruder.

'*Stop!*' Jormah shouted but dared not make a sound. He could not run after him, for fear of further jeopardizing their positions. Holding fast, he watched Tremlo dissolve through the trees and disappear.

The man had wet himself, and the smell of rot, fear, and pain were mixed now with the scent of urine. Tremlo maintained a defensive-posture through his body while his hands worked quickly to untie the Intruder's bonds.

The man's arms gave way, and he collapsed to the ground with relief and astonishment. Through the haze of pain, he tried to focus on who had released him from this torture. At first, there was nothing, but then, for a brief moment, he saw the youthful face of a wondrous being. Hairless, radiant, its eyes were filled with such empathy, it took his pain away. A hand came out of nowhere and gently stroked his face.

You will be all right, its touch said. *No matter what happens. You are not alone.*

A moment later, the vision was gone.

Wilton strained to see what was no longer there. Was it a dream? A trick of the mind? But his hands had been set free and he had been touched, actually touched, by an incredible being. Whether spirit or god, he did not know, but his life was forever changed. From that time forth he would look constantly about, wishing with all his heart to be seen and touched once again.

Jormah waited by the base of the tree and led them quickly away. Rain was coming, and wet ground would leave signs of their passage. He did not know what the Intruders would do when they found their man untied, or what the man might tell them. But the Intruder had seen Tremlo, and if he told the others, they might start looking for them.

Jormah broke into a run, and Tremlo followed close behind. The smell of rot clung to his fingertips, and he wondered why he had touched the Intruder's face in the first place? Why did he have this overwhelming desire to reassure the man that he was not alone?

Tremlo scooped up a handful of dirt and tried to rub the oily remnants away.

They stopped just before the rain came. Jormah sat down in balance-position beneath a large tree, and Tremlo took his place beside him.

'Why did you do it?'

Tremlo had no answer. He did not know whether it was right or wrong, or even whether this act put them in danger. "I… felt the need," he said after a time.

The Intruder's suffering was like the helplessness of his early life. A part of him had set out to free them both.

"Tremlo, I too felt sorry for the Intruder, but it was reckless to intervene. They know now we are here."

And yet, what was it they knew? That someone or something had released the man? Would they believe it was the Spirit-Of-The-Forest? They could look but would find no trace. And yet, something lingered. Tremlo's actions had instilled the man with hope. Even Jormah felt it.

Is this the message we need to carry? Had Tremlo intuited it?

"It may be wiser," Jormah said, "to reveal ourselves in brief moments. The Intruders' own imaginations may help clear the way. Belief in the Spirits-Of-The-Forest would be an easy matter from there."

Tremlo nodded, but was uncertain.

Nothing is decided yet. Anything can happen.

The rain came with a heavy pour. They sat with their backs against the trunk of the tree. In a short time, they were completely soaked. But rather than using their energy to fight the rain as the Intruders did, they simply sat back and immersed themselves in it.

CHAPTER FORTY-TWO

The cleared land spread out as far and wide as the eye could see.

"These fields have grown," Jormah said. "That hilly area half a day ahead is where they once ended."

They had come to the end of the forest. The few trees ahead were huddled together in fear for their lives.

The land itself was sectioned off with gray, chest-high rock walls. Two bordered the path and followed it straight up into the settlement. There it split into two main thoroughfares. One went to the harbor, and the other turned west, branching out into a cluster of pathways flanked by flat-faced structures.

The core of the settlement.

The fields before them were walled off into sections going east to west, and far out of sight. The rhythms of large animals grazing along the section that bordered the waterbody were easily felt.

"Curvedhorns," Jormah said, and Tremlo remembered.

The crops themselves grew in evenly spaced rows. Their linear patterns spoke of the affliction as surely as anything else.

"We'll stay hidden and observe the Intruders' habits before going farther."

Most of the Intruders were in the distant fields to the west. Some moved on foot, some in carts pulled by curvedhorns. They stopped before dusk and returned to the settlement.

The next day, carts carrying workers came into the field directly across from where Jormah and Tremlo were hiding. Four Watchers and a group Jormah called Others. Tremlo counted ten old men, thirteen women, and four youngers. Jormah thought these were the Wollow and the Twie. They were wearing tattered clothing made from some flimsy material.

Strange ropes were tied between their legs.

'Ropes that jingle while they walk,' Jormah had said.

Heads down, bodies hobbled by ropes, spirits by despair. These were the enslaved.

One of the Watchers said something, and they began to crawl through the rows of waist-high plants, pulling out the small vegetation that grew around them. These they threw into flat baskets that they dragged behind.

The Watchers moved to a nearby clump of trees. Two lay down to sleep, while the other two sat down and tried to stay awake. At one point, one of the Watchers left the shade and marched up to a woman in the field. He shouted at her and twisted her arm, taking obvious pleasure in her pain. She dropped to the ground in total submission. The slaves remained rock-still and kept their eyes on the ground. The Watcher kicked over her basket and yelled once more before letting go. The threat, for now, had ended, and the slaves quickly went back to what they were doing.

When the sun reached the top of the sky, the Others were called in to gather round the trees. Thankful for any respite, they were given thin loaves made from grains and vegetables. Some ate quickly, others chewed slowly, the portions barely enough to support their meager frames.

After a short rest, they were driven back into the field.

At the end of the day, the Watchers herded them into the carts and drove away. In the silence that followed, neither Tremlo nor Jormah moved. The bleakness of these Others' lives and the brutality of the Watchers were unfathomable.

How could they redirect the energies of beings as cruel and forceful as these?

Both wished now only to retreat into the arms of the past. But when darkness fell, they disengaged from the safety of the forest.

"We must be careful, even around the animals."

Tremlo remembered. Jormah had told him about the herders.

"They are scurriers, who on command, do the Intruders' bidding and drive the curvedhorns through the pasture."

Animals commanding animals, commanding animals.

They headed east across the open fields, hidden by the dark, and went all the way to the last wall, which bordered the land-of-great-water.

"Let us rest now."

With few places to hide, it would be too dangerous to sleep during the day.

The next morning, the Intruders gathered and dispersed through the fields as usual. Jormah and Tremlo followed the wall north, ready to drop into a defensive-posture at any moment.

Black-bodied curvedhorns were grazing up ahead, and two Intruders moved towards them. They were dressed in loose-fitting clothing, beige in color, belted at the waist, legs left bare. They did not have weapons. They did not walk with despair.

Neither Watcher nor Other.

One was easily twice as old as the other.

Father and son?

They moved through the herd and stopped beside a calf who was limping along. The older Intruder moved to distract the animal while the younger tackled it and brought it down onto its side. The animal cried out, but the Intruder would not let it go. The older man used a small cutter to dig out a stone lodged in its hoof. As soon as this was done, they released the animal, and it ran off to join the others. They both laughed and continued their walk through the herd.

The exchange was refreshing compared to what Jormah and Tremlo had seen before. If there were these kinds of Intruders, perhaps there was hope after all.

The narrow band of trees standing along the cliffs of the waterbody formed a natural windbreak.

"If we get into trouble or are forced to separate, here is where we will meet."

Tremlo stopped and looked all about.

"What is it?" Jormah asked.

Tremlo did not know.

"Do you sense danger?"

"It feels like a river coming to a place where it gets very narrow."

"This line of trees is narrow."

"Yes."

"The narrower it becomes the fewer choices we have?"

"Yes."

"We will reach the inlet with the wooden path tomorrow. Is that it?"

Tremlo closed his eyes. His body tingled with the collective throb of the Intruders, but nothing more.

They slept that night along the tree-line, but Tremlo did not sleep well. The feeling that something was about to happen would not let him be.

Tomorrow.

CHAPTER FORTY-THREE

"Good journey."

Gremar and thirty members of the tribe set off for a trip to the edge of the Tribal Body.

"When we stand together," Whaet had said, "Our connection to the currents is strong." He believed they should wait for Jormah and Tremlo's return.

"Change is coming," Gremar countered. "We must be flexible and go where it takes us."

"And where might that be?"

"We don't know."

Exactly, Whaet thought. *If this be our end, let it be as we are and have always been. Let us not descend. If we hold true to ourselves, a way will be revealed.*

"This change tests our character."

"We go to explore, Whaet. Nothing more."

Whaet knew Gremar would use this journey for his own purposes. If he forbade him to go, those who were curious would fail to see Gremar's scheming.

It would be best if they discovered it for themselves.

"Good journey," Whaet said again and waited until they were long out of sight. A quiet sense of yearning settled over those who had remained behind. "Be at peace," he told them. "We are the roots that allow the branches to grow."

In the past, Gremar had taken small trips to the northern edge of the Tribal Body with little consequence to anyone. Now he was taking a large group with him. It wasn't the size of the group that he counted a success; rather, it was three of the individuals who were coming with him. With these three in place, everything would follow.

He had planned for the first two. Kenectka was Mahtwah and would bring peace of mind for both those going, and those staying behind. She needed little prodding, and with her coming, he was certain Stelbin would follow. Sure enough, before he could ask, Stelbin declared his intention. No matter the reason, here now was the tribe in microcosm with Mahtwah, Kwaman, and him as Leader.

But when Reena came forward and said she would join them, Gremar could not believe his good fortune. She was the Mother-of-Tremlo. Beyond giving birth to him, whatever touched Tremlo lingered in her. She was often seen listening to invisible forces. She, who dined on finer energies, who sensed things they could not begin to understand, cast her own light. Whenever she appeared, the people drew near.

"What brings you with us?" Gremar had dared to ask.

"What is it you wish to hear?"

"Only what you wish to tell."

Reena nodded absently. When others spoke, she had to force herself to listen. Lately, most of what they said seemed meaningless.

Many were listening now. She felt the push and pull of them. Even Whaet, standing so still, more shadow than substance.

What am I to say?

That part of her that was attached to Tremlo sensed an impending danger. She did not know what it was but needed to know more.

"I go to hear, to see, to smell, to touch. I go to listen. Nothing more, Gremar."

"We are honored to have you with us."

He smiled at her words as if they supported him.

Whaet smiled at her words as if they did not.

Despite her efforts, she had been used.

They set off with Tsute and Railly at the head of the line. These two had gone with Gremar to the southern end of the Tribal Body long ago. Railly's face and body still bore the scars of that awful experience in the swamp. But to the younger members of the tribe, these disfigurements were like badges of courage.

Gremar kept to the middle of the line at first, appearing more like a participant to soften any concerns others might have. Tomar, for one, was one of Whaet's most trusted friends and had come with them.

As they wove their way through the forest, Stelbin felt an openness directed towards himself. Everyone was reaching for a new footing. They might ask Gremar a question, but they would look to him for confirmation.

"The less you say the more they will count upon your words," Donan had told him. *"Do not lead nor follow."*

Stelbin tread ever more lightly and drifted back to where Reena had placed herself.

They coasted along in silence for a time, a conversation all its own. A part of Reena was here on this path, another far away. He listened, his memory of her then, his sense of her now. She was marked by deeper strands.

"You have felt something," he said, keeping his eyes ahead.

Reena took a moment to consider. Their roles were changing. She had always harbored a tender spot for Stelbin, especially for the kindness he showed Tremlo early on. He had matured quickly these last few years.

"What has the Kwaman said?"

"He waits and watches, as we all do."

Donan had gone into seclusion shortly after Jormah and Tremlo left. Stelbin was the only one who saw him these days. Reena thought Donan's influence on him was obvious, but there was something else just as strong, and in that moment, she realized she did not know Stelbin at all.

He has become Kwaman.

"Two days ago, I awoke to a pressure, inside," she said touching her abdomen. "As the day passed, it grew stronger."

"You think they're in trouble?"

"There is a rising tension. The farther they go, the more pronounced it becomes. Tremlo is worried. With each step, there are fewer possibilities."

"In what way?"

"The flow of the currents is contracting. When the compressed energy is released, it feels like a whole new set of circumstances will burst forth. More than that I cannot say, and even this I am unsure of."

What she perceived loud and clear was not even a whisper for him.

"Do you fear for them?"

"I am... wary."

Stelbin nodded and thought a moment,

"What do you think of this journey we are taking?"

"It is irrelevant."

Was she speaking of now or the future?

Stelbin did not know.

They approached the edge of the Tribal Body, and it withdrew from their collective weight. Many would have been content to stop, but Gremar had other plans.

"We all know of the disorientation that occurs when we step outside the Tribal Body. If we stick close together, it may have less of an effect upon us."

If we stick together, we may be able to create an intralife all our own. And if so, how much stronger his position might be.

He lowered his shoulder and led the way straight through the edge.

A burst of air. Released and exposed simultaneously.

Dizzying.

Everyone drew closer, except for Reena. Pinned beneath a mountain of unbridled sensation, she dropped to the ground and sat where she had stood. Gremar came back, but she waved him away. Kenectka was beside her and placed a hand on her shoulder.

It was only Stelbin who reached out to the north and tried to gain some sense of what it was she was sensing.

"Are you alright?" Kenectka asked.

"Yes." Her voice was thyck.

"It doesn't sound so."

"It will pass."

Kenectka stepped back and signaled everyone to make space.

Reena allowed the sensations to take full possession of her. To resist them would only prolong them.

'*It begins,*' she said to Stelbin with a look.

It begins.

"We will stay here for the night," Gremar declared. "Tomorrow, if Reena is feeling better, we will move on."

"I'm feeling better now," she said, insisting they set off once more.

Unsheltered by the Tribal Body, they kept close together, almost touching. Soon, all began to feel a subtle energy surround them.

Lighter than air, a collective sigh.

The hint of an *intra*life all their own.

CHAPTER FORTY-FOUR

"Commander, one of the slaves is missing."

"Missing? From where?" Kriiton demanded. He was tired and heard the irritation in his own voice. Incidents of resistance and outright refusals were occurring more frequently. But this was the first attempt at an escape in many years.

"From the new diggings."

Bettrie had arrived with a mandate from the Emperor and set them to digging an immense basin where she would train the beasts.

"When?"

"Early this morning, we think."

"You think?"

"A section of the wall collapsed and buried seven slaves. The first three they uncovered appeared dead. They dragged them to the side and went back to rescuing the others. It was not until later that they realized one of the dead was missing. Apparently, he had not been dead as first thought."

"Apparently. And when was this discovered?"

"Not too long ago. He's had about half a day's start."

"In what direction is he headed?"

"South, we believe."

"I see."

"Shall we use Bettrie's hounds?"

"No, not yet. Let's see how efficient our Augmentors are. Have them set up a roving patrol along Main Row."

"Understood. He's probably wounded, Commander. We should have no trouble getting him back before long."

"Let's hope so. I don't want a full-scale rebellion on my hands. The slaves must remember there is no escape, save death. Make sure he is caught and brought back alive. Do you understand? I want him back alive! Send a physyck along to make sure."

"Understood."

"And send word when you catch him. I will have the slaves assembled to witness his return."

"Understood."

"Who is it, by the way?"

"The one called Telt, of the Carooh."

"I should have guessed. They've been trouble from the start. Does this Telt have any family?"

"His mate died last year. They had no offspring that we know about."

"Find out who his closest friend is. If they think they can do what they please without repercussions, they still have much to learn."

"Understood."

Kriiton was not immune to the slaves' plight. Perhaps, in an ideal world it would be different. But there was a natural order to life. The pattern could be seen in every aspect of nature, and man was no different. One ate or was eaten, whether one realized it or not. There were the powerful and the weak. If you were listened to, you were the eater; spoken to, the eaten. Kriiton valued life, and if the slaves would just accept their role, it would ease their burden, and he would not be forced to take such harsh measures.

Why don't they see this?

When Telt was dragged out from under the collapsed wall, he wasn't breathing. The wind had been knocked out of him, and he lay there frozen. His shinbone was broken, but worse, his knee was crushed.

As he lay there, unmoving, he knew this was the end of him. In a day or two the leg would turn green and then black. They would have to amputate the leg or he would die. Ontarans had little use for one-legged cripples and would probably kill him outright. Or if they let him live, he would become a burden to his people.

It will be better to end it now.

This was not the cataclysmic struggle he imagined would end his life. Just a simple thought. As easy as saying he was tired or that he did not want to eat. Knowing now that he would die, his only wish was to choose its time and place.

He dragged himself into some nearby bushes. From there, he crawled on one knee with his bad leg trailing painfully, heavily, uselessly, behind. Beyond the bushes was a small wooded area where he fashioned a crutch. His bad leg cried with each step, but he would not stop. He would take back his life, and in that final moment, know that it was his.

He came out of the woods and crossed over the central path the Ontarans called Main Row. From there he headed off to the field that bordered the sea. Once he reached the high bluff, he would stop and wait, and at a moment of his own choosing, throw himself into the wet-and-waiting arms of the water far below.

A surge of pressure. Tremlo's ears popped. Immense forces were crushing the world to a standstill. He waited, watching, barely breathing.

A ripple of pain shattered the air and split the world in two. Intruders were rushing about at one of their diggings. Another surge came, and then another, and another. A multitude of paths converged through a single point in time before bursting into the fragments of things to come.

It begins, he thought, drifting through bits and pieces of a nearby future.

Tremlo. Tremlo?

"Tremlo," Jormah insisted, pulling him back into this moment. "Keep close to the wall."

They headed towards the harbor and arrived at an area where the ground reached its highest point. In the distance, a single being was heading towards them. His movements were erratic. Farther behind, and out of sight, a group of Intruders were coming on fast.

'*Let's stop here,*' Jormah signaled.

They sat before the wall that bordered the waterbody and disappeared into full defensive-postures.

The air filled with the oncoming man. Dressed in dirt-covered rags, limping painfully.

One of the Others, Jormah thought. Something oddly familiar about this one. His overall size and carriage, the irregular motion disguising much of whom he might be. Details of his face became clearer the closer he got.

Telt moved as fast as he could. There was a flat ledge beside a group of trees just ahead. It was clearly visible to any who might pass by. He would wait for the Augmentors there and show them that he would rather die than live under the weight of their rule.

That is where I will live. That is where I will die.

He went right past Jormah and Tremlo, and Jormah saw without a doubt that it was Telt.

But how?

The truth dawned on him and tore at his heart.

"Telt," he called out after him. "Telt!"

The old man heard his name, twisted round in fright and fell to the ground. An explosion of pain!

"Telt. Telt," Jormah said, kneeling beside him.

"Bhytoe?" Recognition spread over Telt's face and body. "Bhytoe!" He grabbed his arms. "Bhytoe!"

A whirl of words.

Save me. Save us, he begged, tears flowing down his face.

"Telt," Jormah said, helping him to sit up. "Telt," his voice filled with compassion.

The agony of Telt's body, the collective agony of his people. Wave after burning wave of it. Jormah tried to steady him with his eyes.

When Telt finally stopped crying, words came pouring out again, fast and furious, telling of their capture and all that had happened.

"The Intruders ambushed the Carooh," Jormah repeated softly to the air about them, "and brought them here."

Telt looked but saw no one.

"His leg is ruined, and if left like this, it will kill him. I know of no remedy but to cut it off, but he refuses. He means to die here. You may show yourself."

Tremlo slowly released his posture, and Telt gasped at the sight of him.

"He begs us to go forth and help the Others."

"Is there nothing we can do for him?"

"We can make him comfortable. He was heading to that ledge."

Tremlo pointed to the Intruders, who were out of sight but drawing near.

"Yes, I know.

"Will they kill him?"

"I don't know, but there is no place for us to hide him. We will stay close and see what can be done."

'Help me.'

They lifted Telt over the wall and carried him to the ledge.

"Save the others," Telt begged. "Please, Bhytoe, save the others."

"We will try," Jormah said.

The Intruders were almost there.

"We must leave you now."

Telt nodded, and the two moved to the nearby tree they would hide in. Jormah turned to wave goodbye and the shift in his weight caused a small twig to snap beneath his foot.

An instant later, the ground lifted up around them. He leaped sideways to push Tremlo out of harm's way but fell through empty air.

Tremlo had assumed the posture-of-speed and vanished.

Jormah scrambled to get up.

A giant web, constructed from layers of rope and attached to a tree limb yanked him straight up into the air.

He compressed his chest and hurled himself into the posture-of-speed. But his leg had slipped between two layers of rope and was locked tightly in place. The sides of the web were already up over his head. As long as he maintained the posture, the web would be as hard as rock and hold his leg fast.

"I'm stuck," he said.

Tremlo was standing beneath him, radiating at the same speed.

"I will have to release this posture to free my leg."

But by the time he freed it, the top of the web would be closed.

"I will climb up and together we will cut you free."

"No. Watchers are almost here. I am caught. You stay hidden. Together we will find a way, but for now you must hide."

Jormah released the posture, and the net snapped up and over him.

"Slave-trap," Telt was wailing. "Slave-trap! Bhytoe! You are caught in their net!"

Jormah freed his leg and tried to cut through the net with his cutting stone, but the rope was strong and resisted his blade.

"Look! By the ledge. There he is!"

Both Tremlo and Jormah assumed defensive-postures and disappeared. The Intruders would find their trap sprung but empty.

Telt was standing as best he could, inches from the ledge. He was going to take his life, but now that the Bhytoe was in danger, he had a reason to live, even if it was just for a while longer. If he could distract the Augmentors, perhaps they would not look too carefully at the slave-trap.

Nine Augmentors spread out before him.

"Halt!" A voice from the rear. It was Regert, one of the less brutal Augmentors. "Telt," he called out. "Do not be afraid. We will not kill you."

Telt laughed a false laugh.

"You see my leg? How can you kill someone who is already dead?"

Regert came forward from the left, drawing Telt's attention to him.

"Be careful, you might fall. Trust me, we will not harm you. We've brought a physyck along with us. He will tend to your wounds."

Another Augmentor closed in from the right. He kept low to the ground and inched forward, unfurling a lightweight man-catcher.

"Telt," Regert said. "What happened today? Were you injured in the diggings? What are you doing here? Did you think—"

The Augmentor sprang forth, throwing the net over Telt's body. A quick pull on the rope locked it, and caused Telt to fall forward, howling in pain.

"Be careful with him!" Regert shouted, turning his attention to the slave-trap. The net was swinging gently in the breeze. It was empty, and yet, the spring-limb was bent as though something heavy was inside.

"Telt, what happened here?"

"I fell near the edge and set off the trap. I just managed to roll off."

Regert wondered how that could be. The trigger stick was always placed near the middle. The net was empty, but there was something odd in Telt's voice.

"Commander," one of the Augmentors said. "Just as we came over the hill, I could've sworn there was something in the trap. I couldn't see what, but, but now I guess I was wrong."

Regert nodded. There was nothing to be seen, yet the shape of the net was irregular. He moved closer to investigate.

"My leg!" Telt began to holler. "You said you'd help me with my leg!"

Regert looked back at Telt. *What is he trying to hide?* He took a spear from one of the Augmentors and carefully poked it through the bottom of the trap. Jormah was standing near the back with his legs parted. The spear came through the front of the net and passed several feet in front of him. The second pass was closer and the third closer still. Each pass moved with that methodical precision characteristic of these Intruders. In another pass or two the point of the spear would touch him.

As the Watcher withdrew the spear and prepared for another pass Jormah assumed the posture-of-speed. Tremlo appeared a moment later on a branch beside him.

"I am caught."

"We can try to cut you out together."

"It will take too long."

"Maybe he will stop."

"No, not this one. If I move to another part of the net it will begin to swing from the weight of me."

"I could divert their attention."

"It will do no good to reveal your presence. We have come to see if we can guide these people. Sooner or later, we have to interact with them. Now is as good a time as any for me to do so."

Tremlo said nothing. The sound of that twig snapping was an integral part of the chain of events he had been sensing all along.

Knowing without knowing.

"It's my fault," Jormah said. "Had I trusted your abilities, I would have assumed the posture-of-speed when you did and we would not be in this predicament."

But Tremlo saw only that they were in the midst of a current far more powerful than themselves. Everything that happened could only have happened this way. He did not know what would come next but sensed real danger elsewhere.

"I will know you are near, and together we will find a way. Stay close. Be careful, but no matter what happens to me, keep hidden unless I call you."

Tremlo nodded.

"If I should die, if they should kill me, you have to get back and warn the others."

Jormah pushed his fingers through in the net. "Come closer, so I might touch your face."

Tremlo climbed over, and the Kwaman traced the ancient sign across his forehead. The touch of his finger gave Tremlo a chill. Jormah was performing the final ceremony that declared a Heart, Kwaman.

"You have owned this sign since the day you were born. You are still young, but you have the ability to become one of the greatest Kwamen of all time. Let your perceptions be your guide. Be what fate has given you."

Tremlo was fighting back tears.

"Go now. I cannot hold this posture much longer. Get into position and hide."

Tremlo dutifully climbed down and hid behind a nearby wall.

Regert was about to push the spear through the back section of the net when it started shaking. A form materialized, and they all jumped back.

What is that?

It sat down in a casual manner and stared at them.

Jormah kept his attention squarely on their Leader.

Where the head goes the body will follow.

He held Regert with a gaze that was neither soft nor threatening, but curious. Inviting. All encompassing.

I will be a cup for you to fill. Make of me what you will.

For the longest time, no one moved. The creature's body was vaguely green in color and also blended in with the net. It was covered in a wondrous material that looked like both leaves, and a layer of skin.

Leaves or skin? If leaves, they were a kind Regert had never seen before. He took a tentative step forward and raised his spear in a threatening manner.

Jormah felt no malice. The Watcher was testing him, and he remained quite still.

Regert pushed the spear slowly through the net and thought to touch this creature with the tip. The serene expression on the creature's face did not change

"Stop! Stop!" Telt cried. "Do not harm him. He is the Bhytoe. The Spirit-Of-The-Forest. He is the Bhytoe. The Bhytoe!"

"The what?"

"The Spirit-Of-The-Forest."

Jormah did not understand most of the words Telt used, for they were not Carooh but Intruder. But he did understand the word Bhytoe.

"Telt," Jormah said. The depth of his voice conveyed a sense of calm to all. "I will be fine."

Regert withdrew the spear and turned to Telt, "Did this Bhytoe help you to escape?"

"No! I came here to die. It was only here in this place that he suddenly appeared."

Telt called it the Bhytoe, the Spirit-Of-The-Forest. *Did that mean it was some sort of god? Had it come to collect Telt? Or save him? Was it caught in their net or just pretending to be?*

"You have met this Bhytoe before?"

"He came to us long ago and lived with us for a season."

"Are there others like it?"

"Only him. He is the Bhytoe. Nothing in the forest will harm him, not even the Kurr. He is the Spirit-Of-The-Forest."

Regert turned back to Jormah.

The creature's body was trim and its arms and legs well defined. Its muscles, however, were not particularly large or bulging. Not exactly the body of a warrior. Yet there was a sense of power in this creature, like a weapon at rest.

Its face was smooth; its body hairless. It possessed a soft feminine quality, but Regert thought that it was male in nature. The creature did not seem to be afraid. The fact that it was caught in their net did not seem to bother it in the least. Was this a bluff or foolishness? Did it not know the power of Ontar?

Or is it so powerful that we count for nothing?

"Who are you? What do you want?" he demanded.

The Intruder's language was gruff and the overall cadence different from the Carooh's. If there were common words, they were almost unrecognizable.

They do not know what to make of me, Jormah thought. *Not knowing is making them fearful.*

Fear was a useful tool, but their fear would keep him held captive in this net. He thought of Tremlo's encounter with the Watcher tied to the tree. Easing the borders of his body, he tried to follow the emotional path of this Intruder.

"Speak," Regert said, his voice trailing off. The creature somehow appeared more familiar and less threatening than a moment ago.

"Telt," Jormah called out. "Tell them I felt their weight upon the land and came to see what manner of being they are."

Telt translated what he said.

"Tell him this is our land," Regert replied harshly, "and he is trespassing."

"The land belongs to the land," Telt said translating the Bhytoe's response, "no matter who might claim it. But do not worry. He says he will not interfere."

Regert did not know what to make of this. The Bhytoe was speaking from a position of strength. Yet he was caught in their trap.

What would Kriiton do?

The men were standing about, their uncertainty growing.

"Grath," he called out. "Run to Kriiton. Inform him that we are returning with the slave and that we have found something else as well. Go! We will carry both of them back with us."

The Augmentor ran off.

"Drusoe, go to the nearest relay post and signal everyone that we found the slave. Then catch up to us."

"Understood."

Regert turned to the others. "Make preparations. Lower the net but do not let this Bhytoe out. Make sure the top is secured."

The Augmentors did as ordered and added extra topknots. Jormah remained seated in balance-position as the net was lowered. Afterwards they inserted two carry poles through the top and hoisted them up onto their shoulders.

"He's a lot heavier than he looks," one of the Augmentors said as they headed back towards the settlement.

The Bhytoe sat so still, there were moments when he seemed to disappear.

"It's hard to see him clearly."

"But he's still there, right?" another asked.

"So far."

Those Augmentors walking along the side kept their swords drawn. None of them noticed the slight rustle in the air that followed along the rock wall. Nor did they notice the blades of grass that lay down only to spring back up a moment later.

Tremlo is too close, Jormah thought. He turned his head in such a way that only Tremlo would notice.

Move back.

But Tremlo wanted to keep as close as possible.

Get back, Jormah's body said again with greater urgency.

Tremlo slowed and allowed them to move on, but he would not let them get too far ahead. Following in the stalking manner, he assumed a new defensive-posture with each step.

They came to a place where there was a small break in the rock wall. It was gated and one of the Watchers went ahead to open it. They left the field and proceeded on along the central path that led directly into the settlement.

Jormah could feel a shift in motion ahead. Word was spreading and Intruders gathering.

People lined up along either side of the path to wait and see the slave the Augmentors had caught. There was just enough room to allow the procession to pass between them.

Tremlo could not hide within an area so thick with people.

If something terrible were to happen….

He scaled the wall and rushed forward, trying to keep parallel along the outside.

"Make ready!" Regert said as they approached the people.

"There's the slave!" someone called out.

"What's that in the second net?" another asked.

"I can't tell."

Jormah felt the bite of a hundred eyes.

"It looks more like a bush than a man!"

Some laughed as they passed by. Some stepped forward with knives drawn, acting as if they were going to stab Jormah through the net. Others shouted or made threatening animal noises.

The tension in Regert and his men increased. They readied themselves to drive the crowd back at the first sign of trouble.

They fear the actions of their own people.

This was a realm of violence. Nothing was safe, not even the sanctity of their own kind.

Once they passed, the onlookers on either side quickly fell in line behind them. All were hungry for a better look at this strange creature.

Tremlo circled wide to avoid the growing throng and lost sight of Jormah and the Watchers carrying him.

Through everything, Jormah did not move. He held his gaze straight, his mind clear, and his body free from the chaos about him.

CHAPTER FORTY-FIVE

"Commander," Randol said. He was now Kriiton's Second after Martel took sick. Unbeknownst to him, Kriiton was considering making the appointment permanent.

"Speak."

"Word has come. They found the slave and are bringing him back."

"Alive?"

"Alive."

Kriiton nodded. The quicker they were done with this business the better.

"Who is the Charge?"

"Regert."

"Good. He'll follow my orders. Have all the slaves brought to the practice field."

"Understood. There is something else. They found Telt sitting near one of the slave-traps along the high bluff. The slave-trap was sprung, but empty. Regert poked the net with his spear, and a creature suddenly appeared inside."

"Suddenly appeared?"

"I'm only repeating what the messenger has told me."

"Is he here?"

"Yes."

"Bring him in."

The Augmentor was brought in from the next room.

"What is your name?"

"Grath, Commander."

"What nonsense is this, Grath?"

"It's truth, Commander."

"Smell his breath!"

Randol did as ordered.

"Free of drink, and his eyes are clear."

"All right, Grath, tell me exactly what happened."

"We came up to the net, and it was empty. But the spring-limb was bent, like there was something inside. Regert started poking around and next thing we knew, the net began to shake. Out of nowhere the Bhytoe appeared."

"The Bhytoe?"

"That's what Telt called it. He said it was the Spirit-Of-The-Forest, and that no one could hurt it. Regert made like he was going to stab it, and Telt screamed for him to stop."

"Where is this Bhytoe now?"

"They're bringing it here with Telt. They're both netted."

"What does it look like?"

"It's kind of blurry and hard to see."

"Hard to see? Does it have arms and legs?"

"Yes. It looks like a man, but it's different too. It doesn't have hair, and its color is, well, it's hard to say. It seemed to be covered with leaves."

"Leaves?"

"Or maybe it's skin. I wasn't there long enough to get a good look. The slaves believe he's a god or something."

"A god? Caught in one of our slave-traps? Ha! I doubt it. Leave us."

Randol waited until Grath was out of the room. "Commander, do you think it wise to bring this Bhytoe here now? The slaves are in such a state of unrest."

"If they believe it to be their god, and we can control it, controlling them will be that much easier."

"But what if it is a god?"

"Are you superstitious?"

"Just raising the question."

"And right you should. However, if it is truly a god, it does not matter what we do. It will do whatever it wants to do. Therefore, I see no reason to delay. Bring it here. We'll expose it for what it is, and put an end to this rebellion once and for all."

The outskirts of the settlement were threaded with canals. Some filled with water, others still under construction. Regert led them across a wooden bridge that arched over several. Tremlo was forced to circumvent it and fell farther behind. Jormah's presence was nearly drowned out now by the punctuated rhythms of those around him.

One part of Tremlo felt the stillness in Jormah. There was no sense of fear in him. Another part was far ahead. Here lay that sense of *knowing without knowing.* Fear was not called for, *not yet.* But danger was coming, and he needed to be there when it happened.

Others were being herded into open field.

So many, Jormah thought, a dissonant hum, too numerous to count.

The character of the Intruders around him was changing as women and children joined the fray. Taunts and threats were giving way now to curiosity. Through all the noise and confusion that surrounded him, Jormah kept a portion of his senses trained on Tremlo. The faint traces of his movement helped ground him. But if real trouble came, he did not think Tremlo would be close enough to stop it.

"Let them understand the futility of escape," Kriiton said once all the slaves were in the practice field. "Line them up in rows so they can all see."

The sooner they accept their station in life, the better their lives, and the safer for all of us.

Three complements of Augmentors surrounded them. If there was any trouble, the slaves would be driven inwards and made to collide with one another.

The entourage led by Regert came into view, and Kriiton went forward to greet them.

Jormah recognized the man almost immediately. This was the same one he had seen long ago. Older now and no longer dressed in white, but his bearing was the same, with his long dark hair tied back in a tail. The deference in the others at his approach confirmed he was their Leader.

Regert called a halt to the procession, and the Watchers carrying Jormah put him down rather hard. The Leader looked past them to the large group of Intruders that had been following and barked out a command. This mass of people rapidly moved past them and stopped beside the field ahead.

"Congratulations, Regert. You have done well," Kriiton said, purposefully ignoring the creature in the net. "Tell me everything that happened. Facts first, then your impressions."

Regert carefully related all that transpired. Twice Kriiton stopped him with a question. When Regert finished, Kriiton turned to Telt.

"When will you learn there is no escape? If you accepted your fate, all would have gone as destined. Now your actions will cause many to suffer."

Kriiton turned away in disgust and took a moment before turning his attention to the creature. He dropped down on one knee and looked directly into Jormah's face.

Jormah stared quietly, unhesitatingly back.

Here is the one who will decide my fate. Here is the one I must convince.

The Leader gave him a menacing look.

Fear was something these Intruders understood well.

My lack of it confuses them.

Each took the full measure of the other. Jormah easily felt the man's reflex point and thought of the game of armrue.

What if I closed my mind around it? What would he think if his hand rose up of its own accord and grasped his face?

Jormah nearly laughed aloud at the prospect. But the Leader might see it as an act of aggression, and Jormah had no doubt the Intruders would kill him if they felt threatened.

Softening the borders of his body, he absorbed the emotional tones of the one before him and reflected the familiar sensations back to him.

Kriiton decided the hairless creature looked more like an innocent child than a supposed god. The open expression on its face, the exquisite green eyes and delicate features. The slow expansion and contraction of its chest. Despite himself, he began to feel compassion for it.

Standing abruptly, he walked around to study it from another angle. The clothes the creature wore clung to its body like skin, just as Grath described. *Clothes or skin?* The color shifted in subtle ways as if possessing a life all its own. Even as he looked, it seemed to be green, then brown matching the net, shading into gray, then green again, making it difficult to see it clearly.

Regert said the net was empty when they first came upon it. It would have been hard to see anything like this from below. That made more sense than the creature materializing out of nowhere. Besides, it appeared so soft and reserved, there was none of the strength or vibrancy he imagined a god would possess.

It is a creature, Kriiton decided, feeling somewhat reluctant for what must follow. *Unique certainly, even special, but a creature just the same.*

"Bring them both!" he commanded. "If the slaves believe this is a god let them see how it fares when confronted with a power such as ours."

The slaves saw the small group of Augmentors coming towards them, carrying two nets. In less than a day, they had captured Telt and brought him back. The message was clear. There was no escape.

But who, they wondered, *was in the second net?*

Bka glanced quickly left and right. Vazdi and Aelor did the same. All three leaders looked at each other.

Not one of ours.

The Carooh were last to be captured and still the most obstinate. Bka's body was covered with scars of resistance. His acts of rebellion had gained the respect of the other slaves and brought him authority amongst the three tribes, but he had been unable to inspire them to similar acts of defiance. They had been here too long, and he came to understand that blatant resistance to these Ontarans did not work. They were too well schooled in the art of enslaving others. The only way of defeating them would be to watch and learn and master their ways.

Bka had studied them carefully this past year, and in their ardor for organization he had found a flaw. Once a pattern was established, they almost neve,r varied from it. Their weakness was in their consistency. Knowing their forms, one could find the cracks, and in so doing make a viable plan for escape. But they needed to be brave and patient, and they needed more weapons. To date, they had two swords and one spear hidden in the slavetrees. But that was not nearly enough.

There were endless discussions about the best route for escape. Some said north, others said west, through the land of the Kurr. It was reasoned that southern regions were too well developed and patrolled. But the north was a daunting place, comprised of rugged mountains and bitter cold winters. Aelor of the Wollow had suggested escape by water. If they got enough of a head start, they could paddle northward and follow one of the inland river-ways west all the way to Clear Water Lake.

But Bka had seen the power and speed of the Ontarans' sailing ships. They could easily overtake those paddling a stolen boat. Even if they were unsure as to the direction the slaves had taken, they need only send two boats out, one to the north and the other south to quickly capture them.

No, we will have to forge our own little army.

Surprise would be on their side. From the established patterns of the Augmentors, Bka saw the possibility of capturing the night guards and their weapons. From two swords they might increase their lot to six, then ten in quick succession. If they captured enough of the important men, or their families, they would have something to bargain with. And even if they failed, he would rather die taking many Ontarans with him than bear a lifetime of slavery.

The Augmentors carrying the two captured slaves were drawing near.

But who was the other one? A tribesman who managed to keep himself hidden all this time? Or some poor soul who inadvertently wandered into this accursed land?

Telt was shouting something, but with all the murmuring and noise Bka could not make out his words.

"Bka th...b...Bh....bk...b...toe."

Bka tensed up. Telt was frantic. Whoever was in the second net did not move, making it impossible to see him.

"Bka! T..Bh...toe."

The hair on the back of Bka's neck stood up.

Bhytoe?!

He took several steps forward.

"Bka!" an Augmentor called his name in warning.

"The Bhytoe," a Carooh called out from somewhere down the line. "It's the Bhytoe!"

"The Bhytoe?" Bka called out. "The Bhytoe?"

"THE BHYTOE!" he screamed, recognizing Jormah at last.

The guards surrounding the slaves felt the sudden tension.

The Augmentors carrying the nets stopped.

And then the Carooh charged.

The Wollow and the Twie had heard stories of the Spirit-Of-The-Forest but only half-believed the Caroohs' tales. Now the Carooh were declaring this creature the Bhytoe, and they trailed after them.

The Augmentors closed ranks in front, and those from the sides pressed in, driving the slaves into themselves with clubs and whips. Those who tried to fight back were pressed into the throng of their own people. The Wollow and the Twie were quick to stop, but the Carooh did not. Bka was felled by two quick blows. They threw a choke-rope around his neck and tied his hands behind his back. The other Carooh, men, women, and even children, fought on, trying to get to their beloved Bhytoe.

Kriiton was annoyed. This new captive should have reemphasized the almighty power of Ontar and reminded the slaves of their place. Instead, it was having the opposite effect. Once open rebellion of this sort began, it would be nearly impossible to stop without killing many of them. This was something he did not want, nor could afford to do.

Drawing his sword from its sheath, he turned to his personal guard. "Aim your spears at the creature's heart and await my orders!"

The Carooh surged forward, and Kriiton thrust his sword through the net, placing it against Jormah's throat.

"I will kill him!"

That stopped them. Some began to cry; others dropped to their knees and begged.

Jormah knew Kriiton's maneuver was a threat, for it did not feel like he meant to kill him, but he would leap into the posture-of-speed if need be.

Tremlo moved swiftly from object to object, working his way closer. Outwardly, this threat appeared real enough, but he too did not feel that Jormah's life was in jeopardy.

Let your perceptions be your guide.

Real danger was coming, of that he felt certain. Just not yet.

And not here.

The Carooh dropped to their knees and bowed in submission. Kriiton nodded and slowly withdrew his sword.

We have to get rid of this creature, he thought, realizing that whatever happened, its very existence threatened the colony. They couldn't kill it outright for fear that it would spur the slaves into an all-out revolt.

It cannot die by our hands, but their god must die just the same.

"Bring Bka!"

Two Augmentors dragged the bound Carooh over and dropped him at Kriiton's feet.

"Bka, is this the one you call the Bhytoe?"

Bka nodded. The sight of Jormah in their net filled him with unspeakable sorrow.

"And you believe it is what you call the Spirit-Of-The-Forest?"

"Yes. He is the Bhytoe."

"And nothing in the forest will harm it?"

"Nothing."

"Well then, we certainly don't want to hurt it either. If what you say is true."

"It is true."

"Why should I take the word of a slave?"

"I was not always a slave."

"True enough. And we all wish to know the truth. Untie Bka!" Kriiton ordered. "And bring forth ten slaves." He looked back at the creature. It had not moved a muscle. Even when he placed his sword across its throat, it had not moved.

Bka's bonds were undone, and he rushed over to Jormah.

"Bhytoe, you have come back!"

"It is good to see you, my friend."

"We will not let them harm you! We will all die first!"

"I do not wish you to die."

"We are prepared to do so all the same."

"I see much has happened since last I came this way."

"We found the warning you left on the cave floor, but we did not understand its meaning. We prayed for you to return to explain it, but years passed. Then, as one warm season approached, we heard the Ontarans coming and sent eyes to see. They also sent eyes and found us. When we left our caves for the trek to the hunting grounds, they were waiting for us. Some of our people ran back to the caves. But the Ontarans had snuck up behind us and were there waiting for them. They killed three, tortured more and then brought us here. We have been here ever since."

"What can you tell me of these Ontarans?"

"They are a harsh and terrible people. Each moon more arrive. They come from a place far away, on the other side of the great-water. There they are said to be as bountiful as the leaves in the forest."

"Why have they come?"

"To take possession of the land and everything on it."

"So it seems."

"Have you come to save us?"

"I am here to learn their nature and see what changes can be made."

"You will help us?"

"If it is within my power to do so, I will."

Kriiton stepped forward.

"I see your Bhytoe speaks your language." He turned to Jormah. "Do you understand mine?"

The creature seemed to think a moment.

"Bka, tell your Bhytoe what I just said."

Bka did as ordered and then translated Jormah's reply.

"The Bhytoe says he does not yet know your words, but he senses the meaning behind them."

What does that mean? Kriiton wondered. *Such a strange creature. It's a shame we won't have time to study it.*

"Bka, I give you and your people my solemn promise that your Bhytoe will come to no harm by any Augmentor's hand."

"Why should I believe you?"

"I have never lied to you. We will not kill him. If anything, you will."

"Never!"

"Your words have already condemned him. Charge! Return the slaves to the trees."

The slaves lived in primitive huts built across the tops of trees stripped of their leaves and branches. Beneath the trees lay a field of poisoned spikes. There was only one way up and one way down. Those who tried to escape met certain death.

"Bka and these ten slaves are to come with me."

"Understood."

A group of Augmentors surrounded them and Kriiton led the way, signaling the two carrying the netted creature to follow.

When they came near the first bridge, he called a halt to the procession. Two Augmentors were sent on ahead before they resumed. Kriiton dropped back to walk alongside the Bhytoe. The creature was still holding that relaxed pose, barely moving within the sway of the net.

Jormah felt deception in each step Kriiton took. Far ahead, the two Augmentors veered off the main path and moved towards a tall, conical structure. They opened its massive door. From inside came the distant but unmistakable scent of a Yarka.

He looked at Kriiton. A faint smile came to the Leader's face. A moment later it was reflected in his own. Kriiton quickly turned away, and by this action confirmed everything.

A small path split off from the one they were traveling on. At some secret signal, the Augmentors closed in around the slaves and drove them onto the small path.

"The pit! They're taking us to the pit!"

Yes, thought Jormah, hearing the fear in their voices. "Bka, tell the others not to be afraid. The Intruders are not going to harm them."

"But what of you?"

"I am not afraid."

Bka told the others, and the tension in their bodies turned to concern for him.

"Bka," Kriiton asked. "What did the creature just say to you?"

Bka hesitated and looked over at the Bhytoe.

"You may tell him," Jormah said, surmising Kriiton's question.

"The Bhytoe said we are not to worry. That you are not going to harm us."

"Your Bhytoe is correct."

"And for himself," Bka added. "He is not afraid."

"Good," Kriiton said, keeping the irritation out of his voice. He wondered if the creature was trying to cast doubt in his mind. It acted like it knew what was going to happen, but if so, how could it not be afraid?

We'll find out soon enough. Soon enough indeed.

The structure ahead was made of shaped stone, its beige surface smooth and crafted.

Like the work of the ancestors, Jormah thought. The interior walls were also smooth and amplified the rhythms of the two beasts in the pit.

It was there that the Intruders expected him to die.

It is there that much will be decided.

To his right, just off the path, came a reassuring tone.

I am with you.

Tremlo had felt that terrible moment fast approaching, and it was no longer just a feeling.

I am with you.

Jormah nodded ever so slightly.

Around the final bend, and there it stood. The entrance was open and the beasts, sensing their approach, roared in anticipation. The Augmentors pushed the slaves inside and lined them up around the waist-high stone wall rimming the pit.

Kriiton expected a violent reaction, and the Augmentors were prepared for a fight. But instead, the slaves grew quite still. Some were afraid to peer over the edge, others curious about the Kurr below, but none acted as though this was to be the end of the life of their beloved Bhytoe.

How can they possibly believe this poor creature will survive the wrath of the Kurr?

The beasts, circling below, became more agitated with each passing moment. First one and then the other began to leap up. Each jump brought them higher, until their claws nearly reached the soft wooden cross bars.

Good, Kriiton thought. He wanted their rage and their violence. *Let it be over quickly so that the creature does not suffer.*

This last thought took him by surprise. Empathy and compassion were dangerous emotions. They were not ones a leader could often indulge in. He stepped back and signaled the Augmentors to bring the creature in.

The interior was exactly as Jormah felt it to be. The pit itself was deep, its sidewalls pitted. There were no handholds, and it would be nearly impossible to climb out of it.

If the scent does not work, there is always the posture-of-speed. But how will I get out?

Tremlo snuck in, less than a blur, and disappeared against the wall where a coil of rope hung.

The Augmentors carried Jormah to within twenty feet of the pit wall and put him down. They untied the top of the net and stepped back. Their swords were drawn, but if they expected him to run, they were mistaken. Jormah stood slowly, and the net fell away. He stretched, arms, legs, torso. In one way a man, in another, completely different. His movements were indescribable.

Jormah ignored them and kept his attention split between the beasts and the Leader. Kriiton was standing perfectly still. He meant for this to be the end of Jormah, and yet, Jormah caught a whiff of uncertainty. Some secret part of Kriiton wished that it would not be so.

The tension in the room grew palpable. A sigh issued forth from Kriiton's chest. The struggle was over. The look on his face, severe. In the next moment, he would order the Augmentors to throw the Bhytoe into the pit.

I must control the moment, Jormah thought, *not them.*

To their surprise, the creature moved towards the pit of its own volition.

It knows its fate, yet shows no fear!

Jormah stopped beside the stone wall surrounding the pit. There would be little room down below for them to get out of each other's way. The vile creatures' eyes flared with excitement at the sight of him. If he dropped down, they would have him long before he touched bottom. Better to bring forth the scent now before the Intruders had a chance to throw him in.

The Augmentors thought he was faltering. He hopped onto the top of the wall before they made a move against him. Spreading his arms wide, he brought forth the scent with fear-inspired intensity. He shouted it through his body with all his might. From behind, the same rhythm rushed forth to amplify his own.

Tremlo.

One of the Yarkas leaped up to make a grab for him. As it rose up, it breathed in the air to savor the smell of its intended victim. It was halfway up when Jormah's scent hit.

The beast let out a blood-curdling scream and threw its body into contortions to stop its upward thrust. As it fell back down, it batted its nose with its paws to drive this searing smell out.

To those standing around the edge, it appeared as though the Kurr leapt up, saw that it was the Bhytoe, and began to scream in fear. Jormah leaned forward, projecting this smell downwards as best he could. A moment later, both beasts were crying like newborns. It was this sound that frightened the Intruders more than anything. The beasts drove their faces deep into the floor of the pit and piled dirt onto their heads with their front paws.

The Carooh dropped to their knees.

"Bhytoe," they whispered, "Bhytoe. Bhytoe."

Kriiton and the Augmentors were in shock. Some wanted to kneel, others run away. Some tightened their grip on their weapons. Jormah dropped his arms and softened the borders of his body.

Kriiton, at a loss for what to do, stood rock-still. Jormah felt his indecision and his fear. If allowed to fester, he might act rashly.

I must control the moment, not them.

Stepping down from the wall, he walked back to where the net lay and sat down upon it.

Kriiton, waking from a dream, signaled the Augmentors to retie the net. The two who stepped forward kept their heads low, as if apologizing for their actions. They raised the sides of the net gently and tied them together once more, this time making sure that the creature had plenty of room to move around inside.

"Return the slaves to the trees," Kriiton said softly. "Bka, you stay with us."

The Carooh moved slowly past Jormah, aching with love, bowing in homage. The Augmentors did nothing to speed them along. Indeed, some of them were tempted to do the same.

"We will take the creature to the fortress," Kriiton said, careful to avoid the term Bhytoe. "Charge, have Bettrie sent for."

"Understood."

"Now!"

The Augmentors lifted the carry poles onto their shoulders and raised Jormah off the ground. This time, however, they did so with great care.

CHAPTER FORTY-SIX

Tremlo breathed a sigh of relief. It had been a grand demonstration. The door to the Intruders' hearts had been opened.

"Take the side path," Kriiton said.

Word of this incident would spread quick enough without them fanning the flames. He would post guards around the outside of the fort, as much to keep the people out, as to keep the creature in.

Creature.

He could not deny what he had seen.

Could it actually be a god of some sort?

Kriiton was not a religious man. Over the years he had come to recognize a certain symmetry that gave the world its form. Some believed Ontar was the center of the universe, but he dismissed this notion.

We are nothing compared to what has come before, and what will come after.

In his mind, there was the seen world; the realm of sight, sound, and touch, the world of substance. This was the world he lived in, and to some extent could control. The concerns here were for food, shelter, procreation, society. Beyond this was the unseen world. It framed them, and some said made them. Ultimately, it contained them. Its influence could only be guessed at, and by its very nature never truly understood.

There were stories about the birth of the world, and the struggle between colossal forces. Some of these stories were simplistic and designed to comfort children in the dead of night. Others were more complex and tried to account for the terrible destruction that befell the world long ago.

Intervention, some had called it. *Judgment. Providence.* Stories of trials and redemption. The foibles of man held up to ridicule by the gods. Stories to build character. Stories to build philosophy. Stories that tried to make real, imagined ways of being.

Seen verses unseen.

By definition opposites, so how could one version describe the other?

The Way-Of-The-Sane had come out of such stories. It was the religion that bound them to each other, and would prevent an *Intervention* from ever occurring again. It spoke about the realm of man and that of the gods. It taught that there was but one evil and that it always began as a thing of wonder. It began with the Electrix. This was an intelligence outside the physical body of man. It was a force that belonged to the gods, a thing man could cause to do his own bidding and, in so doing, stray from his station in life.

This was the first step on the WayWard Path.

According to legend, the Electrix had given rise to such terrible power that a single man could defeat an entire nation. The gods had allowed it, and the price for man's hubris was the destruction of the world.

Nowadays, anyone found dabbling in the Electrix was instantly put to death and their family and possessions burned. There could be no exceptions and no leniency. Tolerance quickly led to the spread of the WayWard Path.

All this was known and helped keep men in their place.

But in all the stories Kriiton heard or read, there was nothing that described anything like the diminutive creature sitting in their net.

The Spirit-Of-The-Forest.

The description was vaguely satisfying.

The creature had submitted itself to their control, but was it really held captive by their net? Or simply pretending? The incredible effect it had on the Kurr was undeniable.

"Bka, tell me of the Bhytoe. What else can it do?"

"Do?"

"What other powers does it have?"

Bka shrugged, "The Bhytoe is the Bhytoe. He is all-knowing."

Not exactly, Kriiton thought. The creature did not know the Ontaran language.

"Tell me what you know of it. Tell me the stories."

Bka eyed Kriiton with suspicion.

"There are no stories," he replied. "Many years ago, the Bhytoe came to stay with us. He learned of our ways, and then he was gone."

"And that was all?"

"Yes."

"How long did *it* stay with you?" He did not want to commit yet to giving the creature an identity.

"He lived with us for one season and part of another."

"What did it do while it lived with you."

"He came to learn of us."

"Learn of you?"

Bka wondered how much he should say. "The Bhytoe once wrestled with evil spirits that were making us sick and drove them away. Another time, he saved us from starving by telling us where the animals were hiding."

"I see," Kriiton said. "How long since you last saw it?"

"We have not seen the Bhytoe for many years."

"Did it ever tell you anything about the past?"

"No."

"Did it give you a set of rules to follow?"

"Rules?"

"Laws, principles to live by."

"Why should he? He is the Bhytoe. He is he, and we are we."

"I see." Kriiton was convinced Bka was hiding something. He would question him again later, and again, and again until he got it out of him.

Jormah listened to the struggle within Kriiton's body as he tried to fit the idea of the Bhytoe into the context of his world. The machinations of the mind-of-his-body were formidable. It would not let go lightly.

The massive, gray-stone walls of the fortress stood heavily upon the ground with blatant disregard for the currents. As it came into sight, there was a flurry of activity. Huge wooden doors were opened, and several Watchers lined up on either side of them.

Tremlo moved quickly along a drainage gully that ran parallel to the path. It ended a good distance from the structure, and he stopped. The area that led up to the doors was flat and open. He crouched down and waited for the small procession to reach the entrance.

As they carried Jormah through the doors, Tremlo assumed the posture-of-speed, and once inside, found a discrete corner in which to hide.

The courtyard was hundreds of paces long and wide. The sides and back were lined with large wooden shelters whose overall shapes were squared.

Squares within squares. The signature of the ancestors.

The walls were whitewashed and uniform.

In the center of the courtyard was a large garden that stood in contrast to the straight-lined walls. There were bushes bearing brightly colored orange, yellow, and red fruit. Tall plants with rose colored bulbs adorned one section. Several rows of green crawlers with narrow white beans another. Paths were threaded throughout, and there was a deep hole with water near the center.

Three Intruders dressed in simple gray robes came forth to greet them. The Leader issued a quick series of orders. Two went off to a place where food was kept and the other off to one of the shelters.

"Close the gate!"

Jormah felt the guards outside the structure come into place before it.

"Put the creature down."

The Augmentors lowered Jormah gently to the ground and carefully removed the poles. One began to untie the rope that held the net closed.

"Stop!" Kriiton said. "We're not ready to release it yet."

The guard gave Jormah an apologetic look and backed away slowly. Kriiton noted the man's reluctance.

What kind of danger have I brought into our midst?

He made a mental note to send this Augmentor off to the furthest outpost before nightfall.

"Bka, let the creature know we are preparing a room for it. We hope to make it comfortable."

Bka said something, and the creature answered him back.

"The Bhytoe says he would be most comfortable here beside the garden, but the corner room is fine if you wish it."

"How does he know it is the corner room?"

"The Bhytoe says it is the room you have sent one of those dressed in gray to prepare."

"And what of the other two?"

"He says they are in the back preparing food. He wishes to express his appreciation, but he has no need. He eats only his own food."

"Does he know how many guards are outside the fort?"

Jormah paused a moment to count.

"He says there are fourteen standing in front of the gate."

"How does he know this?"

"He says he can feel their presence."

Feel their presence?

"Ask him what I am thinking of at this moment."

"You are wondering what else the Bhytoe knows."

A shrewd observation, but not exactly what he was thinking. Here was another example of a limit to the creature's power. He was not all-knowing.

But is that the mark of a god? That everything is known?

"Is he a god?"

"He is the Bhytoe. The Spirit-Of-The-Forest."

"Ask him!"

The question was one Jormah hoped to avoid. The Intruders were much more sophisticated than the Carooh. As long as the truth was undefined it could be crafted and honed.

"Are you a god?" Kriiton asked again.

Jormah thought for a moment.

"The Bhytoe says that is for you to decide."

"So this is a test of some kind?"

"There is no test. There is no challenge. He means you no harm."

"Then why is h— why is *it* here?"

"To learn of your ways. He says that you should not worry. He will not leave without first telling you."

Again, the presumption of power.

What if I choose not to let you go? What if you can't get out of the net? What if all that you've said is a ploy to convince me otherwise?

Kriiton looked hard at the Bhytoe. It was such a soft and gentle creature. He regretted keeping it in the net.

Why am I feeling this way?

His mind cried out for caution. An unknown force was in their midst. It required clear thinking. He could not be swayed by emotion.

The guard-of-the-gate announced Bettrie's arrival. Kriiton never thought the day would come when he would be glad to see the Animal Trainer. She was such a nuisance. Her arrival in the colony had meant a squandering of resources they could ill afford.

Under Baronuus's stamp, she immediately ordered the excavation of an area to be used for training. This coming winter Kriiton would have to field a large contingency of Augmentors to capture hibernating Kurr cubs, and he anticipated a loss of many men.

Bettrie's face was flush.

"I see word has reached you," Kriiton said. "Let's speak in private."

He led her down into his command room and closed the door.

"Tell me what you've heard?"

"They say you captured a creature the slaves believe is a god. You had it thrown into the pit to prove them wrong, but instead of being killed, the Kurr bowed down before it and cried in fear. Is that so?"

"Who did you hear this from?"

"An Augmentor."

"What else did he say?"

"He asked if it could be true. And he wondered if keeping the creature bound up risked offending it."

"Anything else?"

"The slaves are very restless. Everyone wonders how much longer they can be contained."

"The slaves will be kept in the trees until they calm down. If it comes to it, we will starve them and remind them that their resolve will not sustain them."

"In their current state of mind, they may find their belief in this creature sustenance enough."

"Perhaps."

"It's true then?"

"What?"

"What happened in the pit."

"Close enough. Although I am not sure I agree with the interpretation."

"What exactly did happen?"

Kriiton gave her a detailed account, and when he finished, Bettrie began to ask questions.

"You said the Kurr tried to bury their faces? How?"

"They were covering their heads with dirt."

"Their entire heads?"

"Mostly their faces."

"What were they trying to do? What part of their faces? Their eyes, their noses, their mouths?"

"I'm not sure. The pit is too deep to see clearly. Does this have significance?"

"Possibly. How are they now?"

"I don't know. Randol!"

His Second was stationed just outside the door.

"Yes, Commander."

"Send someone to the pit and let us know if the beasts have returned to normal."

"Understood."

"I would like to see them for myself."

"Later. For now, I want you to come with me and study the creature. It's imperative we understand what we have in our midst and what its intentions are. Afterwards, I want you to tell me your impressions."

"What am I looking for?"

"I want you to tell me whether you think this is an animal or some kind of god."

"You believe the slaves?"

"I believe the truth. The slaves have their version. From what I've seen today, I understand their view. However, we are citizens of Ontar. I need to know what our truth will be. Come. The less I influence you the better."

From a distance, Bettrie could barely see the creature. It was sitting so still, there was little to distinguish it from the net. As they drew near, she slowed her approach and stopped a respectful distance away.

The creature looked directly into her eyes. Its eyes were the greenest of greens. Bettrie smiled softly and gave a slight nod, hello. The creature nodded back and smiled in the exact same way. In motion, it caught all the nuances of her face. Bettrie was surprised. A moment later she saw her own surprise on the creature's face.

I see you, it seemed to say. *I know you.*

Magical. Disconcerting.

She had never seen anything like it.

The creature possessed an ethereal, child-like quality that evoked feelings of care and empathy. The longer she looked, the stronger these feelings became.

An inner hush came over her. She turned her attention to its body and saw how the color of its skin, or clothing, blended in with the surround.

No wonder it is so hard to see.

She moved slowly around to the side, maintaining a respectful distance. The creature ceased to follow her with its gaze.

Look all you want. I don't object.

Its color seemed to change with each step. Back around to the front, she took a step closer and kneeled down. From there she sat back on her haunches just like the creature was doing. She rested her hands evenly atop each leg. There was an elegance to this posture, but her legs began to cramp, and she was forced to sit back on her buttocks.

She smiled apologetically.

The creature returned it in kind.

She matched its breathing in the hopes of picking up on other traits. There was a sleepy kind of stillness here. She had observed this in animals. A special kind of listening that focused on many things at once. But they would snap instantly to a focused attention at the first sign of danger.

A ripple shimmered across the surface of the creature's skin. Stunning in its way.

Was that a reflection of something it was sensing?

Her shoulder twitched and was instantly reflected in the creature's.

Hello.

Its whole body could repeat all that it perceived. No wonder the slaves called him the Spirit-Of-The-Forest. *Is that what you are? A spirit, a god of some sort? And what about the Kurr?* There was nothing those beasts feared. Yet, this unassuming creature had struck terror into their hearts.

Is there a dark side to you?

It was difficult to imagine that the creature posed any threat. Bettrie leaned forward and placed her palm against the net.

Are you substance or illusion?

Jormah saw that she wished to confirm in her body, a question in her mind. He met her hand with his own, matching its texture, tone and rigidity. Bettrie felt as though she was touching a hand like her own.

Solid, firm, real!

Their fingers intertwined through the holes in the net and locked in that embrace.

The same, Bettrie thought. *We are the same!*

Different, Jormah thought. *We are so different.* Bettrie's bones were stiff and heavy and stood within her skin like the branches of a tree. A Rehloy's bones could be kept rigid like this or made soft and pliant.

The moment Bettrie's grip softened, Jormah's did the same. To Bettrie, it felt like they released their grip simultaneously.

We are like-minded.

She sat back, filled with the presence of the light before her, and her heart swelled with possibility.

What wonders might we learn from you? What new ways of seeing, of being?

A connection was already growing between them. She was sure it—

The touch of a hand upon her shoulder startled her. She looked up to see Kriiton's stern face. Standing wordlessly, she followed him back to his command room.

Jormah felt her reluctance to go and her anticipation at returning. He was intrigued by this Intruder. She had approached him in a way unlike any other Intruder. She sat down and tried to adopt his posture. This was how a Rehloy might approach someone new. Within this action lay a sense of compassion.

There may yet be hope for these Intruders.

"What do you think?" Kriiton asked as soon as they were inside.

"Incredible," Bettrie said, barely able to contain her excitement. "I think he is very special."

"Do you think it is a god?"

"I don't know. Have you ever come face to face with a god?"

Kriiton was silent.

"Neither have I."

"Fair enough. So, what do you think?"

"I think he may be a living, breathing being like you and me, but one with extraordinary abilities. The real question is, would a god take on the form of such a creature?"

"And?"

"Given the creature's natural abilities, a god would be better served by one of him than one of us."

"Agreed." Kriiton was beginning to appreciate the subtleties of this Animal Trainer's mind. "So you can't say what it is for sure."

"No, not really. Not yet. Has he said anything?"

"What do you mean?"

"Has he declared what he is, or what he's doing here?"

"I asked if it was a god, and it said that was for us to decide."

"Interesting."

"And it said it was here to learn of our ways."

Both lapsed into silence, one pondering the infinite, the other the finite.

"Do you think it is dangerous?" Kriiton asked.

"The unknown always is, but I do not think he is violent."

"Do you think there are others like it?"

"If he is an animal, there would likely be others of his kind."

Kriiton then told her everything that had happened, including the creature's knowing how many men were standing guard outside the fortress gate.

"They were not there when we brought the creature in. When I asked how it knew, it said it 'felt their presence'. What do you make of that?"

"I think his senses are much greater than ours. Like a beast who can see at night or one that can smell its prey a great distance away. His perceptions may be equal to or greater than any being we have ever encountered."

Again, she thrilled to the notion of what his awareness must be, and wondered then what he might be making of them.

"Do you think it can disappear or become invisible?"

"You mean does he have magical powers? I don't know. Birds fly. That is commonplace. If a man were to fly, that would be miraculous."

"You think we have something miraculous in our midst?"

"Yes. But we do not know yet if he is divine." And yet did it matter if he were a god or not, if he brought one to a godly state? Bettrie shook with possibility.

"What do you think we should do with it?" Kriiton pressed.

"You keep calling him, 'it.'"

"And I will do so until we know differently. Now what do you think we should do with *it*?"

"Communicate with him and learn all we can. We should release him immediately as a show of good faith, whether he's a spirit, a god, a messenger of one, or simply a fellow being."

"I am not willing to do that."

"You may risk upsetting him."

"It seems perfectly comfortable where it is right now."

"I suppose."

"You suppose what?"

"He's doing everything he can to make us feel comfortable. Doesn't that tell you something?"

"No, it does not. Enough talk. Let's go. You can question Bka about the creature to your heart's content."

They left the command room and walked back to the garden where the creature was sitting in that quiet manner of his. Had he moved at all? Bettrie smiled, and Jormah smiled back. Bka was near the front wall guarded by two Augmentors. Kriiton signaled them to bring him over.

"The Bhytoe must be set free!" Bka demanded.

"In good time," Kriiton replied. "Be assured we have no wish to harm it."

"You must set him free!"

"We will, once we understand it better."

Bka spoke to the creature, who answered him.

"You cannot lie to the Bhytoe."

"You accuse me of lying?"

"No," Bka said carefully. Slaves were beaten senseless for far less. "I only say what is true for him."

"So he does not believe me?"

"You cannot lie to the Bhytoe."

"I see. I have three brothers and two sisters. Ask it if this is true."

Bka did as he asked.

"The Bhytoe says he is still unfamiliar with your words. He asks that you speak them once more."

"I have three brothers and two sisters."

As he spoke, his body did not amplify his words. There was an inner shift and a flash of scent, gone as quickly as his words. Once again, Jormah was amazed at how obvious these Intruders could be. They were not a stupid people, but they were blind to the language of their senses. Smell spoke as loudly as words. Thoughts assumed shapes within the body. Surely, given who they were, if they understood how much they gave away, they would take measures to disguise it.

"That is not true."

"I have two brothers and two sisters," Kriiton quickly said.

"No."

"I have two sisters and one brother."

"No."

"What do I have?"

"The Bhytoe says that is for you to say."

Kriiton's mind was whirling.

"I am Kriiton, son of Storen."

"That is true."

"I will live to eighty years of age."

"That is not for the Bhytoe to say but for you to discover."

"I wish to return to Ontar."

A complex mixture of smells issued forth from the Intruder's skin. Jormah sensed layers of competing textures.

"That is both true and false."

"What am I thinking at this moment?!"

"You are thinking of something else entirely."

Again, the clever evasion. However this was nothing compared to the startling fact that the creature could discern truth from lies!

Kriiton signaled Bettrie to come with him. Outwardly he maintained a level of calm, while his mind was nearly bursting with possibilities.

Jormah felt his excitement.

Let the myth grow.

Kriiton closed the door to his command room and began to speak softly, "Do you think it can hear us?"

"I don't know. But he does not know our language."

"So he has said." *He.* He could not hold back the tide any longer. "He also said he sensed the meaning beneath it."

"Given what his awareness must be, that makes sense."

"What do you think of what we just witnessed?"

"It was remarkable."

"Do you understand the implications?"

"Implications?"

"The creature knows if we are lying. How incredible a weapon that would be. Not only can he control the fiercest beast we have ever encountered, but with his aide, truth would prevail. No one could hide from it! Whoever controlled him could control all of Ontar!"

Bettrie grew pale.

"As Newland Commander, I formally charge you with the task of befriending the creature and discovering all you can about him. We need to learn his strengths and, more particularly, his weaknesses. If there are others like him, we need to capture them as well."

A wave of nausea came over Bettrie. She had just begun to imagine the possibility of a new era, ushered in by the advent of the creature's arrival. A new way of thinking, of being and understanding. Kriiton's words were a sharp reminder of the ways of Ontar, and she wished now that the creature was divine, that the net could not hold him, and that he would not succumb to their ways.

Kriiton eyed her with suspicion.

"If I am to befriend him, you have to allow me my methods."

"Within reason."

"What if I wish to free him from the net to gain his trust."

"No. I am unwilling to do that just yet. As far as we know, the net is the only thing that is holding him here."

"That and his good will."

"So he would have us believe. If he is merely an animal with exceptional abilities, then there are physical laws that must be obeyed."

"If he thinks he is a prisoner, he may be reluctant to cooperate. Besides, how will the slaves react to us holding their god trussed up in a net?"

"If we enslave their god, he is a god no more."

"I am not sure they will see it that way."

"Bettrie, are you seriously willing to take a chance and allow him to escape?"

Bettrie was taken aback. The thought of losing something so profound was suddenly so terrible, her insides contracted.

I have to get to know him! To learn from him. To help him to get to know us.

In her heart of hearts, if there was any chance….

"No," she said softly, shamefaced. *Not yet.*

"I would consider manacling him, but not before we are sure they would hold him as well as the net."

"If trust is the issue, manacles are the same as a net."

CHAPTER FORTY-SEVEN

Tremlo and Jormah felt the tension behind the closed door. It was a struggle of wills. Tremlo wanted more than ever to cut Jormah out of the net and be gone.

Wait and see, the Kwaman's posture said. *Wait and see. These are both our forefathers, and children who have lost their way.*

Daylight was fading. Bettrie and Kriiton returned, and Bettrie sat down in front of Jormah. She smiled a sheepish grin. Jormah smiled sheepishly back. Bettrie's smile widened, taking Jormah's with it. They looked deep into each other's eyes. Bettrie was suffused with feelings of care, empathy, and now longing.

"It's getting dark," Kriiton said. "Bka, does he want to stay out here for the night?"

Before Bka could ask, Jormah made a sign with his hand indicating this place in the garden.

Did he just sense the meaning of my words?

"As you wish."

"I will stay with the Bhytoe tonight," Bettrie declared, and Kriiton gave her a look, before relenting.

"Bka, come with me. The slaves are restless. You will assure them we are taking good care of your Bhytoe."

They left for the slavetrees accompanied by four Augmentors.

"We mean you no harm," Bettrie said, hoping some of her words would be understood. "I am trying to persuade Kriiton to release you." *I am your friend.* "Perhaps tomorrow he will listen."

The creature had an expression of care on his face.

Does he understand?

It was getting too dark to see.

Bettrie signaled one of the house servants. "We would like a fire."

They rushed about, and in a short time, a small fire blazed. In the freshly minted dark, the Bhytoe's eyes melted into liquid pools of flickering light. The more Bettrie looked, the farther in she was drawn. Details gave way to hues of feeling. Here lay hopes and dreams of a different life. In the Bhytoe's face she felt total acceptance, in his manner, unconditional love.

"I will not let anyone harm you! Not Kriiton nor any Augmentor. This I promise."

Jormah felt the intensity of her words and saw she was pledging herself to him.

For what purpose? What did she foresee?

One of the servants came tentatively forth and asked a question. Bettrie indicated *yes,* and a short time later, plates of meat, bread, and legumes appeared. She offered Jormah a plate of meat, but the Bhytoe turned his head as if put off by it.

"Take this away," Bettrie said, upset with her blunder.

The servant withdrew, and the Bhytoe seemed to relax.

The Spirit-Of-The-Forest.

It made sense. She offered him bread and legumes. The Bhytoe did not appear offended but took something out from what Bettrie saw now was a pouch. *Clothing, not skin.* Another miracle. The Bhytoe began to eat something greenish-white in color.

They ate separately, together. A quiet moment shared.

Tremlo, hidden in the corner, reached into his own backsack and ate along with them. In the calm of the moment, he felt his own fatigue. The events of this day were exhausting. He needed a place to sleep, but it would be too easy for someone to stumble upon him in this corner.

On the far side, atop the back rooms, a large roof overlapped a smaller one. In the space between was a place he could take shelter in.

Jormah felt a soundless shift of movement and kept his attention on the one called Bettrie. He was prepared to create a distraction if anyone came near to noticing, but he need not have worried. Tremlo flowed forth with no beginning and no end, invisible to all who might chance to look in the dark.

Scaling the wall, he eased himself into a comfortable position under the overhang. From here he had an elevated view of the courtyard below. He took one look around, closed his eyes, and was fast asleep.

"Bhytoe, we have so much to learn from you," Bettrie was saying. "Sitting here before you, I feel as if you know me. Like you have always known me."

A gentle smile crossed Jormah's face.

Be an empty cup for her to fill.

When Kriiton and Bka returned to the fortress later that night, Kriiton sent Bka straight over to them.

"Bka?" Jormah asked. The Carooh's upset was very loud.

"Kriiton said if the slaves rebel, you will be the first to be killed."

"And you believe him?"

"He said Ontarans were not the Kurr and not afraid of you. He tried to have you killed once."

Is this what Bettrie feared? But why do I not sense I am in danger? Even from the one called Kriiton. He keeps his distance, but I feel his constant attention. They do not know what to make of me, but I am highly prized.

Kill me? No. If anything they are afraid to let me go.

"Bka, what did you just say?" Kriiton asked.

"I told the Bhytoe I had been to visit my people."

"And?"

"That was all."

"Seize him."

Two Augmentors grabbed Bka's arms and drove him to the ground.

"Your Bhytoe is not the only one who can tell the truth from a lie!"

Kriiton turned sharply towards Jormah.

"These people are our property. We will not allow them to be taken from us! Bka, tell him what I just said. And from now on you speak to him only as ordered, and only the words we tell you to speak. Do you understand?"

"…Yes."

Bettrie gave Kriiton a hard look.

'*We have no idea how he might react to this!*'

'*Do not contradict me!*' Kriiton's body shouted back.

Their senses spoke all this and more.

Jormah knew this demonstration of violence was meant for him. In the struggle for control, nothing was yet established.

The Intruders must be kept off balance. The power lies in their not knowing.

"The Carooh do not belong to me," Jormah said with a well-placed yawn. "You and they may do what you will."

"But you are their Bhytoe."

"No. The Spirit-Of-The-Forest belongs only to the forest."

We shall see, Kriiton's body said. *We shall see.*

But there was less conviction in him than before. He sat down next to Bettrie. He could not show weakness. The Animal Trainer had to know that.

"What happened since I left?"

"The Bhytoe ate something."

"You gave him food?"

"He refused what I offered but ate some of his own. It looked like the pulp from a plant."

"Where did he get it?

"From a pouch. The leaves on his body are clothing, not skin."

"Well done. That is good to know. So he eats."

"And drinks. I offered him some water which he accepted."

"I see." *Do gods have need for sustenance?* "What else have you learned?"

"Nothing in particular. The Bhytoe and I are just beginning to get to know one another."

"Bhytoe is a slave word. We need to call him something else."

"Like what?"

"Bka. Does the Bhytoe have a name?"

"The Bhytoe says you may call him Jormah."

"Jormah?"

The creature smiled and said his name directly to them.

"Jormah."

It was a strong voice that suggested unsuspected capacities.

"Jormah," Kriiton repeated.

"Kriiton, Bettrie," Jormah said to each. He not only spoke their names, but somehow evoked their natures with his tone.

It was astonishing.

"He…. He knows our…. Did you tell him our names?"

"No."

They lapsed into silence.

Looking at the creature for any length of time was like staring into the flames of a fire. It was easy to lose oneself to ever-changing patterns of possibility.

In lieu of words, a quiet sense of wonder grew.

Kriiton glanced over at Bettrie and saw the look in her face.

Yearning.

It was something he himself felt.

"It grows late," he said gruffly. "Bka will sleep in the room originally prepared for the Bhy— for Jormah. Guard! Bring the slave to the corner room. Chain him and post a guard at the door."

"Understood."

"I will retire for the night. Bettrie, you're staying here?"

"Yes."

"Tomorrow, you will join me at first meal. We will talk then. Goodnight."

"Goodnight," Jormah said.

Both were startled.

"He's a fast learner, or he knows far more than he's letting on. Your task is clear Bettrie. Remember where your duty lies."

Kriiton walked stiffly to his room and closed the door solidly behind him. Despite himself, he was falling under the creature's spell. All he wanted was to sit beside Bettrie and stare at Jormah.

I want his friendship. I want his approval. I want to rip open the net and free him from his bonds!

What is this hunger, this weakness?

"Jormah is an animal just like you," he said aloud. "An animal just like us. Keep your wits about you. Do not give in to the wiles of your heart!"

Even as he said this, he knew he was failing in his duty. The wonders of this creature and the possibilities he presented threatened the very framework of the empire. Here was an enemy that worked not from the outside, but from within.

Kriiton was a citizen of Ontar; a commander in its army and the leader of its new colony. His duty was clear. Jormah should be done away with this very night.

But first and foremost, and before all else, he was a man.

Only a man.

And because of this, he hesitated.

CHAPTER FORTY-EIGHT

As the small band of Rehloy moved through the world beyond the Tribal Body, their bodies reached out to one another for balance and support.

You see? Gremar's body said. *You see?*

Embryonic sensations were creating an *intra*life all their own. Different from what they were used to, surprising in their newness.

"We will go north for a day," Gremar said, "and see what it is like."

Without a word, everyone followed.

Let them gain confidence in what I do. Let them see what is possible.

They followed him in close-knit fashion, testing these new sensations. Caution gave way to fascination. Gremar walked slowly to accommodate the growing weight of their curiosity.

Let them linger and absorb. Let them see how I lead with just the right amount of give and take.

Reena kept to the rear as was her want, and Kenectka came back to join her. When Reena, Arlen, and Tremlo first left the confinement of the still-cave, Kenectka ceased to visit them.

"Tremlo must come out into the world and visit me," she had insisted. As a result, she and Reena spent much less time together in the ensuing years.

Reena recalled the young woman, whose rambunctious and high-spirited nature bore little resemblance to the one before her. Away from the tribe, away from Mortulla, it was even more apparent that Kenectka was a serious presence in her own right.

She is quieter than she used to be, Reena thought. The youthful chatter of her body long gone, in its place a deep and abiding tone.

'How are you today?' Kenectka asked with a look.

Memories drew them closer.

'I am well.'

"How are things for Tremlo and Jormah?"

"Worse."

"What do you mean?"

"I fear some calamity is upon them."

She said no more, and they walked in tandem. These two women who had Tremlo in common.

"You are different than you used to be," Kenectka ventured after a time.

"You have changed as well."

"I have matured, yes. But I remember what you were like before Tremlo was born. You are different."

Am I? She, who had gone through so much, who had suffered along with her son, who even now was shifting and changing.

"It is not that I have changed. Those old parts were an expression of another time."

And now? Kenectka wondered, looking more carefully. Reena appeared simultaneously young and old. The surface of her skin lacked the wrinkles of repetitious thought, while her eyes possessed a *knowing* beyond her years. There was a watchfulness both near and far. Tremlo often had that look. There were many qualities these two shared.

She is not Tremlo, or her old self, but something different.

"It is not that I have become something different," Reena said, as if hearing her thoughts. "It's that I have... let go."

Let go? In what way? "Can you say more?"

"A seed must shed its shell in order to grow into what it was meant to be. If not, the seed will live its life as a seed-within-a-shell, from beginning to end."

Reena felt the ground beneath her feet, the air across her skin, the sky upon her shoulders, marking her own passage through the world. It was right to think of this now.

She looked over at Kenectka with sudden insight.

We are intertwined. Our futures are intertwined.

"We'll stop here for the night," Gremar declared as darkness fell. They made camp and slept beneath the thin cover of this new *intra*life. The next morning everything felt more aligned than the day before.

Gremar anticipated a discussion about where they would go next, but no one said a word. Not even Tomar, whom he thought would voice some opinion on Whaet's behalf. Everyone simply stood, ready to follow, expecting him to provide drive and direction, freeing them to explore whatever they chose along the way. Gremar set off immediately to hide his surprise. It all felt so natural.

By the end of the day, the weight of the *intra*life increased. It was absorbing their experience. What one perceived, they all felt in some subtle way. The wisp was becoming a whisper.

Sitting atop Sky Rock, Donan listened to the whispers of those beyond the Tribal Body and the wisp of the two far to the north. Each in their own way created pathways into the future.

Beyond them, larger forces were at work.

He had ceased speaking once Jormah and Tremlo left the Tribal Body and quickly got out of the habit of thinking in words. The elements were his language now. The contrast between night and day became the beat of his heart, the wind, his breath, the mountains and valleys, his body in repose.

From this perspective, huge swirling funnels of energy painted the sky in great sweeping arcs. He did not know the meaning but felt the danger all the same.

"They came this way," Reena said to Kenectka, stopping before a thick stand of golden-leafed boratta trees.

"How do you know?"

"That rock. Those trees. The feel of this place. I… remember it. Tremlo was here. And the forest is remembering too. Can you feel it?"

"Feel what?" Gremar asked coming up to them. These two had become closer of late.

"Tremlo and Jormah came this way," Reena said.

The extent of her perception was something to marvel at. Gremar often wondered if she could sense the future, and if so, did she know what would happen with him?

Reena pointed to a place in front of the borrata trees, "They were in that very spot."

Gremar flushed with excitement. *We are following in their footsteps.* It would seem preordained, with him as Leader. The more they saw him this way, the closer it would be to happening.

"Which way did they go?"

"North," Reena murmured and said no more.

Gremar walked with them, feeling how he stood apart, softening his edges, easing his way in. These two powerful women. Aligning with them would be felt by others.

Kenectka smirked, Reena endured.

When the path narrowed, he moved to take the lead, but Kenectka blocked his way. He smiled to himself and waited for the path to widen before leaping ahead.

The moment he did so, Kenectka stopped dead in her tracks and would not move until he returned to his place behind her.

She enjoys this dance, Reena thought. *And he comes back smiling each time.*

"You are very happy today, Gremar," Kenectka observed.

"It feels so alive to be out here."

"It is a beautiful distraction."

Distraction?

He knew she was toying with him. She never lingered too long or let things evolve too deeply. Often when she pulled back, she sought Stelbin's company. But Gremar knew he had something she did not get from Stelbin. Despite her posturing, he felt her body's response to his when he drew near. Even now he felt her taking secret pleasure in the arch of his back and the flow of his arms.

Your time is coming, he thought looking directly at her. *You can't have it both ways. You will have to choose.*

Kenectka turned from his gaze and began to pick some mushers lying nearby.

"We will speak later," he said, attempting to keep the connection.

"Yes, we will." The sincerity in her voice surprised them both.

He moved off, and the two women resumed their walk.

"He possesses many good qualities," Kenectka ventured in the face of Reena's silence.

"There is an edge to him."

"It serves him. And stands in his way," Kenectka agreed. "If he can triumph over himself, I think he will become a great Leader."

Reena was not so sure. Whaet possessed an inner strength from which everything flowed naturally. In Gremar, she felt premeditation. He was constantly calculating his effect upon others instead of acting from some whole and secure place. And yet, as Kenectka said, he did have some estimable qualities. He seemed to understand the coming change better than most, and had clear ideas as to what to do when it came.

"I'm not interested in pairing with anyone," Kenectka said, sensing the flow of Reena's thoughts.

"No, but the time may come."

Stelbin drifted back, and Kenectka moved to close the distance between them. The air was easier to breathe when he was near. So different from Gremar, whose presence aroused a certain tension in her.

Reena watched and wondered. A crossroad loomed ahead, with Kenectka as the focal point. Whichever way she went so would the tribe.

Am I sensing truth or possibility?

"Reena?" Stelbin asked, and she, suddenly aware he was standing before her, looked at him.

"Yes?"

"Are you sensing something of Tremlo?"

"Not at this moment."

"The future then?"

She looked at him carefully.

His gaze was steady, his face open.

The answer may lie in you, she thought.

"Perhaps," she said aloud. "We shall see."

CHAPTER FORTY-NINE

Jormah sat in quiet contemplation. It had been four days since his capture.

"Look how he sits."

"Amazing."

"He does not move."

"Not once!"

Here was a measure of control, of power, and presence that could not be denied.

"He barely breathes. You'd think he was dead, and yet you can see – no, *feel* how alive he is."

"And he knows when you're looking! Even if you're standing behind him, you know he knows."

The longer Jormah sat still, the stronger their sense of awe became.

"What is he doing?" Kriiton demanded, keeping watch from the safety of his quarters.

"I … think … he is … waiting," Bettrie replied, her words prolonged, her movements slower.

Kriiton knew this mimicry was part of her strategy to get in tune with the creature, but he wondered if her mind was affected.

"Waiting for what?"

"For … us."

"Us?"

Kriiton purposely kept himself at a distance these past many days. Each morning he got out of bed and crept over to the brown shuttered windows of his quarters. Peering through a crack in the wooden slats, he would look into the garden. There was Jormah, sitting in that special way of his.

Does he know I am looking? Can he sense what I am thinking?

Bettrie had yet to come back with any satisfactory answers.

"How far reaching are his abilities?"

"I… don't know."

"Can he sense our people on the docks or the slaves in their trees? Can he sense things through closed spaces? Where did he come from? Are there others like him?"

"I have no idea." Bettrie's speed faster now, matching the press of his inquiry.

"Ask him!"

"I can't."

"Why not?"

"I'm trying to gain his trust. Questions like these get in the way. We can ask them later."

"How much later?"

"I don't know."

"I won't wait much longer."

"If you're so concerned, why don't you ask him?"

Kriiton shook his head. He did not want to give the creature any indication of what was on his mind.

"Besides," Bettrie added. "How much can we learn from him cooped up like this?"

"We're learning plenty just where he is. Need I remind you that we're still looking for signs of weakness and fear in him."

"He has exhibited none."

"Not yet, but we have learned of his fortitude."

Bettrie had no ready reply. Each day she sat in silence before Jormah, trying to enter his world and communicate with him in some real and meaningful way. *Who are you? What are you? What do you really think? Why have you come? Tell me. Show me. I am here to learn.* But every time she looked, she only found parts of herself looking back. Jormah would speak if spoken to, or reflect something back, but he volunteered nothing of himself.

"I don't believe Jormah thinks like we do. His need for words is slight. He is very attuned to what we are feeling. I don't think we can hide our emotions from him, and maybe not our thoughts."

Kriiton frowned, "I need more than supposition."

"He's not forthcoming because we are holding him prisoner."

"So you say."

"It's a matter of trust."

"You'll have to find a better reason for me to let him out of the net."

"Commander, I don't think he will run away, and I don't think he's a danger to us."

"Of course you don't!"

The tone in Kriiton's voice was harsh and getting stronger. She had to find a way to appease him.

"Jormah," Bettrie asked, "can you tell me where you come from?"

An element of apology in her manner, the echo of Kriiton's voice coloring her words. Kriiton himself was making a concerted effort to avoid him.

"The forest," Jormah replied.

"Can you tell me where in the forest?"

"The Bhytoe says from far, far away," Bka translated.

Bettrie noted that Jormah had pointed vaguely to the south and west.

"But where is his home, exactly?"

"He says his home is where he is. He says this place is now his home."

Jormah would not outright lie, but he did not trust them with the truth either.

"Jormah, are there others like you?"

"The Bhytoe says he is the one who is here."

Through it all, Jormah maintained the bemused look of an adult allowing a child her explorations.

These are not the right kinds of questions you should be asking, his face seemed to say.

Randol knocked on Kriiton's door.

"Commander, the gateman reports a hundred colonists outside."

Each day a small group had gathered on the near hillside hoping to catch a glimpse of the creature. Today their numbers had increased significantly.

The Augmentors outside the fort stood with swords at-the-ready. They had drawn a line across the ground. No colonist would be allowed to cross it.

"I had no idea our citizens took such an interest in the affairs of slaves," Kriiton said, standing before them.

"We have heard this is no ordinary creature."

"But a creature all the same," Kriiton replied.

"It drove the Kurr back with a glance."

"So it appeared. But we don't know why. There may be a simple explanation."

"It's been said one can find peace merely looking at him."

"The same could be said of the ocean."

"Why do you insist on keeping him hidden in the compound? Why isn't he in a slavetree?"

"We may well put *it* in one. At this point we are trying to learn all we can about *it*, free from the meddling of others."

That silenced them.

"As soon as we have answers, you will be the first to know. Go back to your homes and your work. There is nothing more you can do here."

Kriiton stood with his arms folded and waited until they were out of sight. It had been easy to dislodge them this time. But what about the next? They were reasonable people, yet the mere suggestion of what this creature might represent caused them to abandon their work and disrupt the normal routine of the colony.

Once again, Kriiton felt the yearning that lay inside them. It was in him as well.

The longer the creature remains in our midst, the greater the danger.

Jormah distracted himself from his confinement by studying the Intruders. He felt their questions, witnessed their interactions, and through the rhythms of their daily lives, came to see more clearly how their minds worked. Nevertheless, the weight of the net upon his head and shoulders was growing tiresome. His skin itched, but he refused to scratch or allow himself to do anything that might reveal his growing irritation.

In response, the mind-of-his-body was generating a series of emotions to dislodge his determination. Flashes of anger welled up, and with them the requisite thoughts. *This is unjust. Outrageous. An insult!* It did not matter that it was he himself who allowed himself to remain here like this.

Jormah pushed away from these thoughts and sat beside himself. A silent battle was being waged, but none of the Intruders were the wiser.

Late that night Tremlo climbed down from the roof. He alone felt the growing effort it took the Kwaman to keep his head up and shoulders straight.

Jormah felt him coming and checked to make sure Bettrie was asleep.

It will only be a moment.

He assumed the posture-of-speed and found Tremlo sitting there beside him.

"I grow weary of this place," Jormah said with a sigh.

'So do I.'

The sights and sounds and smells of the Intruders had penetrated Tremlo's body. Fear drove them. Subjugating everything before them made it safe.

They would own us.

The impression was strong. And the world this kind of ownership would spawn too real.

"We should cut you free."

"Not yet."

"The longer you are held captive, the more dangerous it becomes."

"In what way?"

"The more they hold on, the tighter their grasp."

"We have come here to learn of their ways. Their ultimate treatment of me will reveal much."

"We can still cut you free." A mounting pressure in his own chest.

"It would be better if they freed me on their own accord."

"If they saw you as the Bhytoe."

"Some already do."

"They wonder and they wish, but that doesn't mean they are going to let you go."

"They fear their Leader."

"As we should. He is hiding something."

"They all are. They do not know themselves and are imprisoned by the limits of their understanding. This we must change."

At these words, a flash of fear passed through Tremlo. He reached out to the very fringes of his perceptions in hopes of glimpsing the future. Flickers of hot and cold. In that rarified air everything was still fluid, yet he could not find a sense of himself. *How can this be?* Was he not looking in the right way?

"Tremlo, you want me out of here."

'Yes.'

"This net is as troublesome for them as it is for us. We are all stuck waiting for the other to do something. I wonder what would happen if I began to blend in?"

Tremlo instantly saw the result. If it worked, the Intruders would be forced to release him.

A wave of fatigue peeled off the Kwaman's body, "Tomorrow, we will start anew."

"Agreed. Until then."

Jormah let go the posture and sagged back into the net. Tremlo's demeanor seemed to have changed overnight. Suddenly he had strong opinions and had said 'agreed' almost like an Intruder might.

I need to get out of here.

Bettrie's ears rang softly with a high-pitched pressure. Half-asleep, she opened her eyes. For an instant, she did not see Jormah, and then the Kwaman was sitting before her. She told herself it was just a dream and fell back to sleep. But the next morning it continued.

"Jormah?" Bettrie could barely see him. "Jormah?"

The Kwaman nodded and smiled. Through motion he could be seen but otherwise....

Bettrie ran to get Kriiton.

"He's fading away!"

"What are you talking about?" Kriiton snapped, annoyed by the tone in her voice.

"Come. See for yourself."

Kriiton followed her out to the garden, holding firm, refusing to allow the creature's plight to affect his judgment. Jormah was in the net as usual, but the borders of his body were defined more by where the net touched him than by the sight of him.

Kriiton strained to see, fighting fascination. Setting Jormah free risked not only losing him but unleashing him.

To see how he walks or where he sits. To see what might attract his attention....

"Hello, Kriiton."

Jormah's voice was soft, like it was coming from some distance away.

"Jormah, what is this?" Kriiton asked, shifting from side to side to see him. Here was a physical reminder of the miraculous nature of the creature. "Are you ill?"

"No."

"What is wrong then?"

"The Bhytoe says there is nothing wrong. He is what you wish him to be."

Was this a threat?

"I wish no such thing."

"As he is, you wish him to be gone."

"I think," Bettrie interjected, "Jormah means by keeping him in the net we are not allowing him to be who he is."

Are you still trustworthy, Bettrie?

"Guards!" Kriiton shouted, bringing them to attention. They had all drawn closer to hear better. "Reset your posts! Don't let me have to tell you again!"

Turning his attention back to Jormah, Kriiton felt a sense of regret. A part of him secretly wished Jormah would escape and spare him any decision he might have to make.

Are you playing with my emotions? Is this a ploy to get me to release you?

"We will wait a while longer," Kriiton declared and quickly retreated to his quarters. The effect the creature had on him was unnerving.

I must keep my distance.

Over the next two days Jormah intensified the posture. Kriiton could barely see him now, and every time he went up to Jormah he felt such remorse, he wanted to order his release.

Why do I feel this way?

He no longer trusted himself.

"All right, Bettrie, you have won. We will let him out of the net, but we will manacle him first."

"Manacle him? And then what, chain him to a wall?"

"No. We'll use a travel chain and attach him to an Augmentor. That way he can move around, and you will get to see more of what you claim you are looking for." *What we all are looking for.* "When he's not moving about, he goes back into the net."

"Kriiton, I really don't think—"

"It's that or nothing! If all goes well, you can take him to the pit and watch the Kurrs' reactions for yourself."

This was the last thing on Bettrie's mind.

"Tell Jormah you have persuaded me to allow him out of the net, but I insisted that he be manacled."

Jormah heard them arguing. *I will be released soon.* But something was not to Bettrie's liking.

"Kriiton has agreed to let you out of the net for a short time."

Jormah listened as Bka translated.

"But he is still mistrustful and insists that you be manacled."

"No!" Bka cried. "Don't let them treat him like a slave. Please."

"We have no choice."

"Bka," Jormah said in a calming tone.

"Bhytoe, they mean to attach a manacle to you and hold you tightly in their grasp!"

"Do not worry, my friend. It has no meaning. I do not wish to leave."

Six Augmentors came in through the gate. Two marched straight up to Jormah. Their manner brisk, efficient, eyes cast slightly aside. Kriiton had ordered them not to look directly at the creature.

The other four spread around the courtyard. Each unfurled a light-weight man-catcher. They would use these nets to snare the creature if it made any attempt to escape.

The Kwaman hardened his bones as the Augmentors fitted his legs with the cuffs. They made what they thought was a tight fit just above the ankle of each leg. A short chain was strung between the cuffs and would limit the length of Jormah's stride. Another chain nearly thirty feet long was attached to a link in the middle. The opposite end was wrapped around the waist of a heavyset Augmentor.

When it was done, the net was untied, and they stepped back to look at him more directly. He did not appear at all dangerous, and these special precautions seemed almost absurd.

Jormah stood up and felt the power of the cuffs. To assume the posture of an object was one thing, to have an object impose its form upon him was quite another.

Kriiton saw a flicker of color flash across his body.

"Don't worry," Bettrie said in a reassuring tone. "These are only temporary measures."

"I have never worn such a thing," Jormah hastened to explain.

He is vulnerable. Kriiton took a step closer. *Despite his calm manner, it is bothering him.*

"Come," Bettrie said. "We can walk around the compound. The Augmentor will follow."

Jormah recalled the effect his movements had upon the Carooh long ago. Taking his first steps forward, he made adjustments to the weight and limitations imposed by the manacle. By his fifth step, a sudden stillness came over those in the courtyard. His movements within the net had only hinted at the elegance and grace now before them.

The lines and color of his body became pools of shimmering light. He did not impose himself upon the surroundings but became the expression of them. Here was radiance, here was light. Here was the essence of the world sung through his body for all to see and hear.

The house servants sank to their knees. Some of the Augmentors looked in Kriiton's direction but none dared do the same.

The Spirit-Of-The-Forest.

The Spirit-Of-The-Forest.

The words rang through all their minds.

Jormah felt the effect he was having upon them and incorporated their hopes and dreams into his own body movements.

He knows me.

He understands me.

He cares for me.

I am not alone.

I am not alone.

Kriiton fought to resist the enchantment.

How can we kill a thing of such beauty?

Jormah moved around the courtyard, floating more than walking. The movements of his body limited only by the obscenity of the manacles, and the dull plodding of the Augmentor behind. If not for those, what wonders might be revealed?

Kriiton stared at the manacles and the Augmentor who followed. Here was relief from the spell the creature cast.

Jormah felt his mounting apprehension and went back to the garden to sit upon the net.

None of the guards stepped forward.

Kriiton watched to see how long it might take. Eventually, the Charge gave the order and guards came forward with their heads down.

Awe. Apology. Shame. Remorse.

All this Kriiton noted and more. *They are bewitched.* Whatever doubts he harbored were gone. The creature was a definite threat to the ruling order.

The dull ache in Jormah's shins filled his legs and blinded them to other sensations. As he sat there waiting, he twice shifted his legs.

He is troubled by the cuffs, Kriiton decided. *Despite his acting to the contrary.*

The Augmentors unhooked the chains, but Kriiton signaled them to leave the cuffs on. Jormah remained still. He knew Kriiton was looking for any sort of reaction. *I can soften my bones and slide them off anytime,* he told himself. But his body felt defiled.

"You are bothered by the cuffs," Kriiton said.

"They are... uncomfortable."

"You will get used to them."

"I'm not sure I want to," Jormah replied and immediately regretted it. The mind-of-his-body had spoken the words before he could stop them.

"You may have to," Kriiton said, relieved to find a reaction appropriate to the cause. This was something he could control and exploit.

"Perhaps you are right," Jormah said, working hard to reflect back the more sympathetic tones within Kriiton's body.

Kriiton turned away.

It's happening again. Even with my back to him, feelings of empathy grow.

"You will be forced to live like this for the rest of your life!" he shouted, spinning round on Jormah. "So you had better get used to it."

"If that is what you wish."

"That is what I wish!"

Jormah said nothing more but continued to look on softly. Kriiton stared back as hard as he could. But what seemed clear just a moment ago was now clouded. Once again, his thoughts and heart were at cross purposes. He turned to the others nearby. The guards had responded to Jormah's movements, just as he had. Afterwards, they hesitated in carrying out their duties.

I should send them to the farthest outposts.

But that would only help spread word of the wonders of the creature.

This is a contagion!

"Raise the purple flag," Kriiton declared. "The fort is under quarantine. No one leaves and no one enters without my permission. Is that clear?"

"Understood."

Late that night, Tremlo climbed down from the rooftop. Jormah felt him coming, but the singular rhythm the cuffs imposed upon his body prevented him from assuming the posture-of-speed.

The guards near him were sleepy and the others too far away to see. Bettrie was on her back and breathing deeply.

Slowly, with barely any movement, Jormah worked each cuff off. He had to rub his shins before slamming his chest tight.

Tremlo was there, a look of worry on his face.

"My legs know the slaves' woe. I can isolate the rest of my body from my legs and try to learn from it."

"Jormah—"

"Tremlo, the Intruders are our ancestors. They *are* the pattern-of-change. If we are to survive, we have to guide them into a more hospitable posture." Jormah's words did little to quell Tremlo's growing apprehension. "Things will not always be as they are now."

"No," Tremlo said brightening. Within Jormah's attempt to cheer him up was Jormah's own uncertainty. *I must not add to his burden.*

"I am here."

"I know."

Jormah released the posture and quickly slipped the cuffs back on. The guards were all in their same positions. Bettrie was turning onto her side, but her breathing remained slow and even.

With the cuffs on, the tingling in his shins returned. He had to find a way to ignore it.

The next day, when they opened the net, he stood up and performed a kind of deewah.

The guards turned away.

"They have been ordered to do so," Bettrie said. "Kriiton believes your motion bewitches them."

"What do you think?" Jormah asked, and Bka translated.

"It does not matter what I think. Kriiton is the Newland Commander. He distrusts everything that he does not understand or cannot control."

"But he holds me here with these devices. Doesn't that make him more at ease?"

"These devices may hold you, or they may not."

She knows, Jormah thought. *She must have seen.*

"But they do not help him understand you."

"You are different."

"I'm not an Augmentor. I was brought here to capture and train the Kurr."

"Why?"

"It is believed that with their help we can bring peace to our homeland."

"Peace?"

"We would use them to defend ourselves and destroy our enemies."

"You would use them to kill others?"

Was that disapproval in Jormah's voice?

"We hope they will strike fear into our enemies' hearts and prevent them from attacking us."

Kriiton had been pressing her hard. She needed to give him something and now seemed as good a time as any.

"Jormah, why do the Kurr fear you?"

It was a question Jormah had been waiting for.

"They are dangerous animals. They are born. They eat. They grow old and die. For the most part, they go where they want. Kill what they want. Live how they want and think only of themselves. In the forest, there is no other beast to challenge them. But in the forest, there are forces at work beyond beasts. Just as in this place there are forces beyond your people."

Jormah made no further claim. The truth was for them to create and he to direct.

"...and that's all he said?" Kriiton asked when Bettrie repeated this to him.

"That was all."

Kriiton walked over to the window and looked out. The courtyard was bordered by the walls of the fort, which were bordered by the land, which was bordered by the sky, which in turn was bordered by the unseen. Could this creature, this Jormah be the link between the two worlds?

"Did he say what forces he meant?"

"When I asked, he merely opened his hands indicating everything about us."

"Do you think he is hiding something?"

"I know you're afraid he will escape. I am telling you he is here because he wants to be here."

"For now, I prefer to think he is here because of the net and the manacles."

You are wrong, Bettrie thought, for in the middle of the night, within the blink of an eye, she had witnessed the truth.

CHAPTER FIFTY

Who are you? What are you? What do you really think? Why have you come? Tell me. Show me. I am here to learn.

Bettrie sat the way Jormah did and remained reasonably still for longer periods of time each day. On this day she had a moment of what felt like real stillness. Nothing in her moved, including her thoughts. The borders of her body fell away, and she spread into the greater world about her.

Am I hallucinating?

Between the beat of her heart, between the breath that she took, she looked at Jormah and saw not some reflection of herself, but Jormah actively sitting there, with a smile on his face.

Hello, it seemed to say. *Welcome.*

The impression lasted only a moment, and when Bettrie looked again, she saw only her own reflection staring back.

Who are you? What are you? What do you really think? Why have you come? Tell me. Show me. I am here to learn.

Jormah sat quietly, hiding his surprise. For an instant the thing that was most truthful in Bettrie had been most present. There was a yearning in her, in all of them for something beyond the beast that lived inside.

"Jormah," Bettrie said. "I am sorry about the net and the manacles. You know I want to sit beside you free of these impediments."

Jormah heard her plea and decided it was time to begin.

"One man is trapped in a broken body," Bka translated. "Another held captive by disfigured thoughts. We are all imprisoned by something. The real question is, *who* is imprisoned? *Who* are we, separate from that?"

Questions of this nature were not totally new to Bettrie, but coming from Jormah, they sent waves of sensation through her body. She held onto it as best she could, and later, when she stood up, there was a soft ringing on the fringes of her awareness. She felt herself not only moving, but also watching herself move, and in so doing was connecting to something far greater than herself. It did not last long, but she was sure now that here before them, and mostly hidden by the net, lay the path to enlightenment.

Jormah left the net twice a day for his walk around the garden. He always stood up in that fluid manner of his and sent a hush through an already quiet courtyard. The Augmentors turned away and avoided looking at him directly. They were too well trained to disobey but soon discovered the creature's movements spoke to their other senses as well. They could almost *feel* the warmth of his presence when he drew near. It was like sunlight touching their skin. A sweet smell would color the air. By not looking at him, they strained their other senses to see him and were rewarded with a growing awareness. As he flowed past, the soft melody of his movement harmonized with their own and filled them with a sense of hope and well-being.

Watching from his room, Kriiton saw the Augmentors holding to their post markers and turning away when Jormah was out of the net.

But for how long?

"Randol, what do you hear from the men?"

"Commander?"

"What do they make of the creature and what we are doing?"

"Theirs is not to question."

"Granted, but what is on their minds? How do they view the creature? Is there a consensus of opinion?"

"They are loyal, Commander. They wonder why you insist on keeping Jormah tied up, but they would not presume to act otherwise."

"I see."

Kriiton was not convinced. The mood of the men was shifting. Over the last few days, a strange sense of quiet had descended upon the fort. Superficial conversations had stopped almost completely. Extraneous movements were kept to a minimum, and in their place, a different kind of attention was arising.

Kriiton peered through the closed window slats. Jormah was in the net, sitting in that special way of his.

Can he sense that I am looking at him? Does he know what I am thinking?

Again and again, the same questions. Fear. Hope.

Bettrie sitting beside the creature, mirroring him.

They barely speak to one another, but something is going on.

In a flash of jealousy, Kriiton opened his door. Bettrie felt the tension spread through the Augmentors. Much of what she was learning from Jormah came not from words but from her powers of observation. The more she tried to emulate Jormah, the stronger this sense of things became.

Kriiton blew over like a stiff wind. He stopped before Jormah and planted his feet.

I will stand as an example. We must hold to who we are.

"Hello Jormah," Kriiton said in a strong voice, ignoring Bettrie completely. That dreamy sense of the world she had had just a moment ago was pierced now by the sharp edge of this reality.

"How are you feeling today?" Kriiton continued, spoiling for a fight.

"It is good to see you," Jormah said, expressing himself as they might.

"Oh? And why is that?"

"You have many questions."

"Obviously, and so do you. What do you think, Jormah?"

Bka translated and Jormah shook his head as if to say he did not know or did not understand.

"I'll be more specific. What do you think about us?"

Jormah sat quite still, radiating a sense of openness.

"Why are you here?" Kriiton demanded.

"I am here to learn your ways."

"So you have said. But for what purpose?"

"To understand your nature."

"Why?"

"I wish to learn the nature of all things."

It was dead quiet in the courtyard. The guards were straining to hear. They were Augmentors, hardened by circumstance and the rigors of battle. Yet each and every one of them had a look of wonder on their faces.

Kriiton frowned.

We must hold to who we are.

"Bring me a chair!"

A house servant rushed inside and came running back with a large wooden chair. Kriiton pointed to a place directly in front of Jormah and sat down on the chair with a flourish.

I am a man. This is how men sit!

Bettrie, on the ground beside Jormah, dared not move for fear of drawing attention to herself.

The Newland Commander stretched out his arms and legs and filled the space around him.

"So, Jormah. You are interested in learning our ways. We too have an interest in learning yours, and those of your people."

"Yes," Jormah said, acknowledging his words.

Now we're getting somewhere, Kriiton thought.

"Tell me about your people?"

"I am my people."

"Are they like you?" Kriiton persisted, the edge in his voice palpable.

Jormah shrugged, "I, am I."

"You are you."

"Yes."

What if we tortured you? Would we get a straight answer? Dare I risk it?

Jormah felt the pressure in Kriiton's gaze. It was a dangerous game they were playing.

"Kriiton...," he said softly, a mother gentling her child.

"Kriiton," he said again, elongating the name, filling in the sound with colorful tones that evoked the essence of the man.

"K r i i t o n ," he sang out, and Kriiton's insides vibrated in recognition.

He knows me. He understands me.

"K r i i t o n ," the lilting tones, sung fully now, a homage to him, to the self within.

It's happening again.

Moments ago, he considered torturing him, now he could not imagine ever harming him.

What is this creature?

"There is much you want to know," Bka translated, "and much to learn."

"What does that mean?"

"If you travel down an unfamiliar river, would you know what was around the bend?"

"No, of course not."

"Then how can you expect to understand everything at once? You must first see how you are placed in the world, not how you want the world to be placed."

If I relinquished control, where would this lead?

'To the unknown' his mind said.

'To possibility,' his inner heart throbbed.

'*To annihilation!*' his fear insisted.

He wished he never started this conversation.

"I don't understand what you mean," Kriiton said, stalling for time.

"You have grown into a race of makers," Jormah replied in a gentle but clear voice. "Wonderful as that may be, you have become trapped by your own inventiveness. You look for answers everywhere but where the truth lies."

This was not what Kriiton wanted to hear, nor the men to listen to.

"The answers to who I am or what I represent resides within yourselves."

Kriiton stood abruptly. He could not allow this. Not here, not now, not in front of the men. He had taken an oath to protect the realm, even with his life. "Interesting words," he said loud enough for all to hear, "especially coming from one who is trapped within a maker's net!"

Kriiton walked briskly around the courtyard, conducting an impromptu inspection. He had to get away from the despair rising in his chest. Stopping before each and every Augmentor, he placed a hand on their shoulder and looked them straight in the eye.

We must hold to who we are.

We must hold to who we are.

They stiffened and nodded, but he did not trust that they would hold for long.

Despite his outward rejection of Jormah's words, he felt the truth of them.

If I am thinking of these things, they are too.

Late that night Jormah assumed the posture-of-speed and Tremlo was there to greet him.

"Kriiton's resistance is weakening."

"But his resolve hardens," Tremlo replied.

Jormah looked at him. Here was a burgeoning wisdom.

"That struggle is in all of them. We need to find a way to soften their resolve."

"The longer you are in this net, the more they will come to understand your vulnerabilities."

"There is a yearning in them. Something is growing."

The Intruders were beginning to use their senses to listen in a new way, and this was a first step. But there was something very dark in them, and Tremlo could not get past the feeling that things were misaligned.

The Augmentor stood before Kriiton with his head down. For the past two days he had debated whether to come forward with what he had seen. The two were alone in the command room.

"You say he vanished?"

"For a few moments, yes."

"With the cuffs?"

"They were on the ground beside him."

"And yet the net still held his form?"

"It covered his body but he, he wasn't there."

"And when he returned a moment later, he slid the cuffs back on."

"Exactly."

"And this wasn't a dream?"

"I witnessed it again last night."

"And you didn't think it important enough to tell me the first time?"

"Forgive me, Commander. It was dark, and the first time I saw it, I wasn't sure if it had happened at all. But now, I'm sure."

"You say he took off the cuffs before he disappeared, is that right?"

"Yes."

"If the cuffs prevent him from disappearing, perhaps the net prevents him from leaving. You said the outline of his body remained."

"I couldn't see his body. It was just the net."

"So he disappeared, but he did not leave."

"I think so, but I have no idea what he was doing."

"Do you think he was trying to escape?"

"He was only gone a moment."

"A moment is a relative term. To a child of two, a year is half its life, to a man of seventy, a brief interlude. I have noticed the cuffs bother him."

"I don't think he likes them. Maybe this is part of the way he sleeps."

"Do you believe that?"

"I don't know. I have no explanation."

"Nor I. Do not tell anyone else what you have seen. Continue to observe and report anything out of the ordinary, even if you're not sure what to make of it. You will be rewarded for your diligence."

"Understood."

Alone once again, Kriiton stared blankly at the wall.

I am running out of time.

He was like a dam holding back the waters. If he gave way there would be no stopping the ensuing flood.

I should have had him killed him outright.

But was that even possible? Should he try now?

There had to be some other course. What else could he do?

He set his mind to working, playing out every scenario he could think of. Jormah was a magical creature, and with magic came belief. If he embraced this new phenomenon and set the people of Ontar on a new course, his duty demanded that it be controlled, and not just for the moment. Forever.

When a solution finally presented itself, a part of him was horrified.

I must prevail! But what if I am wrong?

Kriiton silently cursed the role fate had cast him in.

May the gods forgive me.

CHAPTER FIFTY-ONE

The ground sloped down towards the Valley Forest. A pocket of energy, a world all its own, and they, the invaders.

Gremar reached out, no longer concentrating on the immediate surround, but far ahead, searching for what might come, not just for himself, but for everyone. A Leader's duty.

It was exhausting.

He would have told someone else to do it, but how long would they continue to listen to him if he did that? Certainly, they were scrutinizing him. Testing. Judging. But every time he looked, everyone seemed absorbed in their own pursuits. Even Tomar, who had positioned himself close behind, apparently found it more interesting to pay attention to the reality of things he had only seen in his mind's eye.

"Tsute?" Gremar asked when the two were out of earshot. "How do you think it is going?"

"Different," Tsute smiled. The last time the three left the Tribal Body there had been little forethought and much trouble. They were young and foolish, and Railly had nearly died. Times had changed, and they were older now. "You are inspiring confidence."

"I am?"

"You don't know?"

The Valley Forest seethed with energy, and Gremar brought them to a halt before entering. Whaet often consulted others about practical matters, so why not him? Tomar came up beside him.

"I thought it would be best to take the time to reach out and see if any dangers lurked."

Tomar nodded. The impulsive youth he once knew was a thing of the past.

The people peered into the forest as one, each now caretaker of the rest. There had been no sightings of Yarkas for many years, and it was agreed there was no signs of those frightful beasts now.

Gremar let them listen a while longer before giving the signal. He would not be blamed now if something went wrong. They set off, gently threading their way into the forest as only Rehloy might.

The tribe's reach was extended by those who had left. Distant impressions were becoming more vivid. Each day, another detail was added. New ways replacing old. The ground upon which they walked, shifting.
Whaet saw there would be no cataclysmic event now.
Just a slow ceding.

CHAPTER FIFTY-TWO

"Randol, have five charcarts readied," Kriiton ordered. "Man them with Augmentors from outside the compound. Have them prepare for a journey of eight days."

"Understood."

"And send Bettrie to me."

If anyone saw Jormah removing the cuffs, it should have been her.

"You sent for me?" Bettrie asked, entering his command room.

"Have you noticed anything unusual about the creature lately?"

He's back to calling Jormah, 'creature'.

"What do you mean?"

"How is he adjusting to the cuffs?"

"I don't think he likes them," she said carefully.

"What about his walking about? Anything new in that?"

"Nothing in particular."

"I see."

"Commander, given the circumstances, I'm doing the best I can."

"Are you?"

Bettrie was silent.

"If we can control the Kurr and harness the power of the deadliest creature in the world, why not one with special talents?"

"You know my thoughts on the matter."

"I do." *You are no longer trustworthy.* "I'm leaving to conduct a surprise inspection of the far outposts to steady the troops. Randol will be in charge while I am gone. You will meet with him twice a day and report anything you discover."

"Understood."

"You may go."

Bettrie left, relieved Kriiton was leaving, even if it was only for a short time. It would give her time to think. She had to find a way to soften his resistance.

Kriiton went back to his preparations, satisfied Bettrie did not suspect anything. He continued to keep his thoughts and feelings as far away from Jormah as possible.

Randol came by a short time later.

"Everything is ready, Commander."

"Excellent. What do you hear from the slavetrees?"

"The night passed quietly. They are contained."

Only those who worked in the fields or the diggings had been allowed to come down from the trees. Each day their food was withheld until they returned. If the day passed without incident, they were all fed. If not, they got nothing.

"Any more talk?"

"They wonder what we mean to do. You had Bka warn them, and so far, that is holding. They question how long their Bhytoe will allow you to keep him prisoner."

"What do they think he will do?"

"They don't say. Apparently only the Carooh knew him. The Wollow and the Twie were already ours when he came to stay with them."

"I see."

"Commander, is it wise for you to leave at this time?"

"It's important that I go."

Randol said no more. In the short time he had been Kriiton's Second, he had come to trust the man implicitly. Kriiton would confide in him when he deemed the time right.

"While I am away, you will take my place. Keep your curiosity in check, and maintain your distance from the creature. Is that understood?"

"Yes."

"Secondly, make sure discipline is maintained and all my rules are obeyed."

"Understood."

"Keep an eye on Bettrie. She is under the sway of the creature. And keep the Augmentors busy. Institute combat drills during the day. Swords, knives, and hand-to-hand combat. Every other evening stage a night-fight. And most importantly, keep their attention off the creature. Understood?"

"Completely."

"Good. I should be back in about eight days' time. All will become clear then."

"I will carry out your orders to the best of my ability."

"I know you will. Record your daily observations so that I might read them when I return."

"Understood."

Kriiton left through the gate without a backwards glance. Once outside, he climbed up beside the Augmentors waiting in his charcart.

"Let's go."

The beasts were whipped into a trot.

"He's going to inspect the outposts," Bettrie said and Bka translated.

"What does he hope to find?" Jormah asked.

"He goes to oversee the Augmentors and make sure all is in order. I don't think he wanted to leave."

On the contrary, Jormah thought. *He very much did.*

The dull rumble announced their coming.

Two Watchers in each cart, Tremlo thought absently, following them with his senses.

Ten all together.

The slaves working in the fields beside Main Row paused to watch the procession go by. The oxten carts were in close formation, moving at a fast trot. The Newland Commander stood tall in the lead cart, projecting the sense of the power that was Ontar. The Augmentors in the fields quickly came to attention, and Kriiton made sure to acknowledge each and every one of them with a look or a gesture.

We must hold to who we are.

The Augmentors stood at attention until a cloud of dust was all that remained.

Good, Kriiton thought. *Let them remember.*

He had said it would be a surprise inspection, but Relayers would have flashed word on ahead. To really surprise them he would have to travel incognito.

Let them see that it is me. Let it remind them of who we are.

The first outpost was a mid-sized station. It functioned mostly as a supply depot. They arrived just before dusk, and Kriiton performed a routine inspection. Afterwards, the Charge mustered enough courage to come forward.

"Commander, is it true?"

"Is what true?"

"About the creature. They say it is the slaves' god, and that it has magical powers. They say that the Kurr saw it and were afraid."

"Do they also say that the slaves' god is being held captive by an Ontaran net?"

The Charge smiled.

"If there was any danger, would I be out here inspecting the outposts?"

"No."

"We are Ontarans, not slaves. We have little need for such nonsense."

"Understood."

"And one more thing. The creature may have come through here, and if so, it went by completely undetected by you and your men. Laxity will not be tolerated."

"We will double our efforts."

"Good."

They reached the second outpost the following day. The Augmentors did not ask any questions, for Kriiton's words had been flashed through the forest.

Let them hear it from my own lips.

"You have heard the rumors. I will tell you the truth. We captured a creature the slaves call the Bhytoe. We think it is an animal, like you and me. Unique, different, but an animal just the same. The Kurr were afraid of it, and we don't yet know why. But I am not afraid of it. Our net is not afraid of it!

"Bettrie, the great Animal Trainer, is working to discover what it did, and why the Kurr reacted like they did. But the creature does not speak our language and is trying to hide something from us. It might even be here to stir up trouble with the slaves. Either way, it has remarkable qualities we can make use of. And we will do so on our own terms and in our own way. We are Ontarans!"

A chorus of voices shouted out as one.

"Hail Ontar! Hail Kriiton!"

The Newland Commander nodded his approval.

"Go about your ways," he said, standing tall.

Let them see me. Let them remember.

In this way, he spread his message along Main Row.

They arrived at the third outpost well after dark the following day. This was manned by a full complement of Augmentors. Beyond this were only two small stations.

The Augmentors were assembled and waiting for the inspection.

"Greetings, Commander," the Charge said. "It is good to see you again."

Kriiton smiled at the sight of the old man's face. Harguin's wrinkles were like crevices in a rock wall. One as deep and hard as the next. He had served Kriiton on his last campaign in Ontar and volunteered to go with him to the new world. Steadfast in his duties, he preferred to be stationed in the field.

"Greetings Harguin." If there was anyone he could rely upon, it was him.

"The men have eaten, but we have food set aside, if you care to partake."

"I will make my inspection first, then eat."

Kriiton moved through the ranks looking carefully for any sign of questioning. These were hardened field troops that patrolled a large area. They had little use for gossip.

"You have all heard the rumors," Kriiton said after completing his inspection. "I will now tell you the truth…."

He spoke the same words as before, and in the end, they too sent up a cheer.

"Hail Ontar! Hail Kriiton!"

Kriiton and Harguin sat alone beside a small fire while Kriiton ate. Harguin had not asked one question. None of them had.

"If there is something you would like to know, my friend, now is the time."

"What would you have me ask?"

Kriiton smiled. It was a good answer.

"You're right. It is I who should be asking the questions. What do you know about the doings in the settlement?"

"We heard there were problems with the slaves, and you controlled it."

"What about the creature?"

"It's easy to imagine all sorts of things out here. But as you said, it's in one of our nets."

"What was the talk before I arrived?"

"There was some discussion about what the creature might be. We heard it was caught in the slave-trap and almost invisible. As soon as we heard that, we increased the patrol. We didn't know what we were looking for but looked more carefully just the same. And there was that incident with Wilton, but your words today have helped."

"What incident?"

"None of us gave it any thought at the time. Wilton was caught sleeping on duty. Standard punishment. He was branched and left tied to a tree till morning. However, the next day we found him asleep at the base of the tree. His bonds had been untied. When asked who did it, he said a spirit had come in the night and untied his hands. We thought he was lying to protect someone and so he was branched again. He never did change his story."

"Where is this Wilton now?"

"At the next station on night patrol."

"I want to speak with him."

"I will have him brought here in the morning."

"No. I will go to him."

"As you wish. Do you think it significant?"

"I'm not sure."

In the morning, Kriiton went out with a reduced escort of two char-carts. The Augmentors at the station were assembled for inspection. The man on the left stood with a slight lean. There were bruises on his legs, and his eyes were guarded.

Kriiton made quick work of the inspection and commended the Augmentors on their discipline. The men were dismissed and returned to their duties.

Kriiton drew the Charge aside.

"I understand there were some difficulties with Wilton."

"There were, but he has learned his lesson."

"I would like to speak to him."

It took the Charge a moment to realize he meant now.

Wilton was brought forth, and Kriiton dismissed the Charge with a wave of his hand.

"Thank you. Leave us."

Wilton's head was down, expecting a reprimand, but he didn't care. Not really. Not now.

"I have heard reports as to your conduct, Wilton. But I also understand you have been punished and are now on the mend."

"Yes," Wilton said softly.

"Speak up."

"Yes, Commander."

"Good. We all make mistakes. Some more painful than others."

Wilton nodded ever so slightly.

"I understand you were punished, once rightly and once wrongly. Is this correct?"

Wilton grew wary. Was this a trap?

"We are Augmentors, Wilton. Speak to me as one. Were you wrongly punished the second time?"

"Yes, I believe so."

"Good. So do I." Kriiton waited for his words to sink in. "I'm not insensitive to your suffering. Tell me exactly what happened that night."

Wilton looked at Kriiton. He was not known for cruelty.

"I was tied to a tree and branched. Sometime later, someone untied my hands, but when I looked there was no one there...."

"Go on."

"I looked hard to see who had released me. I blinked several times to clear my eyes. And then, a wondrous face appeared before me. The look in its eyes took away my pain. A hand appeared out of nowhere and touched my forehead. It disappeared a moment later, and I passed out. They found me the following morning. And ... well, you know the rest."

Kriiton nodded.

"Commander, may I ask you a question?"

"Proceed."

Bold now, looking him straight in the eye.

"Did you capture this spirit?"

"The creature we captured is unharmed and apparently quite happy to be with us," Kriiton said, quickly sidestepping Wilton's advance. "What did your spirit look like?"

"He was young, with a face like that of a child."

"A child?"

"Yes, formed, but untouched by time."

Jormah's face possessed a child-like look of innocence. Perhaps in the dark he looked like one, but he was clearly an adult.

Could there be others?

"How large was his face?"

"That's hard to say."

"Well, was it like mine? Smaller, larger?"

"I would say smaller. Yes, smaller by about a quarter."

A quarter? Jormah's face was perhaps equal to his own.

"And it didn't have hair, at least I don't think it did."

"I see," Kriiton said softly.

Jormah is not alone!

"I ask again, Commander, is the spirit you captured the same as the one that I saw?"

The edge in Wilton's voice was unmistakable.

"You seem very concerned about its well-being."

"I am," Wilton replied.

The man is tainted. His allegiance to Ontar secondary.

"The creature we captured is an adult, not a child, and from what you've described, quite different. Thank you for your help. You may go."

Wilton walked away, feeling Kriiton's eyes burrowing into his back.

"Charge," Kriiton called out, and the man came running.

"Commander?"

"I'm returning to the main outpost. Keep your men alert. Report anything out of the ordinary, no matter how strange or foolish it may seem."

"Understood."

There was no doubt now. He had to act before it was too late. If Jormah was not alone, how many more were there? And if there were others, where were they? Could they be inside the fort?

He sped back to the third outpost. Harguin was there to meet him.

"Come, walk with me." It was time to take him into his confidence. "What I am about to tell you is under the Oath-of-Secrecy."

"I comply."

Kriiton spoke then about the creature, its special abilities, and its effect on the Augmentors. He explained the dangers it presented to the colony. And he told him what he was planning to do.

Harguin simply grunted to each thing he said. When Kriiton finished he had only one question.

"What if it is a god, or in league with one?"

"Then we are damned, and it will not matter. If it isn't one, it will be all that matters."

Harguin was a simple man and not accustomed to thinking of things much beyond the moment. In the end, he supposed Kriiton had no choice.

"How many men do you need?"

"Nine all together. Six to replace the guards on duty in the courtyard. One for the diversion and two to secure the attachment."

"It is an extraordinary plan."

"For extraordinary circumstances. Which brings me to another point. Wilton is no longer trustworthy. I believe he was freed by the creature or one of its kind. He has his own version of what occurred and why. He did not threaten me directly but made it clear where his allegiance lies. It has convinced me that we are on the right course.

"He should be sent to the farthest outpost, never to return."

"Understood."

"Good. Now, who is your best weapons maker?"

"That would be Merter. I will have him sent to you."

Merter was a medium-sized man with thick, clumsy looking fingers. As he worked the red-hot metal, Kriiton marveled at their agility.

"The tip must be thin and razor sharp to limit the damage and barbed in such a way so as to make it impossible to withdraw. Cap the top with a round chain-port."

Merter worked the metal late into the night, carefully shaping it while maintaining its strength. When he finished, he held it up for Kriiton's approval. Here was a thin, pointed, triangular barb, mounted on a thin shaft an inch long. At the other end was a thick ring they would attach a chain-link to.

Kriiton tested its sharpness and was impressed.

"It should go in nicely," Merter said. "Once in, it'll never come out, not with that winged barb."

"You've done well."

Kriiton wrapped it in a soft cloth and took it back to Harguin's tent. He and Harguin spent the rest of the time reviewing which men to take and what their roles would be. For the two critical ones, they chose the most vicious men, who would do anything in the service of violence.

"They will be told at the last moment."

"Agreed."

"The quicker it is done, the better."

CHAPTER FIFTY-THREE

Six Augmentors were on guard inside the fort at all times. Once Kriiton left, they looked at Jormah more directly.

"Line up!" Randol commanded.

Those off duty gathered near the center of the courtyard in preparation for combat exercises. The first two combatants came forward wearing full-length, white aprons tied tightly round their bodies. Each held a wooden sword covered with black ash from the fire. The remaining Augmentors from the second and third shifts created a large circle around them.

"Ready?"

They raised their swords.

"Begin!"

The larger of the two men charged and brought his sword down in a high arc. The force of the swipe knocked his opponent's sword to the side and left a thin ash mark across the front of the man's apron. If the blade had been real, this would have been a slash rather than a killing blow.

The smaller man hung onto his sword and spun in a tight circle, slashing at the larger man's exposed side. But the larger man anticipated this maneuver and continued to move to the right, allowing the smaller man to score only a glancing blow.

Back and forth the battle waged until they had taken well over a hundred swipes at each other.

"Halt!"

Each was panting and covered in sweat. In a real battle, one would have been dead and the other badly wounded.

Jormah wondered if this demonstration was meant for him. Sitting in balance-position with eyes closed, he felt each thrust and parry.

How easy it would be to avoid the swipes of their swords.

They were fast, but he was faster, even without the posture-of-speed.

The other Augmentors were caught up in the action and filled with a perverse pleasure. The mind-of-their-bodies drove them, ruled them, and was the very thing that kept him in this net.

Randol spoke to the combatants and discussed what they might have done differently.

The next pair stepped into the circle. The others grew still. Having dined on the violence once, they craved it a second time.

"Ready? Begin!"

This time both charged at once and smashed into one another with murderous intent. Once again Jormah followed the action with his body. It was like a dance and these two his awkward partners. Jormah felt how he could bob and weave, and easily avoid the swipes of their blades.

During the next duel, he became more aggressive and realized he could avoid their thrusts in one movement and touch different parts of their bodies in the next.

These men employed certain repetitious movements. Whether due to the constraints of their bodies or their training, it made it that much easier for Jormah to anticipate their movements and act accordingly.

By the last match, he was swept away by the action and fought them both-at-once. Twisting, turning, leaping, ducking, slamming their heads together so swiftly, so soundly, they wouldn't have known what had hit them.

Jormah's body throbbed with excitement. Here was vindication. Here was right justified by power.

Bloodlust!

How eagerly his body embraced the Intruders' brutal and murderous natures. How joyful it was even now. Proud to battle and craving more.

It was horrifying.

From his perch high above, Tremlo observed Jormah's body responding to the Augmentors' aggression. A time of reckoning was fast approaching. The pressure in his own chest attested to it, but he had no idea what it would be.

"This is not normal," Bettrie said, fearful of what Jormah might make of the battling. Odd shifts of color were passing across his body, punctuated by subtle twitches. "Please don't judge us by the actions of a few men."

The combat exercises continued on a daily basis, reminding the Augmentors of who they were. Each time they did battle, Jormah struggled to hold onto a sense of himself separate from the pull of the mind-of-his-body.

The Intruders would have to do the same if they opened themselves up to the Rehloy's influence. The mind-of-their-bodies sensed this and were fighting back, trying to engage him in battle and preserve their way of being.

My mere presence has invoked it.

Their response induced a like response in him, and despite himself, his body rose to the occasion.

CHAPTER FIFTY-FOUR

The charcarts moved swiftly along Main Row.

"Kriiton is returning," Jormah said, "with different men."

Bettrie asked Randol if he knew anything about it.

"I don't."

Later that same day, the official signal came. Kriiton was returning. No more information was forthcoming.

"Welcome, Commander," Randol said, stepping outside to greet them. "It is good to see you."

"It is good to be back."

Kriiton gave a quick signal to the Augmentors he brought with him. They instantly lined up in a new formation. "I trust all is well with the creature."

"All is as you left it."

"Excellent. I'm instituting a rotation. Harguin will lead."

"Understood."

Randol and the men guarding the gate quickly stepped aside.

Harguin entered the fort.

"Stand down!" he commanded in a strong voice.

The Augmentors on duty regrouped as their replacements marched in. It was an orderly exchange, and the old guard followed Harguin outside. Everything was going according to plan. Kriiton turned to Randol and set the next part into motion.

"Randol, we are going to take the cuffs off Jormah's legs and replace them with something more comfortable for him to wear on his wrist. Have Bka explain it to him and tell Bettrie to go to my command room and wait for me. I will be along shortly."

"Understood."

Bettrie stepped inside the command room, and the new Augmentor stationed by the door closed it forcibly behind her. The man took up a position directly in front. She would not get past him.

Harguin came back inside and escorted one of the six new inner guards over to the creature. The man carried a sack of tools and made sure not to look at Jormah directly.

"Have him put his legs through the net," Harguin said to Bka. "One at a time, so we can remove the cuffs."

Bka translated and Jormah complied.

The Augmentor quickly set to work, placing a soft block of wood beneath Jormah's leg to stabilize it. With hammer and awl, he knocked out the lock pin and opened the cuff.

Jormah was relieved but tried not to show it.

The Augmentor removed the other cuff and took out a new manacle. It was much smaller than the leg cuffs and looked more like a thin bracelet than anything else. This would be preferable to the others.

Should I allow it?

"Tell him to lie down on his back and stick his arm through the net."

Jormah complied and the Augmentor put the block of wood beneath the back of his hand.

Two new Augmentors entered the courtyard and came forward as if to watch.

"Take Bka to the command room to wait along with Bettrie."

The Augmentor who removed the cuffs placed the thin bracelet around Jormah's wrist. Jormah hardened his bones to make them as thick as possible.

"Now!" Harguin shouted. He and the two new Augmentors sprang into action. The heaviest man fell directly on top of Jormah. Harguin himself pushed away the Augmentor holding the bracelet and landed on Jormah's arm. The other Augmentor stepped in, placed the spike in the middle of Jormah's palm and hit it with a hammer.

In one quick blow it was done. The spike went straight through Jormah's palm into the wood block beneath. The large ring at the top kept it from going all the way through his hand. The Augmentor gave the block a half turn before pulling the wood away. The barb was at a right angle to the incision and would never come out.

Jormah, far off to the side in disbelief, no sound, no sensation. It was happening to someone else, not him, but it was him, and he knew it.

His body cried out and yanked him back.

He hurled the Augmentor on top off to the side. The man was thrown a great distance and hit the ground hard. The others backed up for fear of something they did not understand.

"Leave!" Kriiton shouted, rushing up to the net. "I'm sorry," he said, relieved to see there was blood on Jormah's hand, and that it was red. "Let me help." He took out bandages soaked in special herbs to prevent infection. "I'm truly sorry, but there was no other way."

He wrapped the bandages carefully around Jormah's hand. The swelling that usually accompanied broken bones had not yet set in.

"We want you here, and we mean to keep you."

Jormah barely heard him over the roar of his hand. The pain was secondary to the singular sound of the spike. It burned a hole in the middle of his hand.

"Iiiii..." it shouted, drowning out all other sensations. "Iiiii..." It pushed out through his palm and into his fingers. "Iiiii..." The voice of the Intruders. The sound of Ontar imposing its will. "Iiiii..." He recited his buntra-for-selfstenance to prevent its rhythm from moving up his wrist and into his arm.

"Iiiiiiiiii...."

It was daunting.

Tremlo was pressed flat against the wall directly behind him.

Stay hidden, Jormah's body warned, fearing he might suffer the same fate.

But Tremlo had no intention of revealing himself. When Kriiton and the new Augmentors came into the fort, his chest had constricted with fear. He thought to come down from his hiding place on the roof, but the weight of the future held him firmly in place.

He saw the Augmentors leap upon the Kwaman a moment before they did and watched in horror as one raised the hammer.

He could not move. He could not breathe.

It was only after the hammer came down upon the spike that he was released into the moment and rushed down to be near him.

The bones in Jormah's hand were soft. By the sound, they had split apart but were not broken.

I am here, Tremlo's body shouted. An anchor in the sea of chaos. *We will find a way out.*

"You'll be all right," Kriiton said, a model of caring as he dressed the very wound he caused to be made. He tied off the bandage and was satisfied. What little bleeding there was had stopped. "I will have a physyck come tend to the wound. They are most skilled in these matters."

Jormah looked at him with bewilderment.

"Guard," Kriiton called out, seeking refuge from that look. "Release Bettrie and Bka."

The Augmentor opened the door to the command room, and the two came running. Bka dropped to the ground and wailed aloud.

"What have you done?" Bettrie demanded.

"We did what was necessary. We cannot afford to lose him."

"But the net was holding him!"

"Really? And the manacles as well?"

"Yes!"

Kriiton grabbed Bettrie's arm and dragged her to the side.

"You have one chance to redeem yourself, Animal Trainer. And one chance only!"

"I don't know what you're talking about."

"There is another creature like Jormah lurking about. A younger one, and maybe more."

"I— I had no idea."

"No?" Kriiton studied her carefully. "Maybe not."

He told her about Wilton, and Bettrie grew very still. Whatever she might have done on Jormah's behalf, whatever she hoped to do was over for now. Kriiton no longer trusted her. If she did not comply, her own position, perhaps even her own life would be in jeopardy.

"If there is another creature like Jormah nearby," Kriiton continued. "This may bring him to us. Or he might already be here."

"I swear I had no idea."

"So you say. Have you noticed Jormah looking anywhere in particular?"

"No."

"Watch more carefully. Perhaps it will be only a glance or some simple gesture. You are the one who spends the most time with him. Report everything... or else."

"Understood."

"Do you?"

"I comply."

Jormah stared at the hand lying helplessly in his lap.

"I'm so sorry," Bettrie said, near tears and sickened by the sight of it. "I had no idea they were going to do this."

They sat in silence as the gray-light of dusk condensed into the thick-black of night. One of the house servants stirred the fire into life. Another lit the torches interspersed throughout the fort. Soon the courtyard was aglow in a dim and somber light.

The Augmentors stood quite still. They, who were hardened men, who had never seen the creature before, saw how others were affected and were confused. Something disturbing, perhaps even profound had occurred, and they themselves were the cause.

Jormah retreated before the solitary sound of the spike.

"Is there anything I can do?" Bettrie asked.

The Kwaman closed his eyes. He had sensed the subterfuge but never suspected they would commit such a barbarous act. *And with such cunning.* He had little experience with treachery such as this. Tremlo tried to warn him, but he did not listen and, instead, placed his fate in the hands of men he barely understood.

Now it was too late.

As soon as Bettrie fell asleep, Tremlo stepped away from the wall. Jormah compressed his chest, and the pressure spread through his body, but it could not penetrate the hand. The spike pinned him to this moment. Frightened now, he tried to assume a full defensive-posture. This also failed, for his hand was useless and could not follow the rest of his body.

Tremlo quickly returned to the wall. The trap Jormah was in was theirs to share. A sense of a future fraught with despair took a step closer. One blow of the Intruder's hammer had placed them firmly on its path.

They will own us and use us like any other possession.

Jormah's hand was throbbing. Tremlo remained hidden, rocking along with it, radiating a sense of care and confidence as best he could.

We will find a way. We will find a way.... Over and over until Jormah fell asleep.

Tremlo climbed back up to his place beneath the rooftop.

What am I to do?

What can I to do?

A throb all its own.

CHAPTER FIFTY-FIVE

Three Augmentors headed down Main Row.

They had been sent to relieve the men at the last outpost.

Wilton walked ahead of Tainer and Galware. Tainer was a master swordsman and Galware the Charge's Second. When the Charge announced the grouping for this menial task, neither of these two had protested. Even now they lingered slightly behind, keeping Wilton in their sights.

They're going to kill me.

"So Wilton, have you seen any more of your night friends?"

Tainer laughed. "Maybe they'll be more forthcoming out here."

"Why don't you introduce us?" Galware chided.

"I think he wants to keep them all to himself," Tainer replied.

Wilton pretended to ignore them. When he had asked Kriiton about the creature, the Newland Commander was vague, and then abruptly dismissed him. This convinced him more than anything that the creature they captured was either the one of his vision or one related to it.

They see me as an enemy. And right they should if they mean to do it harm!

He stopped abruptly and bent over as if to adjust his sandal. With his back to them he quickly withdrew his dagger and unhooked his sword. Surprise was all he had. As Galware and Tainer slowed to a stop, he swooped up from the ground and drove his dagger straight into Tainer's heart. Galware leaped to the side but not before Wilton's sword caught him along the right side of his body. Galware stumbled and fell, just managing to withdraw his sword from its scabbard. Wilton knocked it to the side as he drove his blood-soaked dagger into his neck.

In a few short moments, it was done.

He dragged each body deep into the woods and hid them in a thicket. At best, he had a day or two's head start before the trackers found them.

His life as an Augmentor and a citizen of Ontar was over. He had killed two of his own. If they caught him, they would systematically torture him and then boil him alive.

Main Row was now far too dangerous to travel upon. If he headed due east towards the ocean, he would be trapped between the water and open ground. His best option was to head west through the forest and make for the mountains. He had two day's rations, which he might stretch to a week. It was said that game was plentiful in the west.

He entered the forest and moved slowly at first, careful to cover his tracks. As the day wore on, he picked up speed, and near its end, he was close to running. There were hounds in the settlement now. The Animal Trainer had brought them from Ontar. It would be many days before they could be employed in the search, and there was a good chance it would rain before then.

The Augmentors, however, were another matter. They would be relentless, even if the trail went cold, they would never forget.

Wilton did not stop until it was too dark to see. He longed to light a fire, but there was a danger it might be seen. Besides, it would leave too many traces. And so, he sat in the dark with his back against a tree. He had the advantage of time, but they had the advantage of numbers. The Augmentors would carry enough food to last a week, and while they tracked him, others could hunt for food. He had to hunt for himself, and lose precious time in the doing. This was the real danger.

That night he was startled awake several times by the sound of small animals scampering about. At one point, he heard heavier footsteps approaching. With his dagger in one hand and his sword in the other, he stood up and banged them together making a loud clanging sound. This startled the animal, and it ran off.

I need to sleep, he thought. Perhaps tomorrow he would climb a tree and tie himself to it.

He was on the move at first light, a man alone. No one to talk to, no one to help or be helped by. The life of a fugitive. And yet, it did not matter, for there was something special in the world. Something that had touched him.

He had to elude his captors, no matter how long it took. Once this was accomplished, he would double back and make his way north to the settlement. He would sneak in and find out the truth about the creature. If it was the one who had set him free, he would do everything possible to rescue it, whether that meant sacrificing his life or banding together with the slaves to foster an uprising. He would do whatever was necessary.

CHAPTER FIFTY-SIX

"Bka, tell Jormah to put his hand through the net. I have brought a healer to tend to his wound."

After a moment, Jormah complied.

The physyck kneeled down beside him and gently removed the bandages. He had been instructed to bring things to treat broken bones and stab wounds. He thought there must have been a brawl of some kind, but when he got to the gate, Kriiton himself came to meet him.

"We are in a state of quarantine. You must take a vow of silence regarding the creature and speak nothing of it to anyone. Afterwards, I will decide if you will be allowed to leave."

"I comply!" the physyck said emphatically. He had no desire to be imprisoned here.

"Your vow is accepted. Follow me. We found the creature had no trouble sliding the manacles off its legs. Last night we used a barbed device to bind it to us."

"A device?"

"A spike."

"I see."

"Keep your eyes averted and focus only on its hand. Direct any questions to the slave, Bka. He will translate and speak for it."

The creature was sitting up in the net and seemed so slight and diminutive, the physyck wondered at the need for such a harsh measure. With the bandages removed, he saw that the color of Jormah's hand was nearly translucent. His elongated fingers possessed the kind of beauty and elegance one might find in sculpted works of art. In the center of the palm stood that mean-looking device. It was an obscenity in the context of what surrounded it.

There was no redness or sign of infection. The skin itself appeared undamaged. The back of Jormah's hand was swollen but not in the usual way. A bulge, half a nub wide, spread round the spike in an almost perfect circle. Unbeknownst to the physyck, this was the part of Jormah's hand that was now most dead to him.

"It's healed," the physyck exclaimed.

"The hand?"

"Yes. Look. I've never seen anything like it."

Here was further proof of the miraculous nature of the creature. Kriiton hid his concern with a question.

"When do you think a lead-chain can be attached?"

The physyck gave him a strange look. "Given the speed in which it's healed, I'd say another day or two to be sure."

"So be it. If we need your services, you will be sent for. Remember your vow. If you break it, the punishment will be severe."

With the physyck gone, Kriiton turned back to Jormah.

"We'll soon have you free of this net," he said brightly.

Jormah felt the guilt in his shoulders, saw the steadfastness of his trunk, smelled the complex odors of fear and relief on his skin.

How little I understand these people.

He knew he had aroused something in them. The guards were opening up, thirsting for something his presence was bringing to the fore. They wanted to set him free. Even a part of Kriiton wanted to release him. But now this.

How did I imagine I could effect a change in such a people? What a fool I have been!

And yet, from the depths of his despair he understood Kriiton's fear.

My very success at influencing them was my undoing.

A tall wooden post was brought in and driven deep into the ground nearby. At its top was a swivel link attached to fifty feet of lightweight chain. The next morning, Kriiton ordered the chain attached to the ring in the palm of Jormah's hand. Afterwards, they untied the net. It fell off his body like an outer layer of skin.

Jormah stood up carefully. The spike was lighter than the manacle but the burden far heavier. He bent his elbow and brought his arm to rest flat against his stomach. It was an awkward position, and he performed a new deewah to compensate.

I am.

No matter what you do to me.

I am.

The new guards watched out of the corners of their eyes. Each phrase melted perfectly into the next. Here was a vision of symmetry and grace they had never seen before. None dared move for fear of breaking the spell.

Kriiton watched, relieved he had acted when he did. He watched now, allowing himself to give in to all that might come.

Jormah stepped away from the net and maintained the tonal quality of the deewah.

"Bka, tell Jormah the chain is fifty feet long. He can move about the pole in any direction he chooses."

Jormah barely heard his words. He backed away from the center pole and extended the chain to its full length. Here were the limits of his freedom. He jiggled the chain up and down and saw how the motion ran to the pole and back. He took a step closer and the waves grew taller. He moved his hand from side to side, and the ripples reminded him of a slither, sliding along the ground. He moved his hand in a small circle, and the chain followed.

Round and round, a soft swishing sound, whispering how it would never let him go.

He spun the chain faster, and the whisper became the buzzing sound an insect might make. Faster and faster, higher, louder. His arm moved swifter than the Augmentors had ever seen an arm move. A blur of detail. The chain howled in protest. The sound was so penetrating, it caused the men to grit their teeth and squint. Here was a demonstration of unsuspected power. The speed and force of the chain would cut them in two if they had the misfortune to get in its way.

Everyone took a step back, even if they did not move.

The mind-of-his-body relished threatening them like this, and spun it even faster. Louder!

No wonder the Kurr are afraid of him, Kriiton thought. Here were strengths and abilities far beyond their own. *Why did he let us do this to him? Why didn't he fight back? Is this a test of some kind?* Certainly, Proutus would see that he had done his duty, wouldn't he?

Jormah felt the shift in those about him.

You are letting them see what they did to you, he thought, appalled now by his actions. He elongated the circles. What was loud and brash softened into a mild breeze.

You let them see what they did to you.

He stopped completely and waited for the stillness to return.

The effect upon the Augmentors had been palpable. A storm of energy drove them away before it dissolved into a series of ever softening images. Jormah walked around the courtyard now with the chain gently in tow. His body spoke softly to reassure them, and they allowed themselves to be soothed, even as a sense of hesitation lingered.

Good, the mind-of-his-body said. *Let them beware.*

The Kwaman turned away, saddened by these thoughts. The spike had penetrated his heart.

Bettrie, Bka, and other house servants' eyes were downcast. The outcry of the chain had filled them with sorrow.

Tremlo felt ill. Beyond Jormah's threatening display, every movement revealed the limits the barb imposed upon his body. With each pass around the post, Jormah's despondency grew, until the strain of keeping up appearances became too much to bear. He returned to the net and sat down upon it. He needed time to collect his thoughts. He needed to find a new way to survive.

Tremlo ached with his despair.

We have to get you out of there!

If only he could speak to him. They might come up with a plan for escape, but that was impossible now.

I am Kwaman. I must think like one.

The spike pinned them to circumstance. Circumstance led to consequence, and consequence required thought, forethought, calculation, manipulation. One small thing imposed its will upon the currents. One small thing acting as though it were all and everything.

It was profane.

"Re-tie the net and remove the chain," Kriiton ordered. Jormah's response to the chain had sent a pall over everyone. Something precious had been lost. Fear of repercussions lingered.

He originally planned to keep the chain on at all times and free Jormah from the net. But being tethered to the pole had clearly upset him. Perhaps having him leashed to an Augmentor would be less offensive.

Kriiton resolved to have a special, lightweight chain made so that Jormah might walk about more freely than before. He signaled two Augmentors to come forth and secure the net. Afterwards they used a special tool to pry open the attachment link and take the chain off his hand.

We'll give him a little more time to get used to the idea before attaching it again.

The net, the barb, the chain, the guards, the fortress, the path, the Watchers; Tremlo's mind raced through a labyrinth of obstacles. Here was a linear way of thinking that went against his very nature.

Don't think, remember. Sense the way out.

He let go his mind and spread out.

From there-and-then, to here-and-now, to all-that-could-be.

An infinite number of pathways presented themselves, and each one led to a different reality. It was impossible to sort out, impossible to remember.

How can this help?

He watched Kriiton moving throughout the fort. The way he held his head and shoulders, the swing of his arms and the length of his stride. He felt it now in his own body.

What if I could think like he does? Would I be able to figure a way out?

Late that night, when Kriiton went to bed, Tremlo snuck down and moved quietly along the wall. He stopped just beneath Kriiton's open window to listen. Rhythms, smells, thoughts, sounds, the heave of his chest. Tremlo absorbed it all until his body was thyck with detail. He then withdrew to his haven on the roof. There the added weight dragged him into sleep.

He awoke to the feel of Kriiton standing up in his room. He felt it in his legs as the Leader stood, in his arms as Kriiton stretched. He felt his body following Kriiton's movements now throughout the day.

Surely thoughts would soon follow.

CHAPTER FIFTY-SEVEN

Bettrie looked at the back of Jormah's hand. The swelling had spread, a near perfect circle, from his knuckles to his wrist, reflecting the shape of the shaft itself.

Blasphemous.

She looked into Jormah's face. The Kwaman returned her expression in kind. If only she foresaw this, she would have done anything to prevent it.

The following day the swelling reached Jormah's fingertips. His hand was now saturated with the rhythm of the spike: thick and sluggish, the hand of another. The hand of his captors.

"The spike is having a strange effect on him," Bettrie said. Something had to be done. She had to do something!

"What is done is done."

"It's diminishing him!"

"I'd rather a diminished version than none at all. Did you find out anything else?"

"I asked if there was another out here like him, and he simply said that there was no one like him."

"Another evasion. Keep asking."

Kriiton outfitted several guards with man-catchers. "We're going to try something new today," he announced to everyone.

From his perch above, Tremlo listened to his words and ingested their syllables.

Some-thing new to-day.

"Open the net," Kriiton said. Two guards stepped forward to untie it.

O pen the net.

"O pen the net," Tremlo said softly, letting the feel of the words roll around his mouth. For the past three days, he had stalked Kriiton like an animal stalking its prey. Each night he snuck down and lay beneath his window. He had Kriiton's overall tone and was working on more intimate colors. If he could get it just right, he felt sure the impressions would create thoughts in his mind and tell him what to do.

"Bring the leash!"

"Br ring the lea-sh," Tremlo whispered, realigning the shape of his throat to that of the Leader's.

An Augmentor came forth carrying a thin chain. One end was attached to the belt he wore. He put an open link through the ring in Jormah's palm.

"Give me the grips," he said.

The tool looked like crisscrossed sticks attached near one end. Holding the longer lengths, the Augmentor placed the shorter ends around the link and pressed his hands together. This closed the link. He stepped back, leaving the chain slack on the ground.

Jormah stood and began his deewah. The mesmeric effect he had had upon the guards was tempered now. A level of stiffness had entered his body.

My hand is lost. The arm is next.

After finishing his deewah, the Kwaman stood in silence.

"You can go wherever you like," Kriiton said, and Bka translated. "You are no longer limited by the post."

Jormah did not move.

"You can go wherever you like," Kriiton coaxed.

You can go where-ever you-like.

Jormah took a tentative step forward. With the guard in tow, he circled the courtyard once before returning to the net.

For the longest time no one moved.

"Are you done?" Kriiton asked.

Jormah made no move to answer.

A sense of disquiet spread throughout the courtyard.

"Very well. Re-tie the net!"

Re-tie the net!

Jormah sat down, and the guard came forward. He opened the link attached to Jormah's hand with a different tool. Tremlo's hands moved in reflection.

That night, Tremlo climbed over the back wall and wove his way through the settlement to the water's edge. His body was swollen with detail. He needed to release and hear what it knew. Covered by the sound of the waves and far from any ears, he spoke aloud the words he learned that day. His voice was higher than Kriiton's, and he heard the lack of depth as he spoke. Adjusting his chest muscles and expanding his abdomen, he brought forth the sound from a deeper place.

"Are you done?"

"Something new today."

"Re-tie the net!"

Again and again, he repeated the words until his body resonated with the lower register. Satisfied, he moved about, maintaining the sound and posture while he walked.

Things were beginning to change. Not as they were, but how he was seeing them.

"Something new today."

"Go wherever you want.

"Are you done?"

He practiced long into the night until the bloat passed. None of Kriiton's thoughts came to mind yet, but he was beginning to see as Kriiton might, and if so, surely his thoughts would soon follow.

He had to try harder.

The next day, Jormah performed an abridged version of his deewah. The numbness in his wrist was pushing into his arm and creating violent images in his mind. When he led the Augmentor around the courtyard, he wanted to wrap the chain around Kriiton's neck and drag him along. How easy it was to become just like them.

Perhaps it would be better to remain in the net than be tethered to a post or a man.

Words collected in the inner recesses of Tremlo's body.

Words. Words. Words. Lying in wait.

He returned to the water's edge that night.

"Bettrie, come here!"

More adjustments were necessary to achieve the exact sound of Kriiton before the thoughts would come and tell him what to do.

They have to come, and soon!

The pressure in the air said so.

"Bka, tell Jormah what I just said."

He memorized the exact spot within his body to project each word. Again and again, he practiced until he was able to do it instantaneously. Still, something was missing.

When the Rehloy assumed a defensive-posture, they absorbed the rhythms of what lay behind them and re-created its pattern on the surface of their skin. But Tremlo needed to create something that lived and breathed and moved on its own.

Standing like Kriiton, breathing like him. Arms and legs stiff, back straight. He ached with the confinement but would not allow discomfort to get in the way. Drawing upon sense memories, he stepped forward and walked like Kriiton walked.

Nothing came to mind.

Don't move like Kriiton. Move as Kriiton.

How?

Purpose.

He needed to move with purpose.

The following day Kriiton called again for the leash.

Give me the grips, Tremlo thought, anticipating his words. Kriiton's will resonated through his body. Looking at the men, seeing the world as he might… waiting for the thoughts to come.

Where are they?

Jormah stood slowly. The solid sound of the spike had captured his arm and was moving up into his shoulder and chest. If he lowered his guard for even a moment, the numbness advanced its cause.

The sound of one, drowning out the voice of many.

Relentless. Unswerving. It was going to take him over, no matter what he did.

What if I simply let go?

Falling off a cliff. Thoughts, perceptions, feelings, understanding. What would happen?

Dare I let go?

What will I become?

Is this the way?

Tremlo felt Jormah's turn of mind and nearly cried aloud.

No! Don't! Hold on. Or we are doomed.

As the light that was Jormah dimmed, it became easier to see him. He was becoming more and more manlike. Kriiton found it somewhat reassuring, and yet, in this Jormah, he saw his own pettiness and hated himself for it.

CHAPTER FIFTY-EIGHT

The pressure was becoming unbearable.

Tremlo raced to the sea, stiffening his arms and legs, running as Kriiton ran.

Slap. Slap. Slap.

Feet pounding, ground sounding.

"Go where you want! Bring the grips!"

Words spilled out of his mouth.

They came without thought.

They came from deep inside.

"Are you done?"

Flow with purpose.

"Something new today."

He sounded like Kriiton. Walked like him, looked like him, smelled like him. Standing tall, he could just about achieve the Newland Commander's height. But the thoughts telling him what to do had not yet appeared. *Thicker. I need to be thicker.*

How could he change his body? No Rehloy had ever attempted such a thing. Perhaps none ever thought to do so. Even now, Tremlo did not so much reason this out as feel his way towards it.

He took a sip of water from his watersack. The fluidity within the currents told him to do so. He drank more. The sensation of water, the borders of his body. He drank and drank until his body was swollen stiff with Kriiton.

He stood now *as* Kriiton.

"Re-tie the net!"

The words, resounding in his chest and body, spread through the currents.

"Something new today. Charge!"

He took several steps forward. This new bulk was as natural as could be. Here was the path that led from now into forever. It came without words. His mind empty. His body filled with *knowing*. All he need do was follow where it led.

He let go the images of Kriiton and broke into a terrible sweat.

It poured out of him like rain.

Water.

His body contracted, wringing out all vestiges of the Newland Commander.

Water was everywhere. The swell of the waves, the glistening on his skin, the weight in the air...

A storm is coming.

It had a peculiar flavor. He tasted this before.

The harbinger.

Two days away.

When it comes...

CHAPTER FIFTY-NINE

Jormah was delirious. The incessant numbness reached across his shoulder and down into his chest.

I cannot hold out much longer.

The past several nights he felt Tremlo leave the fort only to return and hide beneath Kriiton's window.

To what end?

You must leave! Jormah expressed in the parts of his body that were still his own. *If I can find a way to escape, I will. But you cannot stay here and risk being captured.*

Go before the impending change takes hold of me.

Go, before I am forced to let go.

Go. Please. The pain of you witnessing it will be too great to bear.

Bettrie was beside herself. The miraculous nature of the being before her was withering away. It felt like he was dying, and there was nothing she could do to stop it.

I should kill Kriiton! But behind him were thousands more just like him. *I should rouse the colonists. I should help the slaves free you.* Was that possible? Would any of that matter?

In Jormah's face she saw her own panic, and despair.

Please forgive us.

Near tears.

Please.

Forgive us.

Jormah did not blame any of them. Not really. If anything, it was his own fault. Although this did not feel exactly right. There were greater forces at work, and he, victim to them, was in a state of transition.

Only when it was complete could he hope to know what was right.

A light rain fell–moments before it began. Remnants of the future–leaking into the present–.

Will happen–happened.

Will happen– happened.

Tremlo, sensing double, waited for the disparity to condense into one solid present.

"It's beginning to rain," Kriiton said. "Tell Jormah we will bring him inside."

Jormah had refused to leave the net these last few days and Kriiton was trying to make amends.

"I wish to stay here," he replied, indicating the net and this place in the courtyard.

"Very well. Charge! Hang a tarp over him."

The Augmentors drove two tall poles into the ground on either side of Jormah and tied a piece of rope between. Slinging a large, well-oiled cloth over it, they staked its sides to the ground.

"I hope you will be comfortable," Kriiton said.

As day turned to night, the light rain turned to a downpour. The Augmentors took out dark brown hooded cloaks made of a material similar to the one placed over Jormah. The rain-guards covered their bodies from head to shin, with side slits for their arms to reach out.

Bettrie and Bka leaned inwards, trying to keep dry beneath the small makeshift tent. They could not hide their discomfort from the Bhytoe.

"Bettrie, Bka. There is no need for either of you to stay here. The rain is my friend as well as the sunshine. Your discomfort becomes my own. Go inside where it is dry."

"If you need anything…"

The Bhytoe waved them away.

Bettrie went into the side room closest to Jormah. Bka was taken to the corner room and locked in.

Kriiton came back out for a short time wearing the same hooded cloak as the guards. Jormah had made no protest and no complaint.

"Are you sure you don't want to come inside?" Kriiton asked.

Jormah shook his head 'no' in the manner of the Intruders.

"Suit yourself."

I won't ask again.

The rain intensified. The sound of the cloth above Jormah's head grew into a constant *sssss*. It was a protective shell, cave-like, a reminder of simpler times. It merged with the rhythm of the numbness that covered him. Soon there would be a letting go, not just of his body but of the past.

It will have me, Jormah thought.

It will have me.

Kriiton watched from his window. The only light came from the small corner fires that were protected by the overhangs. He could not make Jormah out in this dim light but was certain he had not moved a muscle.

Why won't he leave the net?

Why won't he come in out of the rain?

Is he doing this to spite me?

It felt like he had less control over Jormah now than before the spiking.

Tomorrow we will take away the net and chain you to the post. I don't care if you don't like it. You are no longer master of your fate, and the sooner you understand this the better.

Satisfied, at least for the moment, he left the window and lay down in bed. This rain had a strange dampening effect that dulled the spirit. He was suddenly very tired and closed his eyes, welcoming the respite.

Tomorrow we will begin anew.

Sleep, emanating from Kriiton's body, brought an end to Tremlo's double vision. The time to act had come. From beneath the rooftop, he assumed the posture-of-speed and the world froze in place. Raindrops were now solid objects devoid of movement. He marveled at their individual shapes and the overall beauty of their form.

A beaded curtain of delight.

He touched a droplet. It was solid, and cold, and did not feel like water. He pushed hard. It would not budge. The curtain had become an impenetrable wall, and there were far too many to allow him to weave his way through.

Even if Jormah could achieve the posture-of-speed, it would do them no good in the rain.

Tremlo sat back, marveling at the artistry at work. The currents were a channel, its banks a guiding force. He let go thinking what to do and allowed himself to be carried along.

Releasing the posture, he climbed down the wall and crept over to Kriiton's window. He was soaked by the rain, and his body swelled with memory. He took a deep drink from his watersack and brought forth the sound of Kriiton's body.

Opening the door ever so slightly, he breathed the song of Kriiton.

In and out. In and out, leading the Newland Commander into the deepest of sleeps.

On the floor beside the bed were Kriiton's sandals. Tremlo watched himself tracing the patterns of the straps across his own feet and the color appearing on his skin. The future dictating the present. From a distance, no one would know.

Kriiton's rain-guard hung on the back of the door. Glistening with wet, a small spread of water on the floor beneath.

Easily, silently, removed.

In the dark, in the rain, Kriiton coming out of his quarters and putting on his cloak.

With the hood over his head, Tremlo felt half the world disappear, leaving only his face exposed. He walked straight over to two guards standing beside a small fire beneath the overhang. They snapped into rigid postures, surprised by the Newland Commander's sudden appearance.

"Something new today. Bring the chain," Kriiton said.

For a moment, neither guard moved.

Had they seen through his disguise? Tremlo shifted his arms beneath the cloak, ready to throw it off and leap into the night.

"Bring the leash!" he commanded, using Kriiton's harsher tones.

One guard ran to get it while the other tried to light a torch. The guard returned with the leash and the belt. Tremlo took it from him and wrapped the belt around his own waist just like he had seen them do. The two guards watched him with a look of confusion on their faces.

"Open the net!" Tremlo shouted, setting them in motion so they had no time to think.

The torchbearer led the way trying to keep it from getting extinguished. Tremlo followed, all purpose, no thought, floating along with the currents.

Jormah saw the three approaching and was shaken from the haze of his own preoccupation.

What is Kriiton doing?

Something did not feel right. As best he could tell, Tremlo was not in his usual hiding place. He reached over to Kriiton's quarters where Tremlo had spent so much time of late, hiding beneath the window. He wasn't there. And yet, from inside the room— Jormah could not believe what he was sensing.

Walking towards him was the perfect embodiment of the Newland Commander. No Rehloy had ever attained anything remotely like this. Even with the hood pulled over his head, everything that came through was completely Kriiton.

Do not distract him. It is Kriiton you see in mind and gesture.

"Open the net!" Kriiton commanded.

The guards crouched beneath the makeshift tent and worked to untie the ropes.

"Give me the grips!" he snapped when they finished.

He took the tool from the guard and stepped beneath the cover. Jormah quickly extended his hand.

Tremlo's back was to the guards. He put the chain firmly in Jormah's hand and closed his fingers over it.

Hold this tight.

In the dark, in the rain, with his body blocking their view, the guards would never know he had not attached it to Jormah's hand. Tremlo opened and closed the grips as he had seen it done, his body acting of its own accord, and he, trying not to get in its way.

He backed out and stood up.

"Come!" he ordered.

Jormah moved out from beneath the tarp. He did not know what Kriiton wanted but did not look at him directly for fear of distracting him.

Tremlo pointed towards the gate.

"Go!"

Jormah hesitated a moment, just as he might if this was the real Kriiton. Tremlo pushed him roughly forward and paid out the chain exactly as he had seen the Augmentors do it. The two guards fell in behind and followed along.

"No!" Kriiton commanded, pointing to their former posts. "Go!"

They quickly obeyed, and Tremlo turned his attention to the guards ahead. There were two on either side of the gate and two in either corner. One of these would be the Charge.

Seeing Kriiton and the creature approach, all four began to converge.

"Stop! Open the—" Tremlo suddenly realized he did not know their name for the gate. "Open it!" he shouted to cover his mistake and pulled back on Jormah's chain to stop him. Two of the Augmentors rushed to do so. Once the gate was open, Tremlo pushed Jormah forward.

As they passed through the gate, the guards' confusion turned into wariness.

"Close it," Tremlo said, trying to direct their attention.

They looked at one another.

"Close it!" he shouted, this time pointing for them to stay inside.

Three of the guards looked to the fourth.

He is the Charge. Tremlo thought, facing the man directly.

"Commander, we will come with you."

"No. Charge, close it!"

"Understood."

The Charge signaled them to step back inside and he himself closed the gate.

"Go!" Kriiton commanded Jormah, indicating he should continue along the path that led away from the fortress. To the guards along the outside wall, Kriiton raised his hand to stop them.

"Stay!"

The sharp report of their commander's voice held them in place, and they watched the two disappear into the night.

Once out of sight, Tremlo contained the impulse to run. Pushing the hood off his head, he reached out and felt a solitary figure moving towards them.

"Wait," Tremlo said.

Jormah stared at him. Here was not only the voice of Kriiton but his very face. In the dark, even the hair on his head looked real, but Tremlo did not have hair. Somehow the skin on his head had wrinkled up in places to give it a three-dimensional look.

Here was true Sentience.

"Tremlo?" his voice colored with awe.

"Move on," Kriiton snapped, pulling the hood back up over his head.

Jormah set off as before, and a short time later they encountered an Augmentor coming up the path. The man was startled, but Tremlo took control.

"Something new today. Now go!"

The Augmentor would be questioned when he reached the fortress, and Jormah realized that if they'd hidden from him, this might have aroused suspicion. Somehow everything was falling into place.

Once the Augmentor was out of sight, Tremlo turned to Jormah.

"Give me the leash," he said still in Kriiton's voice.

Jormah handed it to him, and Tremlo ran off to the right where he removed the belt and cloak and threw them deep into the underbrush. Free of these objects, he cocked his head back and felt the rain on his face. His muscles and bones were locked tight, and he had to squeeze Kriiton out carefully so as not to do injury.

The skin on his head, clumped in memory, was last to release its hold.

"Tremlo?"

"We must go."

"They will expect us to head south," Jormah said, marveling at the being before him. "The path is the most direct route there. We should go north instead where their presence is weakest."

Tremlo heard the logic of his words, but he was listening to something beyond words. The north felt thick and heavy. Reaching south, the thought of furskins came to mind.

"The cold season is coming. We will need furskins."

"The path then?"

"No. It feels... the waterbody. Come. We must hurry."

CHAPTER SIXTY

The tide was out, the beach exposed. They ran along the edge of the water, and it lapped up their footprints moments after they passed. Jormah's barbed hand throbbed with the exertion. His arm and shoulder worked against the fluidity of his motion.

'*We must keep going,*' Tremlo urged, leading the way.

"I know," Jormah said, struggling to keep up.

Tremlo eased into a trot to match Jormah's growing fatigue. Late that night, they stopped to rest between an outcropping of rocks.

"Tremlo?" *The way he moves, the way he sits, the stillness, the power.* "What happened?"

The young Kwaman shook his head.

"How did you know what to do?"

"I didn't."

"Then how?"

"I let go. The currents took me."

Jormah understood intuition. He knew what it was like to connect to the rhythms of another, but this was something far beyond that.

"No, it is more than that."

"Sleep now. We will have to move on soon."

They slept for a short time and woke just before dawn. The rain had tapered off, but it was still drizzling.

Tremlo reached back to the compound. There was no real activity.

"Kriiton is still asleep."

Jormah nodded, having no idea. The throbbing numbed all that might have sensed it.

"Let me see." Tremlo took his hand gently in his own. The barb protruded out the back. Its peak and edges were sharp to the touch. They had twisted it to prevent it from being pulled back out. "We must get this thing out of you," he said softly, evenly, to disguise the horror of it. The hand and arm were thick and swollen. The sound of it was spreading across Jormah's shoulder and into his chest.

Invade and possess, the creed of these Intruders.

Tremlo wanted to hit it with a rock and break it off. But he could not see any way to do it without causing Jormah great harm.

He took out his cutting stone and tried to cut into it, but the barb possessed a power greater than stone, and it was his cutter that suffered.

There was a small crack in a boulder nearby.

"Can you fit the barb in there?"

Jormah laid the back of his hand upon it and inserted the tip. He tried to turn his hand to break it off, but the pain and lack of leverage proved too much. If the barb could be broken, this was not the way.

Tremlo searched his mind for a solution, but nothing came.

"I may not get away," Jormah said. "But it is wonderful to be free, if only for a little while."

"We will find a way," Tremlo insisted. *We must find a way!*

Bettrie was first to rise.

She stepped out into the drizzled-gray day. The rain had continued throughout the night.

Has he remained dry?

The muddied ground made squishing sounds as she made her way round to the open side of the tarp. It was still too dark to see clearly, but when she got there, she was startled to find the net lying flat on the ground.

"Where is he? Guard! Where is Jormah?"

"Kriiton came and took him away."

"What? When?"

"In the middle of the night."

"Why?"

"He didn't say."

"Where did he take him?"

"Outside."

"Alone?"

The guard shifted nervously.

"He leashed the creature and took him out of the compound."

"Did he say where he was going?"

"No. He only told us to wait inside."

Bettrie ran to the gate.

"Open it!" she shouted.

Once outside, she looked in all directions. Kriiton and Jormah were nowhere to be seen. Back inside, she questioned the Charge. He confirmed Kriiton left in the middle of the night with the creature.

"He ordered us to stay behind."

It made no sense. Kriiton had taken extraordinary measures to keep Jormah inside.

Why would he risk taking him out?

"Did he say when he would return?"

"No."

Bettrie went to Kriiton's command room to see if she could find anything to indicate what the Newland Commander was thinking.

What is all that noise? Kriiton wondered, waking from such a sound sleep, it felt like he had been drugged. He moved to the window and peered through the shutters. The fogbound drizzle matched his mood. From his window he had a clear view of the open side of the tarp. It was difficult to tell in this light, but it appeared empty.

He hastily pulled on his clothes and burst into the courtyard. The guards leaped to attention, unable to mask their surprise. Kriiton strode up to the tarp and confirmed what he had seen from his window.

"Where is he!" he bellowed. "Bettrie!"

She came running out of the command room.

The guards were trying to explain, but Kriiton refused to listen.

"What do you mean I took him away? Charge!"

The Charge came running.

"Did you see me leave with the creature last night?"

"I— I—"

"Did you?" Kriiton roared.

"Yes, Commander, I did."

"What are you talking about?"

"You leashed the creature and were wearing the belt. You told us to open the gate, and then you went outside and ordered us to stay behind."

"Have you all gone mad?" Kriiton shouted. "I have been in my quarters the whole time! Bettrie, what do you know about this?"

"Only what you do. The guards said you left with him last night."

"And how did I do that again?" he said turning to the Charge.

"Commander, you, you were very insistent."

"Insistent? It was my voice?"

"Yes. I mean it seemed to be."

"Seemed to be? What was I wearing?"

"You were wearing your rain-guard."

"With the hood up or down?"

"Up. But, but it was you, Commander."

Kriiton grabbed the man by the throat.

"In the rain?" he roared. "In the dark with the hood up? Would you stake your life on it?"

He threw the man to the ground and ran back to his room. His rain-guard was missing.

How could this happen?

"Bettrie! When did you find out Jormah was gone?"

"A short time ago."

"Why didn't you come get me?"

"They told me you'd left. It never occurred to me that you were still here."

Kriiton quickly interrogated each member of the guard. They all saw the same thing. Despite their reservations, they had obeyed their leader. "He must have been very convincing," Kriiton snarled. "Bettrie, do you realize what this means? They have the ability to impersonate us. Get your hounds. We are going to hunt them down!"

"With all the rain the hounds might not be able—"

"Do it!" he screamed.

There were eight hounds, and they were eager to begin. Bettrie led them over to the net where they sniffed and sniffed, until they owned it.

"Let's go!"

Kriiton commandeered twenty-four Augmentors and armed them with man-catchers.

The hounds found his rain-guard in a relatively short period of time. Nearby was the belt and leash. There was no tie-link, which should have been attached to Jormah.

"Clever," Kriiton muttered.

From here, the trail grew cold. The rain and wet ground had done much to diffuse the scent. After circling several times, the hounds led them towards the sea. Once there, however, they lost the trail.

It was midday, and the drizzle showed no signs of abating.

"We'll divide into three groups. Randol, take eight men and two hounds and follow the shoreline north. Bettrie, take eight men and two hounds and go south. Since the creatures came from that direction there is a good chance they will head back there. I will take the remaining men and four hounds and go along Main Row. We'll coordinate the search from the outposts. As soon as the sky clears, each group must set up Relayers. With a little luck, we will be able to surround them."

"But if we can't see them, what are we supposed to do?"

"The hounds should alert you. Use your nets even if you see nothing. We know these will hold them. If you are confronted by me, use your net first and ask questions later. We will use the password, 'Hail Ontar.' If you do not get that, you will know it's not me. They have a good head start. It could be days before we catch them. The group that captures them will be rewarded with a bar of avarin."

"Understood."

Kriiton and his group raced back to the fort. He would spread the hounds out along Main Row, all the way to the farthest outposts, to try and cut the creatures off.

If they've gone north, all is probably lost.

There was only one outpost in that direction, and the terrain was most difficult. South, however, there was still a chance.

Just before nightfall, the two hounds in Bettrie's group veered sharply from the edge of the water. They sniffed excitedly around a large outcropping of rocks on the beach.

"What are they doing?" the Charge demanded.

"Jormah and the other one may have been here," Bettrie said. "It's hard to be sure." But she knew it was them. They were racing south, parallel to Main Row.

"We have to let the others know," the Charge insisted.

"Agreed. Send your fastest runner back along the shore to catch Randol. At first light, we'll send someone due west through the forest to Main Row to meet up with Kriiton."

"Understood."

Bettrie watched the runner set off, knowing Kriiton would not have hesitated to send a second man through the forest at night.

Run, Jormah. Run.

Tremlo felt a flurry of activity around the place where they had stopped to rest. Two of the animals he sensed on that ship a lifetime ago were with them.

They can smell us.

Jormah's body was giving off the sour odor of one who was sick or wounded.

"They found us."

"You would know better than I." The bitterness in the Kwaman's voice was unmistakable. The sound of the spike was spreading. He could barely sense the Intruders as a group, let alone pick out individuals. "It must be the hounds. Bettrie spoke to me of their plans to use these animals to hunt down Yarka cubs."

Tremlo reached out. Four others were traveling along the main path in separate carts.

Kriiton is with them.

A twinge of the Newland Commander lingered.

He will try to surround us like one giant net.

If Jormah was well, their abilities in the assumptions and the posture-of-speed would have been all they needed to escape, but now....

"We need to get past the last outpost before they do and find some way of removing the barb from your hand."

"And if there is no way?"

Tremlo was silent.

"You will have to cut off my hand."

A wave of repulsion. On the fringes of his awareness, this was a distinct possibility. There were many choices ahead. Each one leading to a different reality. If only he could *see* more clearly.

"Jormah, you could bleed to death or die from the rot that might set in."

"My hand is already lost to me. It threatens to take my body with it. If we get away, I would rather die as I am than live like another."

"Don't say such things."

Envisioning such a thing was the first step to realizing it.

"Tremlo, you are not just Kwaman. You are Sentient. I can't begin to understand what that means, but you must consider every possibility, good or bad. And there is one more thing you have to consider."

"I will not leave you behind," Tremlo said, emphatically. This was another possibility looming in the not-too-distant future.

"Tremlo, if the Intruders think you are near, they will not rest until they have captured you." Jormah pointed to the barb. "You see how ferocious they are. If I can't escape, then that is my fate. Yours is not to waste away beside me. From you, greater things are expected."

"I'm not sure I—"

"Don't you feel it? The weight of your presence? Things grow still when you draw near. You are a focal point for a gathering force. The moment you were born, I felt you, even though I was far away. I do not know what your purpose is, but meaningless sacrifice cannot be it."

Tremlo had not told him that when he reached into the future, he could not find a sense of himself. Things around him seemed to continue on, but he himself was not there.

Am I going to die?

When Jormah got caught in the slave trap, he feared for the Kwaman's wellbeing. When the Intruder's drove the barb through Jormah's hand, it roused such feelings of fear and despair, he was driven to act. The reasons seemed obvious, but now he felt his desire to get away from this place might have its roots elsewhere.

I don't belong here.

Reaching out to the south and west, he peered high and far and wide through the currents. Somewhere, near the tribal lands, was where he breathed most easily. That was where he needed to be.

"Something is calling. I must get back. And you with me."

We shall see, Jormah thought. *We shall see.*

CHAPTER SIXTY-ONE

Gremar awoke long before the others and stood quietly so as not to wake them.

Here is your Leader, ever watchful, maintaining a protective posture.

Entering the Valley Forest had been seamless. Drawing closer to the northern edge however, the weight of the City became more pronounced, and a vague sense of worry set in. Something felt particularly off this morning.

He reached out to determine the cause. It didn't take long.

Reena.

She was in the sparse land just beyond the Forest.

Why didn't she tell me she was going?

He had been trying to win her over, but no matter what he did, she kept him at arm's length. She and Kenectka were often together and if he approached, Reena always drifted away. As far back as he could remember, the older members of the tribe avoided him in some way. Amongst themselves, there was a sense of ease with one another, a connection, a middle ground, unspoken, aligned. He felt none of this.

The others were waking, and Gremar quickly affected a posture of *knowing*.

"We will come to the end of the Forest today, and have a clear view of the City-Of-Straight-Lines," he said before they had a chance to reach out. "Reena is already there, communing with the currents. We will go slowly to give her time."

He had planned to turn back once they got to the edge of the Forest and avoid the growing discomfort ahead. Reena's leaving changed all that. Where she went the others would surely follow, whether they were ready or not.

Reena had entered the sparse land immersed in the distant currents and oblivious to her surroundings. She found herself sitting upon a thick patch of scrub grass. With daylight came a host of new sensations.

Ahead, the rising tensions of the City. Behind, the soft vibrations of the Rehloy. Within her, maternal instincts raged. She wanted to strike out. She wanted to defend. She wanted to run away.

Let go, she thought. *Feelings are irrelevant. Let go.*
Listen.

Gremar led them to the edge of the Valley Forest.

Rely on me, his body said. *Rely on me.*

They followed him out of the Forest into the unobstructed sight of the mountains. A dizzying array of greens, grays, browns, and blacks rising up to the sky. High atop stood the City-Of-Straight-Lines. Dressed in white, larger and louder than ever before, its sharply wrought forms pricked their skin.

Most recoiled, but Gremar stood firm. The harsh tones hurt, but he would not show it. If this was the potential voice of the future, it would have to be endured.

Reena was sitting some distance ahead, her back to them.

She clearly did not want to be disturbed.

"Let us take shelter just inside the Forest," Gremar said, as if for their benefit, but he wished only to quell the rising discomfort in his own body.

For the rest of the day, they remained safely tucked within the shade.

When the sun set, the voice of the City softened.

Reena made no move to return.

"We will spend the night here," Gremar said.

And sleep within the cool arms of the Forest.

There was nothing to do but wait for Reena to return.

"What do you think she's sensing?" he asked Stelbin when they were alone.

"I don't know."

"Will you tell me if you find out?"

Gremar kept his eyes soft, his expression open and humble like he had seen others do. Stelbin was surprised. Here was a vulnerability in Gremar he had not seen before.

"Of course."

Gremar smiled shyly, keeping his mind and body free of thought and feeling. Later, when Stelbin wasn't scrutinizing him, he would think about what just happened and what use he might make of it in the future.

Stelbin waited until everyone was asleep before moving into the sparse land. Reena was lying on her back with eyes closed, but he knew she was awake. Her body was angled to the north and east, and he sensed she was far beyond the City-Of-Straight-Lines.

He lay down beside her and assumed the same posture.

"What are you sensing?" he asked after a time.

How could she explain what she was feeling? In one moment, she was nearly sick with worry. In the next, centered and more grounded than before.

Something is acquiring weight. Something is growing.

"What are you sensing?" Stelbin asked again, drawing her back to the question.

"It... is difficult to say." Reena sat up. "Something terrible is happening and forcing something greater to unfold."

Stelbin scrutinized her carefully.

"As if," he ventured, "in this very moment, our fate was being decided?"

"Yes!" she exclaimed. "You feel it?"

"I feel a wisp of tension in the air. But what I sense mostly comes from you."

"The struggle has intensified. Energy is shifting, setting new things into motion."

Stelbin reached through the currents.

"I feel it here," Reena said, bringing her hand to the place between her chest and abdomen. This was the place she usually touched when referring to her experience of Tremlo.

"How is he?"

"A storm of events is swirling around them. He is changing."

"In what way?"

How could she give words to something she *felt* but did not *know*?

"A bird soars through the sky. We cannot see how it walks until it lands."

"So, nothing is set?"

Something is acquiring weight. Something growing.

Reena lapsed into silence and listened to the currents, searching for pieces of herself out there, *in here*. From beginning, to middle, to now, her life separate from his.

She had never borne another child, even though she and Arlen had tried. In one sense she was still pregnant with Tremlo and the thing that had touched him.

Forces flowing through him move through me.

Could there be purpose here? Something being asked, something required?

From this vantage point, she was placed differently than Tremlo.

I need to grow beyond our connection.

Did she have to abandon him?

Not abandon. Release.

Her body shivered, but she was not cold.

You have to let go, so something new can emerge.

"I will leave you to your musing," Stelbin said and returned to the others.

Gremar awoke just before dawn and found Reena had also returned sometime in the night. She was sitting in balance-position beside them.

"Do you want to go on to the City-Of-Straight-Lines?" he asked. If she said no, it would appear he was giving in to her, and he would avoid the discomfort they all might experience if they continued.

She looked at him carefully, seeing his question as half genuine and half manipulative. Yet, there was a role here for him to play.

"There is no need," she replied. None of them wanted to go, though they would have done so if she wished it. "There is no need," she repeated, for she received what she had come for.

Gremar looked at her with the same open expression he had used on Stelbin. He looked at her in this new way... and she noticed.

CHAPTER SIXTY-TWO

K riiton reached the first outpost.

"I'm leaving you a hound and a handler. Start patrolling the path immediately. I doubt they've crossed, but the hounds will let you know. The moment the weather clears, set up a proper light path. Now bring us fresh oxten. We have to keep going."

"Understood."

Kriiton and his driver led the way. The other three charcarts followed with driver, handler, and hound. At a certain point, Kriiton sat down upon the floor and covered himself with his rain-guard. The gentle rattling of the wood floor beneath made it easy to fall asleep.

Jormah stumbled and fell. *Exhausted.* The sound of the spike rang loudly in his ears.

"Let me lie for a while," he said, burying himself in the feel of wet ground.

Tremlo smelled the stiffness in his body. Rigid, inert, a moment held in time. For a Rehloy, the sickening smell of death.

This is what the hounds will smell.

He kneeled down and kneaded Jormah's shoulders and back. The muscles were taut, and Tremlo's fingers dug in, hoping to remind them of who they were.

Jormah passed out, but Tremlo continued to work on him, determined to release the numbness from each and every muscle. Soon his own hands burned with the rhythm-of-the-spike.

If only we could rest for a day.

They were nearly even with the second outpost. Kriiton had left the first one and was speeding on through the night. Those on the beach behind were slowing down.

Because of the rain? The soft ground? Bettrie?

"Jormah."

Tremlo had waited as long as possible.

"Jormah."

The sun was rising to reveal a sky still clouded with grey, but the rain had stopped.

"We must leave."

The Kwaman sat up and the rhythm-of-the-spike quickly reasserted itself. The rest had been all too brief.

"When I was trapped in the grassland and going bodyblind, I took some yellow Broezia. It helped me recapture a portion of myself," Jormah said, taking out a large pinch and swallowing it whole.

When the surge hit, it drove the spike out of his body and back down into his hand. He stood up and the world with all its nuances returned. For one blessed moment, he remembered... and then the rhythm-of-the-spike came roaring back, enhanced now by the Broezia. It shot up his arm at a fever's pitch and set him on fire.

Jormah cried out and dove into the water to escape the inferno, but it did not help. Leaping up, he ran along the water's edge, splashing as he went; sight, sound, the wetness beneath his feet. Anything to distract himself from the terrible sensation that had taken hold.

"Jormah." Tremlo raced after him. "Jormah!"

He soon fell behind Jormah's terrible, Broezia-inspired dash. Not until noon did the Kwaman begin to falter, and by the time Tremlo caught up to him, he was lying unconscious on the ground, the life wrung out of him.

The clouds parted, and the sun's unbridled light rained down upon them.

Relayers quickly established communication, and the third outpost burst into life. One group rushed down through the forest towards the sea.

"Jormah," Tremlo said, gently placing his hand upon his back.

The Intruders would reach the beach up ahead and block their way.

Jormah was curled up tight. He looked like a seed about to sprout. The future that would grow up around this reality felt too horrible to imagine.

"Jormah!"

The Kwaman did not stir. The acrid smell of rigidity colored his breath.

"Jormah, wake up!" Tremlo shouted and shook him hard.

The Intruders would split up once they reached the beach. One group would go north and the other south.

We have to get off the beach.

"Wake up!"

Jormah moaned. His body, his senses, his very thoughts ached. What little came forth quickly receded.

Tremlo managed to drape him over his shoulder and stood up. He staggered off the beach to hard ground, and put him down. Returning to the beach, Tremlo smoothed out the sand and erased their tracks. The Intruders would not find them. The hounds, however, were another matter.

The Kwaman was inert, his body hot to the touch.

Tremlo carried him deeper into the forest and stopped beside a small brook.

"Jormah," he said. "Jormah."

Each time the Kwaman came out of his delirium, Tremlo made him drink fresh water.

"Jormah," he said. "Jormah."

The Intruders from the third outpost reached the beach near sunset and took up positions for the night. Several were very near the spot where he had carried Jormah into the forest.

"Jormah," Tremlo said softly. "Jormah." He placed wet leaves on his body when he got too hot, and lay down next to him to warm him when he got too cold. *Kenectka and Mortulla telling him what to do.*

Kriiton reached the second outpost, and the Charge came running.

"Commander! Bettrie's group picked up their trail."

"Where?"

"Near the first outpost."

Good, Kriiton thought. Jormah and his accomplice were heading south along the beach.

"What are the positions of the other groups?"

"Randol's group is about a day behind Bettrie's. A patrol from the third outpost reached the beach and took up positions for the night. Neither has reported finding anything yet."

"Nor are they likely. These creatures can make themselves invisible. I'm leaving you two hounds. Have them patrol the path north and south immediately. I'm taking the last one to the third outpost."

"Understood."

Kriiton set off once more. With any luck, he would reach the third outpost by morning. He did not think Jormah and the other one had gotten that far. With Augmentors on the beach, they would be cut off. It was the forest between the beach and the path that he was most concerned about. It was here that the hounds would prove invaluable.

"Jormah."

The Intruders were too close, and the trail they left behind too obvious.

"Jormah," he said, becoming more insistent.

The Kwaman heard the tone in his voice and came to the surface. The world was a painful place.

"Jormah."

Eyes opened.

Tremlo dragged him over to a tree and propped him up against its trunk. It would leave a trace of scent, but it could not be helped.

"We can't stay here," he said. "I will carry you, but I need your help." He crouched down with his back to him.

The Kwaman leaned forward and wrapped his arms weakly around Tremlo's neck.

"Ready?"

Tremlo grabbed his legs and stood up. The rhythms circulating through the Kwaman's body were irritating, but Tremlo refused to listen. Stepping into the brook, he wove their way through the dark night as only a Rehloy might. Once out, he avoided brushing up against the leaves and brush as best he could, but there were moments when something of Jormah was touched.

Late that night, Tremlo stopped. He was exhausted and near collapse. He put Jormah down. and lay down himself. They were a good distance from the beach and closer now to the path. A cart carrying a hound was coming from the north.

Kriiton.

He would pass them by and reach the third outpost by morning. They would bring the hound to the beach, and the hunt would be on.

"I must rest."

Tremlo closed his eyes. He could not sleep long but had to sleep hard.

CHAPTER SIXTY-THREE

The sensations of morning light filled the forest with sights, sounds and newborn smells.

Tremlo instantly awake, Jormah, coming into consciousness, the Broezia-inspired pain gone. The singular sound of the spike was now woven throughout his body.

He sat up slowly.

His perceptions dim, his body sluggish. He sounded more Intruder than Rehloy.

The sound of the ancestors, Tremlo thought, reaching out to the path. "Kriiton and the hound are almost here," he said "The third outpost is not far off. We will wait for them to pass before we cross."

They sat in stillness, Jormah listening as hard as he could, but only when Tremlo turned to him did he know that Kriiton had passed.

"Can you walk?"

'*Yes.*'

Jormah's legs were stiff, his movements awkward. He left a mark on everything he touched. The Intruders would have no difficulty tracking them now.

Tremlo reached through the currents, desperate for an avenue of escape.

Here-and-now, far-and-wide, spreading into *what-might-be.*

Ground faded, sounds grew shallow, light turned to shade. In this state, the softest of breezes might change the course of history.

Where was the pressure greatest? Where did it hurt the least?

To the west, a narrow corridor.

The ghost of a hound suddenly appeared. Tremlo leaped to the side. The animal did not see him and ran around in a circle before charging off into the woods. A second apparition came up the main path. It stopped across from them before turning sharply, nose to the ground, and raced back down the path to the south. Near the third outpost, several more converged and headed west through the forest with a frenzy in their bearing.

Three streams of energy. Three possible futures. Which one?

Tremlo searched for a memory that did not yet exist.

We can't just stand here.

"Jormah, jump onto my back from where you're standing." His words echoed in his mind. "Blend in with me as best you can."

Tremlo braced himself, not for the Kwaman's weight, but the harsh feel of the rhythm-of-the-spike.

Jormah landed on his back with a thud and propelled them forward onto the path. Tremlo headed towards the third outpost, listening to the ground beneath his feet, determined not to leave a sign. It was difficult to prevent Jormah's sickly smell from circulating through his own body. But he hid it from the hounds as best he could.

Keeping to the middle of the path, he searched for that cut between the trees the last group of hounds had gone through.

Watchers from the third outpost spilled out onto the main path, some were coming back towards them, while others went south. Kriiton was heading down to the beach with men, and more importantly, the hound.

Jormah held on tight. Even with his limited capacities, he felt Intruders just around the bend. At the last instant, Tremlo ducked in between the trees, and moments later, the Intruders passed by the very place they had entered.

Tremlo picked his way swiftly over the coarse terrain. His body cushioned the weight on his back. His feet betrayed nothing beneath. Only when softer ground forced them to leave an impression did he stop.

"It's time," he said, and Jormah slid off is back.

CHAPTER SIXTY-FOUR

They headed due west. Jormah's shoulders were squared. He bobbed up and down as he walked, and when they stopped to rest, he did not sit in balance-position but stretched his legs out in front of him. His leefskin looked more like a husk as his eyes darted back and forth to compensate for what his body no longer saw.

There was a density to him now that was difficult to watch.

"What are they doing?"

"The hounds on the beach found our scent. They are following our trail up through the forest."

Jormah nodded. He was like a child listening to a story. It was his body that would lead the Intruders right to them.

"We need to keep moving."

Here, the hounds were baying. *Here!*

Men came running. After searching the area on either side of Main Row, no one had suspected that Jormah and the other one would have come this close to the third outpost.

Clever, Kriiton thought. It was the last place they had looked for them.

"Bettrie, you lead. We'll take four hounds and their handlers with us. Charge, signal the rest to patrol Main Row in case they double back."

Bettrie nodded as if approving, but neither was fooled. Her slow pace along the beach had not gone unnoticed. Kriiton did not know if it was inexperience, or subterfuge, but he would take no more chances with this Animal Trainer.

"They've gained at least a day on us if not two," he shouted for all to hear. "Two days! We'll have to force-march. If the hounds get tired, we will carry them. We have two days to make up!"

"Understood!"

They set off as fast as the hounds could take them.

"They are onto us."

"Yes?"

"From now on we travel when they do," Tremlo heard himself say, "and stop only if they do."

"It will not be enough."

"If you have the strength, we will keep going after they stop."

"You know what I mean. You will have to cut off the hand or leave me behind."

Jormah picked up a sharp stone and brought it down to his side in one fell swoop. "A small cutter will take too long. A wood chopper would be best. One or two swings and it will be over."

A wave of dizziness came over Tremlo. Severing the hand led to circumstances that gnawed at his insides. He pushed away and reached far and wide for any beasts in the area. If he could find a Yarka and drive it towards the Intruders, it might kill the hounds and send the men running.

How am I thinking this?

"Tremlo."

Jormah repeated the chopping motion. "With a little shaping, this stone will do nicely."

'Tie a thin vine tightly around his forearm to stop the flow of blood.' Kenectka's voice inside his head. *'Once the hand is severed, the wrist must be singed with hot coals. Wrap the wound with strips of bandola soaked in baelo, and relene. Eucra for infection, astra for pain.*

'Jormah will need at least a day's rest before traveling is possible.'

Tremlo pushed away from these thoughts and pressed on through the forest.

"Where are you taking us?"

His body was taking them. A step to the right, Jormah's hand would be cut off. A step to the left, some other tragedy. Treading between the two, fearing both, Tremlo held to a dream in order to manifest a reality.

"What is happening?"

He did not know. Between now and what-could-be, were a host of sensations. Within himself, legions. Each conscious act was composed of a multitude of unconscious thoughts. Inner selves. Inner lives. With the posture-of-speed, he learned he could live a lifetime between one moment and the next.

Was he an inner self to a greater world? Were there other forces within this universe called Tremlo?

Was something watching? Something to do with the Resep?

Or was this just the way of things? An infinite number of possibilities offered up in any moment, condensing into a reality in the next. Time and again, moment by moment.

What to listen to?

Lost in the swirl. The greater pressure behind drove them into whatever lay ahead.

"Tremlo?" Jormah said, raising his hand, threatening once again.

"Sharpen the stone if you must," Tremlo heard himself say, deflecting Jormah's thrust, even as he delayed it. "We need to get farther away from the Intruders."

A day to prepare and chop it off. A day to recover. Two more to spare.

It was appalling, but what choice did he have?

They traveled most of the night and long past when the Intruders stopped. Tremlo estimated they were two days behind them. It was going to be difficult to get the extra days they needed.

The following day the Intruders established a rhythm and pressed on longer into the night. At daybreak, it began once again.

How long will they pursue?

Tremlo flowed along ever faster, focusing on the unfocused state. If he gave into fear, it would be the end of them. The weight of the world pressed in on all sides. Threading his way through an unknown reality, he sought to avoid what felt unbearable.

Reaching far ahead, he was shocked to a standstill.

A solitary figure lurked in the direction they were heading. Definitely a Stiffback, but whether Intruder or Other was unclear. If a Watcher, he might be in contact with other Intruders.

"There is someone ahead," Tremlo said.

"How far?"

The young Kwaman spread his hands wide.

They continued north, ever more cautiously. Tremlo's mind was awash with impressions from ahead and behind. He held to the path, the vision, despite his growing apprehension.

Night fell and he stopped. *'Wait here.'*

Speeding through the forest, all senses alive and listening.

Why this being? Why here? Why now?

He slowed, careful not to make a sound. Closing in, advancing in the stalking manner, he stopped behind a thick tree and peered around.

It was a Watcher.

Is he waiting for us?

The man had dug a deep pit and set a small fire. The flames were hidden and limited his exposure. The man stared into the flames. There were no bundles or sacks lying on the ground. Only this Watcher and a long cutter beside him.

Its sharp edges could cut off a hand.

Could it cut through a spike?

What if this Watcher knew how to get it out of Jormah's hand?

What if I appear as Kriiton and order him do it?

"Come! The creature."

He could point to Jormah's hand. *"Open it! Release him!"*

Afterwards he could send the Watcher on his way. *"Go!"*

If only he had Kriiton's cloak. Instead, he would have to maintain his distance and keep mostly to the dark.

I will have to control this man with Kriiton's voice.

But what if the Watcher knew of the escape?

What if he suspects I am not Kriiton?

Within the man's body was a readiness to strike. Twice he turned his head sharply in one direction or another. There was nothing to warrant it.

Madness.

The Watcher took out a small cutter and scraped thin strips off the stalk of a curta plant. Holding the strips above the fire, he began to chant. It was a lonely sound and pulled at Tremlo's insides. The Watcher dropped the strips into the fire one by one. Each strip sizzled, giving off a greenish wisp of scent before it burst into flames.

After burning the last one, the man stopped chanting and sat very still. It seemed like a prayer of sorts.

After a time, he picked up a small piece of wood and looked in all directions before adding it to the fire. He took out a dark stone from his side pouch and began to slide it carefully along the edge of his small cutter. It made a dry, rasping sound. After several passes, the Watcher tested the sharpness of the blade with his finger. Satisfied, he put the stone away and stared deep into the flames.

Despair.

The quality of the ache spoke of the man as surely as if he had shouted out his name.

The one tied to the tree!

This Watcher was not in league with the others. This was an outcast.

Wilton usually began the memory in the middle of the beating. This time, however, his mind started at the end. He was tied so tightly around the tree he could barely breathe. His back seethed with stripes of pain. His arms, choked of blood, cried out into the night.

Suddenly the rope was untied and he fell to the ground. Looking up, the face of a wondrous being appeared before him. The spirit's eyes bathed him with love and understanding. He forgot the rages of his body.

You will be all right, it seemed to say. A hand appeared out of nowhere and touched his face. *Everything will be all right.*

The feeling was so strong now that Wilton looked up from his thoughts and saw that very same spirit materializing before him.

"Ah!" he cried, leaping to his feet and falling to his knees. Head bowed, he burst into tears. His prayer had been answered.

Tremlo stood before him.

"Tremlo," the spirit said, lifting Wilton's head with his voice.

"Tremlo," the spirit said again, a deep voice, lilting, pointing to himself.

Wilton pressed his forehead to the ground.

I am yours.

Tremlo placed his hand on the back of Wilton's head. After a moment he sat down and waited.

Wilton looked up.

"Tremlo," the spirit said again. There was a quizzical expression on his face, a questioning in his voice. Was he asking him his name?

"Wilton," Wilton said, his voice coming out in a whisper.

"Wilton," Tremlo said, nodding his head in the manner of the Intruders.

"Tremlo," Wilton said lowering his head, afraid to look at him directly.

The Tremlo stood.

Was he going to leave again?

The spirit smiled.

"Come. Come, Wilton."

Wilton stood and took a step towards him.

"Bring," The Tremlo said, pointing to the ground.

"The sword?"

"Yes. Bring the s-word."

Wilton slid it into his scabbard.

"Come," The Tremlo said and led him into the forest.

Wilton extended his arm out in front of him to protect his face in the dark. The Tremlo reached back and took hold of his hand. His touch was unlike anything Wilton had ever felt. It didn't so much hold his hand as envelop it. At times, its grasp seemed nonexistent. And yet, if he stumbled, it was suddenly vice-like and rock-hard. He would never fall while in this hand's possession.

Wilton let go all resistance.

My life is yours.

They headed back in the general direction of Main Row, but Wilton did not care. In the past, he had little regard for his fellow man, and less so for religion, but The Tremlo had heard his prayers and returned. Nothing else mattered.

Use me, he thought. *Let me be of service. Let me make amends.*

Tremlo flowed steadily through the black night as if it were bright day.

Where you lead, I will follow. Forever.

When the spirit stopped and let go his hand, they were standing in a small clearing. The stars above cast a vague light. The Tremlo pointed to an empty place on the ground.

"It's all right, Jormah. I have brought him here to help."

The Kwaman released the feeble defensive-posture and Wilton gasped.

There are two of them!

The Tremlo placed a hand on his shoulder and sat him down.

"Stay, Wilton," he said. Then to Jormah, "He may know how to re-move the spike. If not, his cutter may serve another purpose."

Jormah studied the Watcher. How had Tremlo managed to befriend him?

"We need to make a fire so he can see," Tremlo said.

"I know this one!" Jormah exclaimed. "He's the one you set free."

"Yes."

"How did you know?"

"I didn't."

Tremlo was Sentient. Some part of him had to have known.

"The currents took me where they would."

To Wilton, their words sounded more like singing than speech. If only he knew what they were saying. They lit a small fire, and he got a clearer look at them. Both were covered in what appeared to be leaves.

Were they trees come to life?

The Tremlo sat in such perfect balance he nearly vanished into thin air. The other one was older. He was leaning to one side and seemed bound to the earth.

"Jormah," Tremlo said pointing to the Kwaman. "Jormah." Then pointing to Wilton, "Wilton."

"Wilton," Jormah repeated.

"Jormah," Wilton replied.

"Jormah, show him."

The Kwaman extended his hand, and Wilton's heart sank. The barb protruded out the back in horrible contrast to the elegance of that hand.

"You're the one," he said, filled with shame for what his people had done. "You're the one they caught, aren't you?"

His words were Intruder and scraped against the quiet of the night.

"Yes," Tremlo said, sensing the meaning. He pointed to Jormah. "Wilton, open Jormah."

Wilton understood why he was here and what was needed.

I am yours, forever.

"Open Jormah." Tremlo's voice was gentle, coaxing. "Release him."

"I will try."

Wilton took Jormah's hand and turned it gently this way and that. The barb was meant to be permanent. Its wings lay firmly against the back of Jormah's hand while a chain-ring on the palm side kept it from being pulled through. The shaft was short and created a close fit. It would be nearly impossible to saw through without cutting deep into the hand itself. Besides, he did not have a saw.

The weapon's maker used belomite, the strongest metal known to Ontar. It was difficult to cut and impossible to break. Kriiton had no intention of ever letting Jormah go.

Wilton sat back, head down. He did not have the tools nor a weapon maker's skill. His knife and sword were sharp, but in all likelihood, they would not cut through belomite. Short of chopping off Jormah's hand, he did not know what to do.

Tremlo felt his despair.

'It is late and we are tired. Let us sleep now and see what the day brings.'

He pointed to a place near the fire.

"Wilton, stay."

Wilton lay down where Tremlo indicated.

Tremlo and Jormah took up places farther away and nearly disappeared from sight. For a moment, Wilton feared they would leave him. Yet they remained where they were, and eventually he closed his eyes.

You must free Jormah, he said to himself. *You must free him.* He could not bear the thought of failing them.

Try something. Anything! You must find a way.

On and on his mind went until the air about him grew thick and heavy.

'Sleep, Wilton,' Tremlo thought. 'Sleep.'

CHAPTER SIXTY-FIVE

Wilton woke at first light, relieved to find the two still there. The edges of Tremlo's body blended in with the world about, making it hard to see him.

Jormah was dull by comparison. His spiked hand was stiff like a man's and set the tone for the rest of his body.

"It's all the spike's doing," Wilton blurted out, feeling sick inside. *This is what happens when men lay claim to spirits. They turn them into men.*

He had to do something.

"Put your hand down like this," Wilton said, making a fist and placing his knuckles flat on the ground. Jormah did as he asked. The barb was perpendicular to the back of his hand. Wilton put a piece of wood beneath it to prevent the barb from moving.

He pulled out his sword and took careful aim.

The sharp report of metal hitting metal sent a jolt up Jormah's arm and snapped his head back.

"Sorry!" Wilton cried. "Sorry."

Jormah stretched his neck.

Wilton looked closer at the barb. Not even a mark on it. If this were to work, it would require far more force than he had just used.

Jormah hardened himself to the purpose at hand, *'Again.'*

"Forgive me."

Wilton swung harder this time. Jormah's whole body flinched despite his efforts to resist.

The barb was barely scratched.

"Again."

Tremlo reached for Jormah's good hand to distract him, but the Kwaman refused, knowing Tremlo's sensitivity.

You will feel enough of it as you are.

Wilton took aim and swung again, each time coming down a little harder, until he was employing full swings. It was like trying to cut through solid rock.

"Stop!" Jormah cried. He needed a moment.

Tremlo took Wilton's sword in his own hand. It was heavier than he imagined, its edge sharper than any cutting stone he had ever touched. He swung the sword from left to right. It made a swooshing sound as it split the air. This was truly a force to be reckoned with. Tremlo raised it over his head and brought it down with incredible force, turning it aside at the last instant.

Here was the power to cut off a hand, a limb, a life.

The power of the Intruders.

He felt Kriiton and the others moving steadily through the forest. Less than two days behind.

Inevitable, he thought. *They are inevitable.*

Wilton took out his knife and scraped it against the barb to see if he could find any weakness in the belomite. When this failed, he began to chop at it with short, pointed stabs, but only succeeded in chipping his blade. The belomite was just too strong.

He took out his sandstone and began to grind the chip out of his knife. After the third pass, the idea came to him.

"Jormah, make a fist like this and put it on its side so the barb faces up and down."

Jormah did as he asked. Wilton notched out a slot in a piece of wood and slid it under the bottom half of the barb. Once secured, he began to scrape the sandstone across the protruding wing. The vibration set Jormah's body on edge. This was not the sharp report of the sword but an unnerving sensation that sought to shake him apart.

Back and forth, back and forth. Jormah rocked along, sometimes violently so, but kept his hand completely still.

The edge of the wing grew dull.

"It's working. I think it's working!"

While the scraping sound continued to send waves of dissonance through Jormah's body, it helped ease Tremlo's mind.

At one point, the sandstone slipped and cut into the back of Jormah's hand. Jormah did not make a sound, but a droplet of blood appeared.

Jormah covered the cut with his finger and nodded for Wilton to continue.

A bit of blood had leaked onto the top of the wing. Its wetness seemed to help the sandstone cut through the belomite. How a liquid could make grinding metal easier was lost on Wilton, but from then on, he kept the barb moist with drops of water.

At one point, he stopped to rest. The barb was definitely getting duller, but there was not much to show for his labor. Tremlo took over and attacked the barb with vigor. He moved faster than Wilton ever could, and applied greater force.

Jormah's body burst into harsh smells.

Tremlo immediately adjusted his speed and did only what the Kwaman could bear.

When he stopped, the wing had lost some of its bulk. Jormah was soaked in sweat but made no complaint.

Wilton took over, and they alternated all morning. By the afternoon one side of the barb had been ground away, and by nightfall, the other side was gone. They saw clearly now how tightly Jormah's hand had grown around the shaft. It would not be easy to remove it.

Tremlo went off to gather bandola leaves, eucra, and a large handful of insect webs they called faloneet. Upon his return, he dug a narrow hole in the dirt. Jormah lay the back of his hand down flat and inserted the protruding shaft into the hole. Tremlo placed one foot firmly over Jormah's fingers and the other on top of his wrist. Bending down at the knees, he took hold of the ring in the Kwaman's palm.

"Jormah?"

The Kwaman looked up, and Tremlo straightened his legs with a violent thrust. The foul device went flying off into the woods. He quickly pressed the webs onto both sides of the Kwaman's hand, and once the bleeding stopped, wrapped bandola leaves tightly around the wound.

Wilton watched in awe. Jormah had remained completely still the entire time. It was like he was watching his body from afar.

"Rest now," Tremlo said. The sound of his voice nearly put them both to sleep.

"Intruders are closing in. Tomorrow they will be a day behind. We must leave first thing in the morning."

He handed Jormah some astra for the pain, and the Kwaman dutifully chewed. The pain was a welcome relief from the spike. That foul device was gone, but its presence still echoed through his body.

It's just a matter of time, he thought. *Just a matter of time before it goes away.*

At dawn, Jormah stood and began his deewah free of that physical encumbrance. But he was not free. His hand had swollen overnight, and his movements were affected. Tremlo joined in support. From Wilton's view, they possessed an elegance far beyond the capabilities of normal men. Here was reverence in motion, an expression of things so much greater than themselves, it left him choked with emotion.

Tremlo touched Wilton's shoulder.

You are our friend.

"Please," Wilton begged. "Take me with you."

Tremlo's arm gently stiffened, and his face grew somber.

"Please," Wilton cried. "There is nothing for me here. I have no purpose and no place to go. Let me come with you. I can still be of use."

They did not understand most of his words, but the tone in his voice said it all.

"I won't make trouble, I promise. Please," he said. "Please, please…."

Tremlo did not have the heart to drive him away.

"The Watcher should not come with us," Jormah warned.

"We shall see," Tremlo said. He peeled soft bark off a sapling, and apologized to it as he did so. The Intruders would find this mark, but it would merely confirm what the hounds were smelling. He wove a sling from the strips and hung it around Jormah's neck to minimize the movement of his arm while they traveled.

With that they set off, and Wilton followed.

Jormah's movements were encumbered, but he left less of a mark upon the ground than before. Wilton was another matter. Despite his efforts, he made strong impressions upon the subtleties of the forest.

The hounds rushed back and forth, panting with excitement.

"They were here for some time," one of the handlers said.

"At least a day. Maybe more," another added.

"How do we know that?" Kriiton asked Bettrie directly.

"The sounds they are making. The smell is strong."

"So we're gaining on them."

"Possibly."

"Why would they waste time here?"

"Maybe they did not think we were so close."

"You believe that?"

Bettrie shrugged. Kriiton questioned her every word now.

"Search the area!"

"What are we looking for?"

"Anything out of the ordinary."

The handlers separated, urging the hounds out in four different directions.

"Here!"

"What have you got?"

"I think it's the spike, or what's left of it."

The shaft itself was colored with dried blood, but the wings of the barb were gone. The creatures had managed to grind them down.

But how?

An Augmentor found a piece of wood with a thin slot cut into it. *The work of a blade, and by the color, no more than a day or so old.*

"They had help!"

"It must be Wilton," Kriiton deduced. "They have been in league with him all along. Search the grounds for any sign of him!"

A short time later the call was raised.

"Here!"

The footprints were following the same path the hounds were scenting. The three were traveling together.

"After them!" Kriiton shouted. There would be no stopping to rest until absolutely necessary. A forced-march each and every day until they caught them.

The spirits flowed quickly through the forest, and Wilton fought to keep up. The growing fatigue in his body was nothing compared to the joy in his heart, and he followed without complaint.

It was nearly midnight before they stopped. *We will rest only when they do.* Tremlo and Jormah lay down to sleep, and Wilton prayed they would not steal away in the night.

Early the next morning, Tremlo roused him.

"They come."

Wilton did not know how Tremlo knew this or even how they were tracking them so quickly.

"They must have hounds."

"Yes," Jormah replied knowing the word.

"Then we must go fast!" Wilton cried. Once they got close enough, Kriiton would release the hounds, and it would be all over.

CHAPTER SIXTY-SIX

Jormah's hand and arm ached with memory. It was the second morning since the barb had been removed.

Wilton scoured the area for plants and roots, desperate to find ways of being useful.

"Wilton," Tremlo called. The man came running with a handful of astra. "Kriiton comes."

The Augmentors were little more than a day behind.

"They must be on a forced-march," Wilton said.

Kriiton's determination was legendary. And considering the prize, Wilton knew he would never stop.

They set off quickly through the forest, the spirits taking long strides and he trotting after them just to keep up. But he didn't care. He was connecting to something so much greater than himself; these last few days were like a dream.

Tremlo's body often disappeared in a blend of color, only to reappear in a spontaneous burst. Jormah too was beginning to melt into the forest.

The spirits barely spoke aloud. A casual movement of Tremlo's body might cause a turn of Jormah's head to which Tremlo's shoulder might lower in response. In the growing silence lay hundreds of interactions Wilton was just beginning to notice. It was a language all its own.

He tried to emulate them, walking, standing, sitting. A poor imitation, but Tremlo seemed pleased by his efforts. He wanted to ask where they had come from, what they wanted, where were they going, and always, if they would take him with them, but he held his tongue.

They felt his yearning and saw his questioning looks. In answer to one, Tremlo assumed the posture of an Augmentor and walked stiffly, releasing the posture one step at a time, until he was himself again.

We were once like you.

Wilton nodded vigorously. They began as men and evolved into these divine beings.

"So there is hope for us. Please, teach me. Show me the way. Help me to understand."

Wilton reminded Tremlo of Bettrie. Some of these Intruders possessed a desire to grow, to learn, to master their contrary natures and ascend.

'What are we going to do with him?' Jormah asked with a look.

'I do not know.'

They would have to cut back south soon to harvest the Resep and gather their furskins before the cold season set in.

"He clings to us with a growing passion. It slows us down."

"You would have us leave him here?"

There was something hard in Jormah now that had not been there before. To leave Wilton would be to condemn him in more ways than one. This Watcher, this Intruder, was asking something of them that had far-reaching implications.

Tremlo turned his palm face up.

It is not for us to decide.

They were moving faster now and Wilton struggled to keep up. In one sense, he felt cared for, in another, he was beginning to feel like Jormah's hand.

"We will remove ourselves from the trail," Tremlo declared, when they stopped to rest that night.

Wilton watched them float to the top of the trees.

They appear as home up there as on the ground below.

There would be no more quiet times sleeping close together on the ground.

They signaled for him to come up. He climbed up to the first 'V'. This was as high as he dared, for he could not sleep in a tree without the fear of falling.

"Wilton," Tremlo called out in encouragement. "Stay."

Wilton heard the empathy in Tremlo's voice.

The spirits were a part of the treetops, the sky, the heavens above. He was of the ground. He could move his hand through the air, but never take hold of it. Even as he thought this, a part of him wanted to grab on and take hold of them, *just like Kriiton.*

They were staying with him because he had asked them to, because he needed them to. His neediness was a spike all its own.

When I hold on like this, I doom us all.

He could not see them, but felt their all-knowing presence and tried to let go the parts that were afraid of losing them. The more he let go, the lighter he became. Soon it felt as if he was also rising up into the treetops.

They were showing him a way. And he, tasting the sublime, knew nothing else mattered.

When he returned to the self that was his body, he felt how tired it was. Yet, something new had awakened, and having finally done so, it did not want to sleep.

In the morning, Tremlo and Jormah floated down to the ground, *imposing nothing. embracing everything.*

Can I do the same?

He vowed to live this way for the rest of his life.

There was just one more thing he needed to do. Afterwards, it did not matter what happened. Afterwards he could die without regret.

Both Tremlo and Jormah felt something shift in Wilton. He was loosening up, letting go.

Letting us go.

No words passed between them, but Wilton felt them looking at him in a new way. *They know,* he thought. *They understand.*

Later that day, when they stopped for a brief rest, he took out the one spare piece of clothing he had. The shirt was well worn and dirty. He knew the trail they were leaving was mostly his own and making the trackers job much easier.

"I will go," he said, dragging it along the ground, indicating how he would draw the hounds to him and away from them.

Jormah thought this was exactly what was needed.

"Wilton," Tremlo said. *We would never ask you to do this.*

Wilton heard the sincerity in Tremlo's voice and his eyes filled with tears. No matter what the spirit said, he would leave them and take the Augmentors with him.

Through sacrifice, his life would finally have meaning.

CHAPTER SIXTY-SEVEN

"No, Wilton. Come."

Tremlo led them swiftly through the forest. He could not bear the thought of Wilton risking his life for them. It led to a host of other realities that waited, hungering, and felt unbearable. He still could not see beyond a certain point or think his way through. And so he allowed his body to carry them forth.

They raced through the day, increasing the distance between themselves and the Intruders. The call of a distant river, more a caress than a thought, led Tremlo to it.

Rough water, a good forty feet across, rushed around outcroppings of shiny, gray-faced boulders.

The Intruders will have difficulty crossing here.

The water charged headlong over a nearby falls into a gentle pool far below. There, it curled lazily around itself, a quiet churn, before hurling downriver once more.

Tremlo stepped back and signaled them to wait.

His body exploded into motion, and he ran straight to the edge of the bank. Leaping up at the last instant, the momentum carried him clear across to the other side. It was almost like he could fly.

Jormah followed, the elastic-like quality of his legs stretching and snapping, propelled him across, not as high or effortlessly as Tremlo, but he made it.

Wilton, amazed by their physical abilities, wondered how Jormah ever got caught in the first place.

The only way he himself could get across was to swim. But the current here was too swift. Looking at them across the river was like looking at them up in the treetops.

Had the time for parting come?

Tremlo was at the edge of the slate-gray bank looking down. Beneath the riverbed, beneath his feet, lay a hollow sensation telling him something was there. He dove straight down. The splash marks were carried away by the current, and erased all memory of his entry.

What is he doing? Wilton wondered, holding his own breath.

Tremlo did not surface.

Can he breathe underwater?

Jormah stood with his head cocked to one side.

After what seemed like forever, Tremlo reappeared and climbed out.

"It's a small chamber. The opening is just a few feet beneath this ledge. Holes dug by scurriers along the back wall bring in fresh air. It's mostly dry, long enough to lie down in, and tall enough to sit up."

Jormah understood now. The sooner they rid themselves of the Watcher the better.

"Wilton, come," Tremlo said pointing him to walk upstream and around the bend. The river widened there, and the water relaxed. A little farther it became shallow enough for Wilton to walk across if he was not a good swimmer.

"Come, Wilton." Tremlo said, waiting on the opposite bank, hand extended.

Wilton slogged across, filled with joy and willingness to sacrifice himself. Once out, he followed Tremlo back.

It was a warm day and his clothes dried quickly.

Jormah was sitting in balance-position. Tremlo sat beside him and raised his face to the sun. Currents from the past, flowing into the present, splintering into untold streams of future possibility....

The spirits seemed content to sit beside the river, but surely Kriiton and the Augmentors were closing in on them.

What are they waiting for? Wilton wondered.

Was now the time?

He took out his extra shirt, intent on dragging it all the way back to the settlement if need be.

"Wilton." Tremlo stood in answer. "Come."

He brought him to the edge of the water and acted out *open space below.* His body articulated every detail so clearly, Wilton could almost see the very walls of the chamber.

"Come, Wilton."

We will dive in together.

Wilton cast a nervous glance at the water. Jormah stepped up beside him, and the spirits took hold of his hands. Down they went, guiding him to the mouth of the chamber, and pushing him out of the water and onto its' floor. It was pitch black. He heard Tremlo and Jormah come in on either side. A hand touched his shoulder. He could hear them breathing in this chamber, each in their own way.

"Good, Wilton."

Tremlo's voice so clear, so open, so encouraging. One could live a lifetime in that sound.

Wilton.

Did he just hear them say his name?

In the dark of the chamber with the spirits on either side, it came to him again.

Wilton.

His body hummed. On one side, his shoulder was Jormah, on the other, Tremlo.

Wilton.

In the dark of the chamber, he did not know if his eyes were opened or closed.

Wilton.

There were no thoughts.

Wilton.

Tremlo took his hand and guided it to the wall behind them where his fingers found a small hole. Peering deep inside, Wilton saw the reflection of light coming from around a bend.

It leads to the surface. It brings air. It speaks of day and night.

So fragile this moment, so sublime.

Wilton.

It dawned on him then that the spirits were letting him go. This was a place of hiding. A place he could return to. The place where they would leave him.

Will I ever see you again?

His eyes filled with tears.

"Wilton," Tremlo said aloud, his voice giving structure to the moment. "Come."

They slid over to the edge and back into the water.

The riverbank, the sun's light, the blended mix of sound and sensation. Everything so fresh, so incredibly vibrant….

Wilton.

The spirits were watching even though they were not looking.

"He is reaching out to us," Tremlo said.

"The mind-of-his-body takes up too much space."

"It takes up too much space in all their lives."

Wilton wished he knew what they were saying.

Wilton.

They gathered wood to make a fire that night, heedless of its leaving, knowing it would bring him comfort.

"No," Wilton said. He did not need it. He did not want it. He wished only for the darkness of the chamber and this new kind of light. They sat close together, closer than ever before. Wilton desperately held on to each and every moment until he caught himself doing so.

Wilton.

Here was the place-of-no-place where everything resided.

In the morning, he found himself lying on the ground. He did not remember going to sleep.

"Wilton."

Tremlo drew a wiggled line in the dirt. This was the river. He walked his fingers towards it from the other side.

"Kriiton comes."

As his fingers approached the river, he pointed to Jormah and himself and indicated they would leave before Kriiton and the others arrived.

'You will hide in the chamber. You will be safe there. You will hide until they are gone.'

Wilton nodded, unable to stop the sadness.

"Wilton." Tremlo placed his hand upon his shoulder.

The morning filled with quiet wonder, the three barely moving. The sounds of the river their breath, the warmth from the sun's light their skin, the world at large their body.

Being.

A beginning, not an end.

And then it was over.

Intruders were coming. The hounds would smell their scent. Kriiton would order his men to cross the river, probably where Wilton had crossed. There they would find his scent and would follow it to where they had slept. From there, the trail would vanish.

The Augmentors will split up. Some will go upstream and others down.

"Wilton."

They, standing now on either side, and he trying to keep the ache from swallowing him whole.

I will look for you every day of my life, his body declared.

Tremlo touched his forehead and then his own heart.

We will keep you here.

Hounds were baying.

The time to disappear had come.

They nodded once in the manner of the Intruders and leaped away.

The sharp report of men aboveground penetrated the holy silence of the chamber.

I will look and remember.

Every day.

I swear.

CHAPTER SIXTY-EIGHT

"Damn them!" Kriiton swore. The hounds had lost all trace of them and kept returning to this place beside the river.

"Where do you think they went?"

"I don't know," Bettrie replied.

Kriiton took out a rudimentary map of the region. Unknown areas were colored in green, and there were far too many of them.

If we hadn't wasted years hunting the Kurr, we would have surveyed this region long ago.

"Do you think they're heading home?"

"Wherever that is."

"You said Jormah indicated he came from the southwest."

"He made a vague gesture with his hand. I can't be sure if it was south or west."

"He was known to the Carooh, but not to the Wollow or the Twie. That suggests he came from the west."

"I suppose it does."

"You suppose?" Kriiton's eyes narrowed.

"Kriiton, I do not know."

"We'll take your hounds and go to the caves of the Carooh. If we get lucky, we'll find them, or pick up their trail. Perhaps it will lead us to their land and their people."

"What about our mission to capture more Kurr?"

"You disapprove of this venture?"

"I, I'm merely pointing out that we will miss the season."

"Then we miss it!" This was their only chance at recapturing Jormah and maybe the other one. Once news got back to Proutus there would be hell to pay.

Will he understand why I did what I did? Will he see the real danger as I have?

If they hadn't spiked Jormah, they would never have known about the other one. Perhaps both would be gone now no matter what they did.

"Charge! Send a runner to the nearest relay station. Signal the third outpost to gather enough clothing and provisions to outfit fifty men for winter."

"Understood."

Resep, weeks past its prime, leaned with longing. Tremlo ran his fingers across the drooping leaves and hummed the songs-of-Origin. Here was the song-of-these-plants, the song-of-himself. Together they swayed in the fading light of day.

Tomorrow, Harvest would begin.

The night was cool, and the warmth of a fire would have been welcomed, but it would leave a trace. Instead, they curled around the plants for any warmth that might be had. The Resep blanketed them as they slept with whispers of things to come.

The sound of Donan, the undulating walls – and far ahead…

Junnipur.

Standing before her reflection, brushing her hair, adjusting the robe she hastily threw on.

She knows we are coming.

The room was different. Its walls clay-red and cave-like.

"You've come back!" she exclaimed. Beneath her excitement, a great sadness. "My father died the last time you were here."

Tremlo sagged from the sorrow. She reached out to comfort him, to comfort herself.

"I'm sorry," he said, or perhaps it was her.

"We could not help," Donan said.

"I know."

"What happened?" Donan asked, taking her from then to now.

"I woke up and ran outside. My father was lying on the ground, holding his chest…."

Tremlo heard her words and watched himself listening.

"He was shrinking away. In less than a minute he was gone."

Her words, meaningful to the one who listened, were meaningless to the one who watched. The essence of her, the only truth that mattered.

The Resep had whispered of this.

"I screamed. My mother came running, but it was too late. He was gone. There's an empty space between me and most things now."

Donan took a step closer, and Tremlo saw his own body step closer still.

"I feel better with you both here. Please don't go away again."

The essence of who she was intermingled with the essence of who he was. The mind-of-her-body rose to speak, but Tremlo put a finger to her lips. No words were necessary.

And so they remained in this embrace, in the eternity of the moment....

Tremlo awoke to lingering fragments. Trying to recall the dream caused him to fall back asleep.

You are not meant to think of this now.

The smell of the Resep was strong that morning, its plea unmistakable. It yearned for them to make use of it so that it might live on through them, if only for a little while.

They uprooted the plants and placed them in a pile to allow them to cure as best as a few days would allow.

"If the Intruders see this ground tended, they will know we were here," Tremlo thought and Jormah said.

They blended in debris from the surrounding area until it had a natural, disheveled look. Tremlo examined the ground and took seven seeds from one of the uprooted plants. He threw them up in the air and scattered them like the wind.

"Tremlo, we must leave this place and never return. What are you thinking?"

"I'm not."

Jormah said no more.

They stripped the Resep of its leaves and extracted the malta from its stalks. Afterwards, they laid out the patterns to make fresh sets of clothing.

The Intruders were amassing at the third outpost.

Early morning breath-sign had begun to appear.

It was time to go.

They dug up their furskins, tars, and teegns, and set off. By the time the cold season took full possession of this land, they would be safely tucked away inside the caves of the Carooh.

CHAPTER SIXTY-NINE

Whaet took up the same position he had had when they left, a father waiting for his children to return.

They came into the Common Ground and were surrounded.

The newness, the smell, an intralife all its own.

The youngers were envious.

'What did you see?'

'What was it like?'

'Tell us, show us, feed us.'

In the past, Gremar would have stepped forward and drawn all the attention to himself. Now, he held himself back.

"Good journey?" Whaet asked him.

"Leaving and returning."

"So we see."

We, Gremar thought. Whaet often spoke like this.

To hide in plain sight?

He had much to learn. "Take heart, Whaet. If change comes, *we* will not be defeated."

But Whaet saw that change had already come. Gremar's actions advanced its cause.

"We are all participants," Gremar continued, keeping himself small. In so doing, he shined more brightly, and to Whaet that made him all the more dangerous.

If Gremar represents the future, what new form of being will this spawn? And if so, am I foolishly standing before flood waters?

If only Jormah and Tremlo would return soon.

Hurry. We need you now more than ever.

A swirl of questions surrounded Reena and roped her in. Small things appearing large, and she, hovering far above. Arlen waited until they were alone. She, who was his mate, who was the one he knew more intimately than anyone else, was drifting away.

It started before Tremlo was born and had not stopped since.

Can one ever truly know another?

"How are you?" He could just as easily have asked, 'Who are you?'

She knew what he was asking. It was a question she asked herself.

"I am, I," she replied from the *here-and-now*.

Arlen, her bedrock, who never wavered. With him, she could let go the expectations framed by others.

"Is he in pain?" asked the Father-of-Tremlo.

"He sheds his skin like a slither."

"What lies beneath?"

"It is too soon to tell."

'With you then?'

"It weighs on me."

"Separate from him?"

She loved Arlen. He was a part of her, of them. *The Father-of-Tremlo.*

"Yes."

"In what way?"

She, who was here-and-now, did not want to let go.

"Hold me tight."

They lay down and he wrapped his arms around her, keeping the world at bay. Reena placed her head on his chest and withing two breaths was fast asleep. She slept better than she had in weeks.

When Reena and Kenectka parted, they had done so without so much as a look in each other's direction, but there was a subtle exchange. Mortulla witnessed it. She saw it between the others who had left and returned as well. They were connected to one another by delicate strands of shared experience. This was something new. An *intra*life within the *intra*life.

Upon returning to their cave, Kenectka emptied her sack onto the *sepramat* for sorting. Here were all the plants and roots she had gathered along the way.

"A fine bounty," Mortulla said, fingering the brown crusted mushers. She brought one up to her nose. "They have a boldness ours lack."

"I thought so too."

One particular plant was new to them both, and Kenectka had taken care to bring it back, roots and all.

"Look how proud it is," she said holding it up. Its shale-shaded leaves were laced with white veins, like fingers spread wide. From top to bottom it was about three feet tall. "I found it standing by itself."

"No others about?"

"Some distance away."

"An outcast?"

"A traveler. I felt a readiness."

"It wished to share?"

"I think so."

Mortulla cooed and gently pulled apart one of its leaves to smell the fragrance of its life. Often the strongest smells possessed special properties. This one had an interesting complexity. She touched her tongue to it.

Bittersweet.

A warning and an invitation.

It was reminiscent of *ransen* with a hint of *spira*, but in the main there were darker flavors.

Tantalizing.

Did it possess special properties?

Might she use it to help Donan in his plight?

They discussed its merits and listened for what it might tell them. Its color spoke of inward matters. Drawing a sense of it inside, they felt reconstituted. Something for the bones perhaps? If they listened closely and long enough, the plant might guide them and reveal its secrets.

Later, they would grind up some of its leaves and, separately, some of its branches to make a broth and poultice. These they would experiment with to see what effects they might produce.

Mortulla smiled to herself. *How long has it been since I have felt so stimulated?*

Stelbin stared into the fire, listening to the songs the flickering flames sang. It would have taken years for the wood to decompose naturally. Instead, it raced headlong into the future, entering the realm of spirit through the body of smoke, accomplishing in moments what would have taken eons.

Everything is speeding up.

Donan waited for him to speak. Stelbin appeared more firmly cast. Something had happened on this trip.

Stelbin caught a glimmer of his thoughts.

"I became what they supported," he finally said.

"An interesting observation. And if they did not support, would you be undone?"

"If nothing is done, how can it be undone?"

Donan shrugged. "Gremar changes with the wind, Stelbin. You are the light, not the path. Each must find their way according to their own nature."

"And if the others turn away?"

"The sun does not care if the clouds block its view. The sun *is*. A Kwaman *is*, or should be. Yet, we stand on two legs."

Stelbin flushed. *Was Donan speaking of Kenectka?*

"Truth is miniscule," Stelbin replied. "Illusion grand."

Donan burst out laughing at his own words served back to him.

"Well said, Stelbin." *Be the light.* "And what of Gremar?"

"He too was affected. He is maturing."

"Maturing or scheming?"

It was a good question, and Stelbin realized he still did not know *how* Gremar thought.

"Both."

CHAPTER SEVENTY

*C*old!

The mountain range leading to the caves of the Carooh was actually a chain of five mountains strung loosely together by a continuous ridge that ran across them like a crooked smile.

The Intruders were several weeks back and moving steadily. They were not tracking them exactly but coming frightfully close to taking the same route.

They are heading for the caves of the Carooh.

That part of Tremlo that was Kriiton thought this.

"Relentless," Jormah spat. There was a bad taste in his mouth all the time now. His hand had healed, but there was a scar. The wound inside attested to it. "They are relentless!"

It was this very quality that had propelled their ancestors to great heights and great ruin.

We have to get back to the tribe, Tremlo thought. *As soon as possible.* Jormah needed the warmth and care the Rehloy could provide. But it was he who *had* to get back. There was no time to waste.

We are not where we are supposed to be.

The first winter storm charged in from the east and forced them down the western side of the ridge where they took shelter beneath a low overhang.

The siowt was wet and heavy, and in the morning, they awoke to a world smothered in white. In the newly made silence, it was easier to hear the distant crackle of the Intruders.

Kriiton and his men were nearing the first mountain. The main body of the storm had missed them.

They're gaining on us, Tremlo thought, but Jormah barely took notice. The Intruders were relentless, and that was that.

The skies cleared, and the sun shone squinty-bright. The temperature dropped, and the skin of the siowt crusted with cold. They crunched through the knee-high snow and left a clear trail behind.

"If they come this way, they will know we were here," Jormah said, stating the obvious.

"Perhaps," Tremlo said, wondering if the elements were conspiring against them.

We are not where we are supposed to be.

They moved parallel to the ridge until the siowt thinned out enough for them to change direction. Up to the top they went. The wind blew unopposed here and filled in what meager tracks they left behind.

"Here! Commander!"

A stroke of luck. An Augmentor spotted fresh game below and went down to investigate. There he found tracks, nearly filled in, but clearly the markings of two-legged beings slogging their way through the snow.

Kriiton consulted his best tracker.

"The weather's been cold and dry since the last storm. I'd guess they were here about twelve or fourteen days ago."

"Do you think it was them?"

"The Carooh wear snowshoes. The marks would have been different. These two are definitely not from that tribe."

Two. They got rid of Wilton.

It made sense.

"It's got to be them," Kriiton declared.

From the direction of the tracks, it looked like they were moving parallel to the ridge.

"We're getting closer!" he said, infecting the men with new enthusiasm. "We're definitely getting closer."

Daily temperatures continued to drop. Jormah and Tremlo's fingers and toes were becoming numb and unrecognizable despite the fur that covered their hands and feet. They had to find shelter. A place where they could build a fire and remain unseen to wait out the cold months.

The caves of the Carooh were a mountain away, *but it could be ten,* Tremlo thought, certain now that the Intruders were heading there. The backside of this mountain seemed to be the only option. Its steep face was dangerous, made even more so by slippery patches of newly fallen snow.

There were no caves on this side of the mountain, but there was a deep crevice that offered good protection on three sides.

"We will make a roof and entrance cover," Tremlo said.

Jormah saw as much in his own mind. It was oddly exciting to think about building such a structure.

They scoured the area for fallen branches. Their presence would be marked by the lack of ground-wood, but there was nothing to be done.

Jormah framed out a roof and then a lean-to style cover. He did not follow the flow of the wood but rather imposed a form that was expedient and more reminiscent of Intruder than Rehloy. They wove saplings through each to lock it all in place.

"You would make an able Carooh," Jormah said, stopping to admire Tremlo's weaving. "Now that I think about it, you made an excellent Intruder."

Tremlo smiled uneasily. Jests were uncharacteristic for the Kwaman, and his bright mood felt too bright. Jormah worked with a concentration that ignored everything else. Never had he taken such pleasure in performing a task of this nature.

They filled in the open spaces with whatever debris and dirt they could. Afterwards, Jormah turned his attention to the stone floor. It was slanted to one side.

"Let's gather what small stones we can to fill in the bottom."

Tremlo thought this odd, for the slant was not that severe, yet Jormah was insistent.

They filled in the floor, and Jormah made sure it was as even as possible. Once satisfied, he framed out a mat with thin branches and used soft peels of bark to weave them together.

The singular sound of the spike.

The flat wooden surfaces....

He placed the mat on the ground without measuring and chuckled with satisfaction. It fit perfectly.

When the Augmentors reached the base of the mountain housing the caves of the Carooh, Kriiton ordered them to fan out in a wide arc. They moved swiftly up the mountain and stormed the caves. There was no sign of anyone having been there in quite some time.

"Damn," Kriiton muttered. Too many weeks had passed without a sign of the creatures. "We'll winter here," he declared. At least the men would be more comfortable sheltered in caves.

Kriiton commandeered one of the smaller ones and, once installed, called Bettrie to join him.

"A fine mess, eh, Animal Trainer?" His distrust was one thing, his need greater. He had to bring Bettrie back into the fold.

"I tried to warn you."

"That you did."

"What will you do if we find them?"

"Bring them back. Start over. A new footing."

"You think they would trust you?"

"You certainly don't."

"No."

"We all make mistakes, Bettrie. You disagreed with the measures I took."

"With all my heart."

"Given what has happened, I wish it had gone differently. But Jormah was having his way with you."

"That's not true."

"Oh no?"

"You tasked me with getting to know him. He was showing me the way."

"The way to what?"

"To getting to know him."

"And that was all?"

"You have to go with your gut sometimes."

"Your gut or your heart?"

"I am loyal to Ontar."

"Arister once said, 'He who stands against a superior force will need sufficient interior force to resist, or he will be overcome.'"

"Meaning?"

"You can't have it both ways."

Each was searching for middle ground.

"What if we don't find them?" Bettrie asked. For Jormah's sake, she hoped they wouldn't, but for her own….

"We fail only if we do not try."

"So we are on a fool's mission?"

"You came because you had to know. And so do I. We need to work together, Bettrie."

Despite their struggle, each understood the needs of the other.

"I will send out small scouting parties to the adjacent mountains. In the spring, we will have our best chance of engaging them, and by then we'll have the area clearly mapped."

They are here, somewhere. He was sure of it.
"And you will help."
"Understood."

CHAPTER SEVENTY-ONE

Day in and day out the cold and brittle bones of the world creaked and cracked in crystalline cadences. Trees spoke in frozen gestures. Water stood rock-still.

Jormah could only taste the slow-cold drift of life in brief moments before thoughts returned.

Relentless, inevitable.

He watched them come over him until he watched no more.

He and Tremlo should have been in the caves of the Carooh. Instead, they were held captive on the dark side of the mountain, forced to keep their fire low during the day to prevent their smoke from being seen.

The pain from the spike was gone, but its singular tone had a grip on his heart and would not let go.

Winter storms, striking in earnest, piled huge drifts upon the roof and entrance cover. The siowt kept the heat in and the rhythms of the world out. It was like being in a still-cave and reminded Tremlo of his early childhood. A haven then, a hindrance now. The sense of isolation would be suffocating for the uninitiated.

How did my mother bear it?

Was this his question or her feelings?

He rarely thought about Reena as a person separate from himself, nor his father, nor anyone else for that matter. He simply went from phase to phase without reflection.

Is this a flaw?

Reena, Arlen, Donan, the tribe. They were all there inside, not as some stagnant memory of the past but alive with who they were, growing in ways he could not possibly know but felt all the same.

So much happened. So much changed. His body still growing, his being unfolding. He knew there was a 'he' and a 'they' and something he needed to do for both.

If only he could wrap his mind around it.

For weeks on end, they barely uttered a word. Jormah, drowning in thoughts, left the shelter several times a day no matter how cold it was outside. His dreams were filled with violent images, his thoughts consumed with plots. The mind-of-his-body hungered for revenge. At times, he caught it and stepped beside to watch.

At other times, it had its way with him.

Again and again.

The thoughts were relentless.

Tremlo watched near and far, not knowing if Jormah's struggle would be short-lived or long-lasting. The caregiver in him wanted to remove his pain and reassure him. The *Kwaman* in him saw that sympathy was one thing, empathy another. Sympathy gave credence to the cause and by wishing it was different, strengthened it. Empathy allowed him to remain open to who Jormah was separate from that.

Honor with remembrance.

Be the path for him to follow.

And so they sat side by side in their confinement, one expanding, the other contracting.

The Intruders mapped out the area, hunted small game, cut wood, kept warm, remembered the comforts of the settlement, and longed for the riches of Ontar.

Tremlo felt their every move, while Jormah imagined their every thought, his skin speaking of the world about, while retaining an ashen quality of the world within.

I am turning into one of them.

When the cold loosened its grip, the mountains wept with its easing. It was still cold. Storms threatened, but Tremlo insisted it was time to leave.

We are not where we are supposed to be.

They took apart the enclosure and did their best to spread the debris out to relieve the area of their burden. Even so, this place would harbor traces of their presence for years to come.

Tremlo led the way down and across the base of the mountain. His feet moved with the confidence of prior knowledge.

Being-awareness.

"The land," he said, "is a part of us now."

Jormah did not know what he was talking about. Only that something in him was changing.

They stopped to rest that night. The cold bit with added fervor, and Jormah shivered with new resentment. If only they could light a fire. But Kriiton had sent Watchers throughout the area, and there was a small group at the top of the next mountain.

Wrapping themselves tightly in their furskins, they huddled together for what little warmth that could be had.

The hounds began to growl. Low in pitch, they alerted the men to the presence of something far below. The sun was setting and they could not see in the failing light. After some discussion, they agreed to wait until morning to go down and investigate.

Tremlo and Jormah were hiding behind two thick trees, knowing the hounds had scented them. Were it not for the furskins, they would have proceeded along in the stalking manner and avoided all detection.

"As long as we wear these, their smell circulates through us," Tremlo said, observing the trail of scent they were leaving behind.

"Their hounds will find us," Jormah said, blind to the bitterness in his voice.

"We will be long gone."

"Let's hope so."

They waited for dark and snuck past the Intruders, but Jormah's thoughts lingered, leaving a psychic trail behind.

The next day, Kriiton was alerted. The hounds had found something. The hunt was on.

Tremlo and Jormah swung out of the mountains and came to the moat that surrounded the forest-of-crawling-leaves. A huge branch lay in the moat, a piece of its body still clinging to its mother across the way. Black marks spoke of a lightning strike. The tree itself must have put out the flames.

The mud-red vapor had drained the submerged leaves of their color. The branch itself was an arm's length from where they stood.

Tremlo gently leaped onto the branch to avoid arousing its attention. He need not have worried for it was firmly attached to its mother, and they climbed across without incident.

The edge of the forest, warmed by the sun's light, stood in contrast to the dark interior where it was still quite cold.

Breath-sign returned.

Deadly leafbirds tightened their wings. Leaves and small branches lying in their path blew away.

"The smell of smoke clings to our furskins."

The readiness of the forest to strike was palpable.

The sooner we are out of here, Jormah thought, *the better.*

"Commander, look!"

The green-topped mountain proved to be a forest of gigantic proportions. The trees rose up hundreds of feet. Their massive trunks were covered with ripples of bark thicker than a man's body.

"A single tree could provide enough wood to build a fort!" Kriiton exclaimed.

Gnarled roots had grown together to form a barrier wall that stood nearly forty feet tall. The beauty and immensity of it filled them with awe.

The hounds brought them to a massive branch dangling in the moat.

"They must have crossed here."

"Then so shall we," Kriiton said, leading the way up the branch. The Augmentors followed, one at time.

There was an ominous quality to this place. Wherever they looked, whether high or low, they could find no animal life. No birds, no mungs, *nothing.*

Kriiton peered into the darkness. A soft hissing sound issued forth from deep inside. It sounded like the rustling of leaves, but there was no wind and there were no leaves on the ground around them.

"I don't like the looks of this place," one of the Augmentors mumbled.

"Hold your tongue!" Kriiton snapped, straining to hear the sound. It seemed to be moving away from them. Taking out his short sword, he signaled three Augmentors to follow him. The hissing sound grew louder as they stepped into the darkness.

"Commander," one of the Augmentors whispered. "Is that the wind?"

"A wind that flees before us?"

"Spirits then?"

"Whatever it is, it's running away from us."

Could it be Jormah and his people?

Could this be the collective sound of them in retreat?

Kriiton ran forward and overtook several leaves and twigs scurrying up a trunk.

"Amazing," he said, managing to catch one. The leaf was squirming in his hand. A perfect rendering down to the veins, which proved to be tiny legs.

This was a magical place.

Just the sort to spawn one like Jormah.

"Hounds!" Kriiton called out.

They were brought across and quickly picked up the trail, but their handlers held them back. It was pitch black beyond the first few hundred feet.

"Cold," one of the Augmentors said, extending his hand into its dark body.

"Line up. Double file," Kriiton said. "Let the hounds lead us in."

From far behind, Tremlo felt abrasive tones entering the forest-of-crawling-leaves. He and Jormah were approaching the outskirts of the second City. The temperatures were warmer now. Once past the City, they would rid themselves of the furskins and absorb the posture of the land.

It was there that the Intruders would lose their trail.

CHAPTER SEVENTY-TWO

"Light torches," Kriiton commanded, only to find the trees raining sticky, sap-filled drops upon the flames. All torches were extinguished save one when an enterprising Augmentor shielded it with a rain-guard. If they kept the light from touching the crown of the trees, they could stop them from raining down upon them.

With two torches covered, they continued on through this eerie darkness wondering what other surprises this forest might hold for them.

It was quite cold, and when they stopped to rest, one of the Augmentors thought to start a covered fire. He took an axe to one of the trees to cut some wood. After the second strike, terrifying screeches came pouring down from above.

He looked up. A sharp pain shot straight through his eye to the back of his head. It was the last thing he would ever know.

The Augmentors ran for their lives, as birds with long, lethal beaks and razor-sharp claws fell upon them. Once the men got clear of the tree, the attacks stopped as abruptly as they started. One man had been killed outright, and many others were injured.

"Don't touch the trees! Don't start a fire! Keep the torches covered and let's get out of here!"

They followed the hounds, keeping close together, afraid to stray, afraid to invoke the wrath of this godforsaken place.

When light appeared on the far side of the forest, they started to run and did not stop until they were standing in full sunlight. Never had it felt so good.

The hounds picked up the trail once more, and the men followed quickly, putting as much distance as possible between themselves and the forest.

Ruins of a city appeared in the distance.

When confronted with any evidence of the LongPast, the orders of the Empire were very clear. They were to investigate immediately and destroy any Electrix that might be found. That was the edict driven into them from birth. That was the Way-Of-The-Sane.

The Augmentors fell upon the city with well-practiced formations.

"Keep to the streets," Kriiton reminded them. "Do not enter any buildings."

Advance scouts sped ahead with instructions to return at the sound of the horn. Afterwards, Kriiton would question each one carefully. In regards to the Electrix, no one was to be fully trusted. The weak could use it to control the strong, and their rulers feared this more than anything.

Most of the structures had collapsed into the waiting arms of the natural world. The thoroughfares were overgrown, but their wide, linear pathways were still discernable after all this time. If anything was to be found intact, it would probably require much digging.

The scout who traveled farthest was the last to return.

"The ruins are more numerous to the north and west but equally decayed. Just before returning, I climbed a tree and saw a Spire in the distance."

Spires were structures of immense height. There was nothing the people of today could construct that would stand even half as tall without collapsing.

Unnatural.

It was a part of the sickness. A symptom of the WayWard Path.

"We all know the edict, but we must continue our search for the creatures while their trail is fresh," Kriiton said. "You have my word we will return one day to excavate and destroy whatever remains."

Tremlo and Jormah buried their furskins just beyond the City. They walked on, leaving an obvious trail to draw the Intruders away from that place. That night, they even slept on the ground to reinforce it.

In the morning they set off, free now of furskins and their scent, treading lightly once again. Tremlo left nothing behind, but the mind-of-Jormah's-body wanted the Intruders to follow them. It knew the dangers of the grassland. And despite himself, it was leaving little patches of scent here and there.

"Tremlo, what is happening?"

'Happening?'

The edges of Tremlo's body were easing into the landscape ahead. With each passing day these effects became more pronounced. At odd moments, without effort or intention, he vanished.

"You are becoming indistinct."

"I have never felt more defined."

"You are disappearing."

"But I have never been more visible."

Jormah did not know what to make of his words.

The Intruders followed their trail out of the city. It would have taken them years, if not decades, to reach this place. Instead, it was accomplished in one season.

We have accelerated the change, Tremlo thought. Whether by design or accident. *But if by design…*

The pressure in the currents was intensifying and pointed him towards a place within the Tribal Body itself.

That is where we must be.

The vague trail Jormah was leaving behind had not escaped his attention, but it seemed to be intertwined. As if it had already happened.

One small tendril within a host of many.

Too many.

The grassland, an ocean, that distant inlet beckoning. They prepared themselves to enter these dangerous waters. Tremlo shimmering, the wind, the sky, the light itself.

"Do not worry," he said, his voice the only thing rooting him to this spot. "All is... as it is."

Jormah struggled to see him.

"If we hurry, we will reach the children-of-Origin at just the right moment."

"I'm ready," Jormah replied.

Tremlo smiled. *'They await.'* With that, he entered the plain, as the plain, and disappeared.

Jormah charged after the silent breeze, and they wove their way through the grassland, one in perfect reflection, the other, a poor imitation.

CHAPTER SEVENTY-THREE

"Can you see anything?"

The Ontarans were standing upon the blackest of stone, bordering a vast yellow plain. The only movement came from the wind pushing through in waves.

"A sea of grass," Bettrie said, and Kriiton agreed.

The horizon line was tinted with a reddish hue. No hills or rocks or trees to speak of. The marvels and dangers of this new land were quite something. From beasts of incredible ferocity, to the magical creatures they were pursuing. From forests with murderous intent, to ruins that rivaled the outlands of Ontar.

And now this vast plain.

"Do you think they went in?"

"It would be easy enough to hide in there. They could sleep during the day and travel by night and no one would be the wiser."

The waist-high grass grew in randomly spaced tufts, which would make it easier to move through.

The hounds went back and forth along the edge and eventually came to a place of interest.

"They found something."

A tracker spotted a broken blade of grass. By itself, insignificant, but he stepped in carefully. The experience in the forest was very much on all their minds.

The ground between the tufts was hard and dry. The tracker got down on all fours and crawled forward. Almost immediately, he came across a spot where dirt was displaced.

Had it given way to the weight of a hurried step?

There was no discernable form to it, and yet, a step away he found another slight impression. After that, there was nothing.

"Bettrie, take some hounds and see what you can find." Kriiton sent twelve Augmentors along with her. "The land is flat and will make communication easy. Relay back what you see."

The trail was vague, and the hounds moved slowly. The Augmentors followed, ever cautious. It seemed to be just barren grassland.

The hounds were low to the ground and avoided rubbing up against the grass. The Augmentors, however, did not fare as well. The men were wearing tunic-like travel klotts, and the brittle blades were sharp. Their exposed legs were easily scratched.

"Why not cut a path through it?" one of the Augmentors suggested.

"Make a cut or two, and let's see what happens," the Charge replied.

The Augmentor took a swipe with his long sword and cut the grass halfway down its stalks. The others stood with short swords drawn.

Nothing happened, nor did it raise a cry from any other quarter.

"All right, we're good. Let's go."

The Augmentor hacked through the grass. Its stalks were hollow and dry.

"Our return will be much easier," the Charge said.

When the Augmentor grew tired, a second man took his place, and then another and another. Within a few oras, they were far from the rocky shore.

Red spots appeared on individual blades of grass and intermixed with the yellow to create a bright, orange-like iridescence. Beautiful in its way, the farther out they went, the more prevalent the red spots became, until they were completely surrounded.

"Do you smell that?" Bettrie asked the Charge. There was a slightly acrid odor in the air.

"Yes."

"Let's stop a moment. What do you make of it?"

"I don't know."

The breeze, coming from behind, had driven the smell away. Now that they were standing in one place, it became stronger, and their eyes began to tear.

"Look," the Charge pointed. The grass ahead was beginning to sparkle.

"It looks like it rained."

The red spots were growing moist. Bettrie squeezed one. Soft like flesh, the act of touching caused it to shed a drop onto her finger. She sniffed it. Here was the acrid smell that filled the air. The tip of her finger and thumb began to itch... and then burn. She wiped it off on her klott, but the burning continued.

She took out her water flask and doused her fingers.

"Don't touch anything!"

Several Augmentors had already backed into, or brushed up against the ever-dampening grass. The scratches on their legs became inflamed.

"Let's get out of here!"

They started back along the path they had cut, but to their dismay, large droplets were pouring out of the fresh cut stalks. The dust-dry dirt was turning moist. The bottoms of their feet were protected by their wooden sandals, but the moisture was working its way in between their toes and began to burn.

One of the hounds stopped to lick its paw.

"No!" the handler shouted too late. The hound began to whimper, running its tongue around the outside of its mouth. The handler drew out his flask and gave it some water. This seemed to help, but a few moments later, the animal lay down and curled around the pain that was now in its stomach.

"Leave her," the Charge said. "We have to get out of here or we're dead men!"

The cut stalks were drooling with acid.

They splashed through, their legs turning bright red. The time for following the path was over, and they ran straight through the uncut grass. It was like fanning the flames as the sharp blades multiplied their cuts. What little water they carried was nowhere near what they needed to put out these flames. They ran and ran, fearing they would be burned alive.

"They're coming!" a sharp-eyed Augmentor called out.

"What are they running from?" another asked.

"Gather up!" Kriiton commanded. "We'll cover their retreat."

They entered the plain and took up strategic positions along the way.

"What are they running from? Can anyone see?"

Were there snakes or low-borne creatures charging after them?

"Go back," Bettrie shouted, as they drew near. "Go back!"

"What's happening?" Kriiton called. "What's the matter?"

"... fire."

"What?" There was no smoke. "Where?" He grabbed Bettrie's arm as she tried to run past. "Stop! Tell me what's wrong."

Bettrie's arms and legs were bright red like they were sunburned.

"Water!" Bettrie grabbed Kriiton's water flask and poured its meager contents over her arms and legs.

"What's going on?"

"Acid. Burning our skin."

Bettrie broke away. She could not stop. None of them could.

They raced to the shallow stream just beyond the grassland and jumped in from several feet out. Some landed on rocks, others hit bottom, but it did not matter. They had to put the fire out. The water added an underlying chill to the burning and at first did little to relieve their pain.

Back on dry ground, shivering, the others did what they could to treat their comrades for burns.

"Bettrie, what happened out there?"

She was in shock, they all were, their world the color of pain.

"Grass turned red. Sweated acid. It... it knew we were there and surrounded us."

This terrible liquid burned their skin and ate through much of their clothing. Only the wood bottoms of their sandals were unaffected.

Wood, Kriiton thought. That was the answer.

Had the creatures intentionally drawn them here?

First the forest and now this malevolent plain. If Jormah was truly the Spirit-Of-The-Forest, were these his weapons?

One of the twelve Augmentors who went in, died when too much of his skin peeled away. The rest suffered various degrees of burns and all were beset with fever that left them ranting for days.

You escaped this time, Kriiton thought, *but we are not defeated.*

He envisioned a road made of wood that ran straight down the center of this flat land. Those giant trees would provide more than enough if they could kill the birds that protected them.

No, not a road, a ship! A ship to cross a sea of grass.

It could be flat bottomed, mounted on large wooden wheels and powered by the wind.

If not this year, then the next.

They were not defeated, just delayed. That is what he would write to the Emperor. He would use the discovery of the city and the performance of their duty to justify putting off the hunt for Kurr this season.

However, no excuse would be necessary, for unbeknownst to Kriiton, when Proutus received his report about the creatures, he would order three hundred Augmentors sent to Ontara with the express purpose of capturing them and their people.

We will return, Kriiton thought again, little knowing how soon or how right he was.

CHAPTER SEVENTY-FOUR

Jormah sensed the injury that befell the Intruders and was both thrilled and appalled.

Did Tremlo know?

He felt no recrimination. They had not spoken a word since they entered the grassland, and stepping out now, he stumbled upon the hard ground.

Fragments of the Intruders rang through his body.

Am I becoming a bridge between the two?

Tremlo listened, remembering him whole.

Forces are having their way with both of us, he thought, and vanished before the first tree they came upon.

"Tremlo?"

A smile gave definition to his face and body.

"Tremlo, what is happening?"

"The land is now a part of us."

"I don't understand."

Donan believed Tremlo was Sentient but it was he, Jormah, who bore witness to the true meaning of the word.

Tremlo chuckled. "The children-of-Origin are excited," he said, standing before Jormah, and beside them. "They have grown wild and are a tangled mess."

"What else do you know?"

'The plants unravel with our arrival.'

"Can you sense the tribe?"

"Yes."

"Do you know what is happening there now?"

"In a way."

"Do you know what will happen later?"

"I am not ready to look."

Could he see if he wanted to?

Tremlo felt the flow of events leading into the future, but beyond a certain point, he lost a sense of himself. Either he wasn't in the right place to see, or he hadn't grown enough yet to understand. There was nothing to do but live as he would live and see what happened.

They reached the canyon, and Tremlo walked boldly to the edge. Jormah grabbed hold of his arm, afraid he was going over the cliff.

From far out in the canyon Tremlo felt the Kwaman's fear and returned. Jormah gasped at the weight of him. Tremlo's legs were roots reaching deep into the ground. His body encompassed the canyon itself.

Tremlo smiled, his frame suddenly mobile, his weight once more his own.

By the time they reached the plants, the air was suffused with rich and colorful smells. The stalks and branches sounded deep with malta. The leaves spread wide and smiled a vibrant green. Their edges tittered with blue Broezia.

Harvest ready.

Tremlo said they would arrive at just the right moment, and it was true.

If only I could experience a fraction of what he does.

But the mind-of-Jormah's-body had built a wall around himself.

How dull I am.

Tremlo sat down amongst the plants. Their whispers grew louder and whisked him through the hum of the grassland, the nip of the City-Of-Straight-Lines, the melody of the Valley Forest, the lush tones of the Tribal Body.

Rhythms of individuals washed over him, not as they were, but as they *would* be.

Emptiness.

Here was that point beyond which he could not see.

Is it not yet decided? Is there something I must do? Will I cease to exist?

He tried to push through and felt himself seeping into the ground.

"Tremlo?"

Curled up on his side, fast asleep, the plants hovering over him.

Open to everything, Jormah decided. *That's what he meant when he said 'the land is now a part of us.'* So different from his own experience. Denser forces were taking hold, squeezing him into a different reality.

Is this the measure of things to come?

The sun was setting. Tremlo asleep and the plants drawing closer, a blanket of sorts, whispering *who-knew-what,* taking him *who-knew-where*. Jormah felt out of place and went down to the cave-of-Origin to spend the night.

Junnipur looked straight at Tremlo long before he arrived, yet her eyes were blank. She did not see him. In fact, she did not move at all.

I am too far ahead, he thought, pulling back and slamming into himself. Donan's pitch right beside, they arrived simultaneously at her room.

Jennifer leaped out of bed.

"You're here! Finally! Come in! Come in."

She was taller than before and her voice more mature. A young woman to his young man.

Donan behind, he ahead.

She hugged him fiercely.

Let me know that you are real.

Flesh touching flesh?

Essence seeking essence.

Starving.

He fed her embrace with the energy she sought.

"Yes," she murmured, the root of herself elsewhere.

Across the room, invisible to the eye and senses, her body lay upon the bed.

She left him and went to hug Donan, who remained by the entrance.

"Truman is so much warmer than you, Uncle Donald."

Tremlo nodded. He was not only in this dream but standing beside it. In the flickering lines of her being was something akin to his own.

"Oh, where are my manners?"

The words of another.

"Come in. Please have a seat and make yourself comfortable."

Tremlo walked to the table and sat down beside her. Donan stayed by the entrance, for the room was full-to-bursting.

Tremlo and Junnipur, sitting side by side.

Nothing in that room but each other.

I feel drawn to you in a way I have never felt before.

This was not her thought or his, but both. Two worlds merging. Pieces of one lay in the other.

Junnipur drew closer. Images flooded Tremlo's senses with complexity. Too much to sort out. He retreated back to this place. Simply he, simply she, their interaction a world onto itself.

Bodies spoke form. Minds, thoughts. Essence sang of being.

"I wish that you could stay," Jennifer said.

"I do as well," Tremlo replied.

Who is speaking?

"You will—"

'*—come back soon.*'

"I'm not crazy then?"

"I do not understand."

"It doesn't matter. As long as—"

'*—I return?*'

"Yes. How will I know it is you?"

"How will you not?"

She smiled. These were silly words to draw him out, to hold him close, if only for a moment longer.

"Do you have to leave?"

He touched her face, and she placed her hand on his.

He was standing by the wall. She raised her hand to wave goodbye. He returned the gesture, his hand the last thing she saw.

Jennifer's body, in bed, turned onto its side, even as a small part continued through the wall. The longer she held on, the farther away it took her. Soon she would not be able to let go, even while awake.

Fear yanked her back and placed her beside her father's open grave. He lay there, dressed in his black suit. The only one he had. Her mother stared down, a stern and disapproving look on her face.

People were whispering, the coffin lowered. And then they were all outside the house, trying to get in. The bolt on the front door had somehow been thrown. Jennifer was three years old again and small enough to fit through the tiny cellar window. They lowered her down gently. She liked the feel of their hands on her arms and legs. She raced up the cellar stairs and came to the front door. The bolt was rusted in place and she could not get it to slide back. They were banging on the door, yelling for her to open it. The pounding on the door became the thunder outside. She turned in sleep, her mind briefly acknowledging that it was raining outside....

The cool lick of night thickened with the sounds of the oncoming day.

Dawn.

He was here now, surrounded by the Resep plants.

The dream....

He had had it before. Many times.

A dreaming life.

The details were vague….

Junnipur.

He remembered her name and something of her surroundings. The rest was all feeling, rich in meaning and completely obscure.

Sitting up, his body declared itself. Standing up, it roared.

Here. I am here!

And yet a moment later…

Jormah was sitting in front of the cave-of-Origin.

"What happened last night?" Tremlo asked, coming down from the ridge.

"You lay down beside the Resep and fell asleep. I did not want to disturb you and came down here to wait. I too fell asleep, and the next thing I knew, it was dawn."

Donan awoke to the hollow ring of forgotten thoughts.

He whirled around the High Cave.

Is someone here?

Tremlo smiled. How much he missed him.

"What is it?" Jormah's voice brought him back.

What is it?

He had never reached out with a mere thought and felt a thing so vividly.

I am drifting out of time.

"What is it?"

Tremlo dropped into balance position and lowered his head. Jormah kneeled behind him and kneaded his shoulders.

Jormah was standing several feet away. He sensed Tremlo's disorientation and came up slowly behind him. Tremlo flinched when he placed his hands on his shoulders. He dug his fingers deep into his muscles.

"I am here," Tremlo said softly, but Jormah remained unconvinced.

"I will make you a hot cup of bunoi."

Tremlo drank. The warm flavor traveled down his throat and into his stomach.

When the bunoi was ready, Jormah handed him the cup. The warm flavor traveled down his throat and into his stomach exactly as it had already done.

Tremlo lay down on his side and drew the voice of the ground deep inside.

He dreamed the dream from the night before, but it was only a memory, and it mixed in with other dreams, stitching him back into this time and place.

He awoke moments later. Half the day was gone.

The Resep was calling.

"Jormah. The Resep needs to be taken."

"It's getting late. Let's wait till morning."

"No."

There was no time to waste. So many things were converging into that moment beyond which he could not see. If they were not where they were supposed to be, disaster would follow.

"It must be now," he said, already chanting the songs-of-Origin.

After Harvesting, Jormah made a small fire. Tremlo placed a thick stalk of Resep onto the coals. There was a tautness in the currents. Jormah felt its tension in Tremlo's body.

"We have come a long way," Tremlo replied.

"It is you who traveled the greatest distance."

The stalk began to sizzle. When the malta smelled ready, Tremlo took it off the fire and put it on the ground to cool.

A thick cloud cover lay high overhead, the world one giant cave. Tremlo took his cutting stone and split open the stalk. Malta burst forth in song. A chorus of flavors rang through their bodies as they ate.

In the morning, Tremlo set to work separating the blue Broezia from the yellow. There was far more blue Broezia than they would ever take in a lifetime, let alone one more time. Tremlo wrapped it carefully in a leaffold.

Images, dreams, feelings, memories.

No time to allow the plants to cure.

We are not where we are supposed to be.

They stripped the branches and sorted the leaves.

Tremlo watched himself from high above, thrice removed from his body.

How hard he tries. How naïve. How sincere.

A gentle caress across the back of his head. He languished in its touch long before looking up from his work.

After making new leefskins, they removed the rest of the malta from the stalks. It was a rich crop with more malta than they could possibly carry. Tremlo filled his backsack to the brim and then constructed an outside pouch to hold more.

"Tremlo, we do not need half as much for our journey."

Jormah was right, but he could not stop himself from stuffing the newly made pouch with as much as it could possibly hold.

He filled it to capacity but still felt vaguely dissatisfied.

They cleaned the ground, turned the soil, added fertoe, and planted the seeds.

"Tomorrow, we leave."

"We should wait until the seeds take hold."

"There isn't enough time."

His voice was adamant, telling them so.

CHAPTER SEVENTY-FIVE

The pressure, the noise, the punctuated rhythms of the pattern-of-change. The tribe's overall movements were curtailed by the listening.

"Look at us," Gremar said. "This is what it must have been like for our ancestors huddling against the Onslaught."

The thought rippled through the tribe and brought to mind the time when Yarkas came en mass and forced their ancestors to flee their homeland.

"Kwaman Reja found the solution," Whaet countered. "They built traps *inside* the Tribal Body not outside."

Gremar laughed out loud. "The Intruders are men, not beasts. What kind of trap would you build to stop them?"

Instead of transforming the energy and maintaining awareness, the people were driven to all sorts of speculations.

What kind of trap, Whaet wondered, *are we, ourselves, in?*

Donan and Stelbin listened from above.

"The mind-of-the-body will have its life despite us," Stelbin said. What it concocted seemed so real. One was easily drawn in and carried off.

"Some must resist to prevent the rest from being completely swept away. If not, we will descend as a people."

Stelbin himself was halfway between the dream and *awareness*.

"Maintain the struggle, Stelbin. The rest will follow."

The Kwaman's voice was strong, belying the fact that his body was not. A year ago, the creeping death nearly took him away. He was slow to recover, and now that he was up and moving about, it was apparent how much he had lost in this last bout.

"Reena will come today," Donan said.

How do you know? Stelbin wondered.

Reena had risen before dawn, and as she did each day, took a path up the mountain to a place where no one came. Sitting in balance-position along the ledge, she reached out to the oncoming day while simultaneously listening within. Between the two lay an invisible river with forks and tributaries. One particular branch was already inside her, had been, *forever.*

She felt the thread of her own movement weaving its way up to the High Cave.

Am I being summoned? Has the time come?

She had not seen Donan since Jormah and Tremlo left the Tribal Body. The Kwaman said he was going into seclusion so that he might hear them better. He stopped speaking for a time, or so it was said. Only Stelbin knew for sure, and he recently told her Donan was speaking again.

"He became ill and began to mutter, and when he recovered, he continued to talk."

"What did the Mahtwah say about this?"

"That he was an old fool and that it did not matter if he spoke or not. Lately, he has been focused on the energy surrounding the tribe."

"What does he see?"

"You would know better than I."

What is it I know?

She headed up the mountain. The few people she passed along the way nodded in deference just as they might to a Kwaman. *The Mother-of-Tremlo.* What moved in him moved in her.

Her trek to the High Cave set off all sorts of speculations below.

Where are Tremlo and Jormah?

Does she have something special to tell the Kwaman?

Would he see her?

Will he be coming down now?

The stir from below set off a host of thoughts in her own mind.

And then she was before him, and the light of his attention colored her warm. Here was the delight a parent had watching their child approach.

"Hello Doda," she said, settling into the role his feelings cast for her.

"It has been a long time since I have heard that name," he laughed.

His body was wasting away.

"A long time," she said, sitting beside him. She took his hand firmly in hers and squeezed. "Much has changed, but this will always be the same."

Donan smiled. Emotional memories, an unexpected gift.

"It was not so long ago that you came here to ask about your unborn child."

"Yes," she replied, unburdened now as then.

"You are growing into the role you were made for."

"The Mother-of-Tremlo?"

"Far more. You bring hope, you show what is possible."

She did not see herself that way and did not know what to make of it.

"My role will soon end," Donan continued. "I will be remembered for what we once were. But you will be looked to for what we can become. It is you they will seek out in the coming times."

"What have you seen?"

"Something is going to happen, and sooner than expected."

"The Intruders?"

"Your son."

Her body snapped to attention. "What do you know?" Her voice as calm and steady as she could manage.

"I should ask you the same question."

If she doesn't know, he thought, *that means Tremlo doesn't. And if he doesn't know, our course is still uncertain.*

"What are you sensing?" his voice gentle, coaxing.

"Forces swirl about him."

"He is at the center of a storm."

"He is staying the course."

"And what might that be?"

"I don't know."

Her throat constricted with fear of the unknown.

"Is he afraid?"

She sighed, releasing the tension, watching now to help her body along.

"He is letting go what is, in order to become what will be."

"As we all are."

"Doda, what have you seen?"

"The people hover, keeping closer to one another than ever before. Their movements are constrained. It is a defensive-posture. The energy those two bring will set it into motion."

"I feel that." She placed her hand on her abdomen just below her chest.

"It all hinges on Tremlo's return," Donan continued. "Many things *can* happen, but only one thing will. From there everything will follow. I cannot be sure what, but afterwards it feels like... everything changes."

"Will you stay here?" Reena blurted out. She did not know where the words came from or what she meant.

"There is something left for me to do." *Something I have to resist. Something I have to hold onto.* "And you?" he countered.

"Me?"

"Will you be leaving?"

Both looked deep into the other, searching.

Despite the front Donan was putting on, Reena felt how weak and frail his body had become. His brow was furrowed as he tried to maintain a posture of strength, but he was taking on far more weight than his shoulders could bear. For a moment, he was like a little boy, and she smiled at the look of determination on his face. She took his hand once more, and he smiled back.

"I remember the times before the pattern-of-change," he said. "There was a lyrical quality to our lives. 'To disappear in plain sight.' With the coming change, we fend off what once we would have embraced."

"I fear the coming change, but also have a great curiosity."

"Yes," Donan said, a dry patch of ground soaking up the newly fallen rain. His body swelled, reconstituting itself with the energy that passed between them. It was no longer Kwaman and Rehloy, man and woman, but equals drawing upon each other, reminding themselves of what and who they were.

They lapsed into a prolonged silence and languished in the strange comfort of knowing they had come full circle.

CHAPTER SEVENTY-SIX

*W*e are not where we are supposed to be.

Tremlo and Jormah headed towards the grassland in haste.

"You're carrying enough Resep for three of us," Jormah said, observing the sway of Tremlo's bulging backsack.

Tremlo could not explain why he had packed so much, or why he took comfort in the added bulk, but it balanced him somehow. Each heavy footfall sent a satisfying thud through his body.

The rhythms of the dream had subsided. From several day's distance it came only in spurts and quickly dissolved into a murky past.

Junnipur.

He remembered the room in which she lived. Here were things he could not possibly know.

"My dreams are speaking to me," he said aloud.

"Dreams speak in many forms."

"I think these are echoes of our ancestors."

"Visions? Memories?"

"Impressions of a different world."

"Are you observing them or are you in them?"

"Both."

"And what are you doing?"

"Learning."

"Of what?"

"I don't know."

"If visions of the past, do they speak of our future?"

Was that it? Were they trying to tell him something?

Forces were gathering, pointing to some pivotal event, beyond which he could not see. Was this the end of things? Of seeing? Of being?

They sped through the grassland. At night, Tremlo dreamed the same dream over and over, building a bridge.

What am I supposed to see?

The grassland passed in a blur. He took them straight up the mountain to the City-Of-Straight-Lines as fast as they could climb.

We are not where we are supposed to be.

The first time he came this way he had been blind. Now he looked skyward to where the structures once stood.

The bird's eye view of the land ahead was filled with texture, tone, color and memories. Tremlo's body spread out, devouring every detail.

Starving.

He grabbed handfuls of malta and ate to keep up with this *on-grow-ing-ness.* He ate and ate, continuously now, yet his waist did not thicken, nor his legs, or arms or any part.

Jormah had scoffed at the amount of malta he had packed. But at the rate he was eating, it seemed like it was barely enough.

Here was a gathering force.

Donan felt the energy pressing in from the north.

It's them!

One was certainly Jormah. Beside him, subtle shades belying enormous power. Like looking at the sun hidden behind a thick cloud.

He is evolving. But into what?

Reena, sitting in her cave, felt the walls around her and the sky over the City-Of-Straight-Lines within her.

The inner and outer merging.

She sat quite still, far too large now to move.

They poured down the mountain and sped across the sparse ground leading to the Valley Forest. With each step, Tremlo felt an ever-increasing weight. While his body took small steps, his being took huge ones. The perceptions of the past were nothing compared to the forces he now perceived. Invisible walls of energy were charging in from all quarters. He ate constantly to keep from being crushed.

Lying next to him at night, Jormah thought him as heavy as the land. Yet, with the slightest of movement, light as air.

They reached the Valley Forest and Tremlo swallowed it whole. The last time he came this way the animals felt his presence and came to him. Now, he was everywhere, and they languished in the stillness.

Through the forest, into the wilderness, every corner filled.

How large I have become.

How would he ever fit back inside?

The edge of the Tribal Body caught scent of him and rushed forward, a cloud of dust marking its charge. A strand twenty steps across, burst through the forest and leaped upon them.

HOME!

Moments later, all in the tribe heard it.

TREMLO!

Gone were the awkward and painful tones of his youth. In their stead was sheer radiance. Here. Everywhere.

A mountain, a forest, the sky.

The two were heading towards them. Tremlo all width, from one side of the Tribal Body to the other. Only through Jormah could they judge distance.

Their collective senses washed over the pair. Jormah imagined what they would ask and what he would say.

"The story of our journey will be told for generations to come," he said.

Tremlo nodded, shying away from thought of the future.

Hurry, it said.

Hurry! it shouted.

Everyone reached out and the daily activities of the tribe stopped. Tremlo felt more like a cloud. There were no edges to hold onto. Jormah, on the other hand, was prickly, edgy, *disturbing*. He walked like one harboring a wound.

Neither returned their greetings. It was worrisome. Even Gremar was unsure what to do. Jormah snubbed him the last time he went into the forest to greet him. Then as now there was no invitation.

But the people see me as a man of action.

It was their rising anxiety that finally made his decision for him.

I will do what they are afraid to do.

At worst, he would be rebuked. At best, the Rehloy's admiration for him would grow.

He left that very afternoon.

Some were appalled and feared he would give offense. Others waited to see what happened. But none could deny an underlying sense of relief from his action.

"Gremar comes," Jormah said, wondering what Tremlo would make of it.

"Yes, it was to happen this way."

Tremlo, three days deep, embodying the past, present, and future all at once.

"You have foreseen this?"

"I have felt the possibility."

"What else have you felt?"

"Nothing beyond tomorrow," he said, surprised by a flash of fear that came with the words.

They stopped that night to rest, and Tremlo gathered wood to make a fire.

Will this be my last?

"Tremlo?"

"Yes?"

He was drifting.

Four days deep and growing.

"I remember another time," Jormah said, trying to hold him here. "It was the night before Harvest long ago. I was out here alone."

Tremlo's body, soaking up everything in its path.

Six days deep and growing.

"The trickling sound of water appeared out of nowhere and woke me. It was coming from that ravine nearby."

The ravine, less than a day away.

Tremlo, flowing back in time, heard it himself. He was inside his mother's body. It was that very sound that brought him into consciousness and caused him to differentiate.

"That was the beginning," he said aloud to himself.

"Yes, it began there," Jormah replied. "I remember the color and the feel of the water as if it were yesterday."

They had come full circle.

"Tremlo?"

The young Kwaman looked up from his thoughts. He had been everywhere, even then.

"Tremlo?"

It was the middle of the night, and their fire was almost out.

"I'm here."

Jormah lying beside him, unsure if he himself was still awake. Tremlo growing even as they slept.

The land, the topography, the sound of his birth, the perceptions of his early life.

He eased into the Common Ground. The area smaller than he remembered. Most of the Rehloy were in their caves asleep. Those sitting outside were infected by the rhythm of his sleep and passed out.

Donan felt his presence outside his cave. He stood up and caught sight of him by the entrance. The young Rehloy was not only taller than he expected, but he had filled out as well. Tremlo smiled and moved towards him.

His movements, so delicate, so eloquent, took Donan's breath away.

Tremlo stood before him, and Donan hugged him. What was once familiar stretched out far beyond recognition.

"You've changed," he said.

"I've grown."

The melodious layers within his voice suggested unimagined depths.

"You are no longer a younger and far more than Kwaman."

This was beyond awareness. This was ascension.

"I have learned the lessons and become the forms."

Donan's skin gave off a yellowish scent. Here was the wasting away of his body.

Come in, Donan signaled, realizing he was lying on his mat asleep.

Tremlo stepped inside, entering all their caves at once.

Tremlo? Tremlo. Tremlo!

Reena and Arlen, sleeping, their combined tones echoing softly off the walls. An oval sound whose timbre lay deep within him.

Home.

It made that very sound.

Home…

The ghost of himself seemed to inhabit the walls and the floor. Tremlo crept up beside them. Reena's face was reflected in his own. When she turned her head, she did so with the motion he himself might use. Beside her, Arlen stirred. Along his shoulders and back Tremlo felt the curve of his own. Within the mannerisms of their bodies lay the mixture of parts he had combined to create himself.

How much of them I carry.

The warmth of his mother's attention spoke to him.

She knows I am here.

She, who had felt his thoughts, who knew him as no other, endowed him with more of herself than she would ever know. She mother to him, that child a part of something far greater now.

As he, so she.

Arlen's tones were more distant and yet, these were the very ones Tremlo clung to when he felt overwhelmed. These two, the roots of his existence. He saw them clearly, separately, and beyond this he saw the roots of other forces that had taken hold long before his lungs filled with air.

Reena was standing beside him, watching him watch Reena and Arlen as they awoke to his presence.

"Tremlo!" his mother cried, sitting up.

"It's good to see you, son."

"Look how you've grown."

The Reena standing beside him chuckled and placed her arm across his shoulder. She had grown far beyond the memory of the Reena sitting before them. She was mother to Tremlo, but he was also mother to her and the self she was becoming.

"How are you?"

I am well.

"What has happened?" Arlen asked.

Words were getting in the way.

Images and memories faded. Reena was her true-self now.

You are at the heart of a tempest, her hand said touching his face, feeling all that he felt.

Yes....

Tremlo stepped inside, entering all their dreams at once.

Tremlo? Tremlo. Tremlo!

Here was the troubled boy Kenectka remembered and the special connection between them. She intended to take hold of him like she had when he was younger, but stopped short. The one before her was no longer a child. Quite the contrary, he had grown way beyond his years.

He smiled at her surprise.

"I have missed you," she said....

Tremlo stepped inside, entering all their caves at once.

Tremlo. Tremlo? Tremlo!

Stelbin saw the one he remembered metamorphosize into the one that now stood before him. He spread his arms wide with wonder.

Tremlo smiled with light.

Tremlo stepped inside, entering all their dreams at once.

Tremlo? Tremlo. Tremlo!

Gremar was in the forest, sleeping on the ground, rife with contrasts, a tapestry of strengths and weaknesses. He felt Tremlo beside him and was startled.

Yes, Tremlo smiled. His presence invoked the essence of Gremar separate from the machinations of Gremar.

Gremar sighed with relief and sat up.

Tremlo stepped inside all their dreams at once. He felt their pain and their sorrow, their wonder and their happiness. He felt the best and the worst of them, and because of this, he saw what they would do, what they would grow into and become. In a glance, he saw their future. There was no preference or condescension, just acceptance. He saw them, and they basked in the light of unconditional love.

Hunger gently tugged at him, but the people did not want to let go.

Hunger tightened its grip, but they fought just as hard to hold on to him.

Hunger yanked him out of their dreams and back into his body. Jormah was lying on one side, the tribe on the other, all sleeping.

I am awake.

Starving!

He tore the Resep from his backsack. There was no time to cook, and he stuffed the malta into his mouth. He felt relief only as he chewed and swallowed. If he stopped for even a moment, the pangs would consume him.

He ate and ate, compelled now to eat far beyond his capacity. He ate and ate, knowing he would do so until the only thing left in his backsack was the blue Broezia.

An hour before dawn, he swallowed the last piece of malta and lay back exhausted. The forces around him were arching back, creating a space in their midst. Through this emptiness flowed the river whose energy flowed through him.

It was daybreak. He sat up, and as he did so, so did everyone in the tribe.

They stood as he stood and began to perform their deewahs. Afterwards, they gathered in the Common Ground, shrouded in a haze from the night before.

"I dreamed of Tremlo last night," a younger chanced to say. "He came to our cave."

Her words pierced the darkness, and suddenly everyone remembered having dreamed of him.

In the years ahead, it would come to be known as *the presentment*.

For now, they felt released. Something was happening. And almost as one, they poured out of the Common Ground and raced into the forest.

Arlen started to go after them, but Reena grabbed his arm.

"Our place is not with them."

The gravity in her bearing could not be denied. He fought against the pull of the others and sat back down beside her. Only then did he feel the rightness of it. Their presence here, a counterbalance. And they were not alone. Donan remained above with Stelbin by his side.

It was left to the four of them.

We have to resist. We have to hold and keep everything in place.

Tremlo and Jormah were on the move, Tremlo taking long purposeful strides deep within the river. A burst of energy that once would have made his head spin, now merely filled his mind with shapes and colors.

A short time later, another spasm of sensation, and then another. Bursts coming more frequently. Fragments of meaning, disjointed, powerful, calling.

Called!

The faster he went, the more rapid the bursts. Soon it was one long stream of color, shape, sound, and smell.

Tremlo blew through the woods and headed for the ravine.

Jormah ran after but could not keep up. For each step he took Tremlo must have taken three.

The Rehloy raced through the forest, running as hard as they could. They could not stop. If they slowed for even a moment, it felt like they were being dragged.

The four that remained behind braced themselves, digging in, holding back, fighting against the pull of forces that threatened to carry them all away.

It was coming now as surely as night followed day.

In the soft quiet of the woods, a high-pitched whisper, like the trickling sound a brook or stream might make.

The waterpool!

Jormah heard it and ran harder.

There. Nearly There.

Tremlo flew up the hill. *Here!*

A golden pool of water. Fed by oceans of energy. Night and day merging. All that had happened from before his birth until now led to this very moment in time.

The moment he could not see beyond.

To his back, the known. Ahead, a plea, a cry in the night….

Was there a choice?

The world holding its breath….

How could he refuse?

Jormah raced up to the top of the hill. The brilliance of the water below caused him to squint.

Tremlo, at water's edge, his back to him, a shadow in relief, his arm raised as if to say farewell.

And then he dove.

"No!" Jormah cried. "Nooooo!"

Torrents of energy swept Tremlo straight towards the bottom, but his bulk too large to be carried down by it alone.

He began to swim. The water thick. The deeper he went, the thicker it became. He pulled and kicked and squeezed his way down until he could go no farther. The weight of multiple worlds pressed in from all sides, holding him fast.

Just out of reach, lay the rhythms of the future, behind, those of the past. His lungs soon burned with desire.

He tried to turn and swim back to the surface, but the forces pushing down were too great.

I'm trapped! the mind-of-his-body cried out.

He reached frantically about. From below lay the sound of Resep, the tone of the dream, the open mouth of the cavern. If only he could get to it.

The sound of the Resep!

That was the key.

He remembered, understood, had known all along.

Blue Broezia.

He concentrated on its rhythm and projected it through his arm with all his might. The pressure eased just enough for him to reach back into his backsack, to the leaffold that held the blue Broezia. The burning in his lungs was spreading. If it reached his mind, he would lose consciousness.

He brought the Broezia to his mouth. There was no way of measuring it out. No time to be sure. The burning was in his shoulders and moving up the back of his neck. He sucked it into his mouth with some water as well, surprised by the sweetness.

The Broezia traveled down his throat, relieving the pressure around it. Down into his stomach, up through his chest, into his limbs… He was sliding forward now, carried down by torrents of energy, the walls expanding just enough for him to slip through.

Below him an opening, widening, just out of reach. His lungs screaming, his mouth opening, driving out the last of the stale air. He held on, refusing to take a breath until his mind went black. His chest expanded and drew the golden liquid inside.

Dark to Dawn to Light.

Alive!

His heart beating, and yet… he had stopped breathing. Mouth wide opened, lungs full of water keeping his chest in place, a steady flow of air blowing through.

The undulating walls of the tunnel surrounded him. Wave after wave of energy propelling him forward at ever increasing speed.

Like the dream. Just like the…

The forms in his mind lost their edges to the steady hum of the tunnel walls. Suddenly very tired.

Just like…. Just… like…. With that, he entered the flow… of the dream.

"Noooo!" Jormah cried as he ran down to the waterpool. He leaped after it only to fall upon dry ground.

There was nothing now.

Nothing at all.

It had taken Tremlo and left without a trace.

Donan, Reena, Arlen, and Stelbin collapsed at the same moment. Those running through the woods fell, tripping over a sudden and terrible emptiness.

Jormah lay on the floor of the ravine, near the center, where the waterpool had been.

He stayed there not knowing what to do.

After a time, he felt the motion of the tribe.

They were coming.

With Tremlo gone he felt broken. Unprotected. What would they make of him? What would they see? Would they find him tainted? Repugnant? Would they turn away?

Gremar was closest. It appeared like he was leading the way through the forest, and they, following.

Something was gone. Lost. A hope, a dream. The thing that had held them in place for so long was gone. Anything could happen now. Already a sense of imbalance was descending upon them.

LONG BEFORE AND EVER AFTER

The sound was coming. It got steadily stronger each night. It was coming from a great distance away and seemed to take years. Just hearing it was vaguely comforting, and the fact that it was getting stronger filled Jennifer with a sense of anticipation.

What is it I'm waiting for? she wondered, realizing she had been feeling this for a very long time. She had grown up with this sound.

As it grew louder, the pressure on her chest increased. It was becoming hard to breathe while she slept. And then suddenly the sound filled her room and blew past. It was coming now from behind the house in the hills where the woods were thickest, where she still grew Wildflower, her secret friend. She hastily pulled on her jeans and hiking boots and grabbed a flashlight from the kitchen drawer. This an afterthought, for she could almost see in the dark, or at least *feel* her way. She was never quite sure how she did it, but she had this strange ability that no one else seemed to have.

She heard the gurgling sound of water long before she got there. The plants she secretly grew were nearly ready to be harvested. Beside them was a deep gully. It was there that the sound was coming from.

The sound of my dreams.

She was standing over it now and looking down. Water was oozing out from the rocks below, forming a small puddle. She took her flashlight and shined the light on it. The water had a strange golden afterglow. It began to bubble forth faster and faster, filling the gully as if fueled by a torrential rain. The sound of her dreams and the sound of this water were merging. The water continued to churn until it filled the entire gully, and suddenly stopped. The surface now quite still.

She felt compelled to touch it.

So smooth, and yet so thick, *like molasses.* Its temperature matched the touch of her hand.

There is something I must do.

Suddenly, her hand plunged deep into the water.

Instantly the grasp of another took hold. It squeezed hard, and she squeezed back just as hard.

Simultaneously, the water began to recede.

Bending her knees, she leaned back, using two hands now, holding on as if her life depended upon it.

"I will not let you go!" she cried out. "I will not let you go!"

The sound of her dreams and the sound of this water were one and the same, and she could not tell if she was actually here or still in her bed. She held on as tightly as she could and felt the water recede. She held on as tightly as she could, feeling the walls of her bedroom surround her.

She held on as tightly as she could, feeling the water and the walls recede, and as they did, she felt the form of a body ... slowly ... but surely ... emerge.

ACKNOWLEDGMENTS

Book Two is launched and Book Three is waiting in the wings. Alas, the series, which was supposed to take a few years, took a few decades to complete. I remain indebted to so many people along the way. Their support, wisdom, and guidance added to the writing, and ultimately the author, who had to grow into the person who could write these books.

A special shout out to my wife, Carolyn Alper, for her care, support, and who, with Sophia Shiffman, provided excellent grammatical oversight. Beth Freed for her brilliant suggestions. Vicky Mesrie for her red pen. Paula Joudry, whose quiet observations roared. And to all the others whose feedback and enthusiasm helped sustain me throughout the years.

A quick list of other notables: William Bentley, Jamie Bruno, James Conboy, Pam Dennison, Larry Epstein, Adam Green, Peri Basel, Alice Goldsmith, Fred Gross, Zelda Gross, Harvey Helms, Raphael Infante, Rick Lite, Jim Longo, Janna Makaeva, Michael Malloy, Vin Marmoratto, Kathy Mickel, Benjamin Moore, Jonathan Moore, Stephenie Magister, Thadi Murali, James Powers, Lisa Queen, Adriana Restrepo, Jason Rockwood, Sarna Cohen-Ross, Jeff Siegel, Hane Selmani, Peggy Stitzenberg, Robert Swift, Lindsey Van Wagenen, and to all those striving to bring the light of consciousness to humanity. Your spirit feeds my own.

ABOUT THE AUTHOR

In a past life, Todd David Gross had an extensive background in music and was a member of such rock groups as The Burning Sensations, The Band Next Door and The Shout! He performed primarily on bass, sometimes keys, sang, wrote songs, hauled equipment and performed in downtown clubs, (usually after 2am on a work night), hauled equipment back, and sometimes saw the sunrise.

Along the way he discovered esoteric literature, and for decades has been a student of philosophical and psychological studies, embracing both Eastern and Western traditions.

Eventually he traded one keyboard for another and wrote several plays including *The Visit, Life In The Park,* and *Sense Memory,* all of which were performed in New York City. *Them Within Us* ran Off-Broadway at Theater Row Theater, (alas, now Theater Row Diner), and was published by Broadway Play Publishing.

Thereafter, he set about writing *Loy,* which has grown into this series, his most extensive achievement to date.

www.ToddGrossAuthor.com

CHAPTER THREE

The old, red, rust-splattered pickup truck swerved off the dirt road and skidded to a stop. A cloud of dust spread before it, the ghost of the path the vehicle might have taken.

Jennifer pressed her head against the steering wheel and waited for the dizziness to pass. This was the third spell today. They were coming faster now. Reaching into her pocket, she pulled out a small piece of pulp, taken from the plant she called Wildflower. She popped it into her mouth and began to chew. The 'mara', her nickname for the marrow of the plant, didn't stop the dizziness, but speeded her up and made it less jarring.

Something is wrong with me.

This was a persistent theme in her life. If the spells grew much worse, she might go see the doctor, even though she doubted it would do any good. Throughout her life, doctors had never been able to help her.

"She's healthy as a horse," one told her mother.

"There's nothing physically wrong with her," another declared. "I would recommend you take her to Doctor Alper."

She was nine years old when the psychiatrist put her on medication. Over the course of the next thirteen years there had been many different prescriptions. She had taken them as long as her mother was alive. But the drugs had little or no effect and only seemed to make her feel dull or irritable.

"You're too sensitive," her mother would say. "You're just too sensitive!" As if this was something she could control.

"Extreme hypersensitivity," the last doctor had said after running several tests on her, some of which sent small electric impulses across her skin. "I've never seen anything like it."

Her father died when she was seven years old. Most of the therapists believed this was the traumatic event that set off her hallucinations.

But for her, she had always been the same. Her father's death had been painful and frightening, but merely one incident in a long line of many. The fabric of her mind and what they called her "sensitivities" had always been the same. By fourth grade, however, her flights of fancy were no longer tolerated.

What changed were the adults' expectations of her.

Over time, she learned not to speak about the voices in her head. Over time, she came to understand that in comparison to others, there was something wrong with her.

She was twenty-five years old now and living alone in the isolated farmhouse in which she had been born. Her mother had died three years before. The neighbors felt sorry for her and came around for a time, but Jennifer was never good at small talk. She felt their mounting discomfort as they struggled for things to talk about. It was painful for all involved, and she just couldn't wait for them to leave. Thankfully, they finally got the hint and stopped coming round.

The dizziness was passing, the energy that flashed through her body gone, the sweat on her brow all that remained. She wiped it off with the back of her hand, and put the truck back in gear.

The dirt road that bordered the McAlisters' farm was the long way back, but it was quiet, solitary. When she finally came to the lone stop sign, she dutifully stopped.

There was no one around for miles.

Turning left onto the paved road, she headed back towards civilization.

She had never fit in, not with her peers, not with adults. She thought if she died, it would be weeks, if not months, before someone noticed. Probably the mailman would be first. Not that she got any letters of a personal nature, but there were bills and junk mail addressed to 'occupant', or once in a while, one to her dead parents.

Others might think her a loner, but strangely, she did not feel alone. All she need do was drive slowly through town. From the safe haven of her truck, she could feel the emotions of the people walking about. This was the madness. This was the thing that separated her and drove her both towards and away from everyone.

Different locations were colored by different sensations. The gas station was about suspension of movement. Impatience was often the prevalent tone. The supermarket was a multicolored affair marked by everything from deliberation, to acquisition, to the emotions of the hunt. It often ended in frustration at the checkout counter, where people waiting in line roared at one another in silence.

The beauty parlor was rich with a different kind of energy. Here, the strong flavors of hope, eagerness, vulnerability, and fear reigned.

The local bar changed depending upon the time of day. The afternoon exuded an overall sense of refuge and exhaustion. At night, the contrasting rhythms of power, competition, love, and despair abounded.

All these created a sense of ongoing-ness that allowed her to feel she was a part of something human and alive.

If she got out of her truck and walked around, the impressions often became so vivid that her mind filled with voices. But from inside the truck, everything was softer and more manageable. From inside the truck, she could feel what they were feeling and not be overwhelmed.

In the fall, she would go to the high school football games and remain in the parking lot. There she would lie across the seat of her pickup truck to avoid being seen. She could feel the exhilaration of the crowd without distraction and live it as if she were there in the stands.

Jennifer pulled up to the traffic light and signaled right. A small, bright blue car pulled up beside her. Windows down, music blasting, it was one of those new sporty models. The brand and details were something she never paid attention to, but the song was vaguely familiar.

Hot flashes of desire filled her.

A young couple, by the feel of them, but she dared not look. The moment the light changed, the car screeched forward. The couple's sense of urgency marked their path as clearly as the tires marked the road. She saw them through their rear window, two heads close together, forming the outline of a heart.

She had never had a lover. Not that she didn't want one, but the few boys who came circling scared her. At the heart of their interest was something predatory, and she ran from them, but not only them. How people acted and what they truly felt were often at odds with one another. It so confused her, it was just easier to be alone.

At the end of the road was the turnoff. She would be home soon. The driveway, if one could call it that, was a narrow, unpaved path, worn brown along the edges where the tires tread. Between them sat a hump of green grass. Bushes and trees encroached on either side. The soft sound of leaves scraping the sides of her truck were the sounds of *home*. It was these very same sounds that kept most of the cars away.

The farm had ceased to function like one when her grandfather sold off most of the land to a developer. It had never worked well as a farm anyway. The soil was too thin and the stone-filled landscape barely able to provide enough grazing for cattle.

The white house, stained gray with age, was tucked away at the base of a small mountain range. The rugged vista out back, insured that it would never be encroached upon. She pulled the truck in beside the dilapidated brown barn, which had ceased to house animals long ago, and parked. The ground directly beneath the truck was black from years of sporadic oil drips that declared this "parking spot".

Another wave of dizziness hit as she opened the door. It was louder than before, and she grasped the handle tightly to keep from falling. Breathing deeply, again and again to steady herself, the sensation flowed through her body and into the foothills out back.

She was sure now that it wasn't something inside her head. It wasn't the result of a tumor or some other physical malady.

It's coming from outside of me.

Wary now, she got out of her truck and looked around.

Something is going to happen.

She had had premonitions before, but never anything as strong as this.

Inside the house, everything felt different. The floors, the walls, even the furniture were colored by a sense of temporality.

Something is going to happen.

She was in the front parlor, sitting on the faded, floral-patterned couch, when the next wave hit. She was there in the parlor, and yet, for several moments could have sworn she was lying in her bed.

When the sensation passed, she felt the sound of it, for it had a sound now, retreating into the foothills out back.

She did not move. For the longest time, she barely breathed. This last wave had been the strongest yet, and she felt pinned to this place, this couch, this moment.

Jennifer was three years old when she found the solitary plant growing inside a hidden cavern out back. The entrance was more like a crack in the hill than an opening, and secreted behind the old evergreen tree. She could not fit through that opening now, but as a child of two, it was manageable. That was when she first met Wildflower. The plant soothed her somehow. When she played grownup, she would soak its leaves in water to make pretend tea. It seemed the more she drank the tea, the more the plant hummed to her. It did not use words or sounds, and yet, she could somehow hear it.

When she was ten, she tried eating some of the pulp that filled its stalks and branches. Almost immediately, she was able to hear the songs of Wildflower more clearly. But not just Wildflower. It was as if the body of each person she met sang how it was feeling, even if the person's words or actions were completely different.

Over the years, Wildflower grew smaller, for the leaves and branches she broke off never grew back. Just before its end, Jennifer picked the pod that housed its seeds and planted them out back in a hidden part of the woods. She did not know how she came up with this idea. It almost felt like Wildflower told her what to do, or maybe she dreamed it. Either way, she was greatly comforted by the plants that grew there. In an odd way, they that had become her friends.

Jennifer got up off the couch and went into the kitchen to prepare a light dinner of vegetables and rice, mixed with Wildflower. As usual, she set the table for two, though it had been years since she had eaten with anyone. When she was feeling low, the empty plate stood in testament to her loneliness. When she was feeling more balanced, it comforted her. As long as she kept setting the place someone would eventually come. *But who?* Today, it made her nervous.

She ate in silence, the sound of knife and fork reverberating loudly off the walls.

After eating mara, her perceptions were always enhanced for hours on end. Lately, she had been eating it more regularly and today almost constantly, driven to it by the waves of dizziness.

She cleaned up after dinner and went around the house making sure all the doors and windows were locked. It was still early, and she wasn't tired, but she felt the need to be upstairs in the comfort of her bedroom. The light on the staircase was out. She had forgotten to change the bulb, but it didn't matter, for she could pretty much see in the dark or at least feel her way. She was never quite sure how she did it, but she had this strange ability that no one else seemed to have.

Once inside her bedroom, she closed the door. She felt safe and contained by its dark walls. Over the years, she had changed its color many times, each time going a bit darker. Her mother had held her back, but after she died, Jennifer painted it a dark brown. Her room was cave-like now, and the place that made her most happy.

She emptied her pockets and placed the remaining pieces of mara back inside the large wooden jewelry box on top of her dresser. The box had several compartments and a small drawer in the bottom. It was here that she kept the blue sparkle dust. This was the pollen that formed on the edges of Wildflower's leaves. She had tasted it once long ago, but it was so strong, it burned her tongue and she spit it out. Even so, she was left feeling disembodied for days.

She resolved never to taste it again, but the dust fascinated her. It glowed in the dark, sparkling in all manner of blues. Sometimes bright, sometimes soft, always changing as if it were speaking a language all its own. Whenever it was time to harvest the new plants, she would scrape the blue sparkle dust off the leaves and put it into this ziplock plastic bag. The bag was now about a quarter full. There was something so alive about it. For that matter, something so alive about Wildflower. She always thought of it as a person, not just a thing.

Wildflower.

She kept most of its leaves in the bottom drawer of the dresser. It was almost empty now, and it would soon be time to harvest the new crop. She took two leaves out and placed them in the glass of water she kept beside her bed. Where others might use mint or lemon, she craved this flavor.

Jennifer yawned loudly. The waves of dizziness had taken much out of her. She pulled out the bag of sparkle dust and placed it on the nightstand before lying down. She often looked at it before she went to sleep. It was very bright tonight, so much so it seemed to illuminate the room.

Bright and agitated, the language of light.

She could watch it for hours, but tonight, its pulsations had the strange effect of putting her to sleep.

In sleep, she heard the sound, remembered it, felt it getting stronger. It was coming from a great distance away. It had been coming for years. She had grown up with this sound. Just hearing it was vaguely comforting, and the fact that it was getting stronger filled her with a sense of anticipation.

What am I waiting for?

It was growing louder now, like a freight train roaring down a track. It seemed to be heading straight for her.

The pressure on her chest increased. She could not move. She could not get out of its way.

The floor, the walls, the bed, her body, filled with the sound. She gritted her teeth. She clenched her fists.

Piercing.

In another moment, she would shatter into a thousand pieces.

And then it blew past, bellowing as it went, deeper and deeper, charging up into the hills where the woods were thickest to the very place where Wildflower grew.

Jennifer threw off the covers and jumped out of bed. Pulling on her jeans and hiking boots, she raced down the stairs and out the back. She ran all the way, hearing the gurgling sound long before she got there....